ABOUT THE AUTHOR

David Walker is a retired executive who turned to writing late in life. He is a keen amateur historian with a particular interest in the First World War. He was born in Hamilton, Scotland, the home garrison of the Cameronians. David attended Hamilton Academy, Edinburgh University, and Imperial College, before embarking on an international career in the energy industry. He now lives in Guildford, Surrey.

ALSO BY DAVID D WALKER

TORRES DEL PAINE

Torres del Paine is set in the spectacular Chilean national park of the same name. The story begins in the early part of 2020 in the Southern Hemisphere's summer, which, in the park, is extremely windy. Inspector Ignatius Hernandez, aka Nacho, has to solve the apparent murder of a visiting US senator while the park is isolated due to weather-related incidents. A range of suspects from various nationalities, using a variety of possible killing methods, are investigated and discarded before the crime is solved. The characters represent several newsworthy themes and viewpoints, and all have a reason for killing the senator. All the action takes place against the backdrop of the beautiful mountains and lakes of some of the world's greatest scenery.

BLACKMAIL
ERPRESSUNG
CHANTAGE

A Jamie Brown Story

DAVID D. WALKER

Matador
9 Priory Business Park,
Wistow Road, Kibworth Beauchamp,
Leicestershire. LE8 0RX
Tel: 0116 279 2299
Email: books@troubador.co.uk
Web: www.troubador.co.uk/matador
Twitter: @matadorbooks

ISBN 978 1800461 734

British Library Cataloguing in Publication Data.
A catalogue record for this book is available from the British Library.

Printed and bound in Great Britain by 4edge Limited
Typeset in 11pt Adobe Garamond Pro by Troubador Publishing Ltd, Leicester, UK

Matador is an imprint of Troubador Publishing Ltd

For Janet
My much suffering companion in a retirement of writing

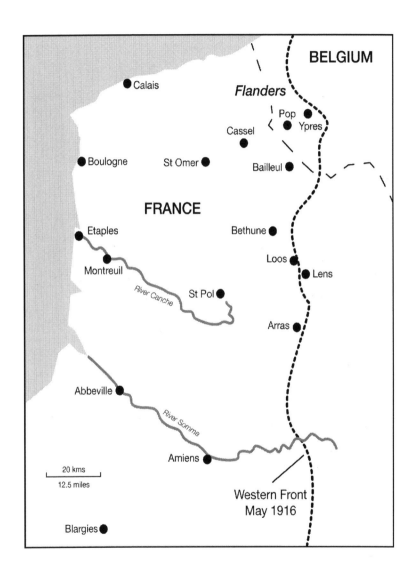

BELGIUM

Flanders

Calais

Pop

Ypres

Cassel

Boulogne St Omer Bailleul

FRANCE

Etaples Bethune

Montreuil Loos

Lens

River Canche St Pol

Arras

Abbeville

River Somme

20 kms
12.5 miles

Amiens

Western Front
May 1916

Blargies

PROLOGUE

'What's he done now?'

Rather than reply, Lord Wokingham handed over a large photograph.

'My God!' the King exclaimed, his eyes wide, his face white behind his dark beard, the hand holding the photograph shaking.

Wokingham then explained how and why the photograph had come into his possession.

'Has the boy no shame? Where was this taken?' the King demanded.

'Somewhere in Paris I believe, Your Majesty, but I don't yet know where.'

'Does the boy not know they call this "The German Disease"? Is the family not being criticised enough these days for our German ancestry without this?' asked the King, as he waved the photograph at Wokingham.

'Perhaps he was not aware, Your Majesty.'

'And what about my dear brother Eddy? Does the boy not remember "The Cleveland Street Scandal"?'

'To be fair, Your Majesty, he wasn't even born then,' said Wokingham, remembering that "Eddy" was the Royal Family's patronym for the late Prince Albert.

'Well, what are we going to do about it?'

Lord Wokingham had served the King as an adviser for long enough to understand that his monarch meant "What are you, Wokingham, going to do about it?". Indeed, his ability to iron out such sensitive issues for the King had earned him the nickname of "Grand Vizier" in the Royal Household.

'I hope Your Majesty will forgive me, but I have already taken steps. I have talked to one of our confidants in France, and he has suggested a way forward.'

Wokingham outlined the recommended course of action.

'Why don't we just shoot the traitor by firing squad?' demanded the King.

'We could, Your Majesty, but he would have to be charged with something serious, and then there would have to be a court martial at which he could speak out. It would involve too many people.'

'I'm not sure my cousin, Wilhelm, will be too pleased.'

'I think that's the least of our problems regarding this issue, if I'm honest, Your Majesty.'

'And our friend is sure this is safe?' asked the King, a slight tremor in his voice.

'He assures me it will be totally safe, Your Majesty.'

'And the negatives?'

'We'll take care of those too, of course.'

'And what about the Prime Minister? What about General Haig?'

'I suggest we leave Asquith out of this at the moment, and just keep it to your close friends, Your Majesty. I can inform Haig if you like.'

'Yes, better Haig should know the basics, but not the details of what the boy's been up to. You know, there will be the devil to pay if this gets out!'

'Yes, Your Majesty, but I believe the risk to the monarchy warrants the action I've described.'

'I suppose you're correct, Wokingham. And I'll deal with the boy. He must understand that royal scandals are best avoided.

The outcome of the plan you've described will show him that his irresponsible actions can have deadly consequences.'

'Thank you, Your Majesty, I believe that would be appropriate.'

'And it's not as if we haven't enough deaths to deal with. Have you seen the latest casualty lists?' asked the King, tapping a copy of *The Times* on his desk in front of him.

'Quite, Your Majesty.'

'Then you can proceed.'

'Thank you, Your Majesty. I will clear your diary for the trip. It may take a fortnight to arrange everything. In the meantime, we'll stall paying the demanded monies.'

'Speaking of diaries, I must go and get ready for the Good Friday service at Westminster Abbey.'

'If I may be excused attending, Your Majesty, I would rather address this urgent matter.'

'Yes, of course. You do realise there will have to be some sort of inquiry about this incident to placate the press? They'll want to know how such a thing can happen. You can't just do what you're suggesting and expect them not to look for scapegoats. You know how our dear press love a scapegoat.'

'Yes, Your Majesty, and I've taken the liberty to address that, too. General Maldon will arrange for a unit called Section X of the Army's Intelligence Corps to look into it. They handle special investigations, apparently. Maldon's looked at their personnel files. He's made sure that none of their experienced officers will be used, and he's pushed for a novice investigator to be assigned to the case. We'll then make sure this new chap will find the answers that we want him to find. He'll be presented with a fait accompli. The press will then be given an outline of his independent inquiry. The selected candidate is a former infantry subaltern only recently seconded to the unit, and who's never done this sort of thing before.'

'Good. Does this fellow have a name?'

'Yes, Your Majesty. His name is Lieutenant James Brown.'

Saturday,
6th May 1916

CHAPTER 1

I was used to being stared at.

I was used to being stared at by grieving mothers and black-clad widows with red-rimmed eyes that seemed to say, "Why are you here and my Billy is gone?".

I was used to being stared at by pompous harridans who quickly hid their stupid white feathers in embarrassment when they saw my blue armband and walking stick.

I was used to being stared at by men too old to serve, who took jingoistic pride in my sacrifice, but were glad it wasn't theirs.

I was used to being stared at by young men, guilty that they hadn't yet answered Kitchener's call to arms, worried now that their complacency had been shattered by the introduction of conscription, and frightened that they'd end up with a limp like mine – or worse.

And I was used to being stared at by small boys who shouted, "Hey, Mister, are you a pirate?" because of my eyepatch.

I was therefore used to being stared at by civilians back in Blighty, but I had not expected to be stared at by others dressed like me, in khaki, now that I was in Flanders.

'Can I help you?' I asked the stranger doing the staring.

The man standing next to me was in his late forties, thin-faced, with wire-rimmed spectacles and a regulation moustache.

'Unusual uniform combination you've got there, Lieutenant,' he said.

My uniform tunic, whipcord breeches and riding boots should have solicited no comment within the crowd we were in, so I thought he was referring to my black buttons, my vertical black belts instead of a standard diagonal Sam Browne, and the Glengarry on my head.

'Cameronians,' I said, by way of explanation.

'The Scottish Rifles; yes, I know. I meant the green tabs.'

I'd forgotten about the little green patches of cloth on my collar which indicated my new role.

'Intelligence Corps,' I told him, and realised as I did so, that he was wearing a captain's uniform, but with an armband that indicated he was a war correspondent.

'*Scheisse*,' I muttered. Shit, indeed! This was all I needed, an interrogation by a member of the Fourth Estate on my first day with my new unit.

'You're a war correspondent,' I said. My words had sounded like an accusation and I realised how stupid they were given he was the one wearing the armband. I certainly wasn't displaying much intelligence.

'Usually. Today I'm a royal correspondent,' the journalist replied, nodding towards the party of horsemen assembling on the knoll in front of us. 'I'm William Beach Thomas. I work for Lord Northcliffe on the *Daily Mail*.'

'Jamie Brown,' I said in exchange, and we shook hands.

'Looks like my man's almost ready to take his first picture,' said Beach Thomas, pointing at the photographer, a nervous corporal, positioned in front of the mounted group.

I looked at the horsemen and understood why the corporal was anxious. I recognised King George of course, his naval beard clashing with his British Army uniform, but looking very distinguished as a field marshal, his khaki embellished with splashes of red and gold. He seemed a bit stiff, no doubt still in pain from his riding accident last autumn on a previous visit to the front. I knew General Plumer on the King's right from photographs, and presumably he was there since we were in his sector of the line. There was a red-faced general I didn't recognise on the King's other side, and one or two brass hats filled out the party. A French Army officer in a horizon-blue uniform was presumably some sort of liaison wallah.

The party was being arranged in order by a lieutenant colonel wearing tartan trews. This colonel was obviously on familiar terms with the King as well as his senior officers, and there was a lot of banter going on. The line-up was completed when an officer was placed at the left end of the row as I looked at it. The choreographer then went to the other end.

An escort of Indian cavalry had formed up behind the knoll, their traditional orange turbans replaced by drab khaki-equivalents. The only splashes of colour were the pennants on the sowars' lances and a guidon for aligning the horses. The pennants hung limp, for it was a still, clear day.

The royal party was now face-on to the photographer and his large wooden-bodied field camera on a tripod. He was trying diplomatically to get the horsemen and their mounts to stay still long enough to be recorded for posterity. Given the fine late-spring weather, the lighting was perfect for him. It was a great opportunity for the press to show their avid readers back in Blighty a regal photograph of the King-Emperor commanding Imperial martial might, surrounded by his generals, and against the backdrop of an Indian cavalry squadron.

Just as it seemed that all was organised to good effect, and the photographer dropped his hand to indicate that he'd taken his first picture, a rifle *cracked*, and the officer on the far left of the party fell to the ground. After a brief silent hiatus, pandemonium ensued.

The Indian lancers grabbed the reins of the King's horse and formed a protective shield around him before charging at the crowd, which parted like the Red Sea to let the scrum of horsemen through. Most of the royal party followed helter-skelter down the knoll after the monarch.

One officer of the party, however, wheeled off in the opposite direction, pulling out a pistol and shouting, 'To the woods!'

Those of us watching had dropped to the ground after the horsemen had fled, trained for crossing no-man's land and therefore awaiting further volleys. Only the photographer seemed frozen, as if in one of his own productions.

From a small wood a few hundred yards away came two further shots, followed by a screeching cacophony as a black cloud of disturbed crows rose into the sky before silence again descended.

As I got back onto my feet, the mounted officer who had charged into the wood emerged from the trees brandishing a rifle with a telescopic sight on top. He trotted back to the knoll. As he got closer, I could see it was the lieutenant colonel who had been ushering the horsemen into line.

'Two snipers. I got them both. My God, they could have killed the King!' declared the colonel to the crowd.

On the knoll lay the slumped form of the victim. His horse must have bolted with the rest of the herd when freed of its burden. From the absence of rank badges on his cuffs and the red tabs on his collar I concluded that the casualty had been a staff officer. The red band on the remains of his cap confirmed this. It was now a crumpled heap of millinery rags having been trodden under hoof by the departing stampede.

A medic went up to the fallen man and it didn't take him long to pronounce his diagnosis. 'He's dead. Shot through the head.'

A mix of anger and disbelief lit the faces of the crowd as the words sank in. Then the onlookers began to disperse, their excited chatter seeming to me to be at odds with the sad image of the lifeless body, prone on the grass. On the other hand, these men were used to death on the Western Front, and better it was a dead brass hat than one of their chums.

'Attempted regicide; what a scoop!' I heard Beach Thomas mutter. My journalist companion was writing furiously in a notebook, a smile on his face, no doubt pleased that, despite the fatal outcome, he had an exclusive news story. As I was leaving, he asked his photographer to realign his camera on to the corpse.

'I'd hate to be the poor bastard who's got to sort this mess out,' said a major in front of me, and, lacking foresight, I could only agree with him.

CHAPTER 2

I went in search of my driver, Private Bob Hodgson. I had only met him earlier that day when he'd picked me up in Calais, along with my friend, Archie Dunlop, a brigade major. We'd dropped Archie off in Poperinghe, after crossing the border into Belgium. It was there that we'd heard about the royal visit, and I had decided to try and see the King before heading on to my new posting.

When I found him, Hodgson was drawing heavily on a Woodbine beside our Ford Model T staff car. He was in his late twenties, looked like a large sack of potatoes dressed in khaki serge, and wore his service cap in the crushed "gorblimey" style. He had a plump ruddy face partly masked by a black walrus moustache. His several chins spilled over his collar and its Army Service Corps badges. The ASC were known to all and sundry as "Ally Sloper's Cavalry" after the eponymous comic-strip character, and my driver would not have looked out of place in the humorous cartoon. I'd have to do something about smartening him up.

'Terrible thing, guv. Somebody trying to shoot the King on our territory. Who'd have believed it possible?' said an obviously rattled Hodgson in his cockney accent.

'Yes, you're right, Hodgson. I expect somebody's going to get a rocket up the backside for this debacle,' I told him.

'Where to now, guv? I mean, sir,' he asked.

'Head for Montreuil, Hodgson. In a strange way, I'm going back to university.'

Hodgson cranked the starter, and we set off south-west across the border, back into France.

*

After four hours of driving we finally found ourselves on the outskirts of Montreuil-sur-Mer as dusk was descending. I had never been there before, but, in the half-light, it looked to be an attractive market town, still partly surrounded by medieval ramparts, and with the sea in its name obviously having receded many miles away.

Montreuil had recently become British Expeditionary Force Headquarters under General Haig, and was known simply as BEF GHQ. From my schoolboy knowledge of French geography, the town seemed well situated for this new role as it was on the main route from London to Paris, via the cross-Channel ports, and within a safe, but reasonable, distance of the portion of the Western Front held by the BEF.

I had been sent a map and used it to direct us to the driveway of a small chateau on Montreuil's outskirts. The chateau's wrought-iron gates were blocked by two armed sentries wearing the letters "IC" on armbands and with a green band round their caps. I showed them my pass, and they let us in. Hodgson parked the car on the gravel outside the chateau's ivy-covered frontage.

'You wait here,' I instructed Hodgson before entering the building.

After receiving directions from a clerk in the entrance hall, I knocked and went into an office with a sign saying "Adjutant" on its door.

'Yes? Can I help you, Lieutenant?' asked a rather pasty-faced, thin-haired captain sitting behind a large desk. Since he was the room's only occupant, I presumed he was the adjutant.

'Yes, thank you, sir. I'm Lieutenant James Brown. I'm here to see Lieutenant Colonel Ferguson.'

'Are you, by Jove? And what gives you the right to such an audience, old boy?'

I handed over my paperwork as the man scrutinised my uniform, the eyepatch, and the medal ribbon. He lowered his gaze to the letter and file that I'd given him. I wasn't invited to sit, so I leant heavily on my lacquered Japanese walking stick, a present from my Uncle John on my last home leave, and a souvenir of his time as a missionary in the Far East.

'So, you're the new recruit, eh? I hope you're up to the mark, Brown. This is not a retirement home for has-beens you know, and God knows we've got enough of you Scotch here already.'

I decided that it would be better not to correct the adjutant's application of "Scotch", the whisky, to "Scots", the nation. From his demeanour and tone, I didn't think a smart-alec reply would be appreciated.

He proceeded to read my file and in it I knew he'd find out that I had been seconded to the Intelligence Corps. He would also discover that I had volunteered as part of Kitchener's New Army when the 10th battalion of the Cameronians had been formed in September 1914 in Hamilton, my birthplace twenty-seven years previously, and where I'd gone to school at the local Academy. The adjutant would also see that my education had been completed by a first-class honours degree in law from the Old College of the University of Edinburgh. My medical history form would show him that I'd been signed off for re-engagement, was seventy inches tall, and that I allegedly weighed 170 pounds, although my tight waistband suggested that was now a bit optimistic.

'Hmm, not Oxbridge then, but one of the Old Man's students from Edinburgh. Nepotism's a wonderful thing,' sniffed the adjutant. 'Your file says you speak German and French. How come?'

'I speak reasonable French after studying for a few months in Paris, but I'm fluent in German, sir. I spent part of my childhood in Germany.'

'You're not a sympathiser of the Kaiser by any chance then, are you?' asked the adjutant, sitting back and raising his eyebrows in mock horror as he made his inquiry.

'Yes, of course, sir, and I'm so sympathetic that to make my cover as realistic as possible I had his chaps blow me up.'

'Very funny, old boy. You could write for *The Wipers Times* with that line in sarcasm,' observed my sparring partner. 'And why were you in Germany as a boy?'

'My father is a mining engineer. He went to the Ruhr to learn new extraction techniques and to buy the latest equipment for the collieries back home. The whole family went with him, and so I went to school in Duisburg for a few years.'

'And you're to have a driver *and* a batman it says here on this chitty. My goodness, you do come well looked after, don't you? That explains this,' said the adjutant, handing over an envelope. 'Your man is in detention. You do seem to associate with some unreputable types, Brown.'

I opened the envelope and found it contained a copy of a charge sheet and an address.

'Now, let me see…,' continued the adjutant, but before he could ask his next question, a side door to his office burst open, and a large, balding, bespectacled, and slightly dishevelled lieutenant colonel advanced into the room, arms extended towards me.

'Jamie! I thought I heard your dulcet tones. So good to see you at last. Looks like all the paperwork I sent over to you in Blighty worked, and you got here okay. Welcome to the Intelligence Corps.'

'Hello, Colonel Ferguson. Good to be here at last, sir,' I said, smiling at the familiar figure of my old university professor.

'Well, if you'd listened to me in the first place you wouldn't have ended up in the Poor Bloody Infantry getting yourself blown to bits.'

'I survived, sir, but many didn't,' I said, a bit more tersely than I meant to.

'Aye, true, too true,' acknowledged the Colonel in his soft Edinburgh tones, his eyes misting over as he said it.

'Oh, I'm sorry, sir, that was crassly put. My condolences on your loss,' I replied, cursing myself inwardly for remembering too late that the Colonel's son, Andrew, had died with the Gordon Highlanders at Neuve Chapelle the previous year.

'Ah well, we've all had our losses. It's hard though as a parent to have your child, grown up or not, die before you. I gather your brother, Hugh, was also killed in action?'

'Yes, sir. From what I understand, he was ordered to undertake some suicidal attack against a German redoubt last October. He didn't make it. He left behind a wife and two young daughters. My parents haven't really got over it yet. They weren't too pleased about me coming back here, to be honest.'

'Right, come into my office and I'll tell you all about your new duties,' said the Colonel, and he stood aside and ushered me through his door before turning to the adjutant. 'Villiers,' he said, giving the man a name for me, 'make sure you sort out accommodation for Jamie and his men.'

'Yes, sir. Of course, sir. It will be my pleasure,' said the adjutant through clenched teeth. I was sure I then heard Villiers mutter, 'I'm not a bloody hotel concierge, you know.'

The large room that we had retired into had a desk in its bay window and two comfortable armchairs either side of an impressive stone fireplace flanked by bookcases. It stank of stale pipe smoke. The Colonel embraced me once more. Up close, I could smell who the guilty pipe smoker was. I'd forgotten the dreadful smell of the Turkish tobacco blend he used.

'It really is good to see you, you know,' said the Colonel. 'It's not just Andrew, but so many of my old students have been killed in this damn war. We get all sorts of statistics here in this unit. I saw one the other day. The average lifespan of a subaltern at the front is six weeks. Six weeks! Can you imagine? Your generation will be gone before it's made its mark on the world at this rate. Our role in the Intelligence Corps is making sure GHQ gets the best information to make the right decisions to get this conflict over with as soon as possible.'

'Thank you for inviting me to join, sir.'

'Don't keep calling me "sir", for God's sake. Behind closed doors you can call me "Prof", just like in the old days. And why did you come back, Jamie? Presumably with your wounds you could have been invalided out?'

'Let's just call it unfinished business. After Hugh was killed, plus losing so many of my men at Loos, I still wanted to continue to serve somehow. I'm obviously not fit for the trenches, so I took you up on your previous invitation to join you here. An old medic friend from Edinburgh on my medical board passed me fit for rear echelon duties.'

The Prof went over to a side table and poured two large whiskies from a bottle of Laphroaig and then passed me a glass.

'To absent friends,' toasted the Prof.

The taste of the peaty, smoky Islay malt reminded me of tutorials in the Prof's rooms when we had finished discussions on arcane points of Scots Law, and he would treat his students to a dram. The Prof saw it as compensation for having to put us through some of the more boring aspects of jurisprudence. That was a lot of boredom, so quite a volume of whisky was consumed during my degree course.

'Anyway, now to business,' said the Prof. 'Sit yourself down. How are your wounds? Are you in much pain?'

'The pain comes and goes. I can still walk, but with a limp, and I'm doing exercises to get my fitness back. I'm improving day by day, but I doubt I'll be able to play tennis again. I'm still hoping to have the odd round of golf.'

'Or "a good walk spoiled",' said the Prof. 'Golf is not a game I understand or have any ambition to play, I must admit. Now, let me brief you on your new role. The Intelligence Corps is responsible for field intelligence in direct support of the BEF as opposed to the organisations derived from the old Secret Service Bureau in London, like MI.5 and MI.6, who look after stuff like counter-espionage and security in Blighty, and overseas spies, and so on.'

The Prof proceeded to give me details of our corps' organisation, its duties, its different specialised sections, and how its structure aligned with the BEF's. It was a bit like being back at university as the Prof prattled on. I forced myself to pay attention, just as I'd had to do in his lectures.

'All of this is classic military intelligence and fed into GHQ and Brigadier General Charteris, who is Haig's chief of intelligence and de facto commandant of the Intelligence Corps. He's usually referred to as the BGI. However, there's also Major General MacDonogh back at the War Office reporting into the Imperial General Staff.'

'Sounds complicated to me, Prof.'

'Things can get a bit political between the two, but my job is to protect you from all that nonsense. Then, just to add to the complexity, although the corps is controlled and tasked by Charteris and Haig's staff, it is actually administered by Alston Fenn.'

'Make that *over*-complicated, Prof,' I said, trying to get my head around what he'd described.

'It is what it is. Most of our lot are located with Charteris down at the old military school in Montreuil itself. However, you're now in Section X. We're a sort of special investigations unit that reports directly to Haig and the War Office in London. Our job is to investigate enemy, allied, or internal activities that might affect the BEF's high-level security. Since we deal with sensitive issues, we've been posted out here to this chateau, away from GHQ. I've recruited largely ex-police officers or lawyers like yourself who are good at analysing and investigating.'

The Prof went over to his desk and pulled out a large brown envelope from its drawer. He passed over the contents of two armbands and a pair of officer's rank pips to me.

'Congratulations, Captain Brown, you've just been promoted in the field. A captain gets more attention than a mere lieutenant. The admin has been taken care of, and you'll see a raise the next time the Pay Corps deems it fit to reward you for your labours.'

'Thank you, Prof,' I said, surprised, but delighted by the unexpected promotion. 'The pay rise is really appreciated. I need all the money I can get. Next time I'm home on leave, I plan to buy an engagement ring if my girlfriend, Jeanie, will still have me.'

'I'm sure she will. Have you seen her since you were wounded?'

'Yes, I saw her only last week on my home leave. She didn't seem too put off by my wounds. In fact, she thought the black eyepatch was rather dashing and was glad it matched my hair colouring. She made it sound like a desirable fashion accessory.'

'Speaking of fashion, most new officers around here are commissioned via the 10th Royal Fusiliers, but we allow established officers to retain their original unit's uniforms if they wish to. I presume you'll wish to remain with your old regiment?'

'Yes, I'm actually rather proud to be a Cameronian given their long history and local connections to my home town.'

'Fine, then those collar tabs you've on will suffice. Have your men put those armbands on. They're marked with the corps' initials.'

'Thank you. My batman's not here yet; I need to pick him up tomorrow.'

'Now, I've been requested to specifically assign you to the area of Second Army as their liaison with us. Do you know anyone over there?'

'Not that I'm aware of, Prof,' I said, trying, and failing, to think of anyone I knew on the staff.

'Strange. I wonder why they asked for you? No matter. Tomorrow, you should go and visit General Plumer. Here's a letter of introduction.'

'I actually saw General Plumer today, Prof, but admittedly at a distance.'

I went on to tell the Prof about the day's assassination attempt on the King and the death of a staff officer instead of the monarch.

'My God, that's terrible. It seems like the Huns will stop at nothing. Attempting to kill the King! I dare say the Intelligence Corps will be asked to investigate how that was allowed to happen. Now, drink up, and then you can get yourself settled. We dine at eight.'

'Thank you, Prof,' I said, putting all the materials into my briefcase.

'Oh, and one last thing. Don't be put out by Villiers. He may be an ass sometimes, but he's a very efficient ass, and a bloody good adjutant. He's got a great network in GHQ and indeed across the whole British Army, both here and in Blighty. I haven't dug too deep, but I suspect his old man pulled some strings so that his only son and heir didn't go to the front, and he ended up here instead. As the father of a dead son, I can't say I really blame his pater. Villiers is no coward, and he's still keen to see some fighting, so he could be a bit jealous of you.'

'I'm not sure that getting blown up is something to be jealous of, Prof!'

'Huh, of course you're right,' said the Prof with a chuckle. 'I'm glad you've still got a sense of humour, anyway.'

'Well, you know what they say, Prof? "If you don't laugh, you'll cry".'

As I left, the Prof was staring at the silver-framed photograph of a young highlander on his desk, absentmindedly filling a pipe. Villiers' chair was vacant in the outer office, and I wondered how the adjutant would take to me now being of equal rank. He'd seemed to enjoy swanking it over me in our meeting earlier.

*

Later that evening after dinner, the Prof called me over in the mess bar.

'I was right about us getting involved in investigating the assassination attempt on the King. Since it was in General Plumer's sector, he's been tasked with finding out how it was allowed to happen. He's requested our assistance and that means you, Jamie, as his assigned investigator. Tomorrow, you'd better hotfoot it over to his HQ at Cassel and get a briefing from him. I'm sorry to be throwing you in at the deep end, but I'm sure you'll manage.'

After I'd retired to my room, I poured myself a dram of Talisker malt whisky from the cache of three bottles I'd brought with me to France. As I sipped my drink, I thought about what the Prof had said before I'd left him in the bar.

CHAPTER 3

"I'm sure you'll manage," had been the Prof's exact words. *I hoped that he'd meant the words in respect to me being new to his unit and not in relation to my physical condition. I also thought about my conversation with him earlier about why I had come back to serve again, despite having had the option of being invalided out. I had trotted out the line about "unfinished business" several times before to others asking the same question about my returning to service, but I knew it wasn't true. It wasn't that I was back in khaki despite my wounds, as everyone seemed to suppose, but that I was back because of my wounds. I needed to prove to myself that I was not a good-for-nothing war cripple. I didn't want my new disabilities to define me.*

I was confident enough in my own mental ability to do my new job. School dux, a first in law, an early call to the Scottish Bar and a series of court wins attested to that, although I knew these attributes also made me sometimes seem arrogant to others. I had always been a bit too quick with my tongue. My frequent smart-alec comments at school had led to corporal punishment on several occasions, and I'd been belted with a tawse for my sins.

A quick and sarcastic wit had certainly alienated some of the girls that I'd courted before I'd met Jeanie. I recalled one girl telling me that, "There's no point in having a silver tongue if it's razor sharp at the edges".

Thankfully, Jeanie had seen past that, and although she seemed as loving as ever on my last leave, I still fretted that she'd find herself attracted to some undamaged final-year medical student on her university course.

Professionally, I'd learned to hold my tongue after a few run-ins with High Court judges who had exerted the power of the bench to silence a young upstart like me. However, they were as nothing in their fierceness compared with the drill sergeants I'd encountered during my officer training. An angry, burly man sticking his face to only a few inches from your own while spraying you with spittle, and battering your eardrums with graphic epithets – and all the while politely calling you "sir" – was by far the most effective restraint I'd come across for speaking out of turn.

Now that I wasn't fit for combat, I hoped the Intelligence Corps would give me the opportunity to demonstrate my more cerebral abilities that had lain dormant during my time as an infantry subaltern. Nevertheless, there remained the traditional aspects of soldiering and I wasn't sure how I'd fare if I had to visit the front line again, or deal with the dead and dying. My fear was generated by the many nights of tortured sleep I'd endured since Loos, the previous September, when a German shell had put paid to my left eye, lacerated my left side, and given me a permanent limp. During the day, I was generally fine, but I now found myself dreading turning off my light and what the darkness would bring. The nightcaps of whisky were my response to the threat of nightmares; alcohol being my preferred drug to induce sleep.

I drifted back to the day's events. I wondered what the investigation into the assassination attempt on the King would reveal. How had German snipers got through our lines, and how had they known the King would be at that particular spot, at that specific time? Over the coming days, these were the questions I'd need to answer.

Sunday,
7th May 1916

CHAPTER 4

After my usual nightmare-riven sleep, I went out next morning to find Hodgson standing beside a very large staff car instead of the Model T.

'I think there must have been some mistake, Hodgson. Where did you get this monster?'

'That Model T was a bit dodgy, guv, so I went to the ASC lorry park to get a replacement. Turned out that the quartermaster sergeant was from my old bus depot in London, and I persuaded him to give me this instead.'

'It's an impressive piece of machinery,' I said, running my hand over its khaki-coloured bodywork.

'It's a 1914 Lanchester 40 tourer, guv. Nice runner. Forty horsepower. It was donated to the War Office by some landed gent. It's a bit of a rarity, I'm led to believe, as they didn't make many of them before the balloon went up.'

I was to learn in the coming days that Hodgson was very knowledgeable about all things mechanical, especially vehicles powered by combustion engines. I became convinced that his ambition was to be an expert in his Lanchester down to its last nut and bolt.

'Junior officers don't normally swan about in beasts like this. Are you sure you're not going to get me arrested for stealing some general's chariot?'

'We should be all right, guv. I've got a chitty that says it's ours.'

'Well, if you've got a chitty, then possession is nine-tenths of the law, Hodgson, even in King's Regulations, and I should know as I was a lawyer by trade before I joined up,' I said, as I climbed in and sat in the back.

'I've put your valise in the boot, guv. The ASC mechanics have removed the dicky seat and welded on this trunk, so we've plenty of space,' said Hodgson as he settled himself behind the steering wheel. 'Best thing about this motor is it's got an electric starter, so no need to crank the engine. Where to now, guv? I mean, sir.'

'Hodgson, we're going to jail,' I informed him.

*

The jail in question was in Étaples, the vast British Army base that swamped the coastal town of the same name some ten miles north-west of Montreuil. Those ten miles took us nearly an hour as we competed with the sheer number of Tommies in lorries, on horseback, and on foot, travelling to or from our destination.

Covering over five square miles, the base area we entered was the largest military centre Britain had ever built overseas. Its scale soon became evident. There were rows and rows of wooden huts and lines and lines of bell tents. There were fuel dumps and quartermasters' stores, parade grounds and recreation pitches, YMCA canteens and hospitals. Ominously, there was also a large cemetery for those who had died of wounds in those same hospitals. And then there were the infamous bullrings.

The bullrings were where Tommies received their combat training under the watchful eyes of screaming canaries. These canaries were drill instructors, so called because of the yellow armbands that they wore. As we drove past one such bullring, infantrymen were going through bayonet practice, stabbing with varying levels of enthusiasm at hessian dummies suspended from wooden frames. The exhortations of the canary leading the demonstration could clearly be heard above the Lanchester's engine, even though the instructor was a hundred yards away.

I directed Hodgson to the detention camp on the west side of the base. After exchanging salutes, I showed the sentry at the gate a letter. He let me through and I went inside. As I glanced back at the car, Hodgson was leaning his ample backside on the front wing of the Lanchester and lighting a cigarette. It was a pose I was to become familiar with in the days that followed.

Twenty minutes later, I was let out of the gate. I was accompanied by a small, swarthy private. My companion was in his mid-twenties and had dark eyes above a drinker's nose. He sported a scar on his right cheek that ran from the ear to the edge of his moustache and it gave him a slightly menacing air. Despite being bandy-legged and carrying his pack, he walked with a certain swagger.

'Hodgson, this is Rifleman McIlhenny, my batman. McIlhenny, this is Driver Hodgson,' I said, doing the introductions when we got to the car.

The two privates eyed each other warily before McIlhenny broke into a grin, and extended his hand, saying, 'Any pal of Mister Broon's a pal of mine.'

'For the umpteenth time, McIlhenny, I'm not your pal. We're in the army now in case you hadn't noticed,' I chided him.

'Next thing ye'll be tellin' me there's a war on, sur,' chuckled McIlhenny. 'And anyways, Ah saved yer life at Loos. If it wasn't for me, ye'd still be out there now, a bag of bleached bones, beggin' yer pardon, sur.'

What McIlhenny said was true. I was briefly transported back to the smoke and mud of the battlefield where I had lain wounded until I'd heard my batman's familiar voice shout, "Hey, stretcher-bearers, get yer arses over here double-quick. Ah've found Mister Broon, and he doesn't look too good". It was the last thing I remembered from that day before I blacked out.

'True, McIlhenny, and I just saved you a long stretch in the glasshouse for punching a canary, even if both you and the victim were drunk.'

'The Welsh bastard deserved it, sur, if ye'll pardon ma French. Ah was havin' a wee Friday night bevvy in the town with some of ma chinas from Glesga who're in the HLI. This Taffy called me and ma mates a bunch of circus midgets as he shuvved past us with his drinks. We're not bantams, for God's sake! He spilled ma drink and then refused to buy me another one. Then he tried to punch me, so Ah gubbed him. He started it, not me.'

I could see that Hodgson had only understood half of this conversation, finding McIlhenny's strong Glaswegian accent a formidable barrier to comprehension.

'Excuse me, guv, is he talking English?' Hodgson asked me.

'Although McIlhenny is from Glasgow, he is speaking the King's English, I can assure you,' I told him.

'Aye, well, the King's certainly not Scottish with a name like Saxe-Coburg whatever it is, that's for sure, sur,' rejoined McIlhenny.

'Strictly speaking, McIlhenny, your name's not Scottish either; it's Irish Catholic.'

'Don't start me on religion, sur. It's been bad enough puttin' up with all these Orange bastards in the regiment the last couple of years, believe me. No offence, sur.'

'I'm not sure I'm following this,' said Hodgson.

'The men he refers to as "Orange bastards" are members of the Orange Lodge, a Protestant organisation, found in Scotland and Ulster. I don't think they're big in England. They were the ones against the Free State in Ireland during last month's uprising. Our regiment, the Cameronians, is, historically, a staunch Protestant regiment, and so McIlhenny, as a Roman Catholic recruit, is somewhat unusual,' I explained.

'Ah was drunk and didn't know who Ah signed-up for. Ah just said to the recruitin' sergeant to stick me in with the rest of the blokes in the hall. Turns out they were all Proddies joinin' the Cameronians. And me a Roman Candle too! Ah'm not sure that takin' the King's shillin' was such a great idea,' said a downcast McIlhenny, shaking his head.

'Thanks for the history lesson, guv. You'd have thought they'd have got over all this religious nonsense after a couple of hundred years,' observed Hodgson.

'You don't know the half of it yet regarding this particular religious divide. Just don't start him on football.'

'Aye, don't start me on fitba'. Well, anyways, thanks for gettin' me out, sur.'

'With the character reference I gave you, McIlhenny, how could they not release you? Mind you, if half of what I said about you in there was true, the Pope will have you canonised.'

'Ah think we've got a St Peter already, sur,' laughed McIlhenny.

McIlhenny's humour was always infectious and I couldn't help but laugh too.

'Right, before we go any further, there are one or two things we need to sort out,' I told them.

'We're going to be together a lot, just the three of us in the car, and frankly it will be a bit inconvenient for you two to ask me for permission to speak every time we have a conversation and so on. However, if any other officer is present, I expect you to revert to the regulation etiquette. Do you understand?'

'Aye, thank ye, sur.'

'Thanks, guv.'

'And the same goes with the use of "guv", Hodgson. It's insubordinate language to a superior officer and would normally carry a three-month sentence in jankers.'

Hodgson turned pale. I felt sorry for him. I actually quite liked being called "guv" as if I was some sort of East End gangster, and, after all, I now called my own superior officer "Prof" in private.

'Sorry, sir. It's a habit. I used to be a London cabbie and "guv" or "guv'nor" was what we always called our fares.'

'Well, be sure not to call me that when other officers are around, or else I'll have to be seen to act.'

'I promise. Thanks again, guv.'

'We're all now in the Intelligence Corps and from time to time

25

you may be exposed to secret information. On no account must you divulge what our work is about to anyone. If you do give anything away, you could end up spending a very long time in the Aldershot Military Prison, assuming you've not been shot by firing squad. Do you understand that, too?'

'Aye, sur.'

'Yes, guv.'

'And just to be quite clear, McIlhenny, that means when drunk as well as when sober!'

'Aye, sur, Ah get it, Ah get it.'

'There's no special uniform as we're just seconded into the corps, and so you'll have to wear these with your normal uniforms,' I said as I passed over the two IC-marked armbands the Prof had given me.

'Where to now, guv?' asked Hodgson when my lecture was complete.

'Now, we're off to see a knight in his castle. By that, I mean General Sir Herbert Plumer at his HQ in Cassel, about fifty miles away.'

CHAPTER 5

Hodgson put his new colleague's kitbag in the boot and all three of us got into the car, with McIlhenny in the front beside Hodgson, and we set off.

As I sat in the back seat, I listened to the two privates chatting as they explored each other's personal history and interests. I knew McIlhenny's background from our time together in the Cameronians, and before that from when our paths had crossed as lawyer and client back in Scotland.

By eavesdropping, I learned as we drove along that Hodgson was from the East End of London and was a married man with two young children. He'd only joined up because his wife had cajoled him into it after her brothers had volunteered. Her siblings had accepted Kitchener's invitation after their uncle, an old seadog, had gone down with the *Lusitania* in May 1915 when it was sunk off Ireland by a German U-boat.

As a result of his driving skills, Hodgson had been posted to a Motor Transport Company in the ASC. These skills had been honed while working for the General Omnibus Company, and before that as a taxi driver. Earlier in his career, Hodgson had driven a horse-drawn hackney cab, working his way up from a livery stable boy after leaving school at fourteen. He didn't really like being in the army, and he missed his nippers terribly, but his wife less so. Once in France, he'd been assigned to a unit using buses requisitioned from his former employer to ferry troops up to the front, and back to rest areas. Hodgson's superiors apparently thought he was quite a good driver, and so he was eventually put on staff car duties, hence his current assignment.

Overall, he sounded a nice, dependable fellow and I was happy to have him. He was certainly a good driver, his gear changes were seamless, and he avoided braking heavily, anticipating problems on the road before they arose. In the coming weeks, I frequently dozed off, such was the smooth ride he delivered.

After about three hours, we reached the outskirts of the hilltop town of Cassel, climbed past its many windmills, negotiated its security checkpoints, and were soon parking the Lanchester outside Second Army HQ. I learned that General Plumer was busy and so, while we waited, I had McIlhenny sew on my extra pips, making me a captain in appearance as well as payroll.

*

Later that afternoon I was granted an audience with General Plumer. Up close, the General proved to be quite portly, with ruddy cheeks, a drooping white moustache, and a monocle in his right eye.

'Come in, Brown, take a seat.'

'Thank you, sir,' I said accepting the offer after saluting and removing my Glengarry.

The General sat at a large desk with a huge map of his command's sector behind him. The Ypres Salient was the standout feature of the map. The British battle line bulged into enemy territory with German guns on the higher ground to the east. The map had a grey blob at its centre representing the remains of the old Belgian cloth town of Ypres itself.

'Glad to have you with us, Brown, and good to have a real soldier with green tabs for a change. Where were you wounded?' asked the General.

'Loos, sir.'

'Regiment?'

'10th Cameronians, 15th (Scottish) Division, sir.'

'Good division, the 15th. You took Hill 70, didn't you? Furthest penetration of German lines by one of our divisions on the first day of the battle, wasn't it?'

'I believe so, sir, but I didn't make it that far with them.'

'I see. And the gong?' he asked, referring to my Military Cross ribbon.

'Charging a machine-gun post which was holding up our advance near Fort Glatz on the edge of Loos village, sir. A bit before Hill 70.'

'Brave thing to do,' acknowledged the General.

'Stupid thing to do, sir. I couldn't see where I was going in my smoke helmet until I was almost on top of the gun. Then a shell burst close by, and that's all I remember. Except…,' I found my voice trailing off.

'Except?'

'Except sometimes at night, sir, when I relive the experience over and over again.'

'Yes, well, good effort, Brown,' said the General, who seemed suddenly uncomfortable with where our conversation was going. I presumed that this was because he was a man who had to send thousands to be wounded or to their deaths as part of his job. I felt glad to be a relative peon as I wasn't sure I was mentally up to that sort of thing. 'Now, I have a task for you, Brown. Your corps has sent you here as a special investigator and I have an assignment for you that I need answers from as soon as possible.'

'Thank you, sir. I gather you requested I be assigned to your command.'

'Not me. I think you must be mistaken,' said the General, shaking his head and frowning.

If it wasn't General Plumer who had asked that I be assigned, I wondered who it had been. I didn't think I knew anyone on his staff. It was all very odd.

The General meanwhile was explaining that there had been an assassination attempt on the King the previous day which had resulted in the death of a Brigadier General Church-Fenton.

'It's a bit off trying to assassinate the King, don't you think?' asked the General. 'But then again, these Huns will try anything to gain advantage over us.'

'Yes, sir. I was actually in the crowd. I saw you there, too. German snipers firing from a nearby wood at the King, I gather. A lieutenant colonel shot them and brought back their rifle,' I said, but the General cut me off before I could go further.

'So, you saw it for yourself then. The quick action of Lord Ross, the officer you saw, prevented them getting a second shot off. Now, I want you to find out how those two Hun assassins got through our lines undetected. There will be hell to pay for whichever battalion it was that allowed them through, believe me!'

'Yes, sir,' I agreed, as I'd decided it was best to keep my answers short. General Plumer didn't seem like the sort of man who liked long-winded replies, and he was obviously quite exercised by what had happened.

'Apparently, there was a reporter from the *Daily Mail* present. That's all we need is for Lord Northcliffe to get involved. You saw the power he wields in sorting out the shell crisis last year?'

'Yes, sir.'

'Once the press have got over their indignation that the Germans would try to kill the King, they'll come after us for allowing it to happen in the first place. Northcliffe, as a Fleet Street publisher, has the power to change governments – and BEF generals, too, I don't doubt,' said the General, who had by now taken to walking up and down behind his desk. 'We'll be a laughing stock because of this. Allowing a couple of enemy soldiers to waltz over here and take a potshot at His Majesty. It's unthinkable. The King is none too pleased either, I can tell you.'

'I expect so, sir.'

'The dead brigadier was one of our main liaison officers with the French Army, so it's also embarrassing that we allowed some Hun sharpshooters to kill an officer that the French liked and trusted. Unfortunately, there was a Frog officer in the party, so we can't hide it from them, more's the pity.'

'I understand, sir.'

'I've drafted a warrant that gives you permission in my name to go wherever you choose to get this thing investigated as quickly as possible,' said the General, handing over an already-typed sheet with a barely-distinguishable H and P in the signature. 'Once you've got the answers, we'll decide what to tell the press about how these snipers got through. Get my ADC to set up a briefing on which units were where, and you can start your inquiries first thing tomorrow. I expect answers as soon as possible. That's all, Brown. Dismissed.'

I left the General's office and had a conversation with his aide-de-camp, during which I gathered useful advice on local food and lodgings, as well as fixing an appointment the next morning with a staff officer. After a phone call to the Prof to update him on events, I went outside and rescued McIlhenny and Hodgson from a game of "crown & anchor" with a sly-looking corporal cook from below stairs.

'Where to now, guv?'

'We'll go on to Poperinghe. I gather accommodation is a bit tight here in Cassel. I'll try to stay at the Toc H Club. We need to find the billeting officer to get him to find somewhere for you to stay.'

Monday,
8th May 1916

CHAPTER 6

I felt a bit guilty the next morning as I walked through the rain to climb into the Lanchester. I was slightly hungover after a good night in La Poupée with Archie Dunlop and some of his colleagues. I'd spent much of the evening in competition with my peers, flirting with the owner's famous daughter, Ginger, while drinking too much red wine. Ginger thought my eyepatch made me look "brave and 'andsome".

Our group had got quite drunk, and I vaguely remembered that a few had ventured off afterwards to Skindles, the local brothel for officers, although I had declined. Instead, I had pretended to be sober as I entered Talbot House, or Toc H, as the Tommies knew it. This was a necessary subterfuge as the club had been set up as a Christian alternative to the debauched recreational opportunities in Poperinghe. Somehow, I'd passed the front door test without the landlord, the Reverend Tubby Clayton, refusing me entry and I had retired to my room without the ignominy of being called out as a drunkard. Now I was suffering for my sins after all.

McIlhenny and Hodgson exchanged knowing looks and grins as I settled myself in the back seat.

Hodgson then asked his usual, 'Where to now, guv?'

'I need a briefing back at Second Army HQ. I've an appointment with a GSO in Cassel in an hour.'

*

The General Staff Officer Grade 1 that I met was a lieutenant colonel, and he showed me a trench map of the front-line sector of Second Army. The map seemed more detailed than those I had used at Loos. The GSO explained to me that this was probably due to the denser aerial photograph coverage that was now available, plus more detailed Royal Engineers' surveys and panoramic photographs.

The map looked like two spiders' webs lying side by side. The British trenches in blue ink were on the left of the map opposite the German trenches in red on the right. The trench lines facing the enemy were crenulated in a Grecian key pattern to represent fire bays and traverses. This arrangement of earthworks prevented shell bursts travelling too far down the trench or an enemy firing enfilade along it if it was infiltrated.

On the British side there were three main lines, with the first, the fire trench, directly opposite the enemy, facing out into no-man's land. This was connected at intervals to a supervisory trench immediately behind it, and together they formed the front line. The second line, a support trench, ran more or less parallel about one hundred yards behind the first. This was designed to provide shelter for backup troops, and offered a place of refuge during heavy bombardments. About a quarter of a mile behind the support trench was the third line, the reserve trench.

Communication trenches ran at almost right angles back to the rear and were the entry points to the whole system. These were zigzagged to prevent damage along their length if a shell exploded inside the excavations. Strong points and fortified villages were noted on the map, as well as major dugouts and shelters. The map was also annotated with the aid posts and field ambulances that interlinked to form the first part of a chain to assess and evacuate the wounded.

The German defences mirrored the British lines, but if anything, had even more strongpoints or redoubts. The sheer scale of the fortifications made it abundantly clear to me why any progress was difficult for either side, especially when the defenders of the trench system were backed by machine guns, mortars, and massed artillery, and major attack preparations were under the watchful eye of observation balloons and spotter aircraft.

Despite the comic or homesick titles of the features on the map that had been named by Tommies, such as "Deadman's Corner" and "Old Kent Road", just looking at the chart and the complexity of the trenches in this one corner of the war made me feel quite depressed.

The various units holding the line were marked on the map. The German units according to the GSO were identified from prisoners or field maps captured on raids, rare radio and telephone intercepts, and sharp eyes using trench periscopes to recognise badges and uniform emblems. Since the enemy's divisions were recruited from the various German states, some experts could apparently identify them from the regional accents of their troops as they shouted insults across no-man's land or sang marching songs.

'It's a bit like Professor Higgins in George Bernard Shaw's new play, *Pygmalion*,' explained the GSO.

'I don't think I've seen that one, sir,' I told him.

'Well, it's worth a visit to His Majesty's Theatre, if it's still on in London. It's a romantic comedy. Mrs Patrick Campbell's in it. She's rather good.'

The GSO was obviously a theatre lover, but I was mindful of General Plumer's sense of urgency. The General didn't seem to be a man to disappoint.

'Thank you for the recommendation, sir. Now about the shooting?' I asked in an effort to refocus my theatre critic.

The GSO pointed out exactly where the incident involving the royal party had taken place. I noted the units immediately in front of it. On the British side, the line was held by a battalion of Seaforth Highlanders. According to intelligence gleaned, opposite them was a regiment of *Jaegers*, the German word for hunters.

'This map is a few days old. Based on the planned unit rotation, that Jock battalion should have been back in reserve by now.

However, since the incident, we've kept more rifles in the line and they're still there.' The GSO looked up his records, before telling me, 'The Seaforth's CO is Lieutenant Colonel Lord Ross. He was the chap who shot those German snipers that tried to kill the King, wasn't he? Good man.'

'Right, I'll start by paying them a visit, and then approach their flanking battalions after that if there's no evidence of enemy penetration in the Seaforth's sector.'

The GSO promised to warn Lord Ross that I would be calling in on his battalion headquarters, but, unfortunately, he couldn't offer me a guide to lead me into the trenches. I made several notes and a sketch map in a moleskin notebook before leaving.

As I approached McIlhenny and Hodgson outside, it seemed to me that they were getting on quite well, despite their linguistic difficulties, and were obviously sharing a good joke.

'Where to now, guv?'

'We're going up to the front.'

The grins on the privates' faces dissolved at this sobering news.

*

We drove only a few miles east to the northern flank of the Salient in Belgian Flanders. As we got closer to the front line, our rate of progress reduced considerably. Although the troops were delivered from their disembarkation ports by train, the last approach to the trenches was made on foot and so we had to slow down to pass columns of marching infantry. Many of the battalions sang as they marched, although the words of their ditties varied greatly from the official versions sung in the music halls back in Blighty. A Welsh regiment sang like a male voice choir on the march, and, despite his recent run-in with a Welshman, McIlhenny was quite moved by their rousing "Men of Harlech".

Then we heard the skirl of bagpipes as a highland regiment, kilts swinging, hove into view. The pipers were playing "Blue Bonnets

Over the Border", and I recalled that this was the tune I'd heard at Loos as I lay wounded. For a moment, I was back on the battlefield, with men dropping around me and the din of exploding shells, the tat-tat-tat of machine guns, the wisps of gas, the shouted orders, the banks of barbed wire, and the churned-up earth underfoot, all flooding back.

'Are ye all right there, sur?' I heard a voice ask through my fugue. McIlhenny had brought me back to the present.

'Yes, I'm fine, McIlhenny. Drive on, Hodgson.'

As we approached our destination, we came upon a deserted village. Shelling had damaged many of the village's houses and the interiors gaped open to the elements, displaying a gaudy array of wallpapers and shattered plaster cornicing. All the buildings had been stripped of furniture and timber for firewood or for support woodwork in the trenches. It was a forlorn and depressing sight, made worse by the overcast sky and late-morning drizzle.

We stopped at a field canteen which a sign told us was run by "The Canteen & Mess Co-operative Society". I treated us all to a cup of tea – char in army slang – in preparation for the next phase of our journey. It was not the "done thing" for officers to sit with their men, and so I sat apart from the other two inside the marquee.

McIlhenny bought some cigarettes and a box of matches and he and Hodgson enjoyed a smoke at a nearby table, McIlhenny on Capstans and Hodgson on Woodbines. I had been forced to give up smoking after Loos and I really missed the calming effect of a smoke and would dearly have loved one now before revisiting the trenches. The only upside to my abstinence was that Jeanie hated the smell of smoke on my clothes and had always wanted me to give up. That was a small mercy at times like this.

Instead of smoking, I read a *Daily Mail* that I'd found. The *Mail* was far more bellicose than the average Tommy in its outlook, but its journalists were well connected, and so it often led the news with breaking stories. From the paper, which was dated Saturday, 6th May, I learned that the Battle of Verdun further south had entered its third month with no sign of respite for the French despite General Nivelle being put in charge; that the South Africans were fighting the Germans in East Africa; that the British authorities were executing the Irish Nationalist leaders of the recent Easter Uprising with unseemly haste; and that the Americans were making threatening noises at Mexico.

As always, there was news from the BEF on the Western Front too, although, despite the paper's contacts, I doubted the accuracy of all the claims due to censorship. There was one short piece by Beach Thomas, my war correspondent acquaintance. I finished the paper wondering what he would say about the attempt on the King and was really glad that I'd escaped his clutches as he might have wanted a quote from a witness.

I pulled out my sketch maps and planned our next move. 'Right, you two, let's be having you,' I then told McIlhenny and Hodgson.

'That was a nice wee rest, sur. Thanks. Ye can always rely on the Co-op for a good cup of char and a fag,' said McIlhenny as we set off into the danger zone.

'Thank goodness the rain's stopped, guv,' observed Hodgson. 'These roads near the front are awful muddy. Terrible on the paintwork.'

*

When we finally arrived near our starting point for the trip into the trenches, I told Hodgson to park the Lanchester in the shadow of a destroyed farm cottage. I'd selected the spot as it was some distance away from a siege battery of six heavy howitzers which were being emplaced off the side of the road. I didn't want our precious car being hit by counter-battery fire if the Germans decided to warm things up in this sector. Four of the large guns were already in gun pits and gunners from the Royal Garrison Artillery were spreading camouflage nets over their charges. The last two guns were being hauled into position by Holt caterpillar tractors. These large American machines belched black exhaust fumes as they turned off the road and pulled the guns cross-country to their pre-dug positions.

We all got out and McIlhenny went to the boot of the car. He had converted the Lanchester's storage into a veritable emporium of weapons, equipment, rations, and other supplies. I was actually quite impressed as he'd certainly had to work quickly during our one night in Pop. I thought it best not to ask where all the stuff had come from as I might not like the answer, for my batman was a born scrounger. If unsuccessful at scrounging, he was not above thieving.

McIlhenny passed out three tin hats. These Brodie steel helmets had become mandatory at the front since my battle where the BEF had gone to war in service caps, smoke helmets, and other soft furnishings. He then helped me on with my Burberry trench coat before he donned a waterproof cape.

I put my Webley revolver in its holster on over my coat and checked it was fully loaded. I was relieved to see I wasn't shaking too much as I steeled myself for our planned excursion.

McIlhenny removed a Lee-Enfield rifle from the boot. He proceeded to check the safety catch was on, that the bolt moved freely, and the magazine was full. He put a canvas cover over the breech to keep out mud, before putting the rifle over his shoulder on its sling.

'Just in case the Alleymen decide to visit, sur,' said McIlhenny, patting his rifle. 'Clean, bright, and slightly oiled. Ma preferred condition, too.' For reasons I could never fathom, officers tended to use the word "Hun"' for our opponents, while our men tended to call them "Alleymen", in a bastardisation of the French *Allemands*, or simply "Jerries".

As I watched his professional handling of the rifle, I remembered that McIlhenny had passed the infantryman test of fifteen rifle shots per minute with flying colours, and was a reasonable marksman into the bargain. I was comforted by having him as my escort and was sure that if any Alleymen did visit, he'd give them short shrift.

McIlhenny next slung a water bottle over his other shoulder and then pulled out gas-mask satchels and gave me one. I fervently hoped I wouldn't have to put the mask on. I'd developed claustrophobia after my experience at Loos where I'd had to wear a smoke hood, an early type of gas mask. The irony was that it had been to keep out British gas, released before the attack into a capricious wind, and some of it had blown back into our battalion's lines. The smell of the impregnated chemicals, the broken mica eyepiece, and the hood's damp flannel which prevented me from breathing properly, had somehow conjured up in me a fear of being closed in. Despite the hood, I was gassed when it had been holed by the shrapnel shell that wounded me. My lungs had been affected slightly by the gas, which was why I no longer smoked. I remembered the weird dream-like sensation I'd felt as we had advanced in our white hoods through the smoke of battle, amid the cacophony of shellfire and machine guns towards the German line, my platoon looking like aliens out of an H.G. Wells' novel. For a moment I was back there. I realised that I'd left the present once more when McIlhenny asked me a question and tugged my arm.

'Everthin' all right, sur?'

'Of course,' I countered somewhat gruffly, pulling myself together, although this was easier said than done. Meanwhile, Hodgson was looking distinctly green in hue.

'Are you all right Hodgson?' I asked my driver in turn, to divert attention away from myself.

'Sorry, guv, it's just that I've never been in the trenches before, and last time I was this close, my B-Type got blown up.'

'Your B-Type?'

'Yes, guv. I was driving an old London B-Type bus, full of troops, up to the front. We got shelled and one landed behind us. We'd had the windows removed from the buses and fixed railway sleepers to the sides as protection, but they didn't work. A shell landed too close. A lot of the lads were between me and the explosion. Most of them copped it, but, somehow, I survived without a scratch. However, I still get nervous when I hear shelling.'

'Why didn't you tell us this before?'

'Didn't seem the same as you going over the top and all, guv.'

'Look, it's not a problem. You stay here and look after the vehicle and we'll be back as quickly as we can,' I told the hugely relieved Hodgson. In reality, I didn't need a passenger on a trip into the trenches, and there was no need to endanger him.

As a final act before going into the line, I removed my hip flask from under my coat and gave McIlhenny a swig before taking a draught myself.

'That's a lot tastier than SRD rum, sur, and no mistake,' said McIlhenny, referring to the tot of spirits issued to Tommies at dawn and dusk, or before they were about to go over the top.

'The Chief's own brand,' I informed him, alluding to my flask's Haig whisky, distilled back in Scotland by the family of the British Commander-in-Chief, Sir Douglas Haig.

After our sip of Dutch courage, we left Hodgson, and McIlhenny and I headed into the trenches. My first big test, mental as well as physical, since returning to active duty was about to unfold, and I wondered how I'd cope.

CHAPTER 7

We had to walk nearly a mile overground just to get to the start of the trench system. I felt quite exposed despite the tall canvas screens that had been erected to obscure movement from German observers. It didn't bode well, in my opinion, that the flapping canvas had been shredded in places by shellfire. The recent rain had ensured that the wooden duckboard path to the trench lines was slippery. It ran over glutinous mud, and all around us the shell holes were filled with stagnant rainwater.

It was mid-afternoon when we entered the appropriate communication trench. I would have preferred to have made the journey at night when it was safest, but I needed to press on. The communication trench started quite shallow and deepened the closer it got to the front. The trench signposts along the way gave me assurance that a regiment of Jocks was further down the sunken pathway. Our main route was called the "Caledonian Road", and there were signs with arrows directing us to "Dingwall Drive", "Inverness High Street", and to other similarly-named trenches. Amongst these direction indicators, other signs reminded passers-by about what to do in the event of a gas attack, exhorted them to take abandoned equipment to salvage dumps for recycling, and warned them to keep their heads down due to snipers.

The trudge down the winding communication trench slowly became agonising, and my limp more pronounced. I'd left my good walking stick behind with Hodgson, and I now depended for support on an old bamboo cane that I'd commandeered at Second Army HQ. It was a bit too flexible for what was required and often got stuck in the mud between the slots of the duckboards on the trench floor. As I led us down the trench, McIlhenny tunelessly whistled "Tipperary" behind me, seemingly oblivious to his environment. I envied him.

The duckboards were treacherous for our entire journey, not only due to the recent showers, but the fact that the water table in Flanders was very shallow. The latter resulted in rapid water ingress whenever excavations were made, and the trench walls were lined with wood and corrugated-iron revetting to prevent them collapsing. A cat's cradle of field telephone wires and electrical cables was pinned to the woodwork along the entire length of the trench, hanging limp in places where some passing Tommy had pulled on it to steady himself.

Our passageway was only three feet wide, and, where there wasn't a convenient passing bay, we had to step off the duckboards into the mud proper and press ourselves against the trench wall to make way for traffic coming up from the front. At various times we stepped aside for men going to collect rations, for officers' runners with unnecessary reports to keep HQ happy, and, sadly, for the odd stretcher party. Sadder still was a burial party carrying a corpse to the rear on a plank. The dead soldier had a small, neat wound in his forehead, while the back of his skull was a mess of blood, bone and brains oozing out of a fist-sized hole. No doubt the death was the result of the man's own carelessness and the quick reactions of a German sniper when a head had appeared above the British parapet.

By the time we got to the reserve trench behind the front line after two miles of slipping and sliding along the muddy pathway, I was a limping, sweaty, dirty, foul-mouthed mess. We stopped for a rest in a cutting off the trench, and I had a pull on my hip flask, while McIlhenny lit a cigarette. However, we soon realised from the stench and the buckets of lime nearby that we were at the entrance to the latrines. I saw a sign saying "Highlanders Rest", and pointed it out to McIlhenny.

'We should have guessed what that was for. Let's get out of here.'

My urgency was not driven solely by the insanitary conditions, but by the knowledge that German *minenwerfer* crews looked out for the clouds of flies that attended latrine pits and specifically aimed mortars at the unfortunate Tommies unloading their expected daily four and a half ounces of excrement and eight ounces of urine. Although it was early in the year for flies, I wasn't taking any chances. McIlhenny flicked his unfinished cigarette into the pit where a whooshing noise indicated a minor methane explosion had been ignited.

'Well, that saved some hairy-arsed Tommie gettin' his balls burned off,' quipped McIlhenny and it was a moment of light relief in the day's proceedings.

We next stopped at the Regimental Aid Post in the communication trench. The post was in a large dugout ready to take up to twenty casualties for their first assessment. It was empty of patients for now and in it we found a young medical officer of the Royal Army Medical Corps. He looked more like a schoolboy than a hardened front-line medic. The MO gave us directions to the Seaforth commander's location.

Based on these new instructions, we found the battalion commander's underground dugout. Beside the entrance to the dugout was a large brass shell casing with a claw hammer attached for use as a gas alarm. A chemical sprayer to neutralise chlorine gas was also at hand, along with an anti-gas fan on a broomstick to waft fumes away from the dugout entrance. I wondered about the efficacy of both tools and prayed that they, like my gas mask, would not be needed. A Very pistol hung beside the alarm, ready to send emergency flares high into the sky to signal back to our artillery if supporting fire was required. On the other side of the entrance was a small loft containing a pair of cooing carrier pigeons. Attached to the wooden lintel of the dugout's entrance was a stag's skull and antlers, the regimental symbol of the Seaforths, and below was a hand-painted sign saying "The Laird's Lair".

*

I pulled back the heavy gas curtain to enter the cramped underground space and went down some steps into the shelter. It was a cut and cover dugout, excavated as a large hole, roofed, and then covered over with earth. The low ceiling was of corrugated-iron sheeting over wooden beams, and the walls were panelled with wood from old packing cases. It was quite dark as there was only one weak electric light bulb, although this was supplemented by a few smoking oil lamps and guttering candles. There was a continuous background "putt, putt, putt" noise of a pump struggling to keep the place from being inundated by water. The dugout had a rather fetid smell of unwashed bodies, whale oil, mildew, and earthy soil. I felt my claustrophobia returning.

'Are ye really sure yer all right, sur?' asked a concerned McIlhenny once more.

I was aware I was swaying a bit, so I held on to the wall and lied, 'Fine. Just give me a sip of water and I'll be fine.' I removed my helmet and took a swig from McIlhenny's canteen.

'Is Colonel Ross here?' I then shouted more loudly than I intended, into the gloom. To my surprise I was answered by a loud bark before what appeared to be a large, shaggy greyhound approached me, its tail wagging.

'Don't mind him. Can I help you?' asked a captain from a shadowy corner of the dugout. The man got up from a makeshift desk with a field telephone and an oil lamp on it, and approached us. The officer had close-cropped red hair and, although he was probably only my age, he was greying at the temples, a familiar attribute of my peers who had endured several tours of the trenches. He was wearing a kilt of blue and green tartan covered by a khaki apron. 'I'm Rhori

47

MacPherson, adjutant to Lord Ross, the battalion CO, and this is Gaisgeach, our battalion mascot.'

'Captain James Brown, Intelligence Corps, accompanied by Rifleman McIlhenny. I'm here to see Lieutenant Colonel Ross about the recent assassination attempt on the King. You should have been forewarned I was coming by Second Army HQ.'

'Ah, yes, we were expecting you. I'll tell Lord Ross you're here. He's out on an inspection right now,' said MacPherson, and he sent the only other occupant of the dugout, a runner, to fetch the Colonel.

I patted the hairy mascot while waiting and it seemed friendly enough. 'What kind of dog is it?' I asked MacPherson in an effort to make conversation while we waited.

'He's a deerhound. There are few breeds faster over rough ground, and he's even been over the bags with us. Since you're a Sassenach and won't have the Gaelic, his name means "warrior",' said the adjutant, referring to my accent being from south of the Highland Line.

'Yes, you're right, I've not seen the breed before,' I had to agree. 'We don't have much need for deerhounds near Glasgow.' I must admit I found the other captain's patronising tone a bit grating. Maybe he thought I was just a desk wallah and hadn't taken in the eyepatch and the walking stick. Or maybe he just disliked Sassenachs. Or maybe he was just a sullen bastard all the time.

A few minutes later, Lieutenant Colonel Ross appeared from behind the curtained entrance. Even in the poor light, I recognised the man from the assassination attempt, although this time, like his adjutant, the Colonel was in a kilt, rather than trews. I sent McIlhenny off in search of tea with the runner, while we officers settled in a motley collection of chairs around an old dining table, no doubt scavenged from some derelict French farmhouse, for a glass of something stronger.

MacPherson poured a measure of Glenmorangie malt whisky into three unmatched cracked glasses. The Colonel described it as his local tipple from Tain, not far from his estate in Ross-shire. Ross packed a pipe with tobacco and lit up, while his adjutant pulled a cigarette from a tin of Dunhill's. I declined his offer of a smoke.

'Please yourself. These are the healthy type. Got a little filter on them,' said MacPherson as he applied a match.

Once the preliminaries about the reason for my visit were over, and *slàinte mhath* Gaelic toasts exchanged and whiskies sipped, Ross gave details of his rapid excursion into the woods after the sniper shot. Our conversation had to be almost shouted to be heard above the noise of the pump and the snores and farts of the dog, which had settled below the table.

'I really don't remember much about it,' said Ross, in an accent that was more that of the English upper class, than Scot's highlander. 'I heard the shot and saw the Brigadier fall, and turned and rode quickly into the woods where the shot had come from without thinking. Rather stupid thing to do, on reflection, as someone had just been sniped from there, and I could easily have been the second victim. I saw two Germans running in the trees, pulled out my Webley, and shot them. I dismounted, picked up their sniper rifle, and rode back. That's about it.'

'I'm sorry to have to ask you this, sir, but do you have any indications that those two Germans may have crossed over into our lines via the sector held by your battalion?'

'What a bloody cheek!' exclaimed MacPherson.

'It's all right, Rhori, the Captain is only doing his job. Don't take affront. I'm sorry, Brown, you'll have to forgive MacPherson's manners. He's a foreigner from across the border in Invernesshire,' joked Ross. 'As I recall, we have no record of any such incursions; in fact, rather the opposite. We sent out a number of successful patrols in the other direction and pulled in a few prisoners who we then passed on up the line for interrogation.'

'For the sake of good order, may I see the battalion war diary to confirm there were no breakthroughs.'

'Are you doubting a Peer of the Realm, old boy?'

'Sorry, sir, force of habit. I was a criminal lawyer before the war.'

'Show him the diary, Rhori,' said Ross with a sigh.

Upon receiving the book, I quickly flicked back in the diary to the days before the assassination attempt. It wasn't easy to read in the poor light conditions. There were only two entries different from the repetitive days of routine line-holding. The first was a raid on the German trenches two nights before the key date, which had led to the capture of three prisoners. The second concerned a sentry being caught asleep at his post on the same night.

'This sentry, asleep at his post,' I asked, tapping the entry in the book. 'A Private McNicol. What's that about?'

'McNicol. The man's a bloody scoundrel and a thief,' said Ross with vehemence. 'He's very unreliable. We should never have allowed him to join the battalion. He'll soon get his well-deserved comeuppance after sleeping on sentry duty.'

'You don't think anyone could have sneaked through when he was out of it?'

'Hmm, I suppose it's always possible, but I don't believe so. That bit of the line was held by Sergeant MacKenzie. He's a decorated war hero and hard as nails. I don't see anything getting passed him, although, come to think of it, he was out on the raid that night. He's a bit of a specialist at night raids. He was our head gamekeeper and is used to catching poachers at night.'

'I'd like to talk to him, if I may?'

'Of course. A bit of a warning though, Brown. MacKenzie can be a bit abrupt. He's an angry man these days. He absolutely hates the Germans. His younger brother, Hamish, was in our battalion, too, and was out on a raid one night when he got caught in a bear trap put out by the Huns in no-man's land. MacKenzie knows all about traps being a gamekeeper. Anyway, his brother was caught by the leg and screaming blue bloody murder, and so MacKenzie went out in broad daylight the next day to rescue him. He crawled right up to his sibling and had just released the jaws of the trap to free Hamish, when a German sniper shot his brother through the head. MacKenzie reckons the sniper was watching, playing with them, and just waiting until his brother was free before taking the shot. So, he hates all Germans, and particularly snipers.'

'Where do I find him?'

'His company is in the fire trench, a few fire bays down on the right. Please, go ahead. You look like you've been in a trench before,' said Ross, nodding at the obvious evidence from my appearance, and seemingly more observant than his adjutant.

CHAPTER 8

Exiting the dugout, I was relieved to be above ground again, even in the narrow confines of a trench, and took a couple of deep breaths. At least I could see sky overhead, grey though it was. I put my helmet back on and collected McIlhenny. We made our way down the last hundred yards of the communication trench to the T-junction with the front line. I felt a surge of fear, mixed with excitement, and my already high adrenaline levels seemed to peak, my heart beating faster, and my knees getting weaker. I hadn't felt like this since I'd stood in a trench at Loos and blown my whistle for my platoon to go over the top. With difficulty, I suppressed my flight instinct, helped by another sip from my hip flask, and allowed McIlhenny a similar draught.

McIlhenny, with his rifle at the port position, was in front as we moved off. He suddenly slipped on a wet duckboard and put his hand out to steady himself. This action was followed by a string of expletives as he'd accidentally grabbed a piece of barbed wire protruding from the wall of the trench.

'Fuckin' barbed wire. Ah hate fuckin' barbed wire,' he exclaimed, and he pulled out a handkerchief and wrapped it round his bleeding hand.

We ignored the narrow supervisory trench and turned right at the T-junction and proceeded to zigzag our way through various traverses in the six-foot-deep cutting of the fire trench in the direction instructed. The trench had a parapet of half-filled sandbags on the side facing the enemy, with a step below to be mounted when firing, and a parados of mounded earth on the side away from the Germans to protect from shell bursts. I couldn't help but notice the unique smell of the fire trench, a combination of residual cordite fumes, sweat and flatulence, stale rations, and rotting flesh. Rats scurried around us underfoot, dodging in and out of the drainage sump below the duckboards. As my senses were assaulted by the sights, sounds and smells of the trench, my mind kept flitting back to September the previous year when I'd scaled a ladder, and led my men towards the waiting Germans. Once more I forced myself to concentrate and tried to blot out these old images from my mind.

Off one of the fire bays we found a lookout peering out towards the enemy through a box periscope fixed to the wall of a sap dug towards the Germans. Despite my intruding memories, I couldn't resist having a look and the sentry made way. I put the viewfinder to my good eye. I was slightly nervous as I knew that German snipers liked to aim at the reflections off the mirror at the top of a periscope, and, if this happened, the shards of broken glass would tumble down inside the device into my eye. The last thing I wanted was to lose my remaining sight, but something compelled me to do it.

About twenty yards in front of me lay the barbed-wire entanglements protecting the British line. Two belts of wire, ten to fifteen feet wide and up to five feet high, hung from old wooden posts and newer steel pickets, for all the world looking like giant bramble patches. These were mirrored some one hundred yards away by the Germans' bundles of wire. Broken glass glinted beneath these entanglements, put there to discourage anyone from crawling underneath. The few gaps between these masses had trip wires with tin cans attached to act as alarms, in case of a night raid. The narrow strip of no-man's land in between the sets of wire looked like a chaotic, badly ploughed field from the low angle I was viewing, reflecting a pockmarked landscape of shell holes. As it was still daylight, nothing stirred on the other side. I thanked the sentry and we moved on.

'Ah'm really glad we don't have to go into the trenches any more,' said McIlhenny as we slithered along the wet wooden pathway.

'I didn't expect you to get cold feet, McIlhenny.'

'It's not that, sur. Ah just can't stand mugs of char tastin' of petrol out those cans the ASC ship the water up in. It's diabolical, so it is.'

McIlhenny's ranting on liquid refreshment was halted by an imposing figure blocking the trench. The man's weather-beaten features indicated an outdoor life, while the three dirty white chevrons on his sleeve suggested this was the sergeant we were looking for.

'Sergeant MacKenzie?' I asked.

'Aye, sir, that's me,' said the NCO in a deep highland voice.

'I'm Captain Brown of the Intelligence Corps and, with your CO's permission, I have a few questions for you.'

We sat down on some empty hessian sandbags on the fire step. They didn't provide much insulation and I could soon feel the cold seeping into my buttocks. I looked over at the Sergeant and noted that in the shadows at the bottom of the trench the former gamekeeper cut a menacing figure. I certainly wouldn't have liked to meet him on a moonlit night out on the moors or in no-man's land.

'Four nights ago, you led a raid that captured some Germans. Brave work, Sergeant, and something you're rather good at I'm told.' I'd been trained to put the witness in a good frame of mind before proceeding to the more difficult questions, but I wasn't sure this lawyer's tactic would work on the Sergeant.

'Aye, that's right, sir. We'd been sent out to capture some prisoners for interrogation and to find out which regiment was opposite us. Going out on a raid is like being back home looking for poachers after our deer and salmon. All you need is a club like this to give them a wee knock on the head to be sure they come quietly, and if they don't, then a wee nick on the cheek or a gun in the ribs is usually all they need,' said MacKenzie, brandishing a South African knockberry, a Scottish dirk, and a captured German Luger pistol in quick succession. When added to the Mills bombs, wire cutters, hedging gloves, and signalling pistol the man was festooned with, the Sergeant was a veritable walking Christmas tree.

'What happened that night?'

'Eight of us went over the top. We crawled out through a gap in our wire into no-man's land and lay awhile, just listening. Then we heard some clinking noises and so crawled over in that direction. We found four Jerries digging a sap out from their fire trench. They were setting up a sniper's post, I'm sure. We had a bit of a fight. No guns, just clubs and knives. One of them was killed, but we got the other three subdued and brought them back in for questioning.'

'And what happened when you came back from the raid?'

The NCO's features darkened, even in the shadows, as he replied. 'We weren't challenged by our sentry when we got to our wire. We gave the password, but there was no reply. I came over the top of our bags to find Private McNicol sleeping at his post. I wakened him and put him on a charge. He claimed he was ill. I reported him to my platoon subaltern, who informed the CO. I was told to send McNicol up to the provosts while I was to take the prisoners to the nearest cage. I gave McNicol to my corporal to deliver to the Red Caps. With a couple of my men, I then took the prisoners up the communication trench back to the rear. Two of the Jerries attempted to escape just as we came out of the trench, so I shot them.' The Sergeant said this as casually as he might recall putting a wounded deer out of its misery.

'I gather from your CO that you particularly don't like snipers, and after hearing about your brother, I can't say I blame you, MacKenzie. However, shooting prisoners is against the Geneva Convention, Sergeant.'

'But not escaping prisoners, sir, surely? Not prisoners who refuse to stop running and could cause trouble behind our lines.'

'You say you shot two. What happened to the third?'

'The third was in front of me under another escort. There's a prisoner of war cage nearby. Prisoners go there before getting sent back for interrogation and on to the PoW camps, so he was sent to the cage.'

'What happened to the shot prisoners?'

'They were buried near the PoW cage.'

'Did you see any evidence of other Germans out in no-man's land? Any other patrols? Any cut wire? Hear anything?'

'Not a thing untoward, sir.'

'I realise this is embarrassing for you and the battalion, but do you think it's possible a German party could have sneaked through past this sleeping sentry? I'm investigating the attempted assassination of the King by German snipers, you see.'

'I suppose it's possible,' said the Sergeant slowly.

'And where is Private McNicol now?' I asked. 'I'd like to question him.'

'He's in the glasshouse, sir. But soon, I hope he'll be rotting in Hell if he's put the King's life and the regiment's reputation at risk,' said MacKenzie, alluding to the punishment of death by firing squad for sleeping sentries.

Private McNicol certainly didn't seem too popular around his battalion, and I wondered what he'd done to generate such strong feelings; feelings which obviously pre-dated him sleeping at his post.

'All right, Sergeant. That will be all. It will soon be time for "stand to", so I'll let you get back to your duties,' I said, concluding the interview.

'Cheery lot, these teuchters, eh sur?' opined McIlhenny, using the epithet of a Lowland Scot for his northern brethren. 'Imagin' wearin' a kilt in the trenches. Must be a bit draughty in the winter if what they say about highlanders is true.'

We returned to "The Laird's Lair" and informed the adjutant of our findings. MacPherson was none too happy about my proposition that German snipers could have crossed over into British-held territory past a sleeping sentry of his battalion, but for me it was an obvious possibility. He did seem pleased, however, that the case against McNicol would almost certainly lead to the severest punishment.

*

On our way out of the trenches we stopped at the Regimental Aid Post again. I asked the MO to take a quick look at McIlhenny's hand. Even though the barbs had only made a small cut, the mud, rats, and open latrines made a fertile breeding ground for bacteria and disease, any of which could infect even the smallest wound, causing tetanus or even life-threatening sepsis. The MO cleaned the cut, declared it infection free, and put a small bandage over it.

'By the way, can you please tell me if you saw a Private McNicol a few days ago?' I asked the MO. 'He was put on a charge for sleeping at his post, but he claimed that he was ill. He must have passed this way.'

'As a matter of fact, I did, sir. I was at the door as I knew we'd had a raid on. The man was staggering up the communication trench under the escort of a corporal. I asked him if he was all right, but the corporal interrupted and told me the man had been found asleep on sentry duty. The private said he wasn't feeling well. I pulled him in here and had a quick look at him under the lights. He wasn't one hundred percent, that's for sure. Seemed quite disorientated, in fact. His eyes were wandering all over the place and his pupils were quite dilated and hadn't reacted to the light. However, I didn't get the chance to examine him properly as the battalion adjutant came up and ordered them to "move along". He said he wanted the private – who he called McNicol – in custody as soon as possible. The adjutant was with a party of prisoners being taken to the rear.'

I thanked the MO and we left the aid post.

'The adjutant here's not too popular with the troops, if ye don't mind me sayin' so, sur. Accordin' to that runner Ah had a mug of char with, while the boys were all stuck in the line, their adjutant

57

disappeared for a few days after takin' the prisoners out. They didn't see him again until he pitched up yesterday. They didn't mind the CO goin' to greet the King though. That was a feather in their cap. Apparently, the CO is quite pally with the royals.'

I was only half-listening, as McIlhenny blathered on. Mentally, I was preparing myself for the return trip up the rest of the communication trench. I wasn't sure which was the worst, the claustrophobia of the dugouts, the physical exertion of hauling myself back up the trench, or the fear of being shelled again at any time. I was well aware that communication trenches were favourite targets of the German guns during the so-called "Evening Hate".

As we made our way out in the gathering dusk, we found ourselves going contraflow to a ration party. Pairs of men were carrying either three-gallon dixies or insulated hay boxes full of hot food, which, from the smell, were mostly full of Maconochie's eponymous stew. Other men carried sandbags which I knew would be full of bread, hardtack biscuits, margarine, and pozzy jam. Some hefted two-gallon petrol cans, washed out and now used for drinking water, as McIlhenny had alluded to earlier. The old axiom that an army marches on its stomach remained true, even in the trenches where there wasn't much marching going on. The corporal in charge of the party carried jars marked SRD, full of rum for the welcome evening tot. All of the porters were further loaded due to the regulation that required them to carry rifles and gas masks at all times.

'Smells like stew. Thank God at our new digs we don't have to eat any more of Maconochie's fuckin' stew. Ah hate Maconochie's fuckin' stew, so Ah do,' McIlhenny informed me. 'Mind you, Ah miss the old shot of rum every night and mornin'. Ye know what SRD on the rum jars stands for, sur? "Seldom Reaches Destination". Or maybe it's "Soon Runs Dry",' he chortled.

A few minutes later, as I had feared they would, the German artillery began shelling just as we emerged out of the communication trench onto open ground. By then I was done in, but the wiry, and surprisingly strong, McIlhenny, even burdened by his rifle, half-carried me at a near run the last mile to the staff car. Where he got his strength from, I don't know, but I really appreciated his assistance, although I was embarrassed by my weakness.

'Jack Johnsons. Those are Jack Johnsons. Ah fuckin' hate Jack Johnsons,' swore McIlhenny, referring to the large German shells that emitted black smoke and which were nicknamed after the giant American boxer.

Luckily for us, but not, alas, for the ration party we'd just seen, the Germans concentrated on the trenches and not the immediate rear area. Hodgson had already fired up the Lanchester upon seeing our approach, and we were soon on board and accelerating away from the barrage of exploding shells.

*

As it turned out, we didn't get very far. A different German battery of long-range guns opened up on a busy crossroads on our route away from the front. I could see high explosive shells bursting in the gathering gloom as the enemy artillery zeroed in on the road junction. As we halted with the other traffic at the bottleneck of wrecked vehicles and wagons, the canny Germans raised their sights and proceeded to pour shrapnel onto the four arms of the crossroads for a hundred yards or so in each direction, deliberately obliterating the men and horses of the traffic jam that their initial barrage had caused. Thankfully, the Lanchester was too far back from the crossroads to be hit, but the scene before us was one of complete mayhem as the shells plastered the area.

Behind us, the heavy howitzers we'd seen being emplaced earlier in the day boomed out in reply, and their counter-battery fire soon silenced the German onslaught. In front of us, men and horses lay in pieces, destroyed by the shell blasts, while those still alive and wounded created a chorus of shrill screams, human and equine, that pierced the air.

'*Scheisse, scheisse, scheisse,*' I heard myself swearing. I had learned to curse as a schoolboy in Germany and still used that language to swear when stressed. I'd first adopted this habit thinking that my mother wouldn't understand. A thick ear later proved my assumption wrong. I'd retained my German cursing even now as I found it more expressive than the English equivalent. I surveyed the scene of destruction before ordering Hodgson and McIlhenny out of the car to join me in trying to help the wounded.

Along with those not caught up in the barrage from other vehicles and wagons, we helped as best we could until the medics of the RAMC got to the scene. Hodgson and McIlhenny assisted the newly arrived stretcher-bearers, while I tried to comfort those waiting to be evacuated. This included a pair of severely wounded staff officers whose car had taken a hit. So much for brass hats not visiting the front lines, I thought.

After a mobile section of the Army Veterinary Corps had arrived, an occasional shot would ring out as its orderlies put down wounded horses or mules using humane killers to the skull. Several terrified dying horses, their bellies split with entrails spilled over the road, were thrashing about and too dangerous to approach, so these beasts were dispatched less humanely with several bullets from a rifle. As the worst of the human wounded were evacuated or died from their injuries, the screaming was replaced by the moans, groans, and mutterings of the less badly hurt, interspersed by the low voices of a pair of padres who had arrived to help. One was a Roman Catholic priest and he found a few fatally wounded of the same denomination who required the Last Rites. As the scene got darker and the night took hold, headlights and torches were used to light the debacle, casting long shadows from the stretcher-bearers, chaplains, and veterinarians.

Eventually a pathway to get traffic moving again was cleared by a pioneer company. As there was little more that we could contribute to the tragic scene, I decided it was time we were on our way, leaving the others to collect the body parts, lay out the corpses, wash away the blood, and repair the roads. The Lanchester was pressed into service as an emergency ambulance and we squeezed some walking wounded in beside us to ferry them to the nearest dressing station at Brandhock, a few miles away.

'Where to now, guv?' asked a sombre Hodgson after we dropped off our bloodied passengers.

'The chateau, and don't spare the horses,' I croaked with the little levity I could muster for I was exhausted, physically and emotionally.

The forty steeds under the long bonnet of the Lanchester duly obliged and we headed off into the dark for the long drive west to Montreuil just as the rain started once more. It was in the early hours of the morning before we arrived, tired and weary, back at our base.

My body was aching by the time I finally went to bed. Deciding a whisky alone wasn't going to stop the pain, I swallowed a single quarter-grain morphine tablet with a dram.

*

As I waited for the drug to take effect, I reflected on the day. I had managed to overcome my fears and re-entered the trenches, reaching right up to the front line. By doing so, I had proved something to myself, if to no one else. It had been physically exhausting, but I'd been able to keep my fears under control. Then I'd had to deal with the casualties from the shelled crossroads, and I hadn't flinched at the sight of so much gore and suffering. A few nights ago, I'd been unsure about how I'd react to such a scene, but somehow I'd managed to cope with the blood and the guts, the wounded and the dying. Perversely, the day had therefore proved to be successful for me, in the real world at least. As I drifted off to sleep, I wondered if the same would prove true in my troubled dream world.

Tuesday,
9th May 1916

CHAPTER 9

The next morning, I woke slowly after a deep sleep. I wasn't sure if this was due to exhaustion after the previous day's exertions, my drug and dram nightcap, or some cathartic effect of my trip into the front line. While I was at a late breakfast, Villiers gathered the information I'd requested, including the location of some more individuals I now wanted to interview.

'The first chap on your list is down past Abbeville in Blargies Military Prison. I let them know you're coming,' Villiers told me. 'The fellow at the other end of the line seemed disappointed that his prisoner's court martial would have to be deferred until you'd completed your investigation. Said something about it only being a "stay of execution". Your other prisoner is up closer to the front at this place.' He handed over some map coordinates for the second location.

I went and collected McIlhenny and Hodgson. I was impressed by the former's positive effect on the latter. Hodgson's buttons were almost shining. Almost. McIlhenny had also worked wonders on my mud-stained riding boots and trench coat. Both had been returned to near pristine condition by my batman, who must have arisen very early to complete these tasks. I wished he could have renewed my battered body with such effectiveness. As was his own speciality, Hodgson had wiped the previous night's wounded passengers' blood from the seats and the inside of the Lanchester was clean once more.

'Where to now, guv?' asked Hodgson.

'We're off to prison,' I told him. 'Head south along the coast and I'll give you directions when we need to change course.'

'Fuckin' prisons. Ah hate fuckin' prisons,' said McIlhenny as we set off. 'Ever been in one, Bob?'

'No, Mac, I can't say I have,' replied Hodgson.

'Aye, well, best avoided.'

'I thought I'd managed to keep you out of Barlinnie?' I asked, referring to Glasgow's infamous jail.

'Aye, and ye've done a good job, sur, so ye have. But ma father spent time inside, and he didn't enjoy it at all, Ah can tell ye. Ah visited him once, and Ah don't want to spend long in one again. A few days in jankers is all Ah can cope with.'

We drove south for two hours, parallel to the coast, to Abbeville, and then proceeded inland to Abancourt, a further three hours away. It rained the entire journey to our eventual destination of Blargies on the outskirts of the town. I entertained myself during the drive, if that's the right word, by reminding myself of the pertinent rules and regulations about sleeping sentries in the 1914 Manual of Military Law. Dry books such as this were the staple diet of lawyers, and I usually devoured them, if without much appetite. However, the arcane small print soon had me dozing off. Maybe the Seaforth's sentry had been reading it before MacKenzie arrested him.

*

I got out the car when we arrived at Blargies and left the two privates to enjoy a cigarette while I entered the prison. At the gate, I used my warrant to get access to Private Charlie McNicol. The highlander was brought to me in an interrogation room in a wooden hut by two burly corporals of the Military Provost Staff Corps. McNicol was a slight figure between the two colossi, but looked fit and healthy. One of the provosts remained in the room for the prisoner's interrogation.

After explaining who I was, I emphasised to McNicol that the charges against him were very serious, and included the possibility that his dereliction of duty could explain why two German assassins were able to get within inches of the King's life. I made my speech as legalistic as possible to impress on him the enormity of what he faced and to get him to talk to me. I didn't feel good about it, but it worked.

'You see, McNicol, Section 6 (1) (k) of the 1914 Manual of Military Law states that, and I quote, *A sentinel found asleep at his post while on active service would, if the character and circumstances of the offence were sufficiently grave, be liable to suffer death*, unquote. Now, although so far in this war no sentry has been shot for sleeping at their post, I am sure that, since the King's life was put at risk, and a brigadier killed, the prosecution will press for you to be shot at dawn.' The prisoner looked petrified at the thought. 'Now, McNicol, do you deny sleeping at your post five nights ago?'

'I don't remember, sir, and that's the God's honest truth. I often work at nights. I've got a small croft up in Ross-shire, but it isn't enough to keep me, the wife, and the bairns well-enough fed, so, occasionally, I go poaching on a moonless night. I admit it. I'm good in the dark, and I've never felt sleepy before on guard duty. I do remember getting some tea from the adjutant on his rounds. Then the next thing I know I'm up against the trench wall with Sergeant MacKenzie's face in mine, and him shouting abuse at me for being asleep at my post. Soon after that, I'm here in this glasshouse.'

'Was it usual for the adjutant to bring the sentries tea?' I asked, more than a little surprised at this kindness, which seemed out of character for the man I'd met in the Seaforth's dugout.

'No, sir. Mister MacPherson's not usually what you might call interested in the troops' welfare beyond what's required by regulations. He'd only do inspections for trench foot and the like. I really don't recall much after drinking the tea he brought as I didn't feel too good.'

'What had you eaten earlier?'

'Just some bread and stew, sir. I shared it with the other blokes in my section.'

'Did the tea Captain MacPherson brought you taste normal?' I asked.

'As normal as any trench tea tastes,' said McNicol, echoing McIlhenny. 'You know how it is, sir. You need a lot of condensed milk and sugar to disguise the terrible taste of the water.'

'But you suspect there was something in it that put you to sleep or at least made you groggy?'

'I'm not sure, sir. It can't have been the stew that upset me, as the others had it too and I'm the only one in here. It's just that I know I'm good in the dark and yet that night something happened to me after I drank the tea, I swear it.'

McNicol seemed very sincere and after my experiences of interrogating many prisoners in police cells and in court, both the guilty and the innocent, I felt myself a reasonable judge of when I was being told the truth and when I was being lied to. I found myself believing McNicol, although it might just have been due to my dislike of MacPherson.

'So, after the tea, you next remember Sergeant MacKenzie shouting at you?'

'Aye, we're neighbours up in Ross-shire, but we've never got on. He's a keeper and I'm a poacher, so we were on opposite sides, I suppose. But I thought when I joined up, and we were in the same regiment, we'd be on the same side fighting the Germans, and the past would be forgotten. Well, no chance of that! That bastard MacKenzie was always on the lookout to charge me with something, begging your pardon, sir.'

'Why was that? Why did he persist after you'd both volunteered? He certainly doesn't look like a man to cross, but your CO seems to rate him very highly.'

'It goes back a few years, sir. There was this stag, a twelve-pointer; a "Royal Stag" we call them. This one was nicknamed "The Emperor". He was a bit like that famous painting that was in the papers.'

'I think you mean *Monarch of the Glen* by Landseer?' I said, remembering seeing a photograph of the painting in a newspaper when it was sold earlier in the year.

'I don't know who painted it, but this stag was monarch of our glen, all right. The King had visited the estate to hunt one year, and the Old Laird, that's Colonel Ross's father, promised the King that he could shoot the stag on his next visit. The stag injured himself in a rut the following spring, but the Laird refused to let it be put down as he'd promised it for King George. He said it would make an easier shot for His Majesty. He really didn't need to do that, as I've seen the King shoot, and he's actually quite a good marksman. Nevertheless, somebody shot the wounded stag and put it out of its misery.'

'What's this got to do with your current plight?' I asked, the connection not clear to me.

'I was near where the carcass was found, and MacKenzie caught me. My rifle was warm, and it was assumed that I shot the beast. My gun was hot, right enough, but it was from shooting a smaller buck I hadn't had time to collect. It was my own fault for going out in daylight that day, but the bairns were awfully hungry. The Laird called in the police, but there wasn't enough evidence to prosecute me, so I was let go. It was in *The Ross-shire Journal*, and the Laird, his son, and MacKenzie, were all embarrassed by the affair. They all still think I did it, but I swear to God I didn't, although I know who did.'

'If you know the culprit, why didn't you tell the police?'

'I'm not for getting anyone into trouble. And anyway, the police wouldn't believe me.'

'Why not?'

'Because I heard the shot, and it came from the forest nearly a mile away.'

'A mile away. That's hard to believe!'

'Exactly! See what I mean, sir? I told you nobody would believe me. But one of the Laird's ghillies, Murdo MacLeod, my wife's uncle, he's the best shot in the Highlands, and he could have done it, no doubt about that. And Old Murdo wasn't a man to see a beast suffering, for king or no king. Shot it clean through the head.'

'He sounds like a man we could use at the front.'

'That's unlikely, sir. Murdo must be seventy if he's a day.'

'So MacKenzie and Lord Ross have a gripe against you, and you think that's why you're in here. That means you also suspect that the adjutant tried to drug you at your post? That's quite an accusation, Private.'

'I know, sir. It's my word against MacKenzie and MacPherson's and His Lordship will back them as well. Now you've said that because I was asleep at my post, I'll be held responsible for those German snipers getting through. I'll be a dead man, sir. Then who'll look after my wife and bairns?' McNicol's eyes welled up.

'Yes, I'm afraid it doesn't look too good, McNicol. Usually sleeping sentries get their sentences commuted if nothing untoward has happened as a result. I'm sorry to say that I'm not so sure that will happen here if the prosecution makes the case that your apparent negligence allowed the Germans to attempt regicide. However, there's something odd about this whole affair, and it begins with the adjutant bringing you tea. The MO you saw on the way out of the line says you weren't behaving quite right when he briefly examined you.'

'He's right, sir. I wasn't feeling well, honest to God.'

'Tell you what, you're allowed someone to represent you at your court martial. The so-called "prisoner's friend". If you like, I'd be happy to do so. I was a criminal lawyer and advocate before the war broke out. I'll tell them at the gate here that Captain Brown of the Intelligence Corps, based in Montreuil, will represent you. I have to go now, but I'll be back before your court martial.'

With that, I handed the dejected McNicol over to the less than tender care of the provosts and returned to the staff car. I'd have to work fast to prove McNicol's innocence and it was an additional incentive on top of General Plumer's demands for a speedy resolution of the investigation.

'Where to now, guv?' asked Hodgson for a second time that day.

'We need to get close to the Germans.'

'What, back to the front, sur?' asked McIlhenny, sitting beside an ashen-faced Hodgson.

'No, just the prisoner of war cage closest to the Seaforth's section of the line. Our adjutant, Captain Villiers, has given me a map reference. I'd like to understand who ordered those Germans to kill the King. Monarchs don't usually take potshots at each other, particularly if they're related, like the King and the Kaiser. Head towards Amiens, Hodgson, then St Pol, and then to Béthune. The adjutant has arranged for us to be billeted there tonight.'

*

Having only stopped to refuel, grab some rations, and use the latrines, by the time we got to Béthune, it felt like we had spent most of the day in the staff car. However, after the previous day's experience, I must confess it was nice to sit back and have a bit of a rest. With the Lanchester occasionally getting up to speed when no military convoys were around, it was all a far cry from the trenches

Upon reaching Béthune, I reported to the local headquarters, waived my warrant, mentioned Villiers' booking, and was given billets for us all. We had arrived with just enough light for McIlhenny and Hodgson to climb the town's famous bell tower and look towards the front line about forty miles to the east.

I decided to forgo this attraction as my damaged leg was a bit stiff after the excursion into the trenches and sitting in the car for hours. Instead, I enjoyed a hot bath at my billet, the Hotel d'Or, before going out for a walk. I found an open café and had a cup of watery coffee. In the café I encountered a fellow captain, a Royal Engineer, who waxed lyrical about the French road system with its bordering trees and proceeded to give me a long, unwelcome history lesson on their construction. However, before he left the café, he redeemed himself by offering me his copy of *The New Church Times*, which, the title informed me, incorporated *The Wipers Times*. It was dated the 1st of May, and so was relatively fresh. For me this gift more than offset the boredom of the roadworks' lecture. I therefore enjoyed an hour of comic relief thanks to the magazine's editors from the Sherwood Foresters and their many contributors. Its satirical ribbing of the High Command, the Kaiser, and the politicians back home was a welcome distraction.

When I returned to my hotel, the doorman asked me on the way in if I'd like to buy some *Kirchners* as he had a nice selection. These were saucy postcards and, although tempted, I politely declined. If anything ever happened to me, I didn't want my personal effects being sent back to my parents, and my mother discovering a collection of racy postcards amongst my memorabilia. On the one hand, it wouldn't matter to me as I'd be dead, but I wouldn't want to upset her even more – assuming she'd be upset enough by my demise.

That evening, I enjoyed a liquid dinner of champagne cocktails in the Globe Café with British, Canadian, and Indian Army officers, accompanied by their French liaison counterparts. The café owner claimed that the Prince of Wales was a frequent patron, and he showed us a napkin signed by his royal customer. More cocktails were ordered to toast His Royal Highness. As it turned out, this was not something I'd have done by the end of my investigation.

I returned to my hotel to find that someone had placed a rather risqué publicity flyer on my pillow for Madame Justine's where, apparently, the hostesses helpfully spoke English. My Presbyterian upbringing, and love for my girlfriend Jeanie, made me forgo the flyer's invitation, just as I had the pornographic postcards. However, both had an erotic effect on my dreams that night, which, for once, were not about battles and dead friends, and much more pleasurable.

Wednesday,
10th May 1916

CHAPTER 10

Hodgson and McIlhenny picked me up on time the next morning. McIlhenny told me they'd enjoyed an *erf* and *pomfritz* dinner the previous night, which I translated as the soldier's staple of egg and chips. My batman, however, complained that the thin French beer was "pish", and the "point blank" – presumably *vin blanc* – was like paint-stripper. Worryingly, McIlhenny sounded like a man who knew what paint-stripper tasted like.

'Where to now, guv? You said something about a cage.'

'Yes, head for the front. "March to the sound of the guns" as General Grouchy was told.'

'General Grouchy? Who's he, sur?'

'A French general.'

'One of those gettin' beat at Verdun, sur?'

'No, he was a bit before our time. One hundred years ago to be precise, at Waterloo.'

'That battle's what the station in London is called after, guv. Did you know that?' asked Hodgson.

'Yes, and strangely it was us and the Germans against the French at Waterloo. How things change, eh? Now, that's enough history for today. Drive on, Hodgson.'

Along the way we were delayed for some hours by having to lower our speed as we passed an entire division on the other side of the road. It was very rare to see a whole division on the march at one time and it was an impressive sight. The column was obviously heading to the nearest railhead to be embarked on trains. The 19,000 men and their accompanying horses, guns, wagons, lorries and ambulances took up fifteen miles of road space. The head of the column experienced rain as we passed it, but by the time we got to its tail, it was dry.

As the division passed, McIlhenny hummed along to the troops' marching songs. This entailed quite a repertoire as each of the division's twelve infantry battalions had a favourite tune. The singing was accompanied by the tramping of several thousand hobnailed boots, the clip-clop and sparks of metal horseshoes on granite setts, and the revving engines of the lorries. The yelled orders of officers and NCOs were lost in the din as they tried to make sure that this disparate mix of men, horseflesh and machines, moved forward in some semblance of military order. The cavalcade even left behind its own aroma of sweating men and horse dung mixed with petrol fumes.

Like a schoolboy spotter, Hodgson contented himself with naming the various makes of motor transport in the column, muttering a litany of "Leyland, Albion, Karrier, Dennis, and Triumph". There was an almost equal variety of horse breeds as officers' English thoroughbred hunters were accompanied by cavalrymen's Arab chargers, imported American light draught horses, giant Shire horses from Scotland, Suffolk, and Yorkshire, and diminutive mules of uncertain parentage. All had the War Department's arrow brand scorched into their rumps.

'Poor bastards,' said McIlhenny, commenting on the whole caravan. 'Looks like they're bein' sent off for some offensive. They'll all be up for the high jump soon enough, mark ma words.'

I couldn't help but agree, wondering how many of the division would come back in the opposite direction, as they were obviously being repositioned for the rumoured "Big Push".

We watched in amazement as young French boys dodged in and out of the column, shovelling up the horse droppings into sacks and then dumping their hard-won steaming and smelly treasure into wheelbarrows at the side of the road. I had noticed that most French cottages had a manure heap, and no doubt this free fertilizer was destined for those stinking middens.

'What a palaver, eh?' asked McIlhenny. 'Gatherin' shite for a livin'. And Ah thought Ah'd had some manky jobs in ma time, but that takes the biscuit.'

Teams of pioneers, working as navvies, struggled to repair the damage caused by the passing division, fixing the pavée road surface with new granite blocks. I felt guilty yet again, riding in our large car as we passed the sweating, swearing labourers.

'I bet they never thought they'd be doing this when they volunteered to fight,' observed Hodgson.

'Aye, well, better to be doin' that than gettin' yer arse blown off in the trenches like those other poor buggers we just passed, Bob, believe me,' was McIlhenny's rejoinder.

*

Eventually, we arrived outside a small muddy field of bell tents surrounded by a high barbed-wire fence, adjacent to a ruined barn with a khaki tarpaulin for a roof.

In the barn, I told the provost sergeant in charge of the prisoner of war cage that I wanted to see the German soldier brought in a few days ago by the Seaforths, as I needed to interrogate him for an intelligence report.

Before he went to collect the German, the provost gave me a brown envelope with the prisoner's effects. 'You're lucky, sir, I was just about to pass these on up the line as per standing orders,' he said.

The envelope's contents included a brown paper-covered paybook, which revealed the prisoner was called Otto Flettner, a *gefreiter* or corporal in the 6th Prussian *Jaeger* regiment. The prisoner's special skill was listed as *scharfschütze* or sharpshooter. The envelope also had an oakleaf cap badge, the symbol of a *Jaeger* regiment, and a pair of epaulettes with the number 6 on them. The oakleaf represented the

Jaeger's natural environment, for they were conscripted from hunters and woodsmen, and historically used by the various German states as scouts and skirmishers. There was a letter, too, from a girl called Trudi and a small sepia photograph of a pretty female teenager who I assumed to be the missive's author. I quickly read the letter. I always felt a bit guilty reading my own men's personal letters for censorship and was a bit surprised that the feeling continued even for an enemy prisoner's mail. The letter seemed to be mostly family news and entirely platonic, although it did end "All my love, Trudi".

A muddy individual in field-grey was eventually produced, and I commandeered what passed as an office in the semi-ruin for an interrogation. I ordered McIlhenny in with me, giving him my revolver in case the German got any ideas.

I told the prisoner in German to sit down at the room's only table and then took the seat opposite, placing the prisoner's effects on the tabletop. The young man was surprised to hear his native tongue and he seemed slightly frightened to be addressed by a German-speaking British officer. Maybe I looked a bit menacing with my eyepatch? I hoped so. As the youth was shaking with fear, or cold, or both, and to put him at ease, I cadged a cigarette and matches off McIlhenny and offered them to the prisoner. The German lit the cigarette with relish and seemed to relax a bit.

'I have a few questions for you,' I started. 'I do realise that all you're obliged to give me is your name, rank, and number. So, let's start with your name?'

'You have my papers, so you'll already know that I am Otto Flettner. *Gefreiter* Otto Flettner.'

'What age are you?'

'I'm nineteen,' said the youth, proudly.

'Your cap badge suggests you're from a *Jaeger* regiment?'

'*Ja*, the best hunters were all put into the *Jaegers*. They are like your rifle regiments.'

'I'm actually from a rifle regiment myself,' I told him. 'The Scottish Rifles.'

The youth looked impressed and he seemed keen to talk as he enjoyed his cigarette, so I continued with friendliness rather than menace for now, seeing this a better option.

'Where are you from, Otto?'

'From Silesia in Prussia. I live just outside Breslau. A nice city. Not like this flat and muddy shithole around here. I was a forest guard in the woods nearby. Silesia has a lot of forests.' After saying this, the youth looked suddenly homesick as his thoughts obviously drifted far to the east.

'How were you captured?'

'Four of us were out in the dark making an observation post. We were snipers. We worked in pairs. A spotter and a shooter. But we were surprised by some Tommies. They'd crept up on us and had daggers at our throats before we could react.'

'So, the hunters became the hunted,' I said, but Otto failed to see the joke.

'There was a fight, and my friend Peter was killed by the British raid leader. We were brought back to your lines and thrown over the parapet. There was a Tommy on guard, but he looked like he was drunk or something, as he was staggering about with his eyes closed. He never challenged our arrival, and the Tommy sergeant who'd captured us went mad at him. He was taken away and the three of us were marched off to the rear.'

'What happened next?'

'I was being marched by two Tommies and the sergeant was bringing up the rear with Hans and Friedrich. An officer was helping him. A captain, I think. He had a large dog with him. We got separated on the way back. It was very dark and there was a lot of traffic going up and down the communication trench with work parties and reserves and so on.'

The boy stopped and looked pointedly at the cigarette butt in his hand, then looked at me. After more enforced generosity from McIlhenny, the boy continued his story with his second smoke.

'I was brought here, but Hans and Friedrich never arrived.'

'What do you think happened to them?'

'Once we were out of the communication trench, I think your sergeant shot them. The Tommy sergeant took one of our rifles as a prize from Hans. He must have recognised it as a sniper's rifle. We know you British shoot our snipers if you capture them. I'm surprised I'm still alive. I heard two shots behind me as I was being marched out. Also, the Tommies were "devils in skirts" and they have a reputation for killing prisoners.'

I had heard rumours of British soldiers killing captured snipers. For some reason, Tommies didn't like the fact that German snipers often made life in the trenches even more unbearable by shooting any unprotected movement on the British side. It was felt to be sneaky and ungentlemanly, as opposed to face-to-face combat. Having been the victim of a shell blast from an unseen howitzer, I really couldn't see the difference any more. I'd also heard rumours that highland regiments, who the Germans called "devils in skirts" or "ladies from Hell", would often take no prisoners when fired up in attacks.

'What sort of rifle did your comrade carry?'

'It was a *Scharfschützen Mauser Gewehr*. It's a special version of our standard rifle, but it had a nice four-times-magnification scope on it. I remember it was a Zeiss. They're the best.'

'How far can you shoot with a rifle like that?'

'The scope can be set to compensate for bullet drop out to 1000 metres, but its effective range is really 500 metres. Most of our kills were across no-man's land, so even less than that.' The youth described all this quite nonchalantly, as if killing humans was the same as killing wild boar in his day job back in the forest. In that, he was similar to Sergeant MacKenzie, another outdoorsman.

'Now, tell me, Otto, was there any talk in your regiment about a plot to assassinate the British King?'

Otto laughed, and then said, 'Such talk would be madness, surely? Your King and our Kaiser are cousins, no? I know we are at war, but I cannot imagine such a plan. I remember before the war seeing pictures in the papers of them enjoying holidays together.'

'So, you don't know if any of your comrades were sent over to penetrate the British lines and act as snipers in the rear of our trenches?'

'No, there was no such talk in the regiment about something so absurd! Anyway, how would we know if your King was around? I remember the Kaiser came to visit us once, and we weren't told about that beforehand, so I can't imagine your side telling us that your King was visiting nearby,' scoffed the young German. The Corporal's reply didn't bring me any closer to finding out how the Germans knew the King would be on the knoll on that day.

'And who is Trudi, Otto?'

The boy suddenly looked deflated and sad. 'She's my cousin. She lives in the Sudeten Mountains, just south of Breslau. She's only sixteen, but I hope to marry her one day. I just want to go home now.' The young man's eyes filled with tears. I couldn't remember if marrying your cousin was a good thing or not.

I felt sorry for the poor boy, so I passed the letter and picture over to him, deeming them of no intelligence value. The youth was joyous.

'Thank you, sir. Thank you so much. This means a lot to me. Having Trudi with me will make my internment easier until I'm free when we win the war.'

'Huh, don't bet on that, Otto. That's all.'

I switched to English and told McIlhenny to call the guard to take the prisoner away.

'Thank God for that, sur,' muttered McIlhenny after the *Jaeger* had left. 'Ah'd have been out of fags soon at the rate he was smokin'.'

Outside the cage, Hodgson started the Lanchester before asking, 'Where to now, guv?'

'I'm not sure. I need some inspiration. Let's go back and revisit the scene of the crime.'

*

As we drove along, I thought about Otto, and how like my old friends in

Duisburg the young Jaeger *was. A year or so ago, I had often wondered if any of my former German schoolmates had been on the opposite side when I'd attacked at Loos. Before the offensive I had hoped not, but was sure that many, if not all of them, would be wearing field-grey somewhere by then as a result of Germany having had conscription for many years. However, after having been wounded by German shelling, and after the death of my brother in an attack on enemy lines, my concerns about my old schoolmates had all but disappeared. This realisation now made me feel somewhat contrite and a bit depressed.*

*

An hour after leaving the PoW cage, the Lanchester was parked near the spot of the assassination attempt. The three of us stood with our backsides leaning on the car looking at the grassy knoll where the royal party of horsemen had assembled for the photograph. We shared a packet of Huntley & Palmer's biscuits that had been in a basket of treats from Fortnum & Mason sent to me by my maiden aunt. McIlhenny made tea in a mess tin on a Tommy cooker, a small, methylated-spirits trench stove. The drink was strong and full of tea leaves, but also very sweet due to McIlhenny's generosity with the sugar and the fact he had also added a large slug of evaporated milk. Despite these additions, I thought that McIlhenny was right; the water did taste of petrol. The residue from the water can formed an oily iridescence between the leaves on the tea's surface in our tin mugs. Notwithstanding all that, it was welcome refreshment.

'Those are good biscuits, sur,' said McIlhenny. 'Not like those dog biscuits they give us as part of our rations. Ah'm tellin' ye they're made out of concrete, so they are. Best thing to do with them is boil them in a mess tin and cover them in pozzy jam, so it is.'

As I rested against the Lanchester, I tried to re-enact in my mind the events on the day of the shooting. The grassy knoll in front of me was only a few hundred yards away from the wood the shots had come from, and so was well within the effective range of a Mauser sniper rifle according to Otto. Next, I pictured the line-up in my mind's eye. The late Brigadier General Church-Fenton had been at the far left of the party, as the photographer would have viewed it, and closest to the wood. In the centre was the King, flanked by General Plumer on his right and the unknown red-faced general on his left, with sundry others either side. Ross was on the far right and furthest from the wood.

After finishing our tea, I struggled up the knoll which was slippery from the rain earlier in the day. I would not have made it without my walking stick and McIlhenny's help as my gammy leg was still aching from my exertions in the trenches. I looked around. There was a thick white line painted in the grass, as on a football or rugby pitch, presumably as a mark for the horsemen to line up behind for the photograph. The rain hadn't washed it away yet. I looked along the line towards the woods where the German snipers had been found and killed. To my surprise, it pointed to open ground, with the nearest cover being a sparse copse of spindly trees some considerable distance away. The mess of hoof marks in the disturbed ground showed that the horsemen, like good soldiers, had obeyed the order to line up behind the white stripe in the grass, so I concluded they were not aligned end-on to the wood.

I stood behind the white line where I thought the King had been placed. It now appeared that a sniper in the woods could easily have picked out the King after all. With the horsemen aligned behind the line, the sniper would have had a reasonable, if slightly oblique, view of the monarch. Maybe the assassin was either a poor sniper or his aim had been disturbed? But why would the Germans send across a duff sniper? Where had the Brigadier been hit? That would give me a clue to the shot's origin. Something else nagged at my mind about the event too.

I slid and slithered back down the knoll and Hodgson drove us to the nearest unit's headquarters and its field telephone. I was eventually connected to Villiers in Montreuil.

'I'm not a damn undertaker and I'm certainly not your bloody secretary, old boy! It's not my job to track down your old university chums,' sniffed Villiers when I explained my latest request.

'I really do appreciate your help, Villiers, and I understand the inconvenience, but will you do it?' I asked, slightly exasperated.

'Yes, all right. It's all quiet over here. Only the usual supply of bumpf to deal with. I'll call you back in a jiffy.'

When Villiers called back, he had some good news for me. 'You're in luck, old boy. The dead and the living you require are actually in the same location,' he said and he gave me the coordinates.

'Where to now, guv?' asked Hodgson, when I had finished my call and approached the car.

'Back towards Pop. I need to see a doctor.'

'Are ye ill, sur?' asked McIlhenny, a note of concern in his voice.

'Only sick of this damned war.'

'Aye, well, we've all got that disease, sur.'

CHAPTER 11

We set off in the direction of Poperinghe once more towards our new destination of No.17 CCS, a Casualty Clearing Station. This was located at a place called Remy Sidings, which, with a prosaic name like that, was presumably named by the British and not the Belgians. Villiers had informed me that this was where the Brigadier's body was resting before a planned burial with full military honours the next day.

As we arrived at the CCS, which was a tented village in the grounds of yet another old farmhouse, I saw a familiar figure walking towards the building's entrance. The man was strolling between two pretty nurses in grey serge dresses with red capes and white muslin caps. I recognised the uniform of Queen Alexandra's Imperial Military Nursing Service. Grand name or not, I was beholden to similar nurses who had helped me during the dark days after my wounding the year before, and I had nothing but admiration for them. While I didn't know the nurses, I did know Doctor Iain Sneddon, the lucky fellow sandwiched between them, from our time sharing a student flat several years ago. Sneddon had gone on to be a pathologist for the Edinburgh City Police Force. I called out to Sneddon, and he left the two nurses and came over.

'Jamie, is that you? It's been ages since we last met! I'd heard you'd caught a packet at Loos. Glad to see you made it through. How are you?'

Sneddon grabbed my good right hand and proceeded to pump it up and down with vigour. He had been a flanker in one of the Borders' rugby teams and carried the necessary energy needed for that role into everything he did, including simple handshakes.

'I'm fine thanks, Iain,' I said, flexing my mangled right hand. 'Just a little bit stiff down the left side. Bit of pain now and again. You're a doctor, so no point in fooling you.' I reflected that it was a strange sensation that, even though I hadn't seen Iain since the war had started, it was as if we had never been separated. I supposed that was a sign of a good friendship.

'So, why are you here, Jamie? And by that, I mean over here at all, given your wounds, as well as here at this hospital.'

'Well, I haven't come here for a personal consultation, but I do need some medical assistance. I've been seconded to the Intelligence Corps, and I'm investigating the recent killing of a brigadier by German snipers. The corpse is here apparently, and I need a quick look at it. Can you help?'

'Yes, I'd heard about that. Be glad to show you. Come this way.'

We left Hodgson to find the adjacent ASC motor depot that maintained the hospital's ambulance fleet so that he could refuel the Lanchester, and Sneddon led McIlhenny and me along a path between marquees that served as wards and operating theatres. Eventually, we branched off left towards a group of large tents set apart from the main hospital. Behind them, there was a well-worn path to a small cemetery of wooden grave markers.

'Here is our Panthéon,' said Sneddon, showing us into the first tent. 'You have to be dead famous to be in here,' he added, with black humour.

The smell inside was awful, a miasma of blood, disinfectant, gas gangrene, and rotting flesh. It was all I could do to stop retching from this dreadful stench. There was a row of bodies of all ranks and all sorts of regiments and corps laid out on the ground. Many of the bodies were incomplete, having lost limbs to shellfire or because the surgeons were unable to save their lives even after an amputation. Each body had a label tied to a big toe, if they still had one, with details copied from their aluminium identity discs. I presumed that these would then be copied again on to the temporary wooden cross at their future grave outside. It was a forlorn sight.

'This lot will be taken away later today for burial,' explained Sneddon, as hearty as ever. I supposed that medical officers, having to deal every day with the remnants of fellow soldiers, alive and dead, had to develop some sort of mental shield to prevent themselves from breaking down under the strain. I wasn't sure that I could have coped as well as my friend appeared to.

Sneddon next took us into what he called the posh wing, which was basically a side tent to the main affair. He switched on a pair of overhead arc lamps to improve the light in the tent. In the centre, raised on a table, lay a body under a white sheet. Sneddon pulled the sheet off like a magician unveiling a trick and revealed the late Brigadier General Church-Fenton. I wasn't sure how I'd react after seeing the outcome of the crossroad's shelling the previous day, but, having managed to console the wounded there, and seen so many dead, I now found I could look at the corpse quite dispassionately. Another personal test completed.

There was no label tied to a bare toe here, but someone had tried to tidy up the corpse and the body was still sporting full uniform and riding boots. The tunic was tight around the girth as the corpse had bloated due to the build-up of gases in the guts. The skin had a marbled appearance, the eyes were bulging, and there were flecks of dried blood around the nostrils. Somewhat ridiculously, the corpse's legs were raised slightly due to his spurs still being on the boot heels. Despite the early signs of decomposition, I thought I vaguely recognised the body from the line-up of horsemen, although this was somewhat difficult as there was a gaping wound on the right side of the Brigadier's head.

'The Brigadier was shot four days ago by German snipers as he lined up for a photograph with the King,' I explained to Sneddon, as he began inspecting the body with professional interest.

'That's strange,' said Sneddon, interrupting me.

'What's strange?' I asked.

'Well, there's a large entry wound, obviously, but no exit wound.'

'You mean the bullet's still in there?'

'Probably. The sniper victims we see in surgery – the few that have survived, that is – have both entry and exit wounds. Mostly snipers shoot their victims in the head when some dozy lookout or green subaltern sticks his neck above the parapet, and no one survives that. As a result, we only see the ones where the headshot's been missed, and so sniper casualties here at the CCS all have upper body wounds, not head wounds. A typical German sniper's victim will have a keyhole in their forehead from the pointed bullet, but a huge tear on the other side of the head.'

'Why that discrepancy?'

'It's because when a pointed bullet is fired, it is only the spin imparted by the rifling in the gun barrel that stops it flying tail first, which is where the centre of gravity lies. When it hits its target, the spin stops and the bullet is free to revert to its natural mode of travel. It therefore rotates inside the body, destroying tissue on the way. "Tumbling" we call it. Usually the bullet exits, but by then it's deformed and moving tail first, and that blunt end tears out a big lump of flesh and bone, leaving a larger exit wound than the entry hole. If it hits a thick bone like a femur, it can move off in a totally different direction, well away from the entry wound and be a devil to find. However, that can't be the case in an enclosed space like the skull.' As he spoke, Sneddon was peering intently into the Brigadier's open wound.

Inside the hole, I could see a mush of grey and red. McIlhenny was having a look too. 'Looks like Maconochie's fuckin' stew in there, before its cooked,' I heard him mutter.

Sneddon pointed to the hole and said, 'The bullet that entered here must have lost its kinetic energy very quickly upon hitting the

Brigadier's head through the right parietal bone. That would suggest an expanding bullet which mushrooms upon entering the body, creating a large surface area. This in turn both slows the bullet down by friction and also causes a large wound channel. In this case that all happened across a few inches inside the skull. In other words, we're looking at a dumdum bullet.'

'Gosh. That's interesting, as dumdums aren't allowed under the Hague Convention,' I pointed out. 'Can you get the bullet out to be sure? You used to be a police pathologist, and a good one too, as I recall.'

'Flattery will get you nowhere, my boy. I'm not a pathologist any more, Jamie. I operate on the living now, not the dead.'

'This is a special case, Iain. So please, can you extract the bullet for me?'

'All right, I'll do it as a favour to you, Jamie,' sighed Sneddon and he went off to get what he called his "toolkit".

He returned with a canvas roll of sharp implements that formed the surgeon's tools of the trade. As Sneddon prodded around inside the Brigadier's skull it reminded me of the time he had sneaked me into his anatomy class to watch him dissecting cadavers when we were students. Up until that point, I'd never seen a dead body, and so I had steeled myself to accompany him due to morbid curiosity, fuelled by one too many lunchtime pints in the union bar.

After poking about with a scalpel to locate the bits of lead which were lodged deep against the other side of the skull from the entry wound, and then extracting them with forceps, Sneddon eventually described himself as satisfied that he'd extracted most of the pieces. The main fragment looked like a mushroom where the tip of the bullet had expanded upon hitting the bone of the Brigadier's skull. Sneddon admitted he'd not seen anything like it before. He went off with the evidence to show another surgeon, an older medical officer who he knew had served in the colonial service before dumdum bullets were banned. He wanted to get what he called a "second opinion".

While we were waiting, I sent McIlhenny to check if Hodgson had returned and to collect my personal camera, a Vest Pocket Kodak, from the car. He soon returned with a small pouch measuring only two inches by four inches. The little black VPK folding camera took quite good shots on 127 roll film and was marketed as "The Soldier's Friend". I had actually been quite handy with it, but now found that its small size and tiny shutter controls made it difficult for me to use with my one good hand. Since McIlhenny had been watching ghoul-like as Sneddon had examined the skull, I now enlisted him to take photographs of the two sides of the Brigadier's head. I explained the controls, and McIlhenny's nimble fingers soon got familiar with the fiddly pointers on the tiny camera lens at the end of the fold-out bellows. Under my direction, he was soon snapping away like a professional forensic photographer.

'Ah'm gettin' the hang of this, sur. Ah'll soon be a dab hand,' he claimed.

Sneddon returned looking quite smug and said, 'Old Major Snodgrass confirms it's a dumdum all right. Curiously, he said it was quite big calibre too, not the usual German rifle size, but more like the hunting rifles they'd used in Africa. Maybe not as big as an elephant gun, he thought. I told him I was a bit surprised that even a dumdum would be slowed by the innards across the width of just a human skull. He told me to check bone thickness, but also pointed out that it could have been a shot at extreme range, with the bullet having only just enough energy to breach the skull.'

After another dig around inside the Brigadier's head, Sneddon muttered, 'Hmm, just as Snodgrass suspected. Most skulls have a parietal bone thickness of about a quarter of an inch or less, but your Brigadier here has a skull closer to almost half an inch thick where the bullet came to rest opposite the entry point. You can see where I've pulled the flesh back on that side that it's cracked, but not broken. The sniper must have been extremely skilled in picking his bullet's charge and a bit lucky, too, in that the Brigadier was so thick-headed!'

I got Sneddon to set the bullet down on the table, and had McIlhenny snap it with the VPK, before I wiped it clean and put it in my tunic pocket. The camera had a special narrow flap on the back and a stylus which allowed the photographer to write a brief note to accompany a specific exposure. I had Sneddon attest the last photograph by autographing the film and dating it.

'I must say this whole affair is getting "curiouser and curiouser",' I said to Sneddon.

'That reminds me, old boy, I've got a date in Pop tonight with Alice, one of the nursing sisters here, so I must go and finish my rounds. Don't want to keep a lady waiting.'

After saying our farewells, I returned once more to the Lanchester with McIlhenny. Despite the gruesome circumstances it had been really good to see Sneddon again and we pledged to each other that now we were reacquainted, we'd keep in touch.

'Best check yer wallet, sur, after that long consultation. "Rob all ma comrades". Did ye know that's the RAMC's nickname, sur?' asked McIlhenny as we got back into the car.

As we left the CCS, we passed an ambulance train lined up in the sidings that had given the location its name. Amid the steam and smoke from the locomotive, the train was being loaded, with some carriages receiving walking wounded, and others maimed soldiers on stretchers. It looked like organised chaos as nurses, stretcher-bearers, and transport officers mingled with the bandaged troops to ensure the train was filled to maximum capacity for its journey to a coastal base hospital.

I recalled waking up on just such a train after I'd been wounded and the claustrophobic conditions on board. My bunk was the bottom in a tier of three, with the bed above just inches from my face. The smell had been an unusual blend of disinfectant and vomit. The sounds were a blood-curdling mix of groans, moans, and occasional screams as the train rattled over points or bumpy track. It was not a memory I was glad to recall and I urged Hodgson to leave immediately.

'Where to now, guv?' asked Hodgson, over his shoulder as we sped off.

'Back to the chateau, Hodgson. I've got some thinking to do.'

Since it took nearly seven hours to drive back to Montreuil, I actually had plenty of time to think en route before we arrived hungry and tired at our base.

Thursday,
11th May 1916

CHAPTER 12

After a poor sleep, where I'd dreamt I was entangled in the ropes and canvas of a collapsed marquee of the dead, I went to see Villiers with another special request first thing on the Thursday morning. After a few phone calls by our ever efficient and well-connected adjutant, I was ready for the road again with more useful information and a special appointment.

'Where to now, guv?'

'Head for St Omer. We'll stop there for a break. Then it's on to Bailleul via Hazebrouck, and I'll direct you from my map when we get closer.'

'Bally-All it is, guv.'

Since it was a warm, clear day for a change, we stopped beside the Canal de Neuffosse and had an early lunch of bully beef sandwiches washed down by mugs of tea. McIlhenny commented on how the sandwiches, made with Fray Bentos tinned corned beef and Normandy butter, tasted so much better on the fresh baguettes he'd obtained from the chateau's kitchen that morning, than on the grey loaves smeared with margarine that the meat was usually served up on at the front.

As we sat on the bank in the shade of a large poplar tree, we watched the slow-paced canal traffic pass by, drawn by small steam tug-boats, or pulled by large draught horses on the adjacent towpath. Like every other form of transport, the canal system had been commandeered for military purposes and most of the cargo we witnessed going south was sacks of oats and bales of pressed hay, fodder for the large BEF horse population. Going in the opposite direction were grey hospital barges full of the badly wounded who would not have survived all the way to the coast on the jolting ride of ambulance trains such as we'd seen the day before. Along the canal banks, local fishermen raised and lowered their rods as if in salute, to accommodate these and other waterway traffic.

The sedate barges, the dappled sunlit water, the anglers, and the lines of poplars parallel to the waterway, made for an idyllic scene, and reminded me of a painting by Monet that hung in the dining room of the chateau back in Montreuil. I managed to stir myself from this peaceful reverie and jolted our picnic party back into motion.

*

After nearly sixty miles in a broadly east-north-east direction from Montreuil, I had directed Hodgson to a large flat field enclosed by barbed wire, close to the small town of Bailleul. A number of aeroplanes were parked around the enclosure, or sat under large wood and canvas hangars, indicating that we had arrived at our correct destination – a Royal Flying Corps' aerodrome. We were admitted via a guarded gate on to the field.

As we surveyed the aerodrome, I told my companions that I had attended an early aviation meeting at Lanark Racecourse near my hometown back in 1910. Neither McIlhenny nor Hodgson had been on an airfield before. They were like young children at a funfair, their eyes wide with excitement, as they looked around. Hodgson stopped the car outside an old inn at the edge of the enclosure, and this proved to be the headquarters of the resident RFC squadron.

After I presented my credentials and my request to the CO of the resident 7 Squadron, I was given a dressing down by him. He was none too happy about the assignment I had requested via Villiers, as he felt he had other more important things to do than give joyrides to the Intelligence Corps. He made it plain to me that his pilots and observers were there to support the war effort and not to stooge around behind our lines, instead of the enemy's. After his brief tirade, the old adage that "orders are orders" prevailed, and the CO agreed to provide me with a pilot and aeroplane. This, he said, was despite a pilot shortage caused by the "Fokker Scourge". He then had me kitted out in a leather flying coat, with the buttons fastened at the side like a dentist's smock, and I was also given a leather helmet and gauntlets, and a pair of goggles. When I was all dressed up, I was escorted by the CO to what he called a "kite".

The CO introduced me to Lieutenant Carter-Smythe, my pilot, and the kite, I was told, was a BE.2, usually used for reconnaissance and artillery spotting. The biplane was a yellow-beige colour, and I wondered how the machine had survived without being painted the ubiquitous khaki.

My pilot took me on an external tour of the aeroplane as he did a visual check of its condition before our flight, and he gave me some insights into our future mount. The BE.2 had been designed by the Royal Aircraft Factory in Farnborough and had a wooden frame of Canadian spruce covered in neatly stitched and doped Irish linen, with a large French-designed V8 engine on the front driving a four-bladed wooden propeller of English walnut. These international components had been assembled in Bristol to make our machine, I was told. The only bit that looked substantial was the engine block. There were two cockpits separated by a curved wooden coaming that would not have looked out of place on a yacht. Each cockpit opening had a padded leather surround. The aircraft smelled of dope, oil, petrol and polish. Carter-Smythe jokingly pointed out the large targets, in the shape of the British national blue-white-red identification roundels, that were helpfully painted on the wings and sides of the machine to give the Germans something to aim at. I didn't laugh.

'Your CO said something about the "Fokker Scourge". What's that?' I asked.

'That, sir, is why this machine is nicknamed "Fokker Fodder". The Fokkers are the German monoplanes that have claimed air superiority across the front these last few months. They're quite nimble, and were designed by a supposedly-neutral Dutchman called, would you believe, Anton Fokker. They have a newly-invented device called an "interrupter gear" which allows them to fire a machine gun directly through the disc of their spinning propeller. A Hun pilot therefore just has to aim his entire aeroplane at one of us and press the firing lever on his machine gun to have a good chance of success. That's why they're called the "Fokker Scourge".'

'But why the nickname "Fokker Fodder" for our aeroplane?'

'Well, the BE.2 is too stable to dodge the enemy, and too slow to outrun it, don't you see?'

This was not in my mind a reassuring pedigree, and my enthusiasm for the flight that I'd commissioned waned with every word my pilot spoke. It was finally extinguished by Carter-Smythe telling me that I'd be sitting directly over our aeroplane's petrol tank. It was something to do with the centre of gravity.

In exchange for my familiarisation tour, I outlined for my pilot on a map the exact area that I wanted to get a bird's-eye view of. Carter-Smythe noted the coordinates on his own chart, looked at a weather report, and estimated some compass settings before declaring himself satisfied that he knew where they were going and how we'd get there. He ordered some mechanics standing by to fetch a camera and attach it to our machine.

'Thankfully, the weather's quite good after the mixed sunshine and showers we've had the last few days, so we should be able to get you what you want,' said Carter-Smythe.

He then showed me the large camera in a wooden box which was being strapped to the right side of our aeroplane beside the rear cockpit. The camera had a magazine of eighteen photographic plates with an automatic plate-changer operated by a cord. Carter-Smythe indicated that he would take the pictures on my command. It all sounded straightforward enough. Deciding that we were now ready to go, the pilot waved to a sergeant standing nearby, who barked some orders. Two vehicles then approached us.

'What are those for?' I asked somewhat apprehensively as one appeared to be an ambulance and the other a sort of fire engine.

'Don't worry, sir. One's the blood wagon and the other's the fire tender. They always hang about at take-offs and landings. Bloody vultures! Take-offs and landings are the most dangerous part of any flight – outside meeting the Fokkers. My old instructor at flying school used to call my landings "controlled crashes". But relax, I've done quite a few circuits and bumps since then,' said Carter-Smythe. I was beginning to find his nonchalance a bit wearing.

After a struggle to get into the front cockpit due to my gammy leg and the awkward access via a step onto the lower wing and then a squeeze in between the biplane's wings and bracing wires, I found myself in what was normally the observer's station. With the lower wings in the way on either side, the upper wings above my head, and the long nose and propeller in front of me, for an observation post its visibility was pretty poor. In my mind surely the cockpit positions should have been reversed? I voiced my opinion to Carter-Smythe who explained that it all had to do with the centre of gravity. A lot of things in an aeroplane seemed to have something to do with the centre of gravity I thought, suspicious this was a stock aviators' answer to laymen.

Once seated in my cockpit, I strapped myself in with a web belt. A mechanic positioned a Lewis machine gun on a mounting behind my head, although how I was expected to turn and fire it if needed, and do so without shooting my pilot's head off, or indeed shredding the aeroplane's tail to ribbons, I wasn't sure. Carter-Smythe climbed on board into what he called his "office". I heard him asking me via a voice tube from the rear cockpit if I was ready to go. I used my good right arm to give him the thumbs-up over my shoulder.

Carter-Smythe shouted, 'Contact!' to the waiting ground crew, and a mechanic manually swung the propeller. The engine soon caught, and the BE.2 started forward, waddling across the grass to position itself nose first into the wind. I gave a rather half-hearted wave to the watching Hodgson and McIlhenny, neither of whom looked like they expected to see me again. With the engine roaring, we sedately trundled down the runway and eventually took off and climbed slowly into the sky.

*

As we gained altitude, we circled the aerodrome. I think because it was my first flight that the excitement overcame my apprehension. The wind in my face, the roar of the engine, the odd bump of turbulence, and an astounding new perspective on the world created a totally novel experience for me. On the airfield below I could see the Lanchester and even make out McIlhenny and Hodgson, as well as all the other aeroplanes, the hangar tents, and the inn. As we got higher, I could see the tree-lined roads rich with traffic, canals and railway lines, farmhouses and barns, and then towns. The fear of Fokkers receded in my mind and I pulled down my goggles to stop my good eye watering and maintain my fantastic view.

I knew we were flying north and so looked right towards the east and Ypres. I could just make out the ruins of the Old Cloth Hall, the town's once famous landmark, now a wasted shell. Most of the town had been reduced to rubble and I couldn't help but feel a pang of sorrow for its former citizens.

In the distance, around the Salient, I could see small puffs of smoke, presumably from artillery fire. From this new viewpoint I could really appreciate the military value of aerial observation. I could now see the lurid brown scar of the front line stretching along my right-hand horizon and I wondered at the hundreds of thousands of men down there on both sides, engaged in a struggle that I could only now fully grasp in scale. It was hard to believe that the scar went all the way from the English Channel to the Swiss border. My view looked like the trench maps I'd poured over with the GSO in Cassel only a few days before, being brought to life.

Above the front line floated the occasional observation kite balloon that the soldiers called blimps. These hydrogen-filled balloons were flammable death traps, manned by brave but mad "balloonatics". I had heard that at least the balloon observers had parachutes, and I wondered why we were not similarly equipped in our aeroplane.

I watched fascinated as a train headed up what must have been the Castre to Ypres line, a smoke-billowing locomotive at its head, pulling a tail of French box trucks, no doubt marked *hommes 40/ chevaux 8*, and packed with grumbling Tommies.

After half an hour, the BE.2 was where I wanted us to be according to Carter-Smythe over the voice tube. I asked if we could go lower to get a closer look, and my pilot duly obliged. I quickly got my bearings. I saw the road we'd parked along on the day of the shooting and could make out the knoll due to its slight shadow. As we circled the spot, I could just see the white line and the muddy mess caused by the horses' hooves behind it. Sure enough, the line did not point to the woods, but to the small copse on a rise almost a mile away. The copse had what looked like young birch trees, but with little or no real cover. There was a sunken lane behind it. I asked my pilot to fly low over the copse, but could see nothing untoward other than it appeared to have grown over an ancient ruin. Looking back at the knoll, and imagining the scene on the day, the Brigadier on his horse would have been smack between the rest of the royal party and the copse. If he'd have been shot from the woods, the Brigadier's head wound would have been in the front of his skull and not on the right side. I was now pretty sure the Brigadier had been shot from this copse, but the distance was ridiculous. Nevertheless, I asked Carter-Smythe to take a series of vertical photographs of the whole area and so we climbed to the optimum altitude to fulfil my request. After exhausting the camera's magazine, we decided to head back to the airfield.

The BE.2 climbed and Carter-Smythe had just informed me after we levelled off that we were at 4000 feet and progressing at a steady 70mph, when suddenly our fuselage fabric was ripped by a marching sequence of holes. Our machine was then rocked by a dark shadow flashing past. I felt a sting, then blood running down my cheek. A small monoplane, our obvious assailant, was climbing up into the sky, almost seemed to stop in mid-air, then flipped quickly around and dived back to face us.

'Oh Christ!' said a strained croak via the voice tube from Carter-Smythe.

'What's wrong?' I shouted in alarm. 'Are you hit?'

'It's a Fokker and it's just done an Immelmann turn.'

'What does that mean?'

'It means it's Max Immelmann.'

'What does that mean?'

'It means we're going to die.'

'*Scheisse.*'

Carter-Smythe turned the BE.2 away from the Fokker and dived to pick up speed, but the monoplane followed and raced towards us. I braced myself for the machine gun on the enemy's nose to spit fire, but after a few bullets ripped into our top wing, nothing happened and the German machine shot past again. I was wondering how to turn and fire the Lewis gun, when the monoplane appeared beside us. It was flying parallel in formation only a few yards away, and was a dull olive-green machine with the number "246" on its side. It was decorated with large black crosses on a white background, the motif of the *Luftstreitkräfte*, the Imperial German Air Service. The pilot looked to be a young man, maybe slightly younger than me, with a pencil moustache. The German smiled at us, pointed to his machine gun in front of him and shook his head, then he gave us a friendly wave and peeled off, disappearing towards the eastern horizon.

'His machine gun must have jammed. What a let off! Not many survive a Fokker attack, much less one by Immelmann himself. Let's get back to the airfield as quickly as possible. I need a change of underwear and a stiff whisky after that encounter. Are you all right, sir?' asked Carter-Smythe.

'Yes,' I yelled into the tube, relieved not to have become "Fokker Fodder". 'Just a scratch.'

*

Soon we were back at the aerodrome and McIlhenny rushed to help me from the aeroplane.

'What happened, sur?' he asked me, as I dismounted.

'We were attacked by a Fokker. Seems like we're lucky to be alive. I think I got cut by a wood splinter from our machine. It's nothing serious.'

When I was back on terra firma, McIlhenny wiped at my shallow wound with an already bloodstained handkerchief, presumably the same one he'd used after his barbed-wire encounter in the trenches. I was not sure how sanitary this was and asked him to desist.

Carter-Smythe led me over in the direction of a van parked on the edge of the airfield, not far from the squadron headquarters. McIlhenny followed, along with two RFC fitters who had removed the camera and were lugging it between them. Outside the van, some ground crew were sitting on canvas chairs, smoking and playing cards around a bridge table. The men stopped and stood up as we approached.

'This is our mobile photographic laboratory,' said Carter-Smythe. 'They were introduced last year and are a real boon for getting prints to headquarters as soon as possible after a flight.'

As we neared the van, Hodgson roared up on a motorcycle, with an RFC man on its pillion. 'Hello, guv, I mean, sir. Just been trying out this Phelon & Moore motorcycle. Nice little bike it is. 3.5 horsepower, RFC special model. There's lots of interesting vehicles here, sir. Crossley tenders, Leyland trucks, Model T's, and all,' said Hodgson before stopping as he realised I was bleeding. 'You're hurt, sir!'

'It's just a graze,' I told him, for it didn't feel like anything serious.

'It was a fucker,' claimed McIlhenny.

'It was a Fokker,' I corrected him.

'Aye, that's what Ah said, a fucker,' rejoined McIlhenny.

The RFC men had all obviously heard this pun on "Fokker" many times before, and were rolling their eyes as they waited impatiently for this exchange to finish.

'Right, Sergeant Hope,' said Carter-Smythe to the laboratory's commander, 'get these plates developed *tout de suite*.'

'And you two wait here and then bring the prints when they're ready over to the squadron HQ,' I instructed McIlhenny and Hodgson.

I returned with my pilot to the former inn and we enjoyed a stiff whisky in the officers' mess with the CO to celebrate surviving a dogfight with the vaunted air ace, Max Immelmann. The CO seemed happy to have us both back in one piece, and glad that he'd filled my request without losing a kite and pilot. As we sipped our drinks, I noticed a pencil drawing of a pilot over the mantelpiece in the mess.

'Who's that?' I asked.

'That's Aidan Liddell. He was English, but joined a Jock regiment, like yours. Ex-Argyll's. Won the VC with us up over Flanders last year, but died of his wounds. He's there to remind us of the standards expected by 7 Squadron,' explained the CO.

Carter-Smythe put a record on the mess Decca gramophone and the voices of George Robey and Violet Loraine sang out via the amplifying horn in the duet "If You Were the Only Girl in the World". The CO said this was from the new musical, *The Bing Boys are Here*, which had opened in London the month before, and which he'd seen with his wife on his last leave. The sentimental lyrics made me think of Jeanie.

If you were the only girl in the world,
And I was the only boy,
Nothing else would matter in the world today,
We would go on loving in the same old way.

As we talked, I couldn't help but notice how twitchy the two flyers were, with Carter-Smythe's hands shaking quite openly. Despite their bravado, the pilots obviously had a stressful role, flying in fragile contraptions of wood, fabric and wire, several thousand feet above the front with no parachute, while being shot at by anti-aircraft guns, not to mention dealing with the dreaded Fokkers. In my mind, I made a quick reassessment of my wish to have joined the RFC instead of the infantry when I'd signed up.

Once my aerial photographs were delivered, still slightly damp and smelling heavily of developer and fixer chemicals, I thanked the CO and Carter-Smythe for their help and hospitality and took my leave.

'Ah'm really glad to see ye back, sur. Ah was talkin' to one of the mechanics. He says they call these pilot blokes "Flying Corpses" because most of them don't last more than three weeks!'

'I'm glad you told me that after I've been up,' I replied, thinking that this was half the lifespan a young officer could expect in the trenches, and that was short enough.

'Well, it may not be too great to be a pilot in the RFC, guv, but it's much better to be in their ground crew than to be a regular Tommy, that's for sure,' said Hodgson.

Curious, I asked, 'Why so?'

'The pay's much better for a start. RFC artificers get paid a lot more than we ASC drivers get paid for the same rank. They need more than six ground crew for every airman, so they've got a lot of vacancies. With my mechanical skills, I reckon I could get promoted too. I'd earn over three times my current wages if I transferred to that mob, guv,' Hodgson explained to me.

'Well, if you want to apply, Hodgson, I won't stop you,' I offered. 'That would only be fair.'

'Nah. I'm just saying, guv. I like this job too much. I love driving my Lanchester.'

'In that case, carry on driving, Hodgson,' I said, relieved at Hodgson's loyalty, even if it wasn't necessarily to me, but to his car.

'Right you are. So, where to now, guv?'

'Back to the chateau.'

CHAPTER 13

Once back at the chateau and in my room, I laid out the aerial photographs from my sortie. I made a sort of mosaic from the overhead shots and compared it to my map. Sure enough, the white stripe for the horsemen's mark didn't line up with the wood. If that was the case, then the two snipers that Ross killed were unlikely to be the true assassins. In turn, if those two *Jaegers* really had snuck through past McNicol, then at least he wasn't responsible for the attempt on the King's life, and that needed to be told at his court martial.

I hadn't really taken to Lord Ross, Captain MacPherson, or Sergeant MacKenzie, and I now felt sure they'd framed McNicol in revenge for past misdemeanours on the Laird's estate back in the Highlands. I knew I was now filled with what Jeanie called one of my "righteous indignation" moods, but I was now determined to have Sergeant MacKenzie for illegally killing prisoners under the Geneva Convention, as well as collaborating with MacPherson to frame McNicol on a death penalty charge. I decided I'd better try to find the Sergeant's two victims.

To clear my head, and calm down a bit, I decided to get some fresh air, and so I went out into the chateau grounds. Outside, I found McIlhenny helping Hodgson to clean the Lanchester.

'Hello, sur, anythin' yer wantin'?' asked McIlhenny.

'Nothing now, thank you, McIlhenny. However, you two better be prepared, as tomorrow you're going to be resurrection men,' I told them.

'Ah don't like the sound of that.'

'What's a resurrection man, guv?' asked Hodgson.

'A bit like Burke and Hare.'

'Are they a music hall act, guv?'

'Not quite. In the last century in Edinburgh, to feed the need for cadavers to train doctors, grave robbers, also known tongue-in-cheek by the locals as "resurrection men", dug up the dead to sell to anatomists. To make sure there was a fresh supply of bodies, Burke and Hare took to murdering their fellow citizens. I just want you to do the digging bit,' I explained in case they got any ideas.

'Typical of folk from bloody Embra. Bunch of thievin' bastards the lot of them,' said McIlhenny with the ingrained disdain of a Glaswegian for those from the Scottish capital.

Just then some crows noisily returned to roost in the trees surrounding the chateau. The flock's arrival suddenly reminded me of what had been nagging me when we had revisited the site of the assassination. On the day of the killing, why had the crows there risen from the trees only after the two shots in the wood fired by Ross, and not from the sniper shot that killed the Brigadier if that had been fired from the same location? I vaguely recalled from my school days that the collective noun for such a flock was "a murder of crows". *How appropriate was that?* I thought.

As I watched the black birds circle in the sky, they reminded me of my own flight earlier in the day, and my brush with the German ace, Immelmann. I went back into the chateau and asked a records clerk to find out if there was an intelligence file on the German pilot. Sure enough, the clerk returned a few minutes later with a thin cardboard folder and I took it to the chateau's library and settled in a leather armchair to read it after ordering a pot of tea.

As I sipped my tea and took in the file's contents, I realised how lucky I was to have escaped from my dogfight with only a scratch. The file suggested that *Oberleutnant* Max Immelmann had been responsible for singlehandedly shooting down thirteen British aircraft and had earned the title of "The Eagle of Lille" amongst fellow airmen for his defence of that city's airspace. Immelmann had been awarded Germany's highest military medal, the *Pour le Mérite*, by the Kaiser himself in January. Due to its blue ribbon, the German press had apparently nicknamed the medal, "The Blue Max", in his honour. The ace's record in aerial combat had a pretty sobering effect on me, so I returned the file and went to the mess bar for whisky to toast the anonymous armourer who had poorly prepared Immelmann's gun or ammunition belt that day and had caused it to jam. It was the least I could do.

Friday,
12th May 1916

CHAPTER 14

After an early start on the Friday, we dropped in at the depot of a nearby pioneer battalion to pick up the necessary digging tools for my soon-to-be labourers. My special warrant got us access to the quartermaster's store. The warehouse had a plentiful supply of picks and shovels amongst its tools designed to keep the battalion's pioneers busy and the roads around Montreuil in good shape. McIlhenny looked in awe at this Aladdin's cave of earth-shifting equipment.

'Ah once worked as a navvy for Glesga Corporation and we never had stuff like this,' he told me. 'Ah jacked it in, though. The foreman was a big Irish bastard who worked us like slaves. It wasn't good for ma hands, with blisters and that, and Ah needed ma fingers for ma night job,' he continued, referring to his breaking-and-entering activities after dark.

McIlhenny selected two long-handled spades, which were deemed by him, based on his short labouring career, to be better than entrenching tools for the task at hand. I signed the tools out from the store's quartermaster sergeant, and we were soon on our way.

*

We duly arrived back at the PoW cage we'd visited two days before. I had noted a small graveyard beside the prison on our previous visit and surmised, based on Sergeant MacKenzie's interview, that the shot PoWs would be buried there.

I went in to see the provost in charge of the cage and asked to see the graves of the two men the Seaforths had brought in for burial. He looked in a logbook and then took me out to a forlorn patch of disturbed ground that formed the cemetery where he pointed out two fresh mounds with rough wooden crosses at their heads. The crosses were nameless. I called over McIlhenny and Hodgson and set them to work.

'If Ah'd wanted to be a sapper, Ah'd have joined the fuckin' Sappers,' I heard McIlhenny mutter under his breath.

'At least it's dry,' said Hodgson, panting heavily as he wielded his spade, the dual effects of his sedentary lifestyle and cigarettes taking his breath away.

Eventually, the two cadavers were exhumed after much "effing and blinding" by my pair of erstwhile gravediggers. After several days in the ground in only an army blanket for a shroud and no coffin, decay had set in and the smell off the corpses was something terrible. I had McIlhenny unwrap the makeshift shrouds.

A pair of large rats approached our graveside party. A couple of swipes of McIlhenny's spade later, one lay decapitated and the other scurried away discouraged and with half its tail missing. 'Rats! Ah hate fuckin' rats,' said McIlhenny in a low, menacing voice.

'That guff's something terrible, guv. Permission to have a fag?' asked Hodgson.

I gave the two resurrection men permission to light up cigarettes to keep the smell at bay. I envied the privates their smokes once more as I surveyed the two dead Germans. The once field-grey uniforms on the bodies were stained brown by the wet earth of the graves. Rigor mortis had begun to wear off and the dead men had lost some of the rigidity I had expected and they weren't bloated like the Brigadier's corpse. Much of the men's faces had been blown away. There were no badges on their uniforms, presumably taken as souvenirs by the burial party. The provost had told me that the men had no identification on them when they'd been brought for burial.

I had *Gefreiter* Flettner brought out under guard from the PoW cage to the graveyard. The youth looked at the two corpses and then turned away and vomited. I had McIlhenny give him a Capstan and it seemed to calm the Corporal. After a few drags on his cigarette he looked once more at the two dead bodies.

'Do you recognise these men?' I asked Otto in German.

'It's difficult to say. The faces and unit badges are missing, but from the hair colouring, size, and basic uniforms, I'd say these two are my old comrades, Hans and Friedrich. Hans had big ears like that one, and Friedrich had a missing finger on his left hand like the other one.'

'What were their full names?'

'Hans Wieczorek and Friedrich Kowalski.'

'Those don't sound very German?'

'Silesia has been Polish, Prussian, Bohemian, and even Hungarian over the centuries. Not all our names sound German.'

I thanked Otto, and had McIlhenny give him another smoke as a reward. The guards came to take Flettner back to the wired compound, but I asked that he be taken to the cage's building first and that he be given a pencil and paper to write down the two dead German soldiers' personal details for me.

Afterwards, I transferred the names into the cage's logbook. 'Right, Sergeant, for the record, here are the two names for the escaping prisoners,' I said to the provost.

'But those aren't escaped prisoners, sir. Those are the two snipers who tried to kill the King.'

'What? But I asked for the graves of the two Germans that the Seaforths had brought in.'

'And those are the only two bodies any Seaforths have brought me here, sir.'

'So, none were brought in here before the attempt on the King's life?'

'No, sir,' said the provost. 'See the date in the log.'

'My God, your right, how stupid of me not to notice that,' I said, feeling a bit foolish. We lawyers were supposed to pay attention to detail. 'Thank you, Sergeant, you've been most helpful. Now, do you mind if I take those bodies away? I need to investigate them further.'

'No problem, sir, if you sign for them. As you know, you have to sign for everything. I'll give you a chitty to say you're taking ownership, so to speak.'

Once back in the graveyard, I gave new orders to McIlhenny and Hodgson, while pointing at the two cadavers, 'Right, you two, bundle them up and strap them to the back of the car. We need to take them to the CCS near Pop that we were at the other day. I need Iain Sneddon to take a look at them.'

Hodgson was aghast at the idea that his beloved Lanchester was going to be a hearse for two German corpses. Nevertheless, with McIlhenny's help, and some rope purloined from the PoW cage, the former soldiers of the Kaiser were re-wrapped in fresh blankets and somehow tied to the rear of the car. Thankfully, the rotting smell was carried behind us in the slipstream as we drove over to the CCS. Along the way, when we stopped at various crossroads and checkpoints, we certainly gained several curious glances at our foul-smelling cargo.

*

I soon found Iain Sneddon at the CCS and persuaded him to take on his old pathologist's role once more. The two Germans were brought in and placed on the table where Brigadier General Church-Fenton had lain until his military funeral. The smell in the tent hadn't improved, but I was glad to see there were fewer bodies awaiting burial. McIlhenny accompanied me to the makeshift autopsy with the VPK camera, but Hodgson declined.

'Any idea when they died?' I asked Sneddon as my friend began his examination.

'Difficult to say. They're at ambient temperature and not stiff, so rigor mortis has worn off. There are signs of putrefaction in terms of the greenish skin, the putrid odour, and some swelling from residual gases, although most of that has dissipated. However, I can't see any big blood blisters, the whole body hasn't discoloured yet, and there's no sign of skin slip. I'd say they've been dead for more than three days, but less than seven.'

Sneddon's imprecise timetable didn't really help me as it meant the dead men could have been MacKenzie's dead escapees or Ross's snipers. However, they couldn't be both. I would have to rely totally on Otto's identification and the PoW cage log.

'Well, they've both died the same way,' said Sneddon after finishing his preliminary examination. 'They've both been shot in the back of the head by a small calibre weapon at close range. You can still see the burn marks on the flesh at the entry wound. The exit wounds have removed most of their faces. I'd say we're looking at a pair of executions here,' said Sneddon as he pointed at what looked like a black star-shaped tattoo around each bullet hole.

He then turned the corpses over and showed me the extensive damage inside each man's skull, a task made easy by much of the faces having been blown off. 'This has been caused by the head absorbing not only the bullet, but also the full blast of the propellant gases. These are the tell-tale signs of a contact shot.'

'So, not shot by a galloping horseman some distance away?' I asked.

'No, never. Someone was standing right behind these two when they were shot. A horseman would never be able to take such accurate headshots from a moving horse. Then they'd be firing down on these men, so the bullet entry point would be higher up the head. Anyway, the powder burns that caused this sort of tattoo indicate it was from a muzzle pressed right onto the skull.'

'Any idea on calibre of gun? Was it a Webley?' was my next question.

'No idea, but the diameter of the entry wound, due to the close proximity of the gun muzzle, is almost always the same size or thereabouts as the weapon's calibre,' said Sneddon. 'We can easily check. Take a bullet out of your own revolver and we'll see if it fits, old boy.'

I had McIlhenny extract a bullet from my Webley, but the 0.455-inch calibre bullet was slightly too large to go through the hole in either German's head. I then sent McIlhenny to fetch a ruler from the hospital's administration office. The wooden ruler he brought had both imperial and metric measurements etched on its opposing edges.

'Just as I thought. Just over a third of an inch,' said Sneddon, 'Or, in metric, just under a centimetre. It looks like a 9-millimetre pistol did the trick.'

'Not standard British issue then, but a standard German calibre.'

'Yes. I'd suggest you're looking for an assassin with a Luger or Mauser pistol here. Why would the Germans shoot two of their own?'

'I'm not sure it was Germans who shot them, but keep that to yourself, please, Iain.'

I got McIlhenny to take photographs of the entry wounds and the tell-tale powder burns with the VPK camera while I held the ruler in place for proof of bullet calibre. Once more I had Sneddon attest the negatives, before thanking my old friend for all his help.

As we parted, Sneddon told me that German prisoners were also treated at the British hospital and some did not survive their wounds. I therefore left our two dead Germans to be re-buried with their fallen comrades who had not lived to become PoWs. I passed over their personal details from Flettner so they wouldn't be buried in unmarked graves. God knows, we had enough of those on the Western Front already. I was now convinced that the executed prisoners and the alleged snipers were one and the same. What I still didn't understand was why Ross, MacPherson and MacKenzie had committed this subterfuge.

'Where to now, guv?' came the usual refrain when we emerged from the autopsy.

'That's a very good question, Hodgson. Where to now? I think I need a conversation with our CO.'

CHAPTER 15

Back at our headquarters near Montreuil, I went in to see Villiers. I asked him to get the roll of film I'd taken from my camera developed as soon as possible and to send a telegram I'd composed to an address on Fleet Street in London. I also asked him for a private meeting with Colonel Ferguson that evening before dinner.

Back in my room, I decided to enjoy a few hours off before my meeting with the Prof. I took off my uniform and handed it to McIlhenny for pressing, along with my belts and boots for polishing.

'It's so nice not to have to kill off lice like we had to in the trenches, sur,' said McIlhenny, referring to the pests which invaded everyone's uniforms in the squalid conditions of the front line. These tiny irritating beasties were no respecters of rank, and officers and men suffered their itchy bites in equal measure. The very thought of these parasitic bloodsuckers made me want to scratch myself. 'Still, Ah'll give yer seams a wee dose of Keating's Powder just in case there's any of the wee buggers about.'

I had McIlhenny give me a good, hot, clean shave with a cutthroat razor. I preferred to use a Gillette safety razor when shaving by myself, but McIlhenny was an expert with an open blade and it was nice to sit back, relaxing in my underwear, and have my batman practise his barbering skills. I remembered that I had been somewhat nervous the first time McIlhenny had given me a shave after he had explained that his expertise with a razor was due to it being the weapon of choice amongst his contemporaries in Glasgow. Furthermore, he told me that the scar on his face had been due to a fight using cut-throats in his youth. By banishing the images of this event from my mind, I actually found the whole experience of hot towels, thick soapy lather, the scratch of razor on bristle, and McIlhenny's constant patter quite relaxing, and often indulged myself in this luxury.

The wearing of a well-trimmed moustache was an army regulation and not a fashion preference. It was deigned to make soldiers look more mature and officers more authoritarian. To ensure my compliance with this regulation, I had McIlhenny tidy my facial hair too, and he gave me the full works, with eyebrows being trimmed and extraneous hair in my nostrils and ears being eradicated.

After McIlhenny had drawn me a hot bath and left to attend to my uniform, and before entering the tub, I did the physical therapy exercises I'd been taught by the splendidly-named Almeric Paget Massage Corps as part of my recuperation. The science of physical therapy was still in its infancy in Britain, being only about twenty years old, but, despite it not being a proven cure, I religiously followed my programme even if it often seemed to induce new aches in my battered body. As I performed the exercise regime, I mentally heard the voice of my petite blonde female masseuse in the recuperation hospital on the South Coast barking in my ear to spur me on. I remembered her as more frightening than many parade-ground sergeant majors. Nevertheless, I was relieved to see the exercises were having a positive effect on my left arm and I thought the movement in my hand was slowly improving too.

Following the exercises, I stripped off and eased myself into my tin bath and soaped myself with a new bar of Lifebuoy before sitting back in the warm water. It was a guilty pleasure, as I thought about all my comrades standing in damp trenches, eating monotonous rations, drinking gallons of tea tasting of petrol, being eaten alive by lice, and, while at risk of being shelled at any time, bored out of their skulls for most of their existence.

*

My guilt was offset somewhat by surveying my wounds as I lay naked in the bath. The doctors who had patched me up had told me how lucky I was to have been on the edge of the lethal blast radius of the shrapnel shell that had wounded me. As a result, the flying fragments of hot metal had lost most of their momentum before they'd penetrated my skin. I'd also been thrown onto my right side, meaning my wounded left had been clear of the muck and mud which so easily could have infected my cuts. Since my wounds, though many, were relatively shallow, the medics had managed to get out most of the pieces of metal and the uniform cloth they'd carried with them into my flesh. I'd thus avoided gangrene and associated amputations, and the results of all this were the angry scars up and down my left leg, the jagged red marks on my hand and arm, and the stitch marks in my left torso. I remembered actually being relieved that I had ended up with only a stiff left leg as a limit on my mobility, and how grateful I was to have retained all my limbs. Thankfully, my private parts were also intact, a constant worry of all soldiers in combat.

Despite what the doctors called my good luck, when I removed my eyepatch, I still felt looking in the mirror with my one good eye upsetting. Whenever I did this, the empty socket on the left side of my face stared back at me, and I felt a huge sense of loss. By a miracle, the shell fragment penetrating this eye had not gone any further than the back of the socket. Now that I'd seen earlier that day the effects of projectiles on brains, I appreciated more than ever not having suffered any physical cranial damage. Unfortunately, my regular nightmares sometimes made me unsure if I hadn't received brain damage in another way.

As always when considering my situation, my thoughts turned guilty once more. Why had I survived while others, like my brother, Hugh, and the boys in my old platoon, had not? I often thought of the waste of my fellow volunteers on that awful day at Loos. Many of the men in my battalion had been miners, steelworkers and farmhands from the towns along the Clyde Valley, and were quite fit as a result of their professions. However, several of the recruits in September 1914 had been unemployed pale-faced youths from the slums, or were factory and mill workers who were not used to hard physical labour. By the time we landed in France, many of the men were better fed and healthier than they'd ever been in their lives. Then they'd been slaughtered, just one year after signing on. It was as if we had fattened them up like geese before Christmas. Eventually I could feel the water around me getting cold, and so I decided to get out, which was just as well, as it stopped me from getting even more maudlin.

*

After my bath, I put on a clean vest and long johns, and in a better frame of mind after a shot of Talisker malt whisky, I sat at my small desk in my underwear and tackled the administration required of all officers. This included censoring my men's letters home, as both had handed in mail for me to review.

In the case of McIlhenny this proved an easy task as my batman had simply filled in a Field Service Postcard where he'd deleted inappropriate set phrases such as "I am wounded and hope to be discharged soon" or "I have received no letter from you lately". The card was addressed to Mrs McIlhenny, my batman's mother, for I knew he was unmarried. The postcard now simply read after deletions, "I am quite well. I have received your letter dated 15th. Letter follows at first opportunity."

By contrast, Hodgson's pencil-written letter to his wife covered two sides of notepaper. I learned that his children were called Agnes and Henry, and that Hodgson was obviously worried about his son who had apparently been poorly as a baby. He asked after his old dad and his wife's mum, and about her brothers who were serving in the London Regiment. He told his wife that he was in fine health, and, I noted, made no mention of being under shellfire only a few days before, presumably not to worry her. Hodgson did tell her that he'd got a wonderful car to drive, that he had a new friend called Mac from Glasgow, and that his officer was a fine fellow, which made me smile.

Encouraged by Hodgson's effort and cheered by my passing mention in it, I poured myself another glass of Talisker to help lubricate my mind as I decided to write letters home to my family and Jeanie. After I'd poured it, I thought I'd better keep a watch on my alcohol intake as I'd noticed it had been creeping up. I smiled as I remembered my strict upbringing where my mother, otherwise teetotal, indulged only in the odd glass of sherry at Christmas and New Year to supplement her intake of sipped Communion wine. My father liked a glass of sweet, fruity German hock with his Sunday dinner, but presumably he had now changed his weekly tipple to something French. During my time as a law student in Edinburgh I had soon abandoned my previously abstemious behaviour, although I still blamed my friends like Sneddon who were medics for this more than my fellow aspiring lawyers. In my experience, medics always seemed to drink more, smoke more, eat more, and have sex more than others, despite warning everyone else about the effects of overindulgence.

As I started to write home, I looked at the fragment of lepidodendron lying on my desk. I'd picked up the fossil wood when out for a childhood walk one day with my maternal grandfather many years ago and it always reminded me of family and of home. It was a piece of the local geology and so was literally a powerful physical souvenir of my homeland. I remembered seeing a fragment of the same fossil through the cracked mica eyepiece of my smoke hood as I lay on the battlefield at Loos and wondering at the irony of the shared geology of the place of my birth and what I had then expected to be the place of my death.

I now set pen to paper, but as always, I felt that writing from a war zone was a tricky compromise between giving relatives hungry for news what they desired, but keeping even low-level military secrets from them. I first completed a letter to my parents, assuring them of my well-being. I always felt really bad about asking for anything from home, but on the other hand I knew that my mother loved to send me treats, and so in my letter I asked for some long socks to wear under my riding boots. I stole the idea from Hodgson's letter home of describing my companions and as I completed my pen-sketches I found that I felt great warmth towards McIlhenny and Hodgson. I finished off by guiltily lying that I was not in any danger in my new role, and that I'd been reunited with my old law professor from Edinburgh, whom they'd met at my graduation some years ago.

I then pulled out the small photograph of Jeanie that I always carried in my pocketbook. I found it was easier to write to her while looking at her beautiful face and raven black hair. I had been rebuked in the past by her for writing cold, uninteresting letters during my previous time in France. She'd told me she didn't really care about the weather, what I was eating and drinking, or the historic towns I'd marched through, but wanted to know how I was feeling, and how I felt about her. Jeanie obviously desired warmer and more romantic prose, and thankfully the whiskies helped remove my inhibitions.

*

Later that evening, my administrative chores and letter-writing completed, I went downstairs with my briefcase to see the Prof. I found him in his office sitting by a roaring fire, puffing on his foul-smelling pipe, and with two glasses of malt whisky already poured.

'Hello, Prof, good of you to see me.'

'Not at all, Jamie. Come and sit yourself down and tell me what's on your mind.'

'I think I'm getting an idea of what happened the other day when the Brigadier was shot, but my theory seems a bit preposterous although it fits the evidence.'

'Well, remember what Sherlock Holmes always says, "When you have eliminated the impossible, whatever remains, however improbable, must be the truth". Holmes may be fictional, but Conan Doyle has a great way with words,' said the Prof. 'So, what's your theory?'

I pulled my notes and a map out of my briefcase. 'I need to check out a couple more things first, Prof, if you don't mind. I think I know what might have happened, but not why it happened. I need to understand a bit more about snipers and sniping and what's the art of the possible. You see, I need to know if a man can shoot from here to there,' I said, pointing to the map.

'Ah, I may be able to help you. There's a Captain Hesketh-Pritchard on General Allenby's staff of Third Army who is advocating we form BEF sniping schools. I saw a paper about it doing the rounds a few days ago. Apparently, this term of "sniper" was first awarded to a few English hunters last century who could achieve the rare feat of hitting a snipe, a notoriously elusive and fast-moving bird, while it was in flight.'

The Prof had always been fascinated by etymology – the origins of words – and could wax lyrical about the derivations of certain legal words or phrases for what seemed, to those of us in his audience, hours.

'This Hesketh-Pritchard is teaching Third Army's best marksmen. I'm sure he'll know if the shot you're curious about is possible. I'll get Villiers to send a message down to Captain Selby, our man with Allenby. He'll give you the details about this sniping school. You can set off in the morning and they'll be alerted by the time you get there. Allenby's recently moved his HQ to St Pol, so it's not too far away.'

After downing our whiskies, we set off directly for dinner, and so I left my briefcase and materials in the Prof's office. By the time the dinner was over, I was feeling the full effects of the whisky and was enthusiastic when the Prof suggested we go into Montreuil to watch a concert party called *The Follies* at the town theatre. I noted McIlhenny and Hodgson in the audience as we took our seats.

In *The Follies*, the players delivered a rather bawdy take on Shakespeare where the lines from several plays had been deliberately mixed up for comical effect. This was followed in succession by an act that had to be the world's worst ventriloquist, a bungling juggler, a magician of sorts, and then a comic double act. Like most of the audience, I'd heard the majority of the jokes before, but it didn't hinder me laughing aloud at one or two of the old chestnuts. These turns were followed by a slapstick act moving a grand piano onto the stage with many slips, trips and falls, to the delight of the audience. A pianist in bow tie and tails duly arrived to accompany the star attraction, a drag artist called Bella Epoch. Bella, in his gold lamé gown, and with his high falsetto voice, looked and sounded extremely convincing to the hundreds of soldiers bereft of female company.

The show ended with the pianist and Bella leading the audience in a singalong which began with the old pub songs such as "Where Did You Get That Hat?" and "Ta-Ra-Ra-Boom-De-Ay", moved on to marching songs like "Tipperary" and "Pack Up Your Troubles", then slowed to the maudlin "Danny Boy" and "Keep the Home Fires Burning", before ending with "There's a Long, Long Trail".

There's a long, long trail a-winding,
Into the land of my dreams,
Where the nightingales are singing,
And a white moon beams.
There's a long, long night of waiting,
Until my dreams all come true;
Till the day when I'll be going down
That long, long trail with you.

A deep silence followed and I was sure that each member of the audience, like me, was thinking about their home and loved ones. I felt strangely contented after my letter-writing that I'd let the folk at home know how I felt about them, although that feeling may have been the result of the copious amount of alcohol I'd imbibed.

*

My contentment evaporated upon our return to the chateau. My room was in disarray and it had obviously been searched when I was out at the concert. I looked in vain for my briefcase before remembering that I'd left it in the Prof's office when we'd gone to dinner. Nothing seemed to have been taken. I was wondering who the perpetrators might have been when I heard a commotion outside. I rushed downstairs as fast as my gammy leg would let me and limped out into the grounds. I was met by McIlhenny and Hodgson running from the direction of their billet.

'Some women broke into our room, guv, but we disturbed them when we came back from the concert,' said Hodgson, between gulps for air.

'Aye, they were too quick for us, sur, but Bob here managed to rugby tackle one of them as they escaped,' added McIlhenny.

'I got this, guv, when I grabbed one of their ankles as they made off,' said Hodgson holding out a small knife with a black handle.

'It's a *sgian-dubh*,' I told him as I took it to inspect.

'A what, guv?' asked Hodgson.

'A small dagger that Highlanders keep in their socks as a personal weapon. Its name is Gaelic,' I explained. The version I held in my hand had the motto *Cuidich 'n Righ* etched along the blade.

'Whoever it was must have broken in through the wire. We followed them to where they went out. They might have been good wire cutters, but they were amateur burglars, Ah can tell ye, and Ah'm an expert at that kind of thing,' added McIlhenny.

'Did you recognise who it was?'

'Naw. There were two of them, though. We thought they were women in skirts, but it must have been two blokes in kilts.'

'I thought the legs were a bit hairy when I grabbed them,' added Hodgson, chuckling.

'I didn't recognise them in the dark,' said McIlhenny, shaking his head, and Hodgson mirrored the action.

'My room was broken into as well, but luckily my briefcase and notes weren't there. It would appear that they hadn't found anything in my room and were searching your billet to see if what they wanted was there. Well, as nothing's been stolen, we'd all best get some sleep, as we're off again early tomorrow.'

Saturday,
13th May 1916

CHAPTER 16

After a good night's sleep, despite the previous evening's closing turmoil, but no doubt helped by the drink, I felt quite rested, although I had a mental itch that needed scratching. I got Villiers to have an operator connect me with the field telephone of the PoW cage I'd visited. By questioning the provost sergeant in charge, I found out that the Seaforth adjutant, Captain MacPherson, had asked to be informed if anybody had come to the cage and made inquiries about the buried German snipers. The provost confirmed that he had told MacPherson that an Intelligence Corps' captain by the name of Brown had taken the bodies away.

'When was this?' I asked.

'Yesterday afternoon, sir. Soon after you visited. The Seaforths were marching past on their way out of the line and the adjutant dropped by.'

'Right, thank you, Sergeant.'

Once outside, I pre-empted Hodgson's usual destination question with instructions to set off east for Third Army's HQ. We started off in rain, but it was dry by the time we completed the thirty-mile drive to St Pol-sur-Ternoise.

*

At the headquarters, I was ushered into the office of my Intelligence Corps peer, Captain Selby.

'Good to meet you, Brown,' said Selby in welcome. 'Colonel Ferguson was here the other day and he talks very highly of you.'

'Thank you, Selby, that's very kind. I'm here about the assassination attempt on the King.'

'Yes, of course. Villiers called to warn us. Don't worry. It's all in hand. The plan is coming along.'

'Plan?' I asked, somewhat confused. 'What plan?'

'The revenge attack on the Germans, of course. We've ruled out the Kaiser, as we feel he'd be too difficult to get to, and we don't have anyone close to his entourage to predict his movements. So, instead, we've decided to go for another of the Hun's royals, namely Rupprecht, the Crown Prince of Bavaria. As you may know, he's a general in the German Army. As such, we know where his headquarters are, and, of course, he comes and goes from there frequently, so we're bound to catch him one of these days.'

'But how are you going to pull that off?'

'We've taken a sharpshooter from the sniping school we've established and sent him back to Blighty. He'll be paired up with someone who specialises in operating behind enemy lines. They'll then go over to neutral Holland on the ferry to the Hook and then under the electric fence into Belgium, and finally on to Rupprecht's HQ. We've got some brave undercover Belgians who will help. Bit of a journey, I know, but it's probably the best we can do. Our sniper will then take out Rupprecht. When the Huns have got a dead royal on their hands it will hopefully warn them off trying to get one of ours ever again.'

'Gosh, I wasn't aware of that plan.' To me, it sounded like a suicide mission. 'All I actually wanted was directions to this sniping school you mentioned.'

'Ah, I see,' said Selby, looking a bit discomfited. 'Well, please keep quiet about this other business will you, old boy? I'm not sure even Colonel Ferguson knows of it. Planning it was a direct order from on high, apparently. Anyway, you can always smile when you hear that poor old Rupprecht's had his comeuppance.'

*

Based on the information from Selby, the Lanchester was soon parked beside a field of long grass, populated on one side by some khaki military tents. After inquiries at the gate, I set off across the field with my trusty walking stick and briefcase in hand and hailed a captain who was standing alone in the field. He had a telescope trained on what looked like a row of decapitated heads.

'Captain Hesketh-Pritchard? I'm Captain Jamie Brown of the Intelligence Corps. I wonder if I could ask you a few questions to help me with an investigation?'

Suddenly I stumbled over something in the long grass, and shouted, '*Scheisse*!' as I fell. There was an echoing loudly yelled expletive beneath me as an apparition arose ghost-like beside the site of my fall. Standing over me was a sort of scarecrow that had previously been invisible and must have been lying on the ground until I had tripped over it.

Hesketh-Pritchard was laughing to himself as he came over and helped me to my feet, saying, 'Welcome, old boy. Meet Corporal Fraser of the Lovat Scouts.'

The Captain was quite old for his rank, closer to forty than thirty, was well suntanned, and had a relaxed self-confident air about him. I knew from talking to Selby that Hesketh-Pritchard was a man of many parts having been a first-class cricketer, an author, a big game hunter, and an explorer, amongst other things. Like me, he had a law degree, but had apparently never practised. I felt my own pre-war history was rather boring by comparison.

'Whatever is he wearing?' I asked, pointing to the scarecrow. 'I never saw him lying there.'

Upon closer inspection, the Corporal was in fact wearing exactly the same long grass as the field he'd been lying in, but with it woven into some kind of overalls and a headdress, thus making him invisible, even at close range. In his hands he held a Lee-Enfield rifle with a telescopic sight on the top, offset to the left.

'Fraser is wearing what we call a "ghillie suit". It's named after the Highland ghillies that wear them when hunting or guarding against poachers in the Highlands. It's a mix of hessian and jute twine, with whatever the local vegetation is affixed to it. The headdress is the same, only like a beekeeper's bonnet, with a slot to see out of to aim your rifle. Perfect cover for a sniper who doesn't want to be discovered when taking potshots at the enemy,' explained Hesketh-Pritchard.

'Well, it certainly fooled me,' I said, dusting myself down and flicking grass off my uniform. 'What's with the heads?' I asked, pointing to the gruesome line-up a few hundred yards away.

'Don't worry, they're papier-mâché dummies. We use them in the lines to draw out German snipers to take a shot so we can fix their locations. The idea is that our own snipers then take their snipers out. Tit for tat. Or at least that's the theory. We've even got dummies that appear to smoke. We blow the smoke up a rubber tube into the dummy's mouth. It's quite realistic at a distance. We just use them here for practising headshots. Watch this,' said Hesketh-Pritchard as he handed me his telescope to train on the dummies. His voice changed as he shouted an order, 'Ramsey and Quinnell, pick off two heads.'

Two of the papier-mâché heads exploded, shot by a pair of snipers concealed just yards away from me. I hadn't seen them either. 'Gosh, that's very impressive. I had no idea those men were even down there. And good shooting, too. I can see why we need a school like this if that's the quality of your graduates.'

'It's not going to win us the war, but it's good for morale as our troops will know that they're not the only ones being randomly sniped.'

'Fascinating.' I was glad this expert was on our side, but I needed to dig deeper into that expertise. 'Now, Captain, can I ask your advice on a couple of things?'

We retired to one of the tents where a large tea urn dispensed well-earned refreshment to the trainees and their instructors. We sat at a table apart from the others and, after swearing Hesketh-Pritchard to secrecy, I spread out a map of the area of the Brigadier's assassination, along with my aerial photographs. I gave the other captain only the rudimentary details of my investigation so far and began to ask him a series of layman's questions about sniping.

'What I need to know is if it is possible for someone in this copse here to shoot someone in the head nearly a mile away over here on this knoll? The shot was taken by a rifle of a calibre larger than a German Mauser or a British Lee-Enfield. Dumdum ammunition like this was used.' I produced the bullet from the Brigadier's skull as I spoke.

'At first glance you've got two conflicting pieces of evidence here, Brown. Firstly, it's literally a long shot, and extremely difficult. Especially a headshot. Against that, your bullet here is of a large calibre, closer to the 0.45 of a service revolver, and is possibly from an elephant gun or some other large-bore hunting rifle. Game, though, is usually shot much closer than the distance you've mentioned. More like 300 yards or less, and so a hunting rifle isn't normally used for the sort of long shot you describe.'

'Normally?'

'Yes, but if such a gun is loaded with a Nitro Express cartridge, they pack a hell of a punch. We've proven that these can cut those little steel shields the German snipers use like a knife through butter. From what you've shown me, your sniper may have substituted stopping power for range by adapting a similar type of bullet.'

'Can you make a dumdum out of those sorts of bullets?'

'Yes, an Express bullet could be adapted into a dumdum, and indeed that's how it was first used to hunt big game in Africa and India. Believe me, if a bull elephant is charging at you, you need all the stopping power you can get!'

'So, most likely a British gun then?'

'Well, probably, but not necessarily. Don't forget there's German East Africa, just south of Kenya. The German hunters there will use similar rifles.'

I had forgotten that Germany had colonies in Africa, despite having read in the *Daily Mail* a few days before about the South Africans fighting the Germans on that remote front. I presumed they would have game-hunting communities and wondered if I should revisit Otto one more time to find out if any of the *Jaeger*'s comrades had such a rifle. Meanwhile, Hesketh-Pritchard was continuing.

'Against it being German, though, is the fact that their snipers do seem to have settled on a special version of their standard 7.9-millimetre calibre Mauser rifle. Your chaps in Intelligence have told us that they select the best rifles off the production line, test the guns' accuracy at the factory, add on scopes, and then dispatch them specially packaged to their snipers at the front. I must say, though, that I've never heard of the German snipers using dumdums. Some of our chaps think they do, but they don't.'

'Yes, there is still the issue of the dumdum bullet, a projectile the Germans wanted banned from the battlefield and had it enshrined in the Hague Convention of 1899. So, the dumdum and unusual calibre mean the weight of evidence points once more to non-German, after all?'

'Whichever rifle and ammunition combination was used, it's still a long way to shoot so accurately. Not impossible, but incredibly difficult. Sniping is as much an art as a science. The sniper has to be able to think in three-dimensions.'

'How so?'

'The first dimension is the distance to the target. The range the bullet needs to cover determines the charge in the cartridge. The bullet must retain enough energy upon reaching the target to penetrate it with lethal effect.

'The second dimension is the vertical. Over that distance, a bullet would drop quite considerably due to gravity, so the sniper would have to be highly skilled to allow for that by aiming just high enough and still hit his target.

'The third dimension is the horizontal. The sniper would have to take into account the weather conditions, particularly wind speed and direction. "Windage" we call it. Humidity can be important too, as it affects the air's density, and so the friction on the bullet.

'Also, you'd need a good telescopic sight to see the target clearly, and preferably the time of day has to provide a good front-lit target and not a back-lit silhouette. The scope must be adjustable for all these measures as well as the parallax shift of using only one eye to look down the scope. What you're asking about is quite a complicated piece of shooting. Actually, on reflection, the distance may also suggest this wasn't a German kill we're discussing.'

'Why not?'

'Well, the Germans usually use woodsmen as snipers, and in the confines of their native forests, they're used to taking relatively close shots. That's perfect for sniping across no-man's land, but not so good for long shots. By comparison, our best snipers come mostly from the Highlands or the moors. That is to say, from more open countryside where a long-range shot may be necessary in a hunt. Now, having said all that, there are probably only three people on our side I know who could attempt that shot, although even then it would be a push,' mused Hesketh-Pritchard.

'Who are they?' I asked.

'One's Danny Kelly of the Connaught Rangers. He's from the wilds of Connemara. However, he's on leave right now in London. Then there's Jimmy Wright from the Norfolk Regiment. He learned his trade on the Broads sniping wildfowl. He's not here either, as he's just been seconded to some hush-hush special operation. Anyway, when this incident you're talking about actually happened, he was with me giving a demonstration to the Belgians in Dixmude.'

After talking to Captain Selby, I thought I knew where poor Wright was going to end up, so I asked, 'Who is the third?'

'The other's Old Man MacLeod, as we call him.'

'Old Man MacLeod?' That name rang a bell. Then I remembered that Private McNicol had mentioned a MacLeod when we'd talked at Blargies Prison.

'Yes, he must be the oldest soldier in the British Army. He's over seventy. Lord Ross of the Seaforths recommended him to us when he heard we were setting up this school. He was a ghillie back in Ross-shire, up in the Highlands. He's won all sorts of shooting competitions. A real champion marksman! His Lordship persuaded MacLeod to come over to France to be an instructor here with a promise of no active service and a sergeant's stripes. The War Office gave him a special dispensation because of his age and his special skills. He was enlisted into the Lovat Scouts, who are also appropriately known as "The Sharpshooters". MacLeod's an amazing shot. He's probably the best I've ever seen, and believe me, I've seen many good shots on my travels round the globe.'

'He sounds quite a character.'

'And he's got a fantastic rifle, too. It's a Rigby of London 0.416 bolt-action hunting rifle with a fancy Bausch & Lomb five-times-magnification scope on it that he uses to demonstrate extreme shooting to the students here. Ironically, it's got a German-designed Mauser action on it. It was a parting gift from his old laird, Lord Ross's father, before he came over here. Despite his age, he's a better shot than any of our new recruits, that's for sure. If he were younger, he'd wreak havoc with the Germans if he were in the front line. MacLeod could certainly advise you as to how your shot could be made.'

'Could this Rigby rifle achieve such a long shot?'

'Yes, it could. It's large bore and long range. But obviously MacLeod wouldn't assassinate a British officer, so you've got a bit of a conundrum here, I'm afraid to say.'

The mention of Ross had rung an alarm bell in my head and so I asked to see Sergeant MacLeod in private to get some additional advice.

CHAPTER 17

Soon, a small, elderly soldier whose weather-beaten brown face was offset by bristle-like white hair and a matching moustache arrived at my table. The man's eyes belied these other physical indicators of age and were a striking light blue, clear and alert, a little large for his face, and surrounded by deep crows' feet wrinkles. They were certainly not the rheumy eyes so often seen in the elderly. I introduced myself and asked the Sergeant for his full name.

'Sergeant Murdo MacLeod of the Lovat Scouts, sir.'

'And you live on Lord Ross's estate, up in Ross-shire, I believe?'

'Aye, that's right, sir.'

I explained that I was there to ask for MacLeod's advice on a sniper shot taken a few days ago, just north of our current location, in an apparent attempt on the King's life.

'Aye, I heard a rumour about that. *Jaegers* with a Mauser, wasn't it?'

'Actually, no, it wasn't,' I told him, keenly watching for his reaction. 'I've been told by a *Jaeger* prisoner that a Mauser is only good out to about 500 yards and this shot was taken much further away than that. And then there's this.'

I produced the mushroom-shaped remains of the bullet dug out of Church-Fenton's skull and put it on the table.

'This is the bullet removed by a pathologist from the head of the Brigadier who was shot that day instead of the King,' I told him. 'Your CO here says the Germans have settled on a 7.9-millimetre calibre sniping rifle and this is a larger calibre than that. It's closer to a big game rifle, I'm told. As you can see, it's a dumdum round. The Germans don't use dumdums as a matter of course.'

I was sure that below the tanned face the man blanched a little and looked quite uncomfortable. I wondered why. I got out the map and aerial photographs once more and showed the Sergeant where the wood and the smaller copse were. I told him that I thought the copse was the assassin's hide.

'That's just under a mile away, sir,' said the old man pointing to the map's scale. 'It's about a 1500-yard range.'

'But an excellent shot like you could take that? Captain Hesketh-Pritchard says you're the best shot he's ever seen, which, coming from him, is some accolade. I also heard you once killed an injured stag from over a mile away. "The Emperor" was the beast, wasn't it?'

'Who told you that, sir?' asked MacLeod, his brow furrowed.

'Charlie McNicol told me from his prison cell.'

'What's he in prison for?' asked the Sergeant, suddenly looking bewildered.

'He's in prison accused of sleeping at his post one night when on sentry duty, and thereby letting a German sniper party creep across into our lines. That's the sniper party of *Jaegers* that supposedly tried to assassinate the King from this wood here on the map. But I don't believe any snipers crossed into our territory. The copse, and not the wood, is correctly aligned with the royal party and the Brigadier at its end. The Brigadier was shot in the right side of his skull, which was a profile shot for a sniper in the copse.'

Sergeant MacLeod was now staring fixedly at the map, avoiding my eye.

'Now, you suddenly seem a wee bit anxious, MacLeod. You wouldn't have been the real sniper, would you?' I asked, curious to the man's nervousness and instinctively leveraging my previous experience of dealing with guilty criminals whose behaviour he seemed to me to be replicating.

'Why would it have been me, sir?' asked MacLeod, and I detected a slight tremble in the old man's voice.

'Well, I know it wasn't a German because of the dumdum and the calibre. Then your own CO said he knows of only three men who could even come close to such a feat, and one of them was on leave at the time of the incident, and the other was also elsewhere, which, I'm afraid, brings me to you, Sergeant, and your fancy Rigby hunting rifle.'

'Are you suggesting I shot a British officer, sir?' MacLeod tried to sound indignant, but he couldn't quite carry it off.

'That's exactly what I'm suggesting, Sergeant. I did some calculations when I was waiting for you to appear. Your rifle has a bore of about 11 millimetres, and that's more than a standard Mauser's near 8 millimetres, but close to this deformed bullet here. Look, I can easily check around the school to see if, on the day in question, you were here. But if you weren't on site, then where were you?'

The old soldier looked even more uncomfortable, and I decided to tighten the screw some more. I was in full prosecutor mode by now.

'Sergeant, right now Charlie McNicol faces a firing squad at dawn for his supposed misdemeanour. His wife, your niece I believe, will soon be a widow, and his children will be fatherless, and a man I believe to be innocent will be dead if that happens.'

'Charlie was always good at night; I doubt he ever slept at his post. MacKenzie, the head keeper, he knew Charlie was a poacher, but he could never catch him at it. He hated Charlie with a vengeance and that only got worse after they couldn't prove that Charlie shot "The Emperor". And now you say Charlie himself is to be shot?'

MacLeod let out a low sigh. He seemed to be struggling with something in his mind and so I prompted him. 'Come on, Sergeant, out with it. I know Lord Ross is up to no good here, and you're from his estate and the best marksman he could go to for this. He was the one who placed the Brigadier on the end of the line of horsemen and directly into the firing line. I saw that myself.'

'Ach, it's not fair a young man like Charlie should die an innocent man, and an old man like me continue to go on. I don't like the idea of my niece Peggie being a widow on my account, either. You're right in your suspicions, sir, I did shoot that Brigadier, so please make sure Charlie is set free. I'm sure he was never asleep; someone must have done for him.'

'But why did you shoot a British senior officer? Was the Brigadier your actual target? And if so, why him? What's going on here, MacLeod?' I demanded, wondering what this conspiracy was all about.

'I can't tell you, sir.'

'Look, Sergeant, Private McNicol isn't the only one who could be shot. We're talking about the assassination of a British brigadier general for God's sake. You could be standing beside Charlie facing the firing squad.'

'I really can't tell you, sir.'

'MacLeod, your wife back in Ross-shire will be a widow. Your name will be disgraced. What could be worse for her than that?'

These stark facts seemed to unnerve the old man. He was obviously dealing with something major and troubling in his mind judging from the emotions that ran across his face. A long silence ensued before the Sergeant spoke again.

'Aye, you're right, sir. I wouldn't want my Mhairi to suffer that, but I was ordered to do it, sir. I was only obeying orders.'

'Whose orders?'

'I was ordered to do it by Lord Ross. I didn't want to do it, even after he explained that I'd be doing every Tommy a favour as this Brigadier was one of the most incompetent officers in the British Army. He mentioned the man had been responsible for a few disasters where many Tommies had been lost. He told me this incompetence was a disguise as the Brigadier was in fact a German spy and was deliberately sending our troops into useless attacks. His Lordship said

140

the Brigadier would be shot as a traitor anyway. He said the reason for eliminating the man in this way was to save the BEF from the embarrassment of a spy being seen to reach such a senior position. Even so, I was still reluctant to do it, sir.'

'Church-Fenton was a German spy?' I exclaimed, absolutely astonished. I had never suspected that one.

'Aye, that's what I was told. But I swear I still didn't want to do it. I've shot many a beast and bird in my time, but never a man.'

'But you did it in the end. Why?'

'Lord Ross said that if I didn't do it, then me and my wife, Mhairi, and our children and our grandchildren, would all be evicted from our crofts on his father's estate. Where would we go, sir?'

'So, he blackmailed you into doing it?'

MacLeod nodded grimly and then explained what he'd been required to do. It gushed out of him, as if his confession was a huge relief.

'I agreed. I had to agree. I kept telling myself it was my patriotic duty to kill the German spy and that it was an order. Lord Ross told me everything was to be top secret.'

'What exactly did he tell you to do? Tell me the whole story.'

'I was told that a morale-boosting visit by the King was planned and that there would be a press picture taken on a knoll which would give me an easier shot as the target would have to be still for the photograph. Lord Ross said I would be collected the night before from the school here and taken to a copse near the knoll by someone I didn't know. The next morning, I was to reconnoitre the site to take in the weather conditions, and ensure I understood the sightline and required range. I was told to make myself inconspicuous in a ghillie suit and wait for the royal party to assemble after lunch.'

'How did you know who to shoot? Were you given a photograph?'

'No, sir. I was instructed to shoot in the head whichever officer was on the end of the line, closest to me when the picture was being taken. I was told to use a dumdum bullet to be sure that neither the King nor any other officers would be injured.'

'What about conditions for the shot? How could they be predicted?'

'To help me make the shot I was told to expect an escort of cavalry to be positioned behind the party and that they would have pennants on their lances to give an indication of wind speed and direction.'

'So then, what did you do?'

'As a result of these instructions, I cleaned my Rigby and made up a number of dumdum rounds with different Nitro Express charges, as I couldn't be sure until I got to the site about the exact range to the target or the wind conditions I'd be firing into. Finally, I polished each bullet to make sure they flew as true as possible. After the shot, I was told to wait until dark and then make my way to the sunken lane behind the copse, where I'd be picked up and returned to the school.'

'Did you recognise who picked you up?'

'I didn't recognise the driver of the car for the trip to and from the firing site as his uniform was devoid of rank or unit badges. However, from the man's voice, I think that the driver must have been Scottish, probably a Highlander, and, since he talked like the Laird and ordered me about, I think he was also an officer. I sat in the back and although the driver never turned around, I could see the back of his neck. He was ginger-haired. That was about the only distinguishing feature I could see, sir. I know all the gentry on the Laird's estate, and I'm pretty sure, though, that it wasn't one of them.'

I had a good idea who it was that MacLeod was describing, but asked, 'And there's nothing else about this man you can think may identify him?'

'He smelled.'

'He smelled? What did he smell of?'

'It was a mix of fags and wet dogs. Being a ghillie, sir, you develop a keen sense of smell.'

'Right, thanks. Now, tell me what happened on the day.'

'It went pretty much as Lord Ross said it would, sir. On the day I took the shot, I settled down between two trees at the front of the copse. Although it was a long way off, the target sat still, was presented in profile as expected, and the wind was negligible. From my reconnaissance of the field, I selected a bullet that I thought would cover the distance and just have enough energy to kill. I fired and hit the designated target. The man went down.'

'It was an amazing piece of shooting, Sergeant, I'll give you that. To hit a headshot at that distance.'

There was a glimmer of a smile as Sergeant MacLeod replied, 'Ah well, to tell you the truth, sir, I wasn't going for a headshot at that range. Even I'm not that good. I only had to hit the target from the waist up. The dumdum I fired would have killed him if it had hit anywhere in the upper body, never mind his head.' MacLeod stopped, the smile fading as he relived the event and realised the enormity of what he'd done. He'd shot a British senior officer, after all. 'I swear, sir, I didn't know anything about the supposed German snipers or poor Charlie McNicol. I'm really, really sorry for what happened to all of them. What will happen to me now, sir? I was only obeying orders,' pleaded the old soldier. 'What will happen to my family back home?'

'Nothing yet, Sergeant. You were apparently obeying an order of a superior officer, although it was an illegal order and you were under duress. There's something fishy going on here between Lord Ross and Church-Fenton and I need to get to the bottom of that before deciding what to do with you. Whatever happens, I'll make sure your family is taken care of. In the meantime, say nothing of this to anyone, and do not tell Lord Ross about our conversation.'

The old man looked stricken, his head bowed, and his body shaking.

'That's all for now, MacLeod. I'll be in touch.'

I left the Sergeant, nearly in tears, staring at the table in front of him. I felt sorry for the old man. He had been used and blackmailed by his supposed superiors.

Outside the school, I disturbed McIlhenny and Hodgson on what looked like their fourth or fifth fag to judge by the pile of cigarette butts at their feet.

'Where to now, guv?' asked Hodgson in a croak resulting from his smoking session.

'Back to the scene of the crime again, but I want to view it from a different angle this time.'

*

Using my aerial photographs, I directed Hodgson into the sunken lane behind the small copse growing over the old ruins that I'd detected from my flight overhead. With McIlhenny's help, I scaled the bank, clambered over some tumbledown walls, and entered a sparse growth of young birch trees. Early-blooming poppies were rife on the broken ground covering the ruin under the saplings, offering a splash of colour in an otherwise green landscape. Using my field glasses, I could see the knoll where the horsemen had been lined up. It was indeed a long way away and one hell of a shot the old man had taken.

To come up with this plan, Ross must have had the utmost confidence in the Sergeant and his ability. Looking around I could see no evidence of the sniper's firing position, however I felt satisfied with MacLeod's story, given the strong references on the man's shooting prowess from McNicol and Hesketh-Pritchard.

After descending to the sunken lane once more, I looked around. There were some muddy tyre tracks visible, but little else. As I was about to climb back into the staff car something caught my eye. I went over and picked up a cigarette butt lying near the edge of the road.

'That's from one of those fancy fags, isn't it, sur?' asked McIlhenny. 'Ye know, the ones with the cotton wool filter. Supposed to be healthy. Pretty expensive. Out ma league. Ah think Ah'll stick to ma Capstans.'

'Yes, I do believe it is,' I acknowledged as I put it in my pocket.

'Where to now, guv?' asked Hodgson.

'Back to the chateau. I've a case for the prosecution to put together.'

CHAPTER 18

Two hours later, upon arriving back at the chateau, I sought an appointment with the Prof once more before going for lunch. Later, after settling in my room, I felt energised and in my element. This is what I'd been trained for before joining the army, collecting facts and making a case. I started to put my thoughts together on paper for the legal argument I was about to make to the Prof based on the evidence I'd amassed. When I went down to the Prof's study at the appointed time, Villiers handed over my developed prints.

'You take some pretty gruesome snaps, old boy,' said Villiers, revealing that he'd obviously sneaked a peek at my photographs.

'Yes, well, there's been some pretty gruesome goings-on around here, I can tell you,' I said. 'Now, please can you have someone look at the personnel records of these two for me?' I added, handing over a list with two names on it before I went into the Prof's office and closed the door.

Over two glasses of Laphroaig, I outlined my current, if seemingly preposterous, theory of what had happened on the grassy knoll in Flanders a few days before, using maps and my aerial photographs to help my explanation. The importance of the entry wounds on the various victims was enhanced by McIlhenny's forensic snaps, which, I was pleased to see, were actually quite good. My batman's steady hand and agile fingers had taken several quite clear photographs. Having told my story, it all seemed rather unlikely and my earlier enthusiasm drained away, and I felt myself staring a bit shamefaced down into the dregs of my whisky.

'Well, well,' said the Prof when I'd finished, 'that's a tale and half, I'll say.'

'Yes, I'm sorry, Prof. It all sounds utterly ridiculous.'

'There's also a bit that makes me quite angry in your story. That's the fact that Church-Fenton was supposedly a spy. We in the Intelligence Corps are responsible for counter-intelligence, including the identification of German spies and their activities behind our lines. However, I've never heard of such an accusation against the Brigadier. I need to make a few inquiries of my own, and I need to think about our next step. I won't join you for dinner tonight. I'll have to go to GHQ and talk discreetly to some senior officers, and that, unfortunately, means I'd better not have another one of these,' said the Prof holding up his glass. 'In the meantime, why don't you go over and look at Church-Fenton's billet to see if there is any proof of this supposed German connection.'

*

Based on the Prof's suggestion, I had Hodgson drop me off at the large town house that served as accommodation for the late Brigadier General Church-Fenton according to Villiers' rapid research. My warrant got me past the Brigadier's batman, a Private Leeming, who was annoyed that his plan to parcel up his deceased officer's belongings that evening had been interrupted.

'I'm just looking to round out my inquiries about the Brigadier's death, Leeming. Nothing to worry about,' I told him.

'Yes, sir, but I don't understand why the staff officers or that other Scottish officer who looked in the room didn't just update you.'

'Other Scottish officer?'

'Yes, I didn't catch his name, and I don't recall his rank. He didn't sound particularly Scottish, but he did have a kilt on.'

'And the staff officers?'

'Yes, two of them came over to check the Brigadier hadn't left any secret papers or plans lying about. A colonel and a captain. Sorry, sir, I can't remember their names either, although I do remember the captain's accent was foreign. Probably a colonial, I'd guess. They didn't want any secrets sent back to Blighty with his effects, and into civilian hands.'

I suspected that I knew who the other Scottish officer might have been, and the staff officers' visit seemed a logical precaution.

Leeming showed me to Church-Fenton's room and I turned on the lights as it was now dark outside. The room was quite large, with a half-canopied bed, an armoire, a desk and chair, an overstuffed armchair, a large gramophone on a side table beside a bookcase, and a couple of steamer trunks as its principal contents. It felt cold and damp, as presumably no fire had been lit in its rather grandiose carved marble fireplace since the Brigadier's demise.

I sat at the desk which had a blotter, an old brass shell case filled with pencils, and a photograph on its surface. The photograph was a close-up of the Brigadier and in the sepia image I saw a handsome, if haughty-looking, man of about forty. I briefly reflected on the terrible damage I'd seen done to this fine head by the dumdum bullet that had ended Church-Fenton's life. I also thought it weirdly egotistical to have a photograph of oneself on one's own desk.

I went on to search the desk drawers, but found nothing incriminating in them. In a pile beside the gramophone were recordings of Wagner, Beethoven, and Bach. The records were all Deutsche Grammaphon. I reflected that liking Wagner made a person many things in my view, but it didn't necessarily make them a German spy, and the record label, if not the composers themselves, was circumstantial evidence at best, as the brand was readily available in pre-war Britain. Other than his collection of recordings and a German-English dictionary in his bookcase beside a copy of Schiller's poems and Goethe's autobiography, both of which were in the English translation, there was nothing obvious to suggest Church-

Fenton was a particularly strong Germanophile. Indeed, the rest of the bookcase was a mix of English and French literature, and the deceased Brigadier seemed to show a very strong bias to Britain's main ally. Frustrated in my search, I went to question Leeming.

'Did you ever suspect the Brigadier had any positive feelings for the Germans? Did he ever say anything to indicate that, or did you ever find anything to suggest that in his room?' I asked the batman.

'No, sir, nothing of the sort. He was very keen on the French I'd say, but I never heard him say anything good about the Germans. I never found anything suspicious to suggest otherwise, sir,' replied Leeming. 'Why do you ask, sir?'

'Just checking for completeness. Right, carry on, Leeming,' I said and went to collect Hodgson outside.

'Where to now, guv?'

'Back to the chateau for dinner.'

When we got back to our headquarters, I was handed a note from Iain Sneddon, who, it turned out, was at an RAMC conference in Montreuil and who was available to meet that night. There was a telephone number to call. I rang and invited Sneddon to the chateau after dinner. I did so with some trepidation as Sneddon was a great carouser, and I could ill afford a hangover.

*

When Sneddon came over, we went up to my room where I still had a bottle of Talisker. After I poured two whiskies, we clinked glasses and sipped our malts.

'Just like Saturday nights at the Students' Union back in Auld Reekie, eh Jamie?' said Sneddon.

'God, I hope not,' I replied, remembering some very drunken nights in Teviot Row back in Edinburgh in our university days.

'Those were the days, my friend.'

'Aye, but it was mostly pints of Usher's and McEwan's heavy we were on then and not single malts.'

'You're right. We were lucky Edinburgh had so many breweries. Do you remember how sometimes the weather conspires to create a malty smelling haze over the city? That's the smell of Edinburgh!'

'I remember it well. But why are you here in Montreuil then, Iain?' I asked my old friend.

'I was sent over for a lecture on mobile X-ray machines.'

'An X-ray machine at the front?'

'Yes, you'd be surprised at what we can do now close to the battlefield. Lots of things are possible to help the wounded and save more lives and limbs. Well, that is until we get overwhelmed by sheer numbers by a Hun attack on us, or alternatively, an offensive by us on the Huns. Then it can all go to hell in a handcart.'

'Yes, I've seen the convoys of ambulances, and the trains and barges. You must be pretty busy over there sometimes.'

'We are indeed,' said Sneddon, peering at me, a glint in his eye. 'Now, tell me, have you had a recent check-up yourself, Jamie?'

'No, I haven't,' I had to admit and then felt the need to defend myself. 'I've been rather busy. I may have a gammy leg, Iain, but I'm actually quite fit. I managed a few miles into the trenches and back a few days ago. It was tough going, but I made it. I'm doing physical therapy exercises to get my hand back its flexibility. I think I'm doing all right, thank you very much.'

'I'll be the judge of that,' said Sneddon. 'Now, get your kit off!'

'What?' I asked, startled.

'Get your uniform off. You need a medical examination, old boy. You can't keep delaying it.'

I reluctantly did as the doctor ordered and stripped down to my vest and long johns. Sneddon pulled my woollen underwear about to inspect my left arm, side and leg, before lifting my eyepatch to peer into the empty eye socket.

'Hmm, I'd say you were jolly lucky, Jamie. If you'd have been a yard closer to that shell blast, you'd either have been a goner or an amputee. Wedding tackle unscathed?' asked Sneddon, now pointing at my nether regions.

'Yes, everything's fine down there, thank you, and there's no need for a short-arm inspection!'

'Good, I'm sure Jeanie will be pleased! I assume you're still walking out with her?'

'Yes, I hope to ask her to marry me next time I'm home, actually. I just hope she'll be all right about my current state of disrepair to contemplate getting engaged,' I answered, a hint of worry creeping into my voice.

'What does she do apart from pining for your safe return, obviously?'

'She's actually one of your lot. She's training to be a doctor at Glasgow University.'

'A doctor! Well then, perhaps I should meet her and give her some personal tutoring.'

'Not on your nelly! I remember you giving "personal tutoring" to half the nurses at the Royal Infirmary when we were students. I'm surprised you survived without a slate of paternity suits.'

'If she's to be a doctor, I'm sure she'll see beyond your infirmities and into that walnut in your skull that you call a brain. I mean you're still quite a good catch, after all, with a brilliant career ahead of you in the legal profession. Admittedly that's only thanks to the depleted competition for the top jobs due to the Huns' efforts. I'm sure you'll be Scotland's Advocate General someday. Shame about the eye, although perversely it makes you look more distinguished. War hero and all that. Just wait until you go grey at the temples. By the way, didn't they offer you a glass eye instead of that patch?'

'I was sent to Moorfields Eye Hospital in London, but they said that the way the socket was damaged it wasn't suitable for a glass eye, I'm afraid.'

'Well, Moorfields is the best. Anyway, the finest glass eyes are made in Germany, and for obvious reasons, they're a bit difficult to come by at the moment,' said Sneddon with a grin. The grin faded as he continued. 'You know, Jamie, it's a great pity you went into action before steel helmets were introduced. If you had been wearing a battle bowler you may not have lost that eye. Those tin hats have reduced head wounds from shrapnel by almost seventy-five per cent. They save us a lot of work at the CCS.'

'Well I wasn't, and there's not much I can do about it now. I've got to accept my lot and move on.'

'And how do you feel in yourself, Jamie?'

'Fine, I'm fine.'

'Hold out your hands, palms down.'

I obliged, suspicious of what Sneddon was now up to.

'Good. No sign of tremors.'

'I wasn't planning to do conjuring tricks when this is over, you know.'

'Any ringing in the ears? Dizziness? Blackouts?'

I shook my head at all these questions and demanded, 'Why are you asking all this?'

'We see a lot of troops suffering from battle fatigue. They're physically all right, but their nervous system is damaged. There was an article in *The Lancet* last year by a Colonel Myers, and he used the term "shell shock" to describe the condition. Soldiers' minds are becoming a bit of a worry if they're exposed to too much shelling or, like you, survive a nearby blast. With GHQ though, it's how we'll be sure we have enough warm bodies to put in the firing line, so sufferers of this are not always treated sympathetically, I'm sorry to say.'

'Well, as I said, I had to go down into the trenches a few days ago and it was all I could do to hold it together going in. I'm proud to say I managed it, though. But then we got shelled on the way out, and that was pretty dreadful. But again, I got over seeing all the wounded and the dead. I feel I've come through some sort of test.'

'Do you get headaches, nightmares?'

'I get headaches occasionally, but no more than normal I'd guess, and usually after too much of what we're drinking. The bad dreams I get quite often, I'm afraid, but curiously, less so since I was back at the front.'

'I'm no Freud,' said Sneddon, 'but sometimes it's good to talk about them. What happens in your dreams?'

'Usually something bad happens, and mostly to my old platoon of Cameronians, but they're always already dead. And then I wake up feeling guilty and sometimes can't get back to sleep.'

'You shouldn't feel guilty, Jamie. You did what you were required to do as an officer and their leader. Look, if all this becomes too much for you, you don't have to go on with this. Let me know and I can put you in touch with someone in the RAMC more expert than me. You may be suffering from neurasthenia, a suppressed nervous condition – it's a mild version of the shell shock I mentioned. It's difficult to diagnose and, as I've said, it isn't always treated sympathetically. However, with your physical wounds you could be invalided out.'

'And as I've said, Iain, I'm fine for now. I'm coping. Honestly! My job provides plenty of distractions, believe me.'

'In fact, how come you weren't invalided out?' asked Sneddon, frowning.

'I persuaded one of your former fellow students to sign me off as fit for restricted duties, such as the Intelligence Corps.'

'I'm not sure that was very intelligent,' said Sneddon, his grin returning. 'Who was daft enough to pass you as fit?'

'Walter Moffat.'

'Wee fat Walter Moffat, the human cannonball?'

'Yes, the very same. I'm afraid I blackmailed him,' I said, with a laugh. 'He refused to sign me off, but I reminded him that I knew about that stunt he played in the anatomy lab with the male and female cadavers, and how your professor went completely haywire about respect for the dead and so on. Somehow, that jogged his pen into the necessary signature.'

'We were lucky we all weren't sent down from medical school after that one as nobody owned up to Walter's tableau. Mind you, I think it would have been too embarrassing for the university to write off an entire year of medics!' said Sneddon, joining in my laughter.

'Walter did all right after all that, and he had a practice on Harley Street before the war, would you believe? And not only that, but he's on his second marriage and not yet thirty.'

'Wee Walter, who'd have thought it! But, being serious again for a minute, are you taking anything for the pain or sleeplessness?' asked Sneddon, my attempts at distraction seemingly not working.

'Just this really,' I said holding up my glass of whisky. 'I try not to take the morphine tablets too often as I was told they can become addictive.'

'And you think whisky isn't?' said Sneddon with another grin. 'I'm afraid there's a lot of us taking "the water of life" as a remedy for nerves and pain at the moment. Go carefully, though. I don't want to be treating you for alcohol dependency. And anyway, I may not be sober enough to do it. Having said all that, my glass seems to be empty.'

I poured us both two more fingers of malt and put my uniform back on, and we settled into a walk down the memory lane of our carefree student days. As we enjoyed our recollections of stunts and parties, I found us pausing occasionally as we realised that one or other of our friends who had participated in the fun with us then was now no longer alive. Eventually, Sneddon left after calling it a night when the clock struck twelve. So much for my plan to avoid a hangover, I thought, when he'd finally gone.

Sunday,
14th May 1916

CHAPTER 19

The Prof did not appear for breakfast. Villiers, delivering an envelope in person, interrupted my early morning meal. The adjutant raised his eyebrows as he handed it over.

'Sealed orders from the Old Man. Must have written them himself. Not a usual state of affairs, old boy,' said my erstwhile postman, before heading for the buffet of traditional English Sunday breakfast fare on the dresser.

Inside the envelope I found a note ordering me to appear at a specific meeting room at GHQ at 4pm that afternoon in my best uniform, and to bring my maps and aerial photographs with me, along with all my courtroom skills, to address some senior officers about my findings.

I went out and ordered McIlhenny and Hodgson to stand down as we weren't going anywhere that day until late afternoon. I then retired to my room to rehearse my case once more. I was interrupted by an orderly sent up by Villiers with an envelope marked "Urgent". Inside was a note on *Daily Mail* headed notepaper saying "I hope this is what you wanted? You were lucky I was in London on leave," and signed Beach Thomas. The note was attached to the photograph I had indeed hoped for when I'd had Villiers send the journalist a telegram two days before.

I arrived at the *École Militaire* that housed much of GHQ ten minutes before the allotted time. I was dressed in my finery of Glengarry, black-buttoned tunic and Douglas tartan trews, and had my Japanese walking stick in one hand, and my briefcase in the other. McIlhenny had even polished my black leather eyepatch in a fit of zeal, leaving me to hope that it wouldn't run like bad mascara.

As I entered the former military school building, a delegation of senior French officers was leaving. I thought I recognised one of the generals, a thin man with drooping shoulders, as Brigadier General Weygand. He was discussing something loudly with a short colonel, distinguished by a droopy moustache and a large mole on his right cheek.

'At last they seem to agree with us that action is needed and they're finally on the move. My God, it's taken them long enough,' said Weygand in French as he passed me.

'Yes, thankfully we won't need Plan B now,' replied his companion. Out of curiosity, I wondered what Plan B was.

An orderly showed me where to go for my meeting, and I was surprised to be met by Villiers outside the door.

'I'm the bloody usher, old boy,' said Villiers. 'You've got a brass hat in there, not to mention a civilian gent, and a Jock colonel. I don't know quite what you've been up to, but anyway, it's been nice working with you, old chum.'

Just as I went to knock on the door, Villiers spoke again. 'Oh, I almost forgot. Those two chaps you asked me to look into? Nothing exceptional I'd say, other than they've both been "Mentioned in Despatches". One's done rather well for the son of a town pharmacist, and the other one much as one would expect for a scion of nobility. The details are here,' he said passing over a folded sheet of paper. I quickly glanced at the note, then knocked on the door and the Prof's voice bid me enter.

In the middle of the room was a long table with a row of four seats on one side of it facing the door, and a solitary chair on the other. What very much looked like a panel sitting in judgement occupied the four seats. In the centre sat a distinguished-looking civilian gentleman in formal black frock coat with a white shirt and wing collar, a Guards' blue and red striped tie, and a red rose in his buttonhole. The only thing spoiling his appearance was his crooked nose, which I imagined must be from a rugby or boxing injury. The civilian introduced himself as Lord Wokingham, an adviser to the King. The Peer's voice was that of the privileged English upper class.

On the civilian's right was a red-faced general, the brass hat Villiers had promised. He did not introduce himself, but he had a staff officer's red tabs on his lapels to match his florid demeanour. I vaguely recognised him, and it suddenly came back to me that this general was the one beside the King in the royal party during the Brigadier's assassination. Why was he here instead of General Plumer, I wondered.

Although pre-warned of a Jock colonel, I was still surprised to see Lord Ross occupying one of the chairs. His presence rather put the cat amongst the pigeons given what I was about to say.

The Prof filled the last seat. I saluted and waited at attention. Lieutenant Colonel Ferguson, not the Prof any more in my mind, indicated that I should sit in the lone chair opposite the panel. I removed my Glengarry and got out my papers, maps, and photographs. The Prof introduced me to the other officers and the civilian.

'Gentlemen, this is Captain James Brown. Before volunteering he was one of the youngest and brightest advocates in Scotland – that's the equivalent of a barrister in England. He first served with the Cameronians, was wounded at Loos, and was awarded the Military Cross after the battle for his bravery in the field. He was assigned to the Intelligence Corps only a few days ago. I had a request that he be assigned to Second Army and hence, since the assassination attempt fell in their sector, he was in the right place to conduct the investigation, the results of which he will now share with us. Captain Brown, please go through the investigation you've conducted into the attempt on the King's life.'

'Yes, sir. Thank you, sir. As you are all aware, gentlemen, an assassination attempt was made on the King, which, by the grace of God, failed, but unfortunately led to the death of Brigadier General Church-Fenton,' I began, and my small audience all nodded solemnly before I continued.

'Now, as you will also know, royal visits take some time to set up given the King's busy schedule. It would appear that, despite the secrecy of such a visit, the King's programme, including the time and location of a planned press photograph, was leaked to the Germans. The most likely culprit of this was in fact Brigadier Church-Fenton himself, a German spy, who had been under suspicion for some time due to his reckless use of troops, which in turn had led to substantial losses on our part; losses we could ill afford. The reason Church-Fenton knew about the planned photograph and its location was that he'd been invited to participate in recognition of his important role in liaising with the French. It's not clear yet how, but he passed this information on to the Germans.'

More nods, but no looks of surprise at this news, which in turn surprised me.

'The Germans, upon receiving this information, placed a battalion of *Jaegers*, a regiment of hunters in other words, with all of them crack shots, into the front line opposite where the King was going to visit. The *Jaegers* probed the British line and got lucky. They found a British sentry asleep at his post one night, and a two-man sniping team slipped through with the intention of assassinating His Majesty. I'm sorry to say that the sleeping sentry, a Private McNicol, was from Lord Ross's battalion of Seaforth Highlanders.'

The others in the audience all turned to look at Ross whose gaze was fixed on the table.

'Knowing the location of the planned photograph of the royal party, the snipers hid in a nearby wood. They had a perfect opportunity as the target would have to remain still when the photograph was being taken. Once the King and his party were lined up, the sniper took his shot, but missed the King and ironically killed the treacherous Brigadier instead. Luckily, the Indian cavalry escort on duty whisked the King away before a second shot could be fired.'

'And thank God for that,' muttered the General.

'The snipers would also have been put off by Lord Ross here bravely charging into the wood. Lord Ross shot the two snipers with his revolver from horseback before they could escape. The snipers were then buried in unmarked graves in a cemetery attached to a nearby prisoner of war cage.'

'Well done, Ross,' said the General. 'You'll get a medal for this, I dare say. And I'll make sure the Chief doesn't commute this man McNicol's sentence. He'll be shot at dawn before the week is out. I mean to say, such dereliction of duty, putting the King in harm's way.'

I presumed the General was referring to the fact that the British Commander in Chief, Sir Douglas Haig, could commute any man's sentence, even the death penalty. He was known for approving only very few death sentences, about one in ten, and some of his generals thought him too soft.

'We must release these facts to the press, stressing they're from an official inquiry, so Fleet Street can see there's not been any whitewash over this dreadful incident,' said Wokingham. 'It's a very clear story of a German plot, helped unfortunately by treachery on our side and a lapse of security. I'm sorry, Lord Ross, that this will cause your regiment some embarrassment.'

'There is, however, another version of what happened,' I said, interrupting the Peer. I eyed Ross warily and wondered how he would react to the version I was about to tell.

CHAPTER 20

'What the devil do you mean, Captain Brown?' inquired Lord Wokingham stiffly.

'I actually believe that Brigadier General Church-Fenton was the intended victim of the assassination all along and not the King.'

'Why would anyone want to kill a brigadier when the King was available as a target?' asked Wokingham. 'That sounds very far-fetched, Captain Brown.'

'Perhaps, sir, but I also believe that the killing shot came from a copse on a low rise just under a mile away and not the nearby woods. You see, gentlemen, the royal party had lined their horses up behind a white mark which meant that Church-Fenton, on the far-right flank of the group, was directly exposed in profile to a rifleman in the copse and not the wood where the Germans were found. According to an experienced former police pathologist, it looks like a dumdum bullet was used specifically because it would enter the target's head, but not exit. This seemed to be to ensure that nobody else in the King's entourage was to be hurt.'

'A dumdum bullet, you say?' asked Wokingham.

'Yes, and dumdum bullets were banned for use in warfare by the Hague Convention of 1899 in a vote led by Germany, and so it is unlikely that a German sniper would use such bullets. The Brigadier was placed on the exposed end of the line and therefore put into harm's way by Lord Ross.'

'This is preposterous!' exclaimed Ross.

'Please let me continue,' I said. 'After the shot, everyone's attention was directed by Lord Ross towards the wood a few hundred yards away. But, as I've said, the wood is not aligned with the white line used to arrange the horses. The copse, though, is perfectly aligned. If Church-Fenton had been shot from the wood he would have had a facial entry wound. I have checked this out from above using an aerial survey and have the aerial photographs to prove it.'

I laid out on the table the aerial photographs which were marked up in chinagraph pencil, along with a large-scale map.

'As you all know, the ground is mostly pretty flat in Flanders. The planned press photograph's location on the low knoll allowed the photographer a nice, clean composition with good light. It also helped give a clearer target to any sniper. Having the royal party freeze for a photograph created a still target.'

I pointed out the key locations on the map.

'The wood would have been an obvious place for concealment for a sniper, but as you can see from this aerial view with the white line on the mound and the mass of hoof marks behind it, the mark is not in line with the wood. It is, however, in line with this copse of half a dozen spindly trees over here. I believe the line was painted to ensure the real sniper would get the cleanest shot of the end horseman.'

I drew their attention to one particular image.

'The copse is on a bump, which, as you can see from this aerial photograph, turns out to be the ruin of an old farmhouse or something similar that's now overgrown. It must pre-date the war. It's the only place of concealment nearby other than the wood and it's not much. However, I believe a good sniper in what's called a ghillie suit – a sort of camouflaged overall – could have hidden there.'

Next, I laid out the photograph which had arrived earlier that day in my package from Beach Thomas, the war correspondent.

'Now, as you can see from this *Daily Mail* picture which their photographer took just a second before the Brigadier fell, all the royal party are looking directly at the camera and therefore at right angles to the white line. It means that the Brigadier behind the line was exactly in profile for a shot from the copse. Behind the knoll you can see the Indian cavalry squadron lined up. I believe they were deliberately placed there so the pennants on their lances could give the sniper an indication of wind strength and direction.'

'But you've just said that's nearly a mile away according to your map!' interrupted the General.

'Yes, sir. To be more precise it's just over 1400 yards. I will return to that in a moment if I may,' I said before continuing with my proposition. 'His Lordship claims that he rode into the wood and killed a two-man *Jaeger* sniper party. But here's the funny thing. By chance, I was at this event. After his shots rang out when Lord Ross supposedly killed the snipers, I saw a huge flock of disturbed crows arise from the wood. Why didn't they react the same way a few minutes before to the noise of a sniper if he had fired from the same wood?'

By now, Ross was fiddling nervously with his pipe, filling its bowl with tobacco and tamping it down repeatedly before lighting it.

'Now, after having allegedly killed the snipers, Lord Ross brought back a German Mauser Gewehr 98 rifle with a telescopic sight attached, claiming it was the weapon used in the assassination. A rifle such as that, with a Zeiss scope, had been taken from a *Jaeger* group by a Seaforth raiding party just two nights previously. That Seaforth Highlander battalion was commanded by Lord Ross, and, at the time, it held a section of the front line nearby in the Salient. However, the bullet extracted from the Brigadier's head was clearly of larger calibre than the Mauser's 7.9 millimetre. This is the bullet that killed the Brigadier and was extracted from his skull by a trained police pathologist.'

There was an intake of breath from the audience as I produced the dumdum bullet pulled from the Brigadier's head and the appropriate photographs McIlhenny had taken with the VPK camera. I placed these on top of my other evidence.

'As you can see, the bullet has been deformed into a mushroom shape as one would expect from a dumdum expanding round. By the way, the photographs are attested by Captain Sneddon, now a surgeon in the RAMC and the former pathologist,' I warned them, in case anyone thought I was making this all up.

'The same Seaforth raiders I just mentioned had captured three prisoners, but two were later reported to have been killed while trying to escape by a sergeant named MacKenzie, coincidently, Lord Ross's gamekeeper off his estate. He had been escorting them along with a captain, who I believe was the battalion adjutant, Captain MacPherson. When I inquired, the bodies of the two escapees could not be found. However, two German soldiers brought in by Seaforths had been buried near a PoW cage as the sniping pair shot by Lord Ross. The surviving third man of the captured German trio, who had been separated from his comrades, has identified the buried *Jaegers* as his missing comrades, and the ones MacKenzie claimed to be escapees – the very same ones that Lord Ross claims to have been the assassins in the wood. Obviously, they cannot be both.'

By now, Ross wasn't the only one smoking, and the General had a lit cigarette in a fussy little holder, and Wokingham was puffing on a fat cigar. For some reason it seemed to me they were trying to create a physical smokescreen to go with the figurative one Ross had pulled over the assassination attempt.

'The same pathologist has identified the two *Jaegers* as having been executed by a 9-millimetre pistol placed directly in contact with the back of their heads. They cannot have been shot from above and at a distance by a 0.455 calibre Webley service revolver by Lord Ross from horseback. On the other hand, Sergeant MacKenzie, who supposedly killed the escaping prisoners, had a captured 9-millimetre Luger, the same calibre weapon as that which had killed the men buried as the reported snipers. Lord Ross has testified that MacKenzie had a great hatred for German snipers after they killed his brother before his very eyes, and having met the man, I do not believe he would have batted an eyelid during this illegal cold-blooded execution of prisoners.'

The Prof had unfortunately now lit his acrid polluting pipe to add to the room's fug.

'The surviving *Jaeger* prisoner also claimed there were no orders to his unit to attempt to kill the King or to penetrate behind enemy lines. I therefore believe that needing to provide a sniper party, Lord Ross ordered his sergeant to capture two suitable prisoners when out on a raid. The two *Jaeger* prisoners were then executed, and their bodies dumped in the wood along with the captured Mauser rifle to provide evidence of a sniper party to any official inquiry. In the woods, Lord Ross simply let off two shots from his revolver to pretend to kill them, but in fact they were already dead.'

Before continuing, I now produced the photographs of the *Jaegers'* skulls with the bullet holes and the surrounding tattoos from the powder burns. The images showed the ruler alongside for scale.

'My investigation has revealed that two nights before the assassination, a sentry, the aforementioned Private Charlie McNicol of Lord Ross's battalion, had allegedly fallen asleep in the line near where the killing occurred. I believe he was set up so that it would be assumed by an investigating officer that the sniper party had bypassed him to get inside British lines. The sentry, however, claimed to have felt unwell after having been given tea in an uncharacteristic act of charity by the battalion adjutant, Captain MacPherson. I have a witness that McNicol, a serial night-time poacher, was good in the dark and it's unlikely that he fell asleep. He was supposedly caught red-handed by Sergeant MacKenzie of the raiding party upon its return. It turns out there was a long history of animosity between the sergeant and the sentry, one being gamekeeper and the other poacher, on Lord Ross's Highland estate. I believe the sentry was drugged.'

'Drugged? That's quite an accusation,' said Ross, his eyes narrow, his teeth clenched.

'Yes, sir. However, I know that your adjutant is the son of a pharmacist. Maybe he learned a thing or two from his father? In addition, the medic at the nearest Aid Post saw McNicol on his way out of the line and said he was staggering and acting irrationally, but his examination was curtailed by the passing adjutant.'

'Surely the sentry could tell from the taste of the tea that there was something wrong with it?' inquired Wokingham.

'Begging your pardon, Your Lordship, but you obviously haven't tasted tea in the trenches. The water is often brought up to the front in cans previously used for carrying petrol, and it doesn't taste like a decent cup of Darjeeling, believe me, I can swear to that. You could put all sorts of things into trench tea and nobody would notice.'

'Continue, Brown,' growled the General.

'Private McNicol is now in military prison, awaiting court-martial, and will, as the General here has said, be shot if found guilty of being asleep at his post. It will be alleged that his negligence resulted in a brigadier being killed and the King's life threatened. This would indeed be unfortunate, as no sniper party had actually ever broken though our lines. It had all been a subterfuge. The involvement of McNicol seems like an act of revenge for perceived historic crimes against Lord Ross and his estate. It was an opportunity too good to miss for him and his gamekeeper to settle some old scores.'

Ross was by now looking daggers at me, but I tried to continue as calmly as possible.

'Based on the evidence I've shown you so far, I visited the Third Army Sniping School to get advice on the long-range shot and its feasibility. I was advised by its commander that currently here in France there is only one man who could have taken the shot in question. I believe that Lord Ross ordered the shooting and that it was carried out by a crack shot from his highland estate called Murdo MacLeod.'

'That's ridiculous. MacLeod is over seventy years old,' said Ross.

'That's as maybe, but your ghillie is now a sergeant in the Lovat Scouts and attached to the aforementioned sniping school as an instructor. Sergeant MacLeod has been witnessed in the past as having shot deer over a range of a mile or more, and is a recognised shooting champion in the Highlands. This time he was ordered to kill the Brigadier by Lord Ross since, according to his Laird's son here, Church-Fenton was a German spy. Under close interrogation, MacLeod has now confessed to the killing, but has claimed that he was only obeying orders. He was also under further duress as Lord Ross had coerced him into this act through threatening to evict his family from their crofts on his estate.'

The others were all staring at Ross once more.

'I think MacLeod was taken to and from the copse by Lord Ross's adjutant, Captain MacPherson. The adjutant is from Invernesshire, not off the estate, and is unknown to MacLeod. MacLeod says his driver had ginger hair and MacPherson is a redhead. Another witness said that the adjutant was missing from the battalion for a few days before the shooting, so he could easily have been MacLeod's chauffeur and had the *Jaeger* bodies planted in the wood. Finally, MacPherson carelessly left evidence of his part in all this in the form of a cigarette butt near the copse. It's not a common type as it's got a cotton wool filter. "Absorbals" or something they're called and they're promoted as the "Hygienic Cigarette", I believe. A few days ago, I was offered one by MacPherson from a Dunhill's tin. Now, while those cigarettes are obviously popular with many officers, it seems to me too coincidental that one was found near where the sniper had taken the shot.'

I placed the cigarette butt with its distinctive filter on the table.

'In summary, for reasons as yet unknown, I believe that Lord Ross here, and members of his battalion who were close to him from his estate, plus his adjutant, have somehow colluded, with parties unknown, to have Church-Fenton killed for being a spy. However, I have checked the Intelligence Corps files here at our headquarters and there are no known hints or rumours of Church-Fenton ever having been a German agent. I've also searched his room and found no hard evidence of Germanic leanings. Rather, I'd say he was a committed Francophile. I can only conclude that there must be a personal reason involved for the assassination, of which I am unaware. The whole matter of the snipers-who-never-were seems to have been a well-thought-out plan by Lord Ross that murdered Church-Fenton, and, as a bonus, removed the troublesome McNicol at the same time.'

My audience was silent for a moment. Ross sat stony-faced, if paler than before, staring fixedly at me. The General's face had turned a deeper crimson.

Lord Wokingham, who had listened intently throughout, then exclaimed, 'Well, I'll be damned! The man's got it almost right from start to finish.'

'I told you he was the best,' said the Prof, like a self-satisfied parent at a recital, smiling and winking at me.

'I'm sorry, gentlemen,' I said, becoming very confused. 'I don't understand. There's been a plot to unlawfully execute a brigadier general who wasn't any kind of spy. The officer was shot under an illegal order given by Lord Ross here, and was covered up by a trail of false evidence, but no one in this room seems uncomfortable with this except me? In fact, you all seem to already know what happened!'

Wokingham then spoke up in a low, serious voice. 'What I am about to tell you, Captain Brown, must never be repeated outside of this room and is subject to the Official Secrets Act. Furthermore, do you, Brown, give me your word as a commissioned British officer and a gentleman, that you will hold the information I am about to tell you as confidential for the rest of your life?'

What the hell is going on here? I thought. However, I was intrigued enough to say, 'Yes, sir. Of course, sir.'

'You are broadly correct in your summation of the facts,' said Wokingham. 'We only came here tonight to see if you had made any progress in finding out the real story, and I must confess, when you gave your first version, I was mightily relieved. Now you've given your second version, I'm afraid we have some explaining to do.'

You certainly have, I thought, still perplexed by the situation.

'You see, Brigadier General Church-Fenton was in the process of blackmailing a member of the Royal Family. This could not be allowed to continue. The Brigadier had been threatening an exposé which would have been embarrassing, not only for the King, but also for our whole country in the eyes of the world, and particularly the Empire. We – and by that, I mean His Majesty the King and myself – were worried that it may also have provoked anti-royal unrest in the civilian population. Blackmailing a member of the Royal Family is treason, and we have hard evidence of this crime. As a serving officer and servant of the Crown, the Brigadier had in effect breached his officer's Oath of Allegiance and the Official Secrets Act. Without wishing to sound patronising to a lawyer, you will know that the Act's associated laws preclude the possession of sketches for use detrimental to the State. For sketches, read photographs, and creating civil unrest and embarrassment to the Royal Family would certainly be "detrimental to the State". Don't you agree?'

I nodded, still wondering where this was going.

'Death is the penalty for traitors, Captain Brown, and so, while I realise there was no documented court martial with the Brigadier being present, he was effectively tried *in absentia*. The death penalty was deemed to be justified, but he could not be put before a firing squad as such an event would inevitably leak, leading to questions as to why a senior officer had been shot. A decision was therefore made at the highest level – and here I must stress, *the highest level* – to have him removed covertly. I understand from his superior officers that Church-Fenton may have, in fact, been raised in rank above his capabilities as a field commander, and so he will not be missed. Church-Fenton was unmarried and therefore had no family, which, of course, also made the decision easier.'

My God, I'm embroiled in some sort of conspiracy, I thought.

'The subterfuge you have uncovered was necessary to provide a cover story to give the newspapers showing that the Germans were somehow involved. I therefore contacted Lord Ross here. He is a loyal friend of the Royal Family, and he was conveniently in Flanders near Church-Fenton. Ross came up with the plan that you so expertly summarised for us a few moments ago.'

I looked over at Ross, who was sitting smiling at me like the boy who had just been promoted to top of the class.

'The order to execute a traitor given to Sergeant MacLeod therefore stands as an official order. He was, in effect, a one-man firing squad. As part of the plan, a war correspondent was invited to accompany the royal visit and to take a press photograph. A journalist was therefore on hand to record the first version of the story you described in what I may call the "Official Version". The papers have already published the story that German snipers tried to shoot the King, accompanied by photographs of the two dead snipers and the rifle with its special sight.'

Wokingham passed over a copy of the *Daily Mail* to me. Its leading article was by Beach Thomas, and it described the events on the grassy knoll in Flanders just over a week ago. Sure enough, there were pictures of the two dead *Jaegers*, one of Church-Fenton, and the one I'd just shown of the royal party.

'For the sake of appearances, we've agreed with Lord Ross that his battalion will take the embarrassment of the sleeping sentry; such is his loyalty to the King. General Plumer will be notified, but warned not to take action against Lord Ross or his battalion.'

'The regiment's motto is *Cuidich 'n Righ* in Gaelic; that's "Aid the King" in English. We'll do whatever is necessary to protect His Majesty and his family,' added Ross.

'Ah, so that's what this means,' I said, producing the *sgian-dubh* from my briefcase and showing the panel its inscription. 'I think one of your men left this at our HQ when he tried to get you an unofficial situation report on my investigation's progress, Lord Ross.'

Ross scowled at me, but accepted the knife when I handed it over. 'I'm sorry, Colonel,' Ross said to the Prof. 'Some of my men must have got a bit over-enthusiastic in their desire to find out what was happening. I swear I didn't know about this.'

'To return to the matter in hand,' continued Wokingham, 'once this story was fed to the press, we needed to show our politicians, Fleet Street, the great British public, and, of course, your military colleagues, that the whole matter had been investigated thoroughly, that lessons have been learned, and that such a thing will never be allowed to happen again. That's where you came in, Captain Brown.'

'So, Church-Fenton wasn't a German spy, and you've concocted this whole story?'

'The German spy accusation against Church-Fenton was invented to ensure that MacLeod would kill the traitor. Macleod's a decent man. I wasn't sure he'd do it otherwise,' interceded Ross. 'He still wouldn't do it, and so I had to apply a little bit of extra pressure, shall we say. Please continue, Lord Wokingham.'

The Peer nodded and carried on. 'It is important that you understand, Captain, that this story has additional value, too. It is excellent propaganda. You see, the government is just about to introduce conscription for married men to supplement January's Military Service Act, which introduced it for bachelors. The patriotic fervour an assassination story like this will stir will help make conscription of married men more palatable amongst voters. I have no doubt about that, and so the story is politically expedient too. We need more men in service if we're going to win this war.'

I must confess I was left somewhat stunned by Wokingham's whole explanation. I was very conscious that all the other attendees were watching me intently. I summoned up some courage to speak. 'Thank you, sir, for taking me into your confidence. I'm concerned that two prisoners were sacrificed against Geneva Convention rules as part of your plan. However, I am more concerned that an innocent British soldier stands liable to be shot at dawn in a few days' time for sleeping at his post, when, in fact, it sounds that he was drugged as part of this plan. I'd humbly suggest that this is taking the cover story too far.'

'The man's a felon and a poacher who deserves all he gets,' growled Ross.

'The man has a name, sir. Charlie McNicol. Private McNicol is a husband and father and a patriotic volunteer,' I shot back. 'With all due respect, he doesn't deserve this, sir. This is neither the time nor place to be settling some highland feud.'

'You gave your word, Captain Brown. The cover story is necessary for the war effort. You heard Lord Wokingham. It has ramifications that now go beyond the original purpose of silencing a traitor. Many innocents have died in this war, and I dare say many others will follow before we prevail, but prevail we must,' said the General, sounding like a fully paid-up disciple of Machiavelli, while his cold, dark eyes in his red face made him look like Satan himself, and not someone to cross.

'Captain Brown, I'm sure I can ask the General here to have a word with the Chief if you promise to assist us with a remaining problem connected to this incident,' said Wokingham.

I wondered what was coming next.

CHAPTER 21

Lord Wokingham looked at me steadily for a few moments and then continued, 'Since you have been so successful in unveiling the plan to remove the traitor from our midst, we'd like you to continue your investigation, but on a different tack. The Brigadier's form of blackmail was through the media of photography. He had – how shall I put it? – a rather salacious photograph of a member of the Royal Family caught in an indecent act.'

'Surely this person would not be the first royal to have an affair or a scandal?' I asked.

'You don't understand,' said Wokingham. 'Look at this photograph.'

His Lordship handed over to me a large photographic print taken from a brown envelope in front of him. It was torn across the top so that one of the two figures in the image was headless. From the neck down the headless figure appeared to be in a British officer's uniform. The second figure in the photograph was committing fellatio on the headless officer and was certainly not a member of the Royal Family. To my utter shock, the second figure was a male of Latin features and well-oiled hair, dressed in some kind of smoking jacket, kneeling in front of the headless man.

'My goodness,' I said, aghast. 'That's disgusting!'

'Quite,' said Wokingham as I continued to look transfixed at the photograph.

'And, good God,' I exclaimed, 'it's the Prince of Wales!'

'How the devil can you tell that?' asked the General.

'Well, sir, the man has no cuff rankings, which means he's either of general-rank or a Guards' officer. There are no serving royal generals as far as I know, only ceremonial ones. So, I looked at the cuff button in view. It's difficult to make out, but I think it's the royal cipher as per the Grenadier Guards. That means it's either the Prince of Wales or Prince Alexander of Battenberg. In addition, this man has tabs on his collar plus a striped brassard suggesting a staff officer. He also has a chequered shoulder patch which represents the signal flag for "N", the fourteenth letter of the alphabet. That means he's in XIVth Corps. As far as I know, the only royal who is in both the Grenadier Guards and XIVth Corps is the Prince of Wales,' I said, by way of explanation. My voice trailed away as I observed the consternation on the faces of the three visitors on the panel watching me, while the Prof beamed with paternalistic pride once more.

'Extraordinarily accurate deduction, Captain, I must say. Yes, well, the problem is we only have this photographic print and not the negative,' said Wokingham. 'The Brigadier made contact to let the Prince know he had this evidence and demanded a large sum of money in exchange for the negative which he claimed to have in his possession. The Prince might be rich, but even he couldn't easily get the funds demanded without arousing suspicion in the Royal Household. He therefore pleaded for time with Church-Fenton and contacted me. I informed the King and Lord Ross here. It was decided to remove Church-Fenton and then recover the negative from his possessions. After his death, we had Church-Fenton's billet searched by Lord Ross, but he could find no sign of the said negative.'

This at least confirmed my suspicions as to who the Scottish officer was that had searched the Brigadier's room.

Wokingham continued. 'I am told by a photographic expert, who was shown an innocent portion of the image, that this was almost certainly taken as a plate negative and not on roll film. We don't know where it was taken, or who took it, or where the negative is. We want you, Captain Brown, to answer those questions and to destroy any and all the negatives of this little royal escapade. We cannot afford a repeat performance.'

'Why don't you just ask the Prince where it was taken?' I asked. 'The negatives are most likely there.'

'We have asked. He doesn't remember. He admits to getting drunk on some of his visits to Paris, most recently to celebrate his return from inspecting our troops in Egypt. He has concluded that this was one of those occasions, and this is most likely some sort of bordello. Apparently, he has visited several such establishments, and not just in Paris. Despite what you read in the scandal sheets that he prefers older women, the Prince is rather adventurous, shall we say? I'm afraid that he's not just a ladies' man and is apparently what is called a "bisexual", as he enjoys his pleasures from both the male and female genders. He doesn't recognise this fellow or the location from the photograph, although he's pretty sure it's in Paris. Furthermore, we can hardly ask the French police to visit every brothel in their capital, of which I am sure there are many, with an edited copy of this photograph, and ask them to identify its whereabouts for us.'

'Did he go to this establishment alone?'

'No, he went with a couple of apparently like-minded friends. Buffy Waterton and Simon Caldwell.'

'Why don't you ask them discreetly where it is?'

'I'm afraid that's not possible. They were both killed a few weeks ago before this whole sordid affair came to light. A direct hit on their battalion's HQ dugout,' said the General, in a grim voice.

'What about his bodyguards?'

'The Prince dismisses his Field Security Police escorts when he's in Paris,' the General added, in the same tone.

'Right, I see,' I said, my immediate string of questions drying up.

Wokingham continued once more. 'This matter is further complicated by the fact that in our country, as you may know, homosexuality is called "The German Disease" after the "Eulenburg Affair" of about ten years ago.'

'No, sir, I'm sorry, I didn't know that. I think I must still have been at school then.'

'Well, anyway, with the historic German family connections, and the German name of Saxe-Coburg and Gotha of our Royal Family, accusations of the "German Disease" at the highest level would be very damaging for His Majesty. They would make his dynasty appear even more Germanic and apparently unpatriotic, not to mention, depraved. We are asking men to die for their King and Country – would men want to die for such a king and his family? I can assure you that the King is totally committed to Britain and its Empire, and so we cannot allow another party, one which retains the negatives, to besmirch the Royal Family and repeat this exercise in blackmail.'

'I see,' I said, although I wasn't sure that I did. I wondered why he was telling me all this.

'This is therefore a very delicate matter. So, we'd rather you tried to solve this for us than take the step of getting the French involved. We need the negatives, Church-Fenton's motive for such a dastardly and treacherous act, and whether anyone else was in on this blackmail.'

'We also need to protect the Prince,' said the General. 'As Heir to the Throne, he isn't allowed to fight, as we can't have him killed or captured. However, he frequently visits the front, and those trips are good for our troops' morale. The Prince is very popular, and he's not afraid of getting close to the fighting. His driver was killed in your battle of Loos, when the Prince was visiting the action. Luckily, the Prince wasn't in the Daimler at the time. We've actually decided to award him the Military Cross for his work near the front, and it'll be gazetted next month.'

'Will you help us, Captain Brown?' asked Wokingham.

'All right, sir, I'll try. I'll go along with your "Official Version" and try to help you in this next quest, but it's on the condition that McNicol is released. You can get a medical officer to say he was ill while on sentry duty. I'm sure you can find a doctor to examine him and sign some such chitty to get him out of the stockade. You'll just have to tell the press your story without giving them McNicol's name as a sacrificial lamb.'

'I could order you to do it,' growled the General.

'Yes, sir, and then I may not be very successful in my investigation,' I replied as a warning. 'In addition, I'd like Sergeant MacLeod's mind to be put at rest by someone other than Lord Ross, that his killing of the Brigadier was based on an official order after all. I'd also like Lord Ross to tell MacLeod that his family and their crofts are safe back in Scotland.'

'I give you my word that I shall make sure that your requests are carried out. Now, Captain Brown, I am asking you on behalf of the King to undertake this delicate task. We need that compromising material. Your Colonel here, convinced us beforehand that you would get to the bottom of this despite being new to your role, and so I've prepared the necessary paperwork for you to pursue this second phase in case you proved your worth in the first. I am happy that this is the case. So, I repeat my question,' said Wokingham, 'will you do it?'

'Since you have given me your word as a Peer of the Realm before several witnesses, then, yes, Your Lordship, I will do it,' I said, wondering at the same time exactly what I was committing to.

'Then it shall be so,' confirmed Wokingham.

It was therefore agreed that I would start the next day and that McNicol would be released and sent to another battalion, far away from Lord Ross and Sergeant Mackenzie. MacLeod would be informed that he was in the clear too, and that his family and their homes were secure. I was then relieved of my duties in support of General Plumer and Second Army, and was given another warrant of near carte blanche for my quest to protect the royal, and indeed national, reputation.

As the visitors got up to leave, I spoke out once more, as there was still one thing bothering me. 'Gentlemen, I know it's not my place to comment, but I think your assassination of Crown Prince Rupprecht is not a wise move. Rather than warn the Germans off of attempting the killing of our royals, it may provoke an escalating tit for tat sequence of assassinations. If we kill one of theirs, then this investigation I'm about to launch won't matter a jot if the Prince of Wales is subsequently shot, poisoned, or whatever by the Germans.'

'What the devil are you talking about? What plan to assassinate Prince Rupprecht? Whose idea was this?' demanded Wokingham.

Surprisingly, it was the General who looked sheepish. 'It was just an idea we've been working on. It bolsters the story. The press wouldn't expect us to sit back and do nothing after an attempt on the King's life,' he said, looking angrily at me.

'Well, you can stop working on it right now!' ordered Wokingham. 'While for public consumption, and to stir up national indignation, we will allow the story of the Germans attempting to kill our King to be in the press, the reality is that we have it on good authority, from shared family relatives, that the Kaiser has actually forbidden the Zeppelins bombing London to go anywhere near Buckingham Palace at all costs. Kings and emperors do not kill other kings and emperors, for God's sake!'

'Right, I'll see the plan is shelved,' said the General.

'Thank you, Brown, for bringing that to our attention,' said Wokingham.

'Yes, thank you, Brown,' hissed the General, and he stalked out, followed by the other visitors. I got a nod and a smile from Wokingham, and a grunt and a smirk from Ross as they passed.

CHAPTER 22

After the dignitaries had left, the Prof invited me to have a whisky with him back at the chateau. I certainly needed one. Once there, we settled in the armchairs either side of the fire in his study with a tumbler of malt, and the Prof puffed on his pipe.

'Gosh,' I said, after taking a sip, 'that was quite a surprising turn of events.'

'I'll say,' agreed the Prof. 'I made a few inquiries at GHQ yesterday about who should hear your report, expecting it to be General Plumer, when I was informed that two officials from London would be coming over post-haste by destroyer and was ordered to defer any meeting with you until late afternoon to give them time to get here. I knew it must be really important since the great-and-the-good were willing to give up their Sunday roast dinner.'

'Who was that red-faced general?' I asked. 'He never introduced himself.'

'He's General Maldon. When I found out he was coming, I asked around the staff, and nobody seemed quite sure what he does, but they all seemed to be afraid of him. He sits in the War Office on Whitehall. Apparently, he's a sort of general-without-portfolio. I gather, however, he has the ear of both the Prime Minister and the King. I've also found out that he was the one who originally asked for you to be assigned to Second Army, knowing that you'd then be designated to investigate the shooting. It appears that the plan was to have a novice investigator review the assassination attempt evidence and prepare a report reflecting their "Official Version". Unfortunately for Maldon, your records didn't reveal that you were actually one of Scotland's brightest advocates,' said the Prof, laughing at the General's mistake.

'I hope to God he never gets near a field command, or heaven help the poor Tommies under him.'

'I don't think there's much danger of that. I'm told he's an armchair warrior these days.'

'And to think that my whole investigation these last few days has been nothing but a whitewash to window dress their removal of a blackmailer for the consumption of the press!'

'One more thing, Jamie, related to what they did. It's a word of advice to you as your old professor, and not your CO,' said the Prof, a worried look now on his face. 'You must watch out for these people. The Establishment has a way of protecting its own. You drove a hard bargain in there.'

'Thanks for the concern, Prof. I just couldn't allow them to treat McNicol and MacLeod as pawns in their game just because they were of a lower rank.'

'That sounds like a strongly held conviction.'

'I've never liked bullies since I was at school. There was one in particular. Jack Fletcher was his name; he played front row for the rugby team. His parents were rich enough to send him to Hamilton Academy even though he wasn't the brightest. He picked on me as I was smarter than him and a scholarship boy. One day he beat me up quite badly. My mother was mortified and sent me to see my Uncle John, as my father was away on a business trip. My uncle's a Church of Scotland minister, so I expected to get a lecture on turning the other cheek. Not a bit of it! He took me off to see one of his parishioners, Jimmy McGowan, who ran a boxing gym. Jimmy taught me a few moves, and the next time Fletcher came after me, I laid him out. While the victory was sweet, I've never forgotten what it feels like to be a victim. I suppose that's one of the reasons I joined up after Belgium was invaded by the Germans. Victim and bully, the same as me and Fletcher.'

'Well, you've already got a bit of a reputation for defending the downtrodden, eh, Jamie? Taking on the coal barons in the West of Scotland in your own backyard a few years ago in one of your first cases was a brave action. Something to do with their adherence, or lack thereof, to the Coal Mines Act as I recall.'

'It may have been brave, but it was foolish, too. My father was fired as a mining engineer because of my role in taking the pit owners to court for safety breaches. The mine owner he worked for didn't appreciate the family connection. Luckily, my father's recognised as one of the best engineers in the country, and he got re-employed quite quickly. And then I almost lost my girlfriend, Jeanie, too, because of it.'

'How so?' asked the Prof.

'Jeanie is related to the Watsons, and they own one of the biggest coal mining companies in Lanarkshire. Her uncle owns half the county. Her family forbade her from seeing me. Luckily, when she went off to Glasgow University, they couldn't control her life, and we managed to continue our courtship.'

'Good for her.'

'Mind you, it won't stop me taking them to court if I need to. There are too many miners dying unnecessarily and too many safety laws being broken.'

'You're beginning to sound like the late Keir Hardie there, Jamie.'

'Funnily enough, he and most of the Labour Party founders, Henderson, MacDonald and so on, are from around my home town. Maybe it's something in the water? But I'm not sure I'm a socialist if that's what you mean. I do believe in the Rule of Law and fairness under it. "Justice for All" if you like. Maybe I got indoctrinated during my time as an exchange student over here in France. *Liberté, égalité, fraternité* and so on. Anyway, I suppose that's really why I became a lawyer.'

'Well said, young man,' said the Prof, and he raised his glass to me.

I smiled a bit ruefully in return. 'Jeanie says I sometimes sound like a pompous, sanctimonious old humbug! Must be the whisky talking tonight.'

'It's good to have a cause sometimes, Jamie.'

'I suppose I have a particular affinity with miners. As well as my father, both my grandfathers were miners, and they both lost brothers down the pit due to accidents. Also, my regiment recruited largely from a coal mining area. It was a strange coincidence that so many of them died at Loos, a French mining village. I remember looking across the battlefield at the local pit's draw-works. "Tower Bridge" the Tommies nicknamed it. We were fighting amongst waste heaps and miners' cottages, so that it was just like being at home surrounded by coal bings. It was a really strange sensation.'

'Well, anyway, just remember the Establishment you're dealing with here play for much higher stakes than the Scottish mine owners. I'll do all I can to protect you, but stay alert, for your own good,' said the Prof.

'Don't worry, Prof, I will. Now, is there any more of that Laphroaig?'

*

As I sat in bed that night nursing a nightcap of yet more malt whisky, I reviewed what I knew about homosexuality and decided it was very little, while bisexuality was a new predilection for me. I'd been brought up in a Presbyterian household where sex of any kind was never mentioned, never mind same-gender relationships. I remembered a few boys at school being ribbed about their unbroken voices with puerile comments about their girlishness. I was sure that I'd probably joined in with what passed for adolescent male humour, but I couldn't think of anything other than that on the subject from my teenage years.

A few students at university were definitely quite effeminate and effete in their ways, but I only knew that set peripherally, and some that

I did I know had gone on to get married. My only close encounter with a queer in Edinburgh that I could recall was being propositioned by an elderly gentleman outside the public toilets on the Meadows. I did remember wondering why he had picked on me and whether I'd given off some subliminal signal that I was one of "them". It had caused me a sleepless night, and it was Sneddon who had told me there was nothing untoward about my appearance. I also remembered thinking that this meant anyone could be a closet homosexual and I'd never know, and now that seemed to be true given the Prince and his previous reputation for preferring older women.

I'd learned about the laws relating to homosexuality during my degree course, but there hadn't been many historic prosecutions for sodomy, as I recalled. I remembered that Scotland had been the last jurisdiction in Europe to abolish the death penalty for same-sex intercourse, and that the penalty had been reduced to what was deemed a generous life imprisonment.

During my short officer training, I had been briefly lectured on the relevant passages in King's Regulations relating to homosexual behaviour, and, as usual, it was long on punishment, but short on the proof required to demonstrate the crime. My impression at the time was that this wasn't a topic that anyone cared to admit occurred in His Majesty's Forces as it was too embarrassing to contemplate that our warrior caste could indulge in such practices.

All in all, I decided that I'd either led a sheltered life, was more naïve than I cared to admit, or was oblivious to homosexuals in society, and if it was the last, then did it matter so much?

With that piece of logic, I switched off the light and turned my thoughts to Jeanie.

Monday,
15th May 1916

CHAPTER 23

The next day I awoke with a faint memory of dreams about Jeanie, and I began to wonder if my routine nightmares were behind me. After breakfast I gave McIlhenny and Hodgson a short briefing on the latest stage of our investigation, telling them that some senior officers had been blackmailed by Brigadier Church-Fenton, but that he may have had associates who were going to carry on this plot, and that it was our job to stop it. I warned them once more, quite severely, that they could not discuss anything they saw or heard with anyone else on pain of court-martial.

After my lecture, the three of us went over to Church-Fenton's former billet. I had established the day before that in addition to my own examination, Lord Ross had previously searched the Brigadier's room, and that nothing associated with blackmailing activities had been found by the Seaforth colonel. Since my last visit, the Brigadier's batman, Leeming, had packed his officer's effects into tea chests and trunks, but they had not been sent back to England yet and sat in the middle of the room.

'Right, you two, we're looking for a hidden cache of photographs and papers. It won't be obvious because I searched the room just the other day and, therefore, I don't expect it to be in these packing cases which his batman has just filled. I also know another party has already searched here too for incriminating evidence, and they didn't find anything either,' I told McIlhenny and Hodgson.

'If you found nothing the last time, guv, how are we expecting to find anything this time?'

'Because the last time I did it superficially, Hodgson, and this time it will be done professionally,' I explained.

'And who would do that, guv?' asked Hodgson, looking around to see if we'd been joined in the room by someone else.

'McIlhenny here is a professional; as in a "professional burglar". He's used to finding hidden caches. McIlhenny and I didn't first meet in the Cameronians as you know, but a few years ago at Glasgow Sheriff Court where I successfully got him off a charge of burglary in one of my first cases.'

'Aye, and Mr Broon's helped me and ma family out of a few scrapes since then,' added McIlhenny, nodding and winking at me.

'Right, McIlhenny, with that ringing endorsement of your skills, see if I and the other searchers have missed anything of interest. I'm looking for documents, photographs, photographic plates, or large sums of cash.'

'Ah'm always lookin' for large sums of cash, sur,' said McIlhenny with a smile.

I sent Hodgson out to rustle up some tea and then sat on the desk chair as McIlhenny explored the desk, armoire, and trunks for secret drawers, searched under the bed in case the chamber pot contained our targeted material, inspected the mattress for new stitching in the event that anything had been sewn into it, rolled back the carpet to see if any of the floorboards had been sprung, unpacked and investigated various uniforms for hidden pockets, and looked for any safes behind the ghastly still-life paintings on the walls. All without success.

'Did you find anything?' asked the returning Hodgson, laden with mugs of tea.

'Not a sausage,' said McIlhenny.

'Seems like the Brigadier was a professional at hiding stuff then,' observed Hodgson, soliciting a scowl from McIlhenny. Our driver passed round the mugs, which mollified McIlhenny's temperament somewhat.

After drinking his tea, McIlhenny began a second phase of searching, this time in the en suite bathroom. He climbed on top of the toilet bowl to look in the cistern above it, but there was no waterproofed package within. He inspected below the large enamel claw-foot bath to no avail, and looked for hidden latches in the medicine cabinet to see if anything was behind it, but again in vain.

'Ah'm not done yet,' exclaimed my former client, looking around the room once more, hands on hips, a frown on his face.

While McIlhenny searched, I ordered Hodgson to look through the packing cases for the desktop photograph I'd seen of the Brigadier as I thought it may come in useful in our inquiries. After a quick search of a tea chest, Hodgson found the framed image and extracted the print from the frame for me.

As Hodgson was doing so, McIlhenny approached the marble fireplace. The side pillars were tapped in case they were hollow, but McIlhenny only got bruised knuckles for his pains. He then removed the grate and stepped into the fireplace itself and had a rummage up the chimney.

'There's a loose brick up in here. Ah, got ye!' he exclaimed, and he revealed a soot-blackened brick in his hand. He laid the brick down, and then did the same with two more, and finally after ferreting around for a few moments, he pulled out a small ammunition box. McIlhenny was half-covered in soot by this time, but his grin of triumph shone through the grime as he carried his find over to the desk.

'Thanks, McIlhenny, that's great work,' I told him.

'Yer welcome, sur.'

Hodgson fetched a towel from the bathroom and wiped the box down.

'It's locked,' I said, after trying unsuccessfully to open the tin box.

'No bother,' said McIlhenny, 'Ah've got ma tools with me, as Ah thought they might come in handy today, sur.' He took a set of strange-looking implements on a wire ring out of his tunic pocket. They turned out to be lock picks and he proceeded to open the ammunition box after a couple of attempts.

Inside it, I found two large standard-issue War Office brown manila envelopes, a small moleskin notebook, a bunch of letters tied up with a red ribbon, a photograph in a brown card frame, and a couple of postcards. Much to my disappointment, there were no photographic plates in evidence.

I laid out the box's contents on the desk and sat down to go through the material. The first envelope contained nearly £200 in folded white five-pound notes. The second was, however, much more interesting, and contained four large photographs. I was careful not to show the images to my men who were sitting on the bed watching me intently. I felt like a poker player protecting his hand. The first print was a complete version of the torn image I'd been shown the night before. The Prince in this one had a smile of drunken pleasure on his face. The others were of officers that I didn't recognise. Two of them had cuff ranking insignia, one a captain, and the other a colonel, while the third had the crown and three pips of a brigadier general on his shoulder straps. All were staff officers to judge by the tabs on their collars. The four prints were all of the same sex act being committed by the same fellator, from a nearly identical camera angle. The images were backlit by a large window, with the silhouette of an aspidistra sitting on its sill. Based on the evidence, Church-Fenton seemed to have been blackmailing more than just royalty.

The notebook had been made into a sort of financial ledger with various sums against initials that meant nothing to me, but were no doubt those of the blackmail victims. A small business card fell out of the notebook upon which was typed 'Albert' followed by what I recognised by its spacing as a French telephone number.

Next, after untying the ribbon, I inspected the batch of letters. They looked to my untrained eye to be quite old, and the paper smelled musty and felt slightly brittle, defaced in places by the odd brown damp stain. The letters appeared to be largely schoolboy correspondence as they were on Pevensey College notepaper and were written in neat copperplate handwriting. All seemed to be addressed to "Big Bear" and were from "Bunny", although the homoerotic acts described in them were not from any children's book. Since the letters were found in the late Church-Fenton's possession, I could only conclude that he was the addressee and therefore was Big Bear. It appeared that Church-Fenton was of the same sexual orientation as those he was blackmailing.

One of the postcards was of the Grotta Azzura on the Isle of Capri. Its sender was a certain "Squidgy" and there was a small inkblot after the signature. The writer mentioned meeting various artists, poets and authors on the island, including Brooks, Benson, and Maugham, and that he had run into their mutual acquaintance, Bunny, in Rome. This Bunny character seemed to be a constant thread in the Brigadier's narrative, and indeed the second postcard was from him and had an Ancient Greek scene of two warriors, one with a beard and the other a clean-shaven youth. This card was postmarked Athens, July 1910. On the postcard's back, Bunny compared himself and Big Bear to Achilles and Patroclus, presumably the figures on the front. I wondered what that meant, but having read the letters, I had a pretty good idea, despite my Greek history being a bit rusty.

The question as to who Bunny was, was partially answered by the final item in the ammunition box. I opened the flap of the gold-embossed brown cardboard frame. A sepia portrait showed a young man in a lieutenant's uniform of what I thought looked like one of the old county yeomanry regiments. On the back of the frame in gold print at the bottom was a label, saying "Baker & Hughes, Photographers, Kemp Street, Brighton". When convalescing after my wounds I had visited Brighton to get some healthy sea air at my doctor's suggestion, and I knew that the town and Pevensey were both in East Sussex. If I squinted with my good eye, I could almost convince myself that the cap badge of the soldier in the photograph had six dots on a shield. From my visits to the county I knew there were six martlets on a shield in the Sussex coat of arms, and, at the scale presented in the photograph, these birds would be reduced to just six dots. Scrawled in thick black ink across the photograph's right-hand bottom corner, in the same handwriting as the letters, were the words "Love from Bunny".

If Bunny were still alive, he'd obviously be able to give greater insight into Brigadier General Church-Fenton's life than most others, even if the relationship was no longer warm. The question was how to find him?

I repacked the ammunition box, placed the desktop photograph within it, and then ordered Hodgson to find the Brigadier's batman for questioning. McIlhenny went into the bathroom to dust off the soot.

Under my interrogation, it turned out that Leeming had only been with the Brigadier for a few months before his officer was killed. He had replaced the Brigadier's previous batman who had been run over in an accident in Paris, and subsequently died of his injuries.

'Did Brigadier Church-Fenton go to Paris often then?' I asked Leeming.

'Quite often,' sniffed the batman. 'He also told me he had many friends in Paris. I've been there twice with him. When there, I'd help him get ready for the day, but then never see him again until the next morning. I'm not sure what he got up to, to be honest, sir.'

'What do you suspect he got up to?'

'I'm really not sure,' said Leeming slowly. 'He was a liaison officer to the French Army; I do know that. However, I did see him once when I went out to buy some cigarettes talking to some rough-looking fellows. I remember this, because they were all dressed the same, like a sort of uniform, but clearly not military. They had flared trousers, sailor shirts, and flat caps on. Working-class types, but with nice shoes. I remember the shoes for some reason. They had pretty fierce expressions on their faces, and I thought they should have been in the trenches frightening the Germans with those looks. I was just about to call out to let the Brigadier know that help was at hand in case they were going to rob him when he surprised me by passing an envelope over to them. They became all friendly then, patted him on the back, and ran off round the corner. I asked the doorman at the hotel, who spoke good English, what sort of fellows they were that I'd seen. He called them "Apaches", and told me to stay well clear of them.'

'Apaches?' I asked, not understanding why a French gang should bear that name.

'Yes, you know, like the Red Indians.'

'Did you see him meet with anyone else? You said he claimed to have many friends in Paris. Any lady friends? Any male chums? Did he mention anybody by name?'

'I'm not sure the Brigadier was much of a ladies' man, sir. From talking to the other batmen here, many of their officers, particularly if, like the Brigadier, they're not married, seem to enjoy Paris for its female delights. However, I never saw the Brigadier go out with any ladies or even talk about them. I'm not sure how to put this, sir, but I don't think he was that interested, if you know what I mean?'

'Right, thank you, Leeming. That will be all.'

'Begging your pardon, sir. Are you removing that box from the Brigadier's effects?' said Leeming in an accusing tone, nodding at the ammunition box on the desk. 'I don't remember packing that.'

'Don't worry, Leeming, my warrant allows me to do this. I'm not sure the Brigadier's family would want what's in here.'

'I'm not sure the Brigadier has a family to speak of, sir. As I said, he wasn't married. I've been told to send his stuff to his next of kin, but I'm still waiting for the Pay Corps to tell me who that is and the address. I know the Brigadier had an aunt in Eastbourne. He used to send her bottles of brandy. I'm not sure if she's who I should send all this stuff to?'

'I'm afraid I can't help you there, Leeming.'

'Right, sir. Thanks anyway.'

'Thank you, Private Leeming. Dismissed.'

I confess I emphasised his rank after getting irritated by the man accusing me of stealing something valuable from the Brigadier.

However, I could hardly show Leeming the box's contents to assuage the fellow.

After Leeming had left, we took our booty back to the Lanchester. It had started to rain once more and I was relieved that the evidence I had gathered was safe and dry in the ammunition box.

'Where to now, guv?'

'Back to the chateau for lunch.'

'Back to the chateau for a piece of gateau. It's not only Burns that's a great poet,' claimed McIlhenny, looking pleased with himself and still buoyed by his successful search.

'I think Rabbie can sleep sound in his grave knowing that his place as Scotland's national bard is safe,' I said with a laugh. 'Mind you, William McGonagall's position as our worst poet may be under threat.'

'Which McGonagall, guv?' asked Hodgson.

'He used to play left-half for Celtic. I didn't know he was a poet too, sur?' said McIlhenny, deadpan. Now I wasn't sure if McIlhenny was pulling my leg, instead of me, his.

'Never mind. Drive on, Hodgson.'

CHAPTER 24

While waiting outside the Prof's office at the chateau later, I gave Villiers the scanty information I had on Bunny, the Pevensey College former pupil, to see if he could find him with the Sussex Yeomanry, as well as where they were based, so that I could pay them a visit. Eventually the door to the Prof's room opened and a tall civilian in a dark overcoat and bowler hat emerged with my CO.

'Ah, Jamie,' exclaimed the Prof, 'let me introduce you. This is Inspector Wetherby of Scotland Yard. He's in Special Branch and has been helping us with the Blighty-end of an investigation. He's just leaving for London.'

I shook hands with the Inspector and found my fingers being crushed in a vice-like grip as the policeman stared into my eyes, as if trying to see into my soul. It was a bit disconcerting.

'Come in, Jamie,' said the Prof, stepping aside so I could enter his office before he closed the door. 'Good man, Inspector Wetherby. A useful contact for you to have, I'm sure. Now, before lunch, why don't you bring me up to date with your latest investigations?'

I detailed the information I'd gleaned from my inspection of the Brigadier's room and the ammunition box, and afterwards, the Prof locked the box in his office safe.

*

After lunch, I made an assault on the telephone system. This proved a tedious task due to the complexity of the French civilian and British military telephone networks and their inefficient interface. I was eventually put through by an operator to "Albert" on the number from the business card I'd recovered from the Brigadier's notebook. The French operator had by then told me it was a Paris number. Albert turned out not to be particularly helpful, and kept asking for a *mot de passe* several times before hanging up. Afterwards, I pondered why one would need a password to have a telephone conversation. Next, I went to see if Villiers had had any better luck with his inquiries.

'Sorry, old boy, the Sussex Yeomanry aren't in this neck of the woods. The 1/1st are apparently in Egypt recovering from their exploits at Gallipoli, and the 2/1st are still back in Blighty in Canterbury, never having crossed the Channel,' Villiers told me.

I could tell that despite this bad news, there was more information to come, as Villiers was looking particularly pleased with himself.

'However, I called a couple of old chums who'd been at Pevensey College to see if either of them remembered anyone nicknamed "Bunny", and they coincidently both recalled a Bunny Fairbrother. Don't worry, I gave them some cock-and-bull story as a cover, but I did call the school and told them on behalf of the War Office that their former pupil, Church-Fenton, had died and that I also wanted to contact some of his old schoolmates, including a chap called Fairbrother. The school confirmed that Arthur Church-Fenton and Reginald Fairbrother had been there at the same time, but in different school years.'

'Great work, Villiers. Very well done. Thank you. Pity this Fairbrother's most likely in Egypt or Kent.'

'Ah, but there's more yet,' said the smiling Villiers. 'The school was very happy to tell me that Fairbrother had moved from the yeomanry to the infantry after volunteering at the start of the war, and that he'd been awarded the Victoria Cross at Aubers Ridge last year. He's now with the Royal Sussex. I found out his battalion's location from GHQ. I then called them, adjutant to adjutant, posing as an old friend of

Fairbrother's, and, as it turns out, he is still with them as a major and company commander. They're down near Amiens somewhere in reserve at the moment, billeted in the village of Vignacourt.'

Villiers handed over the details, and I reinforced my appreciation of his efforts once more. The Prof had been correct and Villiers had a network second to none. He was so flattered by my praise that he let me borrow his copy of the latest *Illustrated London News*. The magazine was only two days old, and I enjoyed a cup of tea in the chateau's library while I looked at its sketches and photographs.

*

That evening, Hodgson gave me a lift into Montreuil to the officers' club. When he dropped me off, I told Hodgson to ensure the Lanchester had a full tank of petrol as we had a long drive ahead of us the next day down to Amiens, and that I wouldn't be late, and I'd find my own way back to the chateau. In the club I was glad to enjoy a little gaiety, a cheap meal, a few drinks, and some light music, and these combined to help me forget about my investigation for a while.

I bumped into Villiers at the bar after dinner, and, over several cognacs, we got to know each other a bit better. Villiers revealed his desire to be posted to an active unit and seemed genuinely keen to see some fighting, while I tried to impress on him that it wasn't as glamorous as he thought. I talked about Jeanie and my hopes to marry her someday, but after a few drinks I revealed to my new friend how worried I was that my wounds would put her off. Villiers, equally drunk now, countered that with the wounds and my medal, I would be a hero any girl would fall for, patting me solicitously on the back of the hand as he said it.

We finally left the club just before the ten o'clock curfew inside Montreuil would take effect, and decided to walk back to the chateau as the rain had stopped and the sky had cleared. The pair of us strolled a little unsteadily through Montreuil towards the gate in the walled fortifications that led to our headquarters. We were stopped there by a pair of Military Police sentries who checked our papers. No one was allowed to enter or leave the city between eight at night and five in the morning unless they had a special pass. I could see the Red Caps were itching to put a couple of captains on a charge, but since our unit was based outside of Montreuil, yet was still part of GHQ, the Prof had ensured that we had passes to enter or leave the town whenever we liked. I also knew that we were just the right side of drunk to make the policemen wary. They seemed disappointed that they had to let us through. We were allowed on our way with a warning to "Go carefully, gentlemen".

Out of the town, the country road to the chateau was lined with tall poplar trees which cast dark shadows when the bright moonlight shone through scudding clouds overhead. As we walked, we were passed by very little traffic, although one car didn't pass us, but seemed to hang back a few hundred yards behind us. At first, I thought this was a bit odd, but Villiers presumed the driver was probably a bit drunk like us, and just driving very slowly to be safe.

After half a mile or so, Villiers called for a halt, saying, 'I'm sorry, old boy, I'll have to go take a leak,' and he leapt across the roadside drainage ditch and went behind a poplar.

As Villiers disappeared, the car behind us suddenly accelerated and I had to step back smartish into the ditch to avoid being hit. It had rained earlier in the day and I landed on my backside in a foot of muddy water from the run-off of adjacent fields.

'*Scheisse!*' I remember shouting.

The car stopped a few yards along the road and two men emerged. As I struggled to get out of the ditch, I was offered a helping hand from above which yanked me out. I steadied myself, and as I prepared to thank my helper, I felt a sudden pain behind my right ear and everything blacked out.

Tuesday,
16th May 1916

CHAPTER 25

When I came to, I had a severe headache and a raging thirst. At first, I thought I must have one hell of a hangover. I was also worried that I'd soiled myself in my drunken state as there was a pervading smell of urine and excrement. I forced myself to open my eyes. To my surprise I found myself lying against a tiled wall in what looked like an animal stall. I then realised that my hands were tied together in front of me with a rope that was fastened to an iron tethering ring on the wall behind my head. My feet were also bound and I found I couldn't stand up. Daylight filtered through some high windows, and I could see there was a set of doors at one end of my prison, and what looked like a hayloft at the other. I eventually worked out in my slow brain that I was in a stable block. My walking stick and Glengarry were nowhere to be seen. The stall had not been mucked out recently, which explained the smell, and I was sitting on a bed of dirty, damp, fetid straw. I remembered leaving the officers' club and walking back with Villiers, but then it all got a bit vague. Villiers was nowhere in sight.

'Villiers,' I shouted, 'are you in here, too?' My voice echoed off the bare walls. There was no reply.

I next shouted for help in both English and French until I was hoarse, but nobody came. A few horses' backsides were visible in the stalls opposite, and I could hear some neighing, whinnying, and snorting, as well as the occasional rattle of harness and the stamping of iron-shod hooves. It seemed that although devoid of humans, I had some equine company.

I lay there thirsty, hungry, angry and frustrated. With my uniform already wet from horse piss and smelling of droppings, it didn't seem to add to my discomfort when I had to relieve myself. Eventually the light from the windows faded to dusk, and then darkness, and I began to think that I was being left to die of dehydration and starvation by my captors. I wondered who had imprisoned me in the stable and why. I had to fight to control a rising panic that I'd not felt since lying in the mud on Loos battlefield. I sincerely hoped my life wasn't going to end in this squalid place. I looked frequently at the luminous dial of my wristwatch. The watch revealed that it was nearly eight o'clock when I heard the noise of a vehicle stopping outside, followed by a door creaking open, before the stable was lit by a number of arc lamps.

The approaching footsteps eventually arrived at my stall and I immediately recognised the two men who stood before me as the unknown captain and colonel in the photographs from Church-Fenton's ammunition box. Both had the red tabs of staff officers on their collars, both were armed with revolvers, both were carrying riding whips, and both smiled rather cruel smiles.

'Well, well, seems our prisoner is awake and ready for questioning,' said the Colonel.

'What the hell do you think you're doing, kidnapping a fellow officer? Release me immediately,' I demanded with as much dignity as I could muster while sitting in a pile of shit.

'Oh, you'll be released all right, my dear fellow. Released to wander the Elysium Fields at your leisure and for eternity. Before that, however, you're going to tell us what you've done with the box you took from Brigadier Church-Fenton's rooms yesterday.'

'What are you talking about? Who's Brigadier Church-Fenton? I've never heard of him,' I said with as much conviction as I could muster.

'Come, come, Captain Brown. No need to play the innocent. My batman knows from the late Brigadier's batman, Private Leeming, that you took away a box from Church-Fenton's room. We had searched that room after he died and hadn't found anything. However, you, on the other hand, seem to have been more successful in discovering the Holy Grail. The box contains something we want, you see. Some unfortunate photographs taken at a moment of weakness. Now you need to tell us where the box is so we can retrieve its contents.'

'How do you know who I am?'

'You'd introduced yourself to Leeming and he told my batman your name and described you. There aren't that many Scottish Intelligence Corps officers sporting an eyepatch around these parts, and so it wasn't hard to track you down. We just waited outside your chateau gates until you came out and followed you to the officers' club last night. Then you even made it simple for us by getting a bit sloshed and deciding to walk back to your billet. We trailed you in our staff car. Despite the curfew, the MPs at the gate were reluctant to stop a couple of staff officers in a car couriering urgent despatches to Étaples. Thankfully, they didn't find it curious that we didn't have an ASC driver. On the open road you were easy meat. We've confirmed who you are from your identity papers in your tunic, anyway.'

'Where is Villiers? Is he all right?'

'Your companion, you mean? Is that his name? I'm afraid he tried to come to your aid, but we left him lying in the ditch. It's not good to try and get into a fight when your flies are undone and your willy is hanging out. Makes one a bit self-conscious, I expect. Then again, it was two against one. He won't remember us, though, as we had masks on. Very Dick Turpin we were. Now, tell us where the box is.'

'You'd best let me go,' I tried to argue. 'We know what you and your friend here get up to. You know that behaviour is illegal and that you'll be cashiered and jailed for your sodomy and whatever else you get up to.'

'Ah, so you have looked at the photographs. Not to your taste then?'

'You could let me go and make a run for it without a murder on your charge sheet to add to your other crimes.'

'Replace murder with desertion, you suggest?' laughed the Colonel. 'But it won't be murder, you see. After you've told us where the box is, you'll become the victim of a hit and run accident on the road to your headquarters from Montreuil. You will have been seen drinking last night in the club, and then you got into a drunken scrap on your way home and separated from your chum. Your friend – Villiers, was it? – may deny it, but the evidence will be there. While you may have been missing today, there doesn't appear to have been a search raised for you yet, but I'm sure there will be by tomorrow.

'The search party will find you in a roadside ditch with injuries commensurate with being hit by a fast-moving vehicle, and your uniform will smell of alcohol and shit from the ditch. It will look like your assailants released you, and, still drunk, you were subsequently hit by a car or a lorry. It will be an open and shut case, old boy. I'm sure your family will be told that you died bravely somewhere in France. We'll just go and pick up the box, any evidence of our misdemeanours will disappear, and we'll go back to our jobs of winning the war. Now, again, tell us where the box is.'

'I don't have the box you want. It's been sent up the chain of command.'

'You're lying. If that had been the case, I'd know about it,' said the Colonel. 'Hit him, Cronje.'

The Captain, who had been silent until now said, in a clipped South African accent, 'My pleasure. I'm always up for a bit of sadomasochism.' He advanced and struck me across the face with his whip.

Despite the stinging pain and my bound feet, I managed to kick my attacker's legs from under him and he joined me in the stall's filth. 'You utter bastard,' screamed the Captain as he stood up. 'Look at my uniform. You'll pay for this, you bloody one-eyed cripple.'

He came at me once more, his whip raised, and I steeled myself for the blow. However, the Captain landed beside me once again, this time in response to a gunshot that echoed round the stable.

'That's ma officer yer attackin',' came McIlhenny's voice from the overhead hayloft.

The Colonel, meanwhile, had reacted quickly to McIlhenny's shot and dived behind the wall of the adjacent stall with his revolver drawn. He fired a volley in the direction of McIlhenny's voice and ran into the next stall. I saw him as he crossed over to the other side of the stable to get under McIlhenny and out of the field of fire, reloading as he went.

Unfortunately for him, he backed into a stall with a large Ardennais draught horse tethered in it. The horse kicked out viciously, and the Colonel ended up in the middle of the stable in a heap after the resounding smack of his skull hitting the granite-cobbled floor. A large pool of blood quickly gathered around the Colonel's head.

The personnel door of the stable opened and in rushed Villiers pistol in hand. He approached the Colonel, shouting, 'Don't move,' before retrieving the fallen man's revolver. Only then did he take the Colonel's pulse. 'This one's had it,' he said, before coming over to see if I was all right.

'How are you, old boy? Bit of a messy billet you have here, I must say,' he quipped.

McIlhenny arrived from his perch in the hayloft. He helped Villiers remove the limp South African off me. The shot man was also dead.

'Ah'm awful sorry about that, sur. Back in the Cameronians we were always told to shoot to kill,' said McIlhenny, his face a picture of seriousness, the realisation that he had just shot and killed an officer obviously sinking in.

'Thank God you two arrived. You were in the nick of time. How did you know where to find me?' I asked my rescuers, truly relieved to see them after a day of isolation followed by a rough interrogation.

'Detective work, old boy,' said Villiers. 'Sherlock Holmes would be proud of us. After these two knocked you out last night, I tried to stop them, but they dealt with me too, I'm sorry to say. Before they rolled me into the ditch, I saw their car in the moonlight and managed to read the two letters of the number plate, "E" and "V", but I didn't catch the four digits. When I came round and made it back to the chateau, I roused your men and told Colonel Ferguson. We drove around for a bit, but couldn't see anything suspicious. Back at base, I described the car they'd taken you in to your driver, Hodgson. He seems to know everything there is to know about motor vehicles. He identified the car type as probably a Crossley something or other.'

'Yes, that sounds like Hodgson,' I said, smiling, despite my sorry state.

'Well, I asked him to go to the ASC headquarters and find out which officer had been assigned a staff car of that type with an "EV" number plate. Unfortunately, there were two of them. I tracked them both down through my contacts and went to look at the officers, even though my assailants wore masks. One was a short, fat brigadier who didn't fit my memory of either of our assailants. The next turned out to be your Colonel over there, and he did fit my memory of height and build.

'McIlhenny, Hodgson and I sat watching him and then followed him and the Captain to this place. When they didn't bring you out, we thought we'd better come in and get you, old boy. McIlhenny broke in via the back door. He seems rather good at breaking and entering, I must say.'

'Great job, Villiers. Very well done! And well done too, McIlhenny. Many thanks. It seems like you've saved my life once again.'

'Och, it was nothin', sur,' said McIlhenny with a sheepish grin. 'Ah hope ye didn't mind me borrowin' yer revolver, sur. Ye'd left it in yer room. But will Ah be on a charge now, sur? Shootin' an officer and all that.' McIlhenny's grin had become a look of concern as he contemplated the penalty for killing a superior and he had gone very pale.

'I'll sort it out, McIlhenny, don't worry,' I said, trying to placate him. I'd have to think of a way of hushing this whole thing up.

Using the cut-throat razor he always carried, McIlhenny quickly sliced through the ropes binding me to the wall and helped me to my feet. I immediately felt uncomfortable and embarrassed by the sodden state of my soiled trousers as they clung to my backside, and my condition was reflected in the looks of mild disgust on my companions' faces.

'What are we going to do with these two?' asked Villiers, pointing to my two fallen inquisitors.

'I've been instructed to keep this investigation as low profile as possible, so having two dead staff officers associated with it won't help that. We'll leave these two just as they are. I suggest you, Villiers, go to the Military Police tomorrow and tell them you were walking nearby and heard gunshots and came to investigate and found this scene. The Captain was killed by a revolver shot, so you can suggest to the Red Caps that the Colonel shot him. If anybody examines the Captain, they'll find a Webley's bullet in him and assume it was from the Colonel's pistol, which in turn will have empty chambers from his shots at McIlhenny. They'll see the horseshoe imprint on the Colonel's face, too, and that'll explain his fate. Hopefully, that will satisfy the police.'

Villiers agreed to this plan after I assured him that Colonel Ferguson would approve – at least I hoped he would when I told him. McIlhenny went to fetch Hodgson and the Lanchester. The staff car was apparently parked some way away so that its arrival would not have alerted my kidnappers. When we emerged from the stable into the light spilling from the stable's open door, Hodgson rolled up in the Lanchester and I was pleased that he seemed delighted to see me.

'Mister Brown, so good to see you, guv. I mean, sir,' he said, remembering our adjutant was present. 'See,' he said to McIlhenny while pointing at the other car outside the stable, 'I told you it was a Crossley 15.'

'Yes, good work, Hodgson. Now please get us back to the chateau as quickly as possible. I need a hot bath and a change of clothes.'

Hodgson's attention switched to my uniform upon this order. I looked down and saw a filthy tunic and wet trousers with horse manure attached to my boots. It felt like there was straw embedded in my hair, and I tasted blood running down my face from the whip mark.

'Begging your pardon, sir, but you're not going to sit in my staff car dressed like that, are you?'

'What do ye suggest he does, Bob? Runs alongside us?' asked McIlhenny testily.

'Wait a jiffy, I know what we can do,' said Hodgson.

He disappeared inside. When he came out, he was white-faced and told us, 'There's two dead officers in there, guv. I mean, sir.'

'Forget you ever saw them, Hodgson,' I ordered.

'Yes, guv,' said Hodgson, eyebrows raised, a bewildered look on his face.

Hodgson had returned with two horse blankets. He used one to protect the Lanchester's leather upholstery and the other to wrap my lower half in so that I wouldn't transfer my filth on to Villiers who had to sit beside me in the back seat. With Hodgson's honour satisfied, we drove back to the chateau where he dropped us off before going to see if he could find anything to remove the smell of horses from his precious vehicle.

*

I went up to my room and was relieved to see my walking stick and Glengarry lying on my bed, obviously retrieved by Villiers after the roadside attack. McIlhenny prepared a hot bath for me.

'Ye'd better get into that quick as ye like, sur. With yer arse sittin' in all that wet shite for hours, ye'll be gettin' piles if yer not careful,' advised McIlhenny.

He then took my uniform down to the chateau's laundry to see if he could recover its sartorial condition for me. I thought McIlhenny's admonishment about piles was just an old wives' tale, but after my bath, I found myself checking my arse just in case, unsure how long it took for haemorrhoids to grow. After reviewing my backside, I looked at my face in the small dresser mirror. The weal where Cronje's whip had struck me ran down my left cheek. Luckily, the whip had caught the leather of my eyepatch and as a result the scar was not as long as it might have been and it had only bled a little. Along with the scratch from Immelmann's attack, I was certainly taking more of a battering in this job behind the lines than I'd expected. I dressed in my spare uniform and went down to see the Prof in his study.

The Prof welcomed me and told me to come in for a nightcap, adding, 'And you too, Villiers, you, too.' From his reaction, I gathered that Villiers had never been invited into his CO's office for a drink before, and he positively lit up the room with a beam of delight.

The Prof poured three generous glasses of Laphroaig and passed them round. He almost had apoplexy when Villiers asked for soda in his. The Prof proceeded to lecture our adjutant on the differences between blended and malt whiskies, when water was allowed to be added to whisky and when it was prohibited or had to be in a separate glass, the sacrilegious nature of soda water, and finished up with the anathema of ice. Poor Villiers looked suitably chastened under this lengthy admonishment.

'Right,' said the Prof, 'tell me what happened. You look like you've got a duelling scar on your face there, Jamie? Did you meet some Hun from Heidelberg? Rather than send out search parties for an AWOL Captain Brown, Villiers here convinced me that you had been kidnapped and that he could track you down. In this he was obviously successful. So, what's the story?'

'I think Villiers better tell it, as he was the sleuth in this case, sir.'

Villiers proceeded to tell the tale with great relish, fairly recognising the roles played by Hodgson and McIlhenny in his investigation, but he faltered at the end when it came to the two bodies left in the stable.

'I think, sir, that discretion is the better part of valour here,' I said, intervening. 'We don't want too many people wondering why these two officers wanted to kidnap and interrogate me. Don't you agree?'

'Why did they kidnap you?' asked Villiers.

'I think they must have been connected to Church-Fenton in some way,' I explained. 'They appeared in some photographs he had.'

'We can't tell you the details at the moment, Villiers, sorry. Suffice to say it must have to do with the blackmail case Jamie's working on,' said the Prof. 'Do we know who they were?'

'I don't know the Colonel's name, but the Captain was called Cronje, and he spoke with a South African accent, if I'm not mistaken,' I told them. 'Also, he had some sort of antelope in his cap badge. Leaving the two of them as they are makes it look like they had a falling out and that the Colonel shot the Captain. An investigation will find the Colonel's blood on the horse's shoe along with the mark on his face, indicating that he had an unfortunate accident, which, indeed, is exactly what happened to him. That way we keep McIlhenny in the clear, and I really want to do that as these men obviously had murder on their minds. We don't need the diversion of a court martial where the whole story of why I was there will come out, and McIlhenny acted in good faith, after all, and probably saved my life.'

'Hmm, good points, Jamie, good points,' agreed the Prof.

'We have a story that Villiers will tell the Red Caps tomorrow to get them to go to the crime scene. If you could keep an eye on this for us through your contacts at GHQ and in the Military Police, Prof, and help make sure the right conclusion is reached, that would be most helpful.'

'Yes, of course. I think you've done the right thing and your story's not too outrageous. We could never turn a blind eye to this sort of thing in Civvy Street, but for now, in wartime, we must be pragmatic, particularly with the case in question,' said the Prof and I let out a sigh of relief. 'Now,' he continued, 'who's for another as a nightcap?'

I gladly indulged.

Wednesday,
17th May 1916

CHAPTER 26

'Where to now then, guv?' asked Hodgson on the Wednesday morning.

'We'll go east to St Pol and then on to Amiens.'

'Amends it will be, guv.'

Much to my surprise I felt relatively unscathed by the previous day's ordeal, although my joints were stiff with sitting in the damp, dirty straw for so long. The weal on my face was a bit painful, but the bump on my head had already receded. An MO had come out from GHQ before breakfast to give me the once over, and to put some ointment on my scar, so it didn't feel too bad, all things considered. I hoped that Villiers would satisfy the Red Caps and keep the parts of McIlhenny and myself in the affair at the stables out of their view. While I felt no regrets that the two men had died since they'd planned to kill me, I did wonder at the lengths that men like the Colonel and Captain would go to, to protect their secret, and why they'd been driven to act like that.

After several hours on the road, first to St Pol, where we stopped to eat and visit the latrines, and then on south to Amiens itself, we eventually arrived in the cathedral city and capital of Picardy. As always, the roads were clogged, this time with squadrons of cavalry, convoys of service lorries, and fleets of traction engines hauling huge howitzers at a stately two miles per hour. The much-rumoured "Big Push" that summer was obviously on, but not apparently in Flanders. Most of the traffic was heading further south. I felt that the Germans, despite their focus on the French at Verdun, couldn't help but expect something in the British sector reasonably soon from all this activity.

I reported to the local British headquarters to get a map and directions to the Royal Sussex location, but opted to visit the next day. I was given a room at the Hotel Carlton, with accommodation for the others nearby. As I was leaving the headquarters building, I heard a commotion down the corridor. Several officers, clerks and orderlies were peering into an office.

'What's going on?' I asked.

'It's Brigadier Cranbrook,' said one of the group, looking ashen. 'He appears to have hanged himself.'

'Let me through,' I demanded pushing the gawkers aside.

Sure enough, hanging from a beam in the ceiling was a brigadier, swinging slightly in the breeze from an open window. If it was a suicide, then Cranbrook had got his calculations wrong, and the drop had not been long enough or fast enough to snap his neck. As a result, it looked like he'd died slowly by strangulation, poor devil. Despite the resultant discolouration of the victim's face, I recognised the dead man as the remaining unidentified officer from the photographs I'd found in Church-Fenton's ammunition box. With the Captain, the Colonel, and now Cranbrook, from the photographs all gone, I hoped I'd solve this blackmail mystery before the Prince of Wales was under any pressure to do anything stupid. I lifted a note that lay on Cranbrook's desk and quickly read it:

My friends at GHQ tell me that someone knows our secrets and is hunting us down, one by one. I cannot imagine the embarrassment my past behaviour will have and the effect it will have on my beloved family. Despite my Uranian desires, I love my wife dearly, and hope she goes on to find another more worthy of her than I have proved to be. My love to all my children.

It was signed Frederick Cranbrook.

I found another officer reading the note over my shoulder. 'Being hunted down? Uranian desires? What's that all about?' he asked me.

'I've no idea, old boy,' I lied. 'Well, since I'm only visiting here, I'll leave you to sort it out. Now, for God's sake, someone get a knife and cut the poor man down, and somebody else get a sheet or a blanket to cover him.'

I left the gathering crowd and was about to exit the building once more when by chance I ran into Harry Stewart, an old Edinburgh friend and now, like me, a captain. Harry had gone on from university to become a manager with the North British Railway. This, he now explained to me, was why he'd been assigned to Amiens with the Inspector General of Communications. Amiens was an important railway junction and supplies coming in from Le Havre and Dieppe passed through it on their way to the southern end of the BEF's sector of the front. I told him that I was now in the Intelligence Corps and on my way to investigate some rumours of spying behind the lines. I also told my old friend the shocking news about the unfortunate Cranbrook's suicide.

'That's a shame. He was a good bloke,' said Harry.

'How are you placed for dinner tonight?' I asked.

'No can do, I'm afraid, Jamie. We're very busy at the moment, and I've got a ton of work to do, and, since I'm due to go on leave soon, I've got to get through it. Maybe next time? If you're back in Amiens, call in and see me.'

With that, we parted, and I went out to get McIlhenny and Hodgson. I gave them a pass for the night off, ordering them to drop off my valise at the Carlton and to pick me up outside the hotel at nine the next morning.

A bit shaken by the hanging brigadier and his accusation from beyond the grave that someone was hunting down people like him, I felt myself to be that hunter, and it was an uncomfortable thought. I knew that "Uranian" was another word for homosexual, and that certainly fitted with the photographic evidence of Cranbrook's orientation. I wondered exactly how he had found out that Church-Fenton's blackmailing was being investigated, and if the Captain and Colonel in the stables were all part of some network that had warned him.

I found a café and had a whisky, and, since all that was available was a rather rough 9th Hole-branded blend, I had it with a splash of soda water and made a mental apology to the Prof. After I'd finished my drink, I understood why it was known in the trenches as "barbed-wire whisky". I went for a walk around the town as my appetite had been somewhat doused by the image of the hanging man and the residual taste of the dreadful Scotch.

If I ignored the uniform khaki of half the population as I walked around, I thought that life in Amiens, fifty miles behind the front line, seemed relatively close to pre-war normal conditions. Shops, cafés, and restaurants were all doing a good trade. I decided to visit the famous thirteenth-century cathedral, reputedly the largest Gothic building in France. Like half the cathedrals in the country, this one was dedicated to Our Lady, Notre-Dame. It was certainly a magnificent building, and once inside, the war receded, and I enjoyed the cathedral's soaring interior of high Gothic arches, the little Crying Angel statue, and the stunning stained glass, especially the rose window. My Presbyterian upbringing, however, could not help but make me sceptical that the cathedral's prized reliquary really did hold the head of John the Baptist.

Later that evening, I enjoyed a good dinner at a restaurant called Godbert's. It had been recommended to me by a fellow BEF officer I'd met in the hotel foyer as an alternative to the preferred British watering hole of the Hotel du Rhin. I was told that the latter was frequented by war correspondents as well as officers, and that my green tabs of the Intelligence Corps would make me a certain target for the journalists. At Godbert's the mainly French clientele identified me as a *mutile de guerre*, and so the civilians were quite friendly towards me. One table even sent me over a large cognac in thanks for my sacrifice. An elderly French gentleman recommended

Madame Prudhomme's as the best brothel in town, and, with his ardent enthusiasm, I had to wonder if the old man was still a paying customer. However, instead of accepting the Frenchman's suggestion, I returned to my hotel.

*

As I went to sleep that night after a whisky nightcap, I tried to figure out if my abstinence from female encounters was purely due to my loyalty to Jeanie. Was my self-policed celibacy worth it given the uncertainty around my lifespan, which, given recent events, was not as certain as I had expected in the BEF's rear echelons? As I drifted off, I wondered what Jeanie would think if I transgressed just once.

Thursday,
18th May 1916

CHAPTER 27

Next day, the Lanchester arrived as planned, but with McIlhenny sporting a black eye and Hodgson a thick ear. I was already irritable. My nightmares had returned and the night before I'd had to endure hanging men pointing accusingly at me, with all of them looking like Cameronians of my old platoon, and this had made for an uncomfortable, disrupted sleep.

'All right, out with it, what happened and are you on a charge?' I snapped at them.

'Och, it was nothin' really, sur,' explained McIlhenny. 'Some smart-alec gunners in the café last night asked us what the "IC" on our armbands was for. When Bob here told them it was for Intelligence Corps, they started insultin' us and sayin' we looked too stupid to have anythin' to do with intelligence, and that the Royal Artillery is where all the intelligent soldiers are, what with their geometry and all that. So, Ah asked them if they were so fuckin' smart, how come they never cut the wire in front of us at Loos, or in any other battle for that matter? But they didn't like that, and one of them took a swing at Bob here and punched him in the lughole. Well, Ah wasn't havin' that, so Ah gubbed him, and then all hell broke loose. Luckily for us, a lot of other footsloggers were in the place, and agreed with us about the wire not gettin' cut, and they waded in beside us. In the barney that followed we escaped before the Red Caps came, but only after some bastard lance jack gave me a keeker. Mind ye, he'll not be breathin' very easy today as Ah gave him the old Glesga Kiss.'

'Kiss him? You mean you nutted him and broke his nose!' said Hodgson with a grin of satisfaction.

'All right, all right, stop it!' I shouted. 'Let's hope the Military Police are not looking for two privates with IC armbands on as we drive out of here. In future, I'll be obliged if you two could refrain from causing mayhem behind the lines. I'm sure the Germans have spies for that sort of thing and they don't need your assistance.'

I took out a map from my briefcase and unfolded it on the bonnet of the Lanchester and worked through the route to Vignacourt with Hodgson. It was a fine spring day and McIlhenny helped Hodgson put the car's folding roof down before we set off.

As we drove on through one village on our route, it was clearly home to a British infantry battalion enjoying its time out of the line. While some of the men were having a kickabout with a football on the village green, others were bathing in the duck pond, some were snoozing under trees in a small orchard, and a number were having a game of cards and a smoke. A few keen types were polishing their boots and buttons. A pair of officers were enjoying a gallop and jumps in a nearby field. A few men were obviously on fatigues, sitting beside a large pile of potatoes, peeling away, and throwing the fruits of their labours into dixies. On a makeshift washing line between the apple trees of the orchard fluttered a range of long johns and vests, more grey than white. This almost idyllic scene of a battalion at rest was, however, spoiled by one poor fellow who was stripped to the waist and tied spread-eagled to a general service wagon wheel, his face alive with flies, his eyes glazed, and his body slumped forward.

'That's cruel, that is,' observed McIlhenny as we drove slowly past.

'Field Punishment Number One,' I said. 'I wonder what he's done?'

The lawyer in me wanted to find out if it was deserved as I thought the punishment degrading, almost medieval in its cruelty, and more fitting of the Spanish Inquisition than the British Army. However, it would not do to become embroiled in a battalion's disciplinary procedures. For all I knew, the man may have been guilty of a crime which left his CO no option but to apply the appropriate punishment. Alternatively, of course, the CO might just be a sadistic bastard.

'Move on,' I ordered.

*

As expected, we found the Sussex regimental billets in the next village, Vignacourt, and, after finding the battalion's adjutant in a converted farmhouse, I asked him to locate Major Fairbrother. I explained that I needed to speak to the Major about an ongoing investigation which I felt Fairbrother could shed some light on. McIlhenny and Hodgson went off to scrounge some tea.

'I hope everything is all right,' said the adjutant. 'Major Fairbrother is well respected by his men. They know he's a brave man, his gong attests to that, but what they really appreciate him for is his care for their welfare. He's always arguing with me to be sure his company gets the best billets, plenty of rations, and are first in line for delousing or the bath house, etc. He's popular in the officers' mess, too.'

I assured the adjutant that I just wanted some advice from the Major about an old colleague. After fetching Fairbrother, and introducing his fellow Sussex officer to me, the adjutant lent me his office for the meeting and left us to the interview. We sat down facing each other on either side of the adjutant's desk. The Major was in his mid-thirties, of average build, square-jawed, quite handsome, and was greying at the temples. He was smartly turned out, and looked every inch the image of a wartime leader.

'Congratulations on your VC, Major. Well earned, I gather,' I opened, starting off on a positive.

'I don't know about that. It's up to others to put one forward for such awards, so one's actions are in the eye of the beholder, I suppose.'

'I'm told by your adjutant that your men all feel you thoroughly deserved it.'

'I'm sure you haven't come all this way to congratulate me on my medal, so what's this all about, Captain?' he asked me.

'I'm afraid it's a very delicate matter, sir. It's to do with Brigadier General Church-Fenton.'

A haunted look momentarily passed over the Major's face as his complexion paled, his eyes widened, and he sat back in his chair away from me.

'As you may be aware, the Brigadier was recently assassinated in the presence of the King. As an officer of the Intelligence Corps, I'm conducting an inquiry into how this was allowed to happen. I am here to question you under this official warrant,' I said and passed over my credentials before continuing. 'My investigations have included sorting out the Brigadier's personal effects. I've come to see you as certain matters have come to light after reviewing those items.'

Again, a haunted look.

'I believe you went to school with the late Brigadier?'

'Yes, we were at Pevensey College together.'

'Did you know him well at school?'

'He was several years above me. I was his fag. All the seniors had junior pupils as servants or fags.'

'I see. So, you were very close to him then?'

'What's that supposed to mean?' demanded the Major in a sharp tone.

'Well, let's just explore that, shall we, sir? Among his effects were a number of what can only be called love letters, some describing acts of buggery, from someone called "Bunny".'

The Major was now looking increasingly uncomfortable. I took the letters in their red ribbon out of my briefcase to show Fairbrother that the evidence was real and placed them on the desk. In addition, I placed the photograph of the Major in his old Sussex Yeomanry uniform beside them.

'Based on this photograph, which is clearly of you, Major Fairbrother, and which has the dedication "Love from Bunny", I assume that you are Bunny. Since the letters and photograph were found together and have the same signatures, there must be only one Bunny, and you are therefore the author of these rather graphic missives, are you not?'

The Major sat stock still as if turned to marble. He said nothing and just stared at the letters and photograph on the desk. I continued.

'I'm sure I do not need to remind you that sodomy is a criminal offence under both civilian and military law, and that by your own hand you have clearly convicted yourself of that crime. While I have no proof that as an officer you are still a sodomite, I'm sure that were such an accusation to be made, supported by this burden of proof from your past, that you would be charged under the King's Regulations and suffer the punishment that that entails. That would mean being cashiered with at least two years in a military prison, not to mention a destroyed reputation. The impact such punishment would have on your subsequent civilian life would, I expect, be very significant too.'

The Major still appeared to be made of stone, although there was a single teardrop rolling down his left cheek. On the face of a Victoria Cross winner, I found this quite disconcerting.

'However, if you answer some questions for me, truthfully, I can make this evidence disappear,' I found myself saying.

A glimmer of hope now crossed the Major's face and he licked his dry lips before asking, 'What do you want to know? I can't have my men here think ill of me. We've been through hell together, and I don't want them to remember me as some sort of criminal, even if I think I've really done nothing wrong.'

By now I had become quite uncomfortable myself, although I tried not to show it. The man in front of me was courageous in battle, and was deemed a good leader of men. According to the VC citation that Villiers had passed on to me, Fairbrother had saved the lives of several wounded men by bringing them back in from no-man's land at considerable risk to himself, being under enemy fire the whole time. Could I really destroy such a man's reputation? Who was the winner if I did that? Not Fairbrother, not his men and his battalion, and certainly not the BEF, which would lose a good field officer. I forced myself to refocus.

'Did your relationship with Church-Fenton carry on after school and into recent times?'

'We weren't lovers any more, if that's what you mean. More just good friends. We drifted apart soon after I sent him that photograph. He had become rather reckless in many ways over the years, whereas I'd become more conservative in my outlook, I suppose.'

'Why "Bear"? Why "Bunny"?'

'His name was Arthur. From the Celtic *artos* or bear – like King Arthur and all that. My nickname was rather less cerebral as I had rather large ears in my formative years.'

'Were you aware if he had any money problems?'

'Hah! When did Bear not have money problems? He was the original Good-Time-Charlie when we were at school. He was always gambling. At weekends, when we were allowed out, we'd go to the various Sussex racecourses. Brighton and Plumpton, or even up to Epsom. He was addicted to gambling.'

'But not you?'

'My grandfather taught me that there's a good reason why there's no such thing as a poor bookmaker,' said Fairbrother, smiling for the first time.

'What happened after you both left school?'

'After school, he went to Sandhurst, and I went into the family business in Brighton, but joined the yeomanry. Hence the picture. We'd always kept in touch, and we met a few times at the Lily Pond or the Golden Calf in London – those are meeting places for people like Bear and myself. I then enlisted in the Sussex Regiment when the war started. We've since met a couple of times over here in France.'

'When was the last time you saw him and how was he acting?'

'Actually, I saw him only last month. He was in quite a state. We had dinner together in Amiens and he got rather drunk. Bear told me he'd got into trouble with some French gangsters when he'd been based in Paris with General Wilson some years ago, making the arrangements with the French about the BEF's deployment in the event of a war. Apparently, he still owed these criminals money from gambling debts he'd accumulated from betting at French racecourses. One of them had recognised him upon his reassignment to France, and contacted him again to get him to pay up.'

'Did he tell you how he was going to address this issue?'

'Yes, he claimed that he had somehow gained access to incriminating photographs of British officers conducting homosexual acts, and planned to blackmail them for the cash he needed. He even indicated that he'd hit the jackpot with one particular photograph, although he wouldn't say who it was. I was very angry with him. Here he was, making money out of tortured souls who were the same as us in their sexuality. In my mind it was a sort of treason. Bear was actually betraying people like me. Betraying his own kind. I told him I never wanted to see him again, and we left each other in quite a state of bitterness and recrimination, I have to say. It was a sad way to end a friendship. Still, I'm sorry that he's dead.'

'Thank you, Major. That's all very helpful. Now, this card was found in the Brigadier's possession. Does this telephone number mean anything to you? I know it's a Paris number. Do you know who Albert is?'

The Major looked at the card I had passed over and smiled again. 'That's the number of the Marigny in Paris. L'Hôtel Marigny. It's a special bordello for people like Bear and myself. Albert is the manager.'

'When I called the number, I was asked for a password before anyone would talk to me. Do you know what it is?'

'The password is *hirondelle* on the telephone, and *papillon* at the door.'

'What's the address?' I asked as I wrote the passwords down on the card.

'To be honest, I'm not exactly sure. I've actually only been there twice. The Parisian taxi drivers are very permissive and understanding. I just asked for the *maison close* at the Marigny.'

'That's unfortunate. One more thing, Major, do you know who the man in this photograph is? The one committing the improper act?' I passed over one of the photographs of the young man kneeling in front of Captain Cronje, but with the officer's head torn off.

'Yes, I know him. His name is Valentin. He's one of Albert's boys at the Marigny. From the decor, I'd say this is actually in the Marigny itself.'

'This Valentin chap is in all the photographs that Church-Fenton was using to blackmail brother officers. Will there be a photograph of you too, Major?'

'No, he's not my type. I've met him, but I preferred one of Albert's other chaps.'

In my innocence, I had not envisioned there being more than one type of homosexual, but as I thought about it, I didn't see why they'd be any different to heterosexuals in attraction to a breadth of personalities, physical attributes, etc.

'Now what happens?' asked Fairbrother anxiously after I had been silent for some time as I thought about how little I knew of Bear and Bunny's world. I made a decision.

'Your secret is safe with me, Major. I don't see any reason to take this further. You're a brave and well-respected officer. I don't believe that making a spectacle of you would serve any useful purpose. However, I'd urge you to be careful about your persuasion becoming public. The Army won't be too keen on admitting anything like this in its ranks, so it's not a good time to be seen as being queer in any way, even for VC holders. Here, please take these letters, postcards, and the photograph. They were originally yours anyway. I suggest you burn them,' I said and I passed over the evidence.

The Major could hardly believe his luck and he thanked me profusely.

'One last thing, one of those postcards is from a person called "Squidgy" who claims to have met you in Rome about six years ago, and who was at school with you. I'd like to meet him, too, as another witness to Church-Fenton's activities. He might know where this Marigny is. Any idea if he's joined up?'

'Squidgy is dead,' Fairbrother declared.

'Ah, I see. Which regiment was he in?'

'He wasn't killed in battle. He was killed in a car accident in Italy the same year as I met him in Rome. I was doing a tour of the ancient sites in Italy and Greece and met him purely by chance. He must have died a few weeks after sending this card.'

I tried to figure out if Fairbrother was trying to protect someone by spinning me a tale, but I couldn't detect any evidence from his expression or demeanour, so I asked him, 'What was his real name?' I knew that I could always find out if the Major's story was true from official records via Villiers.

'Freddie Barnes. He was known as the "Squid" at school as he used to get us younger boys up against the wall and it felt like his arms were tentacles feeling all over your body. When he got to know his nickname, he then used to mark his victims with a jet of ink from his fountain pen, like a real squid. Squidgy was Bear's patronym for him, and I think they may have been lovers at one time. He was a bully and never a friend of mine. As I said, I ran into him by chance in Rome, not by preference.'

I decided that Fairbrother was probably telling the truth and decided to end the interview. 'Thank you, Major, that will be all.' As we parted, we actually shook hands as if we'd done some sort of deal, which I suppose we had.

Back in the farmyard, I found my two fellow travellers asleep in the front seats of the Lanchester and roused them.

'Where to now, guv?' asked Hodgson with a yawn.

'We're off to visit a brothel, but we need to go back to HQ to collect some things first,' I told him.

'A brothel! Now you're talking, guv,' said Hodgson with a grin, while McIlhenny turned and looked at me as incredulously as a man with a black eye can look at someone.

CHAPTER 28

On the journey back, I wondered if I'd done the right thing regarding Fairbrother and found myself conflicted. The need to uphold the law was one of the reasons I'd become a lawyer in the first place, and as an officer, I'd sworn to uphold the King's Regulations. Despite this, I'd just handed over evidence to an offender which could clearly have convicted him, and, in doing so, I had become an accomplice to a crime. Fairbrother certainly wasn't what I'd expected – but then what had I expected?

The company commander was obviously a brave soldier to be awarded the Victoria Cross, so his sexuality was no limit on his sense of duty, his devotion to his men, or his patriotism. I was finding the whole subject of what was right and wrong in this particular area of the law quite difficult to reconcile. As I weighed up these facts and emotions in my lawyer's mind, I felt very uneasy, but, as I thought about all that Fairbrother had told me, and reflected on the Major's decency and bravery, I really felt justified that a prosecution in his case would actually have been more like persecution.

As I continued to think about what to do next, I realised that I actually knew little about brothels other than there seemed to be one in every French town I'd recently visited. I was not so naïve as to think that my own troops had not visited such establishments. Indeed, I remembered a horde of men from my battalion on our last Blighty posting in Winchester rushing down to nearby Portsmouth on the train to enjoy their embarkation leave, deeming it too far to return to our native Scotland. As home to the Royal Navy for hundreds of years, Portsmouth had plenty of brothels and breweries to sate the men's desires, just as they had done for sailors over the centuries. I also remembered putting two of my platoon on a charge after they got to France when it was discovered their antics in Pompey's red-light district had resulted in a dose of venereal disease. I knew I was regarded as a bit of a prude in the battalion back then due to my devotion to Jeanie, and I had not joined my fellow officers when one or two of the other subalterns had decided to visit a house of ill repute before going into battle. I therefore decided I needed to talk to my university mentor on all things to do with girls and sex, namely Iain Sneddon.

*

When back at our HQ in the late afternoon, I commandeered an office with a telephone and asked the chateau's operator to find a way of connecting me to No.17 CCS. When I was finally put through, I informed the CCS operator at the other end that I was phoning from GHQ and asked to speak to Captain Sneddon. Eventually, my old friend came on the line.

'Hello, Iain, it's Jamie here. I need your help again, but don't worry, no autopsy required this time.'

'All right, old boy, but make it quick, we've got some casualties coming in from Jerry shelling our lads holding the Izjer Canal,' said Sneddon.

'What can you tell me about brothels?' I asked.

'Nothing, old boy. Never had to pay for it in my life. Look, I know you've been wounded and all that, old chum, but I'm sure I can help find you a young maiden who's willing if you're that desperate and can't wait for Jeanie.'

'It's not for me. It's to do with my investigation.'

'Right oh,' replied Sneddon with a snigger.

'Well, brothels are connected to sexual health, aren't they? Who should I go and see in Montreuil?'

'You haven't got a dose of the clap have you, young Brown?' exclaimed Sneddon.

'No, I do not have a dose of the clap!' I shouted in exasperation. 'I need somebody over here to tell me about brothels and sexual health as part of my investigation, I've just told you. I need to find a specific brothel.'

'Ah, so you have a special fetish then?'

'No, I don't have a bloody fetish!'

'If you say so, old boy. I believe you, but thousands wouldn't. You need to go and see one of the ADMSs at GHQ. That's an Assistant Director of Medical Services. They should be able to help you out,' said Sneddon and he gave me a name.

'Right, thanks, Iain.'

'Not at all. Always glad to help. And remember, if you do need some companionship, I'm sure I can find you a nurse or two to relieve the pain, or a little *mademoiselle* if you fancy something more exotic. Jeanie need never know. Remember what they say?'

'No, what do they say?' I asked, reluctantly.

'Absence makes the heart grow fonder, but abstinence makes you randy. Goodbye.'

"Jeanie need never know" was something I'd been telling myself quite often of late. I tried to banish temptation once more and returned to business by going to see Villiers.

I had him arrange a visit with the specific ADMS in the RAMC that Sneddon had suggested before they shut up shop for the day as it was getting rather late. I then sent for Hodgson and we drove over to the Medical Corp's HQ.

*

I was shown into the office of a bald, rotund, bespectacled brigadier, whose ruddy face had a startlingly large beetroot-coloured nose in its centre and a pure white Charlie Chaplin moustache above thick lips. Brigadier General Poulson looked far from the epitome of health that I had expected in the role of a senior medical administrator.

'How can I help you, Captain?' wheezed the ADMS in a Geordie accent, stubbing out a cigarette in an overflowing ashtray with a nicotine-stained hand as he did so. As I replied, he lit another Black Cat from a near empty tin on his desk.

'Thank you, sir. I believe you are our expert on sexual health and as part of an investigation I am conducting, I need to know more about the brothels our men use, particularly in Paris,' I told him by way of explanation for my visit.

'Brothels, eh? Well, since we are in France, and their social mores are a little less stringent than ours back in England, you have a lot to choose from. Not that we don't have any back in Blighty, of course, but it seems to be a much bigger industry over here and the madames and pimps have a huge captive market of young French and Allied troops to service, that's for sure. There are a lot of women plying the oldest trade in the world over here, and not just the "Mademoiselle from Armentières".

'The French call their brothels *maisons close*, and they're in most major cities and towns, not just Paris. They've sprung up around all our base depots and ports, too. Calais, Boulogne, Dieppe, Le Havre, Étaples – you name it, and you'll find they've all got several nearby establishments. Lots of youngsters trying to break their virginity before they die, and lots of old soaks telling themselves that what the wife back home doesn't see won't hurt her. We give these men in their early twenties nearly 4000 calories a day and make them fighting fit, so they've got to let off steam somehow. When a chap comes out of the line, often all he wants is a drink and a woman. Yes, prostitution is a very lucrative market. While not officially condoning the trade, we are mindful that if we don't, then all that pent-up frustration could result in rapes of our hosts' women, and that would never do. It's a policy of pragmatism in the field over the idealism of religious types back in Blighty.'

233

'Are there different types of brothel?' I asked, feeling that the ADMS was perhaps a bit over enthusiastic about his subject for a man in his position.

'Of course. Like everything else in life, you get what you pay for. Those offering services to officers tend to have a blue light outside, while those for other ranks show a red light, so that's an early warning signal of cost.

'There are some very high-class establishments in Paris, I'm told. You may remember some scandal from a few years ago about the present King's father who was a bit of a playboy in his youth? He frequented Parisian brothels on a regular basis, we were told. He was called Bertie then, before he became Edward VII. No? Well, I suppose it was before your time. Anyway, it shows there are some pretty posh pleasure palaces,' said the ADMS, smiling at his own alliteration before continuing.

'Then there are what the French call *maisons d'abbatage*. That literally means "slaughterhouses". This is the nickname for brothels where the girls service dozens of men a day from queues of ticket holders. It's not unknown for queues of over a hundred men to form outside these places. The men take a ticket and get ten minutes with a wretched girl and then the next client is shown in. Sometimes the poor girls service sixty customers a day! It must be exhausting, poor things.

'We're particularly concerned about such places here at GHQ, of course, as they're literally breeding grounds for venereal disease. That's my speciality. We're averaging about twenty-five cases of VD per 1000 troops at the moment here in France, and that's way too many. It's bad back in Blighty too. The Imperial troops are the worst offenders. Poor old Tommy can't afford the two or three francs a go at these brothels more than occasionally, but with five times the wages, the Canadians and Anzacs are at it like rabbits.'

I knew our brother soldiers from the Dominions were better paid, but I didn't know that this was how they spent their wages. The ADMS was by now in full flow, reeling off a list of statistics.

'Your average Tommy is five times more likely to catch VD than trench foot these days and VD is one in five of our hospital cases. At any one time we can have 10,000 troops in our special VD hospitals and that's close to one division not being available. Think about that! New drugs like Salvarsan to address syphilis help, but it's still a massive problem. An average syphilis case can be out of the line for up to fifty days, so, for GHQ, this is a manpower issue rather than a health or moral issue. That's really why VD is a punishable offence and why wages are docked to pay for the treatment. It's also why there is the continued debate as to whether we should have our own licensed brothels or not, where the girls could be medically inspected regularly to be sure they're clean.'

I wasn't sure the working girls would look forward to an inspection by a sleazy doctor like Brigadier Poulson, but I held my tongue.

'Thankfully, the French are more pragmatic about such things and are regulating and inspecting their brothels. They've been doing that since the last century. Unfortunately, we also have some soldiers who deliberately try to catch VD just before they're due to go up to the front. Gonorrhoea usually appears only five days after contact with an infected woman, so, knowing this, some men time their visit to a prostitute who's not from an inspected brothel to increase their chances of catching a disease, and then getting hospitalised rather than going over the top. We've even had men injecting their urethra with condensed milk to simulate the discharge from the penis as seen in gonorrhoea.'

I winced at the very thought of this. We seemed to be getting off the subject, so I tried to steer the ADMS back to brothels.

'Any more types of brothels, sir?'

'Well, yes, finally, there are the *maisons tolérée* which specialise in the perversions that some men seem to require for their satisfaction. You'll find all three types in Paris.'

'And do you know of any which specialise for those of a homosexual persuasion? Does the Marigny ring a bell?' I asked.

'I'm afraid we don't have any details on any such establishments. Since homosexuality is an offence under Military and Civil Law, and an abomination under God's will according to the Christian Crusaders back in Blighty, it cannot officially exist. I therefore cannot help you there as I have no records of such places,' said the ADMS, with a wink.

'Thank you for the briefing, sir,' I said.

'Not at all. Why are you so interested in brothels anyway?' he asked.

'We're worried that frequenting them may be a source for blackmailing officers and extorting information of use to the enemy,' I lied.

'I'd have thought the list of VD patients might be a better bet for blackmail since VD is evidence after the act, if you see what I mean. Men don't want their wives and sweethearts back in Blighty to know that they've caught a dose of the clap out here. Officers aren't so bad, as many of them use prophylactics, but the Bible Bashers back in Blighty won't contemplate us making condoms available to the men as they say it will only encourage promiscuousness. Maybe you should ensure that the VD records are all locked up?'

'Thank you, sir, I'll see that that is considered. Thank you again for your time.'

'Care for a snifter before you go?' asked the ADMS, taking a bottle of cognac out of his desk drawer.

'Sorry, sir, I've got to get back to my HQ,' I replied, needing to get out of the smoke-filled office for a breath of fresh air. As I took my leave, I heard behind me the glug of liquid being poured and the clink of a glass on bottle. I wondered if the overweight, hard-drinking, chain-smoking ADMS had a life expectancy any greater than the average soldier in the trenches.

I returned to the chateau not much wiser on what the Military Establishment knew about the mysterious Marigny, although well informed about types of brothels and venereal disease. It seemed odd that neither the Prince, nor Fairbrother, nor the RAMC, knew the Marigny's exact location or all pretended not to.

Friday,
19th May 1916

CHAPTER 29

The shot rang out.

King George fell off his horse and crashed to the ground.

The blood from his gaping head wound matched the red tabs on the collar of his khaki Field Marshal's uniform.

The other officers in the royal party gathered round him in a circle and looked down at the fallen monarch. George V's bearded face stared back at them with sightless eyes. I found myself as one of this elite cadre of generals and colonels surrounding the dead King.

The nursery rhyme, Humpty Dumpty, *kept running through my head, "All the King's horses and all the King's men weren't going to put the King's head back together again,".*

Around this calm ring of officers, chaos ensued. Cavalrymen were galloping hither and thither. Bugles were sounding. Sergeants were shouting. Guns were firing.

A red-faced general was pointing at me.

'You there, you'd better tell the Prince of Wales.'

'But I don't know where he is,' I said.

'He's in Paris.'

More shots rang out. The banging of the guns was very close.

I slowly awoke from this dream to find someone pounding on my bedroom door.

'Come,' I shouted, my voice hoarse from sleep.

In walked McIlhenny bearing a tray. 'Ah've brought ye a cup of char, sur,' he said. 'Ye'll have to get up, sur. We've a long drive ahead of us to get to Paris, and ye'll have to be fightin' fit if yer goin' to a brothel.'

'Thank you, McIlhenny,' I said, thinking my batman smelt rather fragrant that morning. 'Are you wearing cologne?' I asked him, trying to keep the incredulity out of my voice.

'Ach, no, sur. It's just Ah went to see the French cook here to see if Ah could get a piece of steak to put on ma black eye to help the swellin' go down. He didn't have any spare, but he gave me some lavender oil to rub in. He said it was an old French cure, so he did.'

'Right, well, I hope it works,' I said trying not to snigger at McIlhenny smelling like my maiden great aunt, and I wondered if the French cook had done this as a joke, or if it was indeed a local remedy.

Following my tea and ablutions, I felt in a better frame of mind to face the world. At breakfast, Villiers informed me that everything had gone well with the Military Police concerning the dead officers in the stable, and that our concocted story had been believed. He told me that the unknown staff officer had subsequently been identified as a Colonel Ellis, and that Captain Cronje was confirmed as the other. Cronje had only arrived at GHQ a few months ago to prepare for the transfer of the South African Brigade to the Western Front from Egypt.

After breakfast, I rounded up McIlhenny and Hodgson, and they packed the Lanchester for a trip to Paris. I had picked up a map of the city from Villiers who had also called ahead to get us accommodation. Hodgson had obtained a full tankful of petrol, as well as a couple of extra cans from the local ASC fuel dump, and McIlhenny had prepared a hamper full of bread, ham and cheese, and so we were well equipped for our journey south.

'Come on now, Flower, settle yourself in the front seat,' said Hodgson to the lavender-smelling McIlhenny.

'Ah'm warnin' ye, Bob. If ye call me "Flower" one more time, Ah'll punch yer lights out, so Ah will.'

'Right children, settle down,' I ordered. 'Head for Amiens first, Hodgson, then on to Paris.'

It was another fine spring day, and occasionally on the drive, where the roads were straight and free of military traffic, Hodgson pushed the Lanchester up to over sixty miles per hour. With the roof down, we were all positively thrilled by the sheer experience of such high speed. Despite these high velocity bursts, it took us most of the day to get to our destination, and it was getting dark by the time we arrived in the French capital.

'Ah'll tell ye what,' said McIlhenny, weary from almost eight hours on the road, 'Ah'm glad Ah don't have piles. Yer arse would be a bloody mess sittin' for that long on these French roads, even in this car, so it would. Ah hope ye're all right, sur, after yer behind was parked in that stable shite all day?'

I confirmed my posterior's health and thanked McIlhenny for his concern.

'No bother, sur.'

'And how's the eye?' I asked as innocently as I could.

'It's gettin' better, sur,' said McIlhenny. 'Ah'll soon be as handsome as ever.' For once, Hodgson, perhaps wary from McIlhenny's earlier warning, refrained from offering a rejoinder.

I guided Hodgson to the BEF liaison office near the French Army's headquarters at the Hôtel de Brienne on the Left Bank of the Seine. Upon receiving our assigned billets, I directed Hodgson to our respective accommodation. My map-reading was made easier thanks to the authorities cancelling the black-out which had been imposed after Zeppelin night raids the year before. Once more, Paris was living up to its sobriquet as the "City of Light"; its famous arc lamp streetlights cast a yellowish hue over the boulevards, side streets, and Seine bridges.

*

That night, I thought about how nice it would be to come to Paris for a honeymoon with Jeanie once the war was over. I soon realised this pleasant fantasy was framed by many "ifs" and "buts" and depended on Britain winning the war, me surviving it, and Jeanie agreeing to marry me. As my thoughts darkened, I poured myself a small dram from my hip flask. Purely medicinal to help me sleep, I told myself. Then I remembered Sneddon's warning and swore I must prevent this becoming a habit. Or had it already become one? Still, it was a shame to waste it, so I decided that since it was already poured, I'd better drink it. I let the whisky warm my throat and help me settle for the night. Again.

Saturday,
20th May 1916

CHAPTER 30

After a breakfast of fresh flaky croissants washed down with milky coffee from a bowl, I met the Lanchester outside my hotel and invited McIlhenny in to do a small sewing job for me with his nimble fingers.

Once we were back outside, I approached the hotel commissionaire. The doorman was an amputee and obviously an old soldier. In my experience, commissionaires and concierges knew everything that was going on in cities, good and bad, legal and illegal, and could provide their guests with advice on most subjects and locations. In French, I asked him for directions to L'Hôtel Marigny.

'Which one?' asked the commissionaire.

'What do you mean, which one?' I replied, confused by his question.

'Well, there's the Baron de Rothschild's town house on Avenue Marigny and then there's the other one.'

'I'm pretty sure it's not the Baron's I'm looking for,' I said, doubting if the Rothschilds needed to earn more money via running a brothel.

'Ah, then I know which one *monsieur* wants,' said the commissionaire, tapping the side of his nose and smiling. 'You want the special one on Rue de l'Arcade. Number 11, I believe.'

'Thank you.' I slipped him a franc. 'And it's not for me, by the way, it's for a friend.'

'*Oui*, of course it is, *monsieur*,' he said, nodding solemnly.

Based on the commissionaire's instructions, I directed Hodgson to Rue de l'Arcade. We stopped outside number 11, a tall Belle Époque-style town house with a sign saying "Hôtel Marigny" over the door. The windows on the ground floor were covered by heavy curtains so passers-by could not see in. The upper five floors had closed shutters. There was a small blue lamp over its door. It appeared that the Marigny was hiding in plain sight.

'Are ye sure this isn't a polis station?' asked McIlhenny. 'What's with the blue lamp, sur? Most knockin' shops Ah know have got a red lamp.'

I explained that it was just another example of the military caste system whereby brothels for officers had blue lights outside to advertise their services, and those for the troops did indeed have red lights. Apart from the blue lamp, there were no other lights showing through curtains or shutters from inside the Marigny, and I could only surmise that we were too early for its normal clientele. I'd decided not to phone ahead. I thought that now was as good a time as any to warn the other two about what sort of brothel this was.

'Actually, this isn't a normal brothel, if there is such a thing. It's a brothel where men seek the company of other men,' I told them.

Both privates eyed me dubiously. 'Ah thought ye wanted to get married, sur? Ah never knew ye were one of these queer types, beggin' yer pardon, sur,' said McIlhenny with some sadness.

'I'm not one of those. It's to do with our investigation. It turns out the Brigadier who got shot was blackmailing British officers who use this place, by taking surreptitious photographs of them in the act, so to speak. That information is secret by the way, and, as I've warned you before, if you ever disclose it, you'll find yourselves on a charge. Our job now is to find out where the negatives of those photographs are and destroy them.'

Hodgson and McIlhenny looked both relieved and curious at this explanation. 'Aye, well, there's a lot of it about,' said McIlhenny.

'Do ye not remember Livingstone and Baird in our old platoon, sur? Ah'm sure they liked that kind of stuff.'

'Really?' I tried to remember them, but there was only a faint memory of my platoon sergeant saying something. 'Maybe Sergeant Hunter did say something about them.'

'Ach, it doesn't matter as they're both dead. Sergeant Hunter, too. His head was blown right off. He was missed after he was killed, so he was. At home, too, Ah expect. His wife was expectin' their seventh bairn. A real shame.'

Hunter had been my right-hand man in our platoon. I did remember looking at the Sergeant's headless corpse lying only a few feet away from me at Loos, presumably decapitated by the shell blast that had wounded me. I forced myself to concentrate on the present.

'Right, let's have a look around Paris until this place opens. I imagine it will be open for business later this afternoon. There must be lots of officers on weekend passes.'

*

With that, I guided them on a tour of Paris, as neither McIlhenny nor Hodgson had been there before. I had learned my French in Paris when I had spent time there in my student days. Scots Law and the French *Code Civil* shared a common root in Roman Law, and I'd studied all three systems during an exchange at the Sorbonne, arranged by the Prof. I remembered my time in the city fondly, not least because of Annette, my French girlfriend for a few months in pre-Jeanie days. I had also got to know the basic layout of the city, if not the details, and so I was able to cobble together a tour that took in the most famous sights.

The city certainly gave the impression of a capital of a warring nation. There were even guns mounted on the Eiffel Tower for anti-aircraft defence. McIlhenny had to admit that Notre-Dame was more impressive than any Catholic chapel he'd been in at home, better even than St Andrew's Cathedral in Glasgow. Famous buildings like the Grand Palais had been turned into military hospitals, and there were many wounded men around, hobbling along on crutches, being wheeled in bath chairs, scrabbling along on trolleys, or being led in sorry columns of the blind with their hands on the shoulders of the man in front. The Arc de Triomphe reminded us of past French military glory, and I had to hope that our Allies would be celebrating another triumph in the near future, although with the Battle of Verdun still raging, I wasn't entirely convinced it would be anytime soon.

The pavements were awash with French soldiers in dull horizon-blue battlefield uniforms, garrison caps on their heads. Occasionally, colour was added through officers on leave in dark blue tunics with red trousers and smart kepis, or by the disparate and exotic uniforms of the *Zouaves, Tirailleurs*, and *Spahis* of the French Colonial Army of Africa. The different police uniforms of the Gendarmerie and the Republican Guard added to the mix. Even the drab khaki of British troops on liaison duties or short-term passes offered some variety.

As we drove around, we also encountered a few marching columns of French infantry in full combat gear, Lebel rifles on their shoulders, and distinctive Adrian helmets on their heads. The fiercest-looking soldiers were undoubtedly those of the Foreign Legion, reinforcing its reputation for recruiting cut-throats and renegades. The troops all seemed to be heading for either the Gare du Nord or the Gare de L'Est for embarkation to the front. I wondered how many of them going to the latter station would return from the mincer of Verdun.

On one of the boulevards we passed a column of cuirassiers. The French cavalrymen had given up their cuirass breastplates and were now dressed in horizon-blue like the rest of the field army, but they retained their sabres and carbines. Their horses looked to me to be in poor shape compared with British cavalry mounts, and I had heard the French treated their animals poorly. Nevertheless, they were an impressive enough sight, and the pavement crowds turned to applaud them as they went by.

'The French eat horses, don't they?' asked Hodgson. 'They'll go hungry if they dine on those nags, that's for sure.'

Not all those in uniform on the streets were military, and we noted several Catholic priests in black cassocks with Cappello Romano broad-brimmed hats or square Biretta caps. Their headwear was, however, outdone by the ladies devoted to the same faith, and the white starched wimples and winged cornettes of the French nuns were something to behold, and to me they looked like galleons under full sail. Hodgson was more prosaic.

'They look like a bunch of bleedin' penguins,' observed Hodgson, commenting on the sisters' black habits and white headgear.

'Don't ye go insultin' nuns, ye Protestant bugger,' said McIlhenny taking umbrage on behalf of his fellow Catholics. 'Ah was taught at school by nuns. They learned me everythin' worthwhile Ah know.'

I could see Hodgson mentally evaluating the quality of the nuns' teaching as he thought of a reply, but he only muttered, 'Well, they didn't teach you very good English, Mac,' under his breath.

'Mind, although Ah liked the nuns, ye'd always to look out for the priests. Some of them were a bit handy with the altar boys, if ye get ma drift,' continued McIlhenny.

I decided I had better intervene before this conversation descended any further.

'Calm down, you two,' I interrupted. 'There are a lot of other women around here worth looking at who are not nuns.'

Those women ranged from the dowdy, to some in their finery, often walking proudly with their beau in uniform. Many, however, were in mourning black, presumably older women grieving for lost sons, while the younger were widows grieving lost husbands or sisters missing brothers. Some of the more frivolous young women were dressed in fashionable takes on army uniforms, mostly based on hussars or colonial troops.

'There's some good-lookin' bints around here, right enough,' opined McIlhenny.

'There's a lot of floozies as well,' countered Hodgson.

We also saw many women working hard at jobs previously done by men. Hodgson was particularly upset to see women driving trams in smart grey and blue striped uniforms. 'Women driving public transport! If that catches on in London, I won't have a job to go back to after the war,' he grumbled.

'It's the same back home already, Hodgson,' I told him. 'If women didn't take these jobs and other roles, such as in munitions factories and so on, we couldn't release men to fight, and then where would we be?'

'Well, things are changing, that's for sure, guv, what with women wanting the vote and everything.'

I was then somewhat surprised by McIlhenny's staunch support for the women's suffrage movement as he countered Hodgson. 'Ah'd give them the vote. Ma mother's the one that runs our close, so she is. Our whole tenement looks up to her. She could show some of those councillors in Glesga Corporation how to run the city, Ah'm sure she could. Bunch of wasters the lot of them. Now that even men like me earnin' a bit of money can vote, why should she not? What do ye think, sur?'

'In my view there's no reason for women not to get the vote. There's plenty of women like your mother, McIlhenny, who organise whole communities, churches, and charities. Now with war work, we've seen that they can do many of the same manual jobs as men. If women can now be doctors and schoolteachers, then they're certainly smart enough to be MPs too.'

'I'm not so sure, if you don't mind me saying so, guv,' said Hodgson. 'Look at the crazy things they've been doing. That suffragette throwing herself under the King's horse just before the war.'

'Ah don't know,' said McIlhenny. 'A few more as brave as that lassie in our ranks and the Germans would be crappin' themselves.'

'Women have had the vote in New Zealand for over twenty years now and it doesn't seem to have done the Kiwis any harm,' I added, although this didn't seem to convince my driver as an argument.

'Huh, they'll be giving the sheep down there the vote next,' muttered Hodgson.

'Well, you'd better get prepared, Hodgson, as I expect women will get the vote once the war is over,' I told him. 'They'll deserve it for putting their protests on hold when the war's on, if for nothing else. Anyway, it seems stupid to me not to get the opinion of half of the population on how to run the country. It's only fair and reasonable, surely?'

'Fair and reasonable! Let me tell you about fair and reasonable, guv. If you had met my mother-in-law...'

Before Hodgson could expand on his in-law's political opinions and capabilities, I had him stop the car and park. I then marched my two companions into the Jardin du Luxembourg. A poster attached to a tree informed me that there was a Saturday concert in the park and I directed the others towards the sound of rousing music. A military band was playing a medley of tunes under a large wrought-iron bandstand in the park's centre. None of us recognised the airs, but they were presumably the French equivalent of the British music-hall standards as the audience was joining in with gusto. The performance ended with a spirited rendition of "La Marseillaise" and I reflected on how uplifting it was as a national anthem compared with "God Save the King", which, perhaps unpatriotically, I always felt was a bit of a dirge.

After a short, but exorbitant lunch in a back-street café where all three of us could eat together without the threat of comments on cross-rank fraternisation from other British officers, we returned in the Lanchester to Rue de l'Arcade and stopped outside the blue lamp. This time it was not the only light burning, and the shutters on the upper floors were open.

'You two park around the corner. I'm off to do a recce. If I'm not out in half an hour, come in and get me,' I said as I got out of the staff car and went up to the door of my very first brothel.

CHAPTER 31

I looked up and down the street to be sure nobody was observing my actions as I knocked on the glossy black door of the Marigny with the ferrule of my stick. I hoped I wouldn't meet anyone I knew inside. A small flap in the door swung back at head height and a deep voice asked '*Mot de passe?*'

'*Papillon,*' I answered.

The door swung back, and I found myself in the entrance hall of what I imagined a Turkish harem would look and smell like, even though I'd never been in one. A very large native from one of the French African colonies was obviously the door guardian. The giant bid me to follow, and I was shown into a poorly-lit room where a man in drag was reclining on a green velvet chaise longue, smoking a cheroot. The African stood behind me. The transvestite was dressed in a red gown, but the feminine effect was somewhat countered by the man's ageing and coarse features. Beside him on a gilded side table were a trio of photographs. The first image was of a young man in Pierrot costume signed by someone called "Jean Cocteau". The second was of a man with a central parting and moustache signed "Marcel" that I recognised as the author, Proust. The third was well known to all Britons after his famous trial and was of Oscar Wilde.

'Good afternoon, Captain. You're new to our establishment I

believe, but, since you knew the password, we must have mutual friends, no? My name is Albert and I am the *propriétaire* of the Marigny, or the "Temple of Shamelessness" as we like to call it. How can we help you?' asked the reclining man in accented English. I noted that he seemed very well versed in British rank insignia.

'Actually, it's my first time in such a place, would you believe, so I don't know exactly what to do. You were indeed highly recommended by a friend,' I squeaked, in my nervousness my voice having gone up an octave.

'I always insist on personal recommendations. They are the best way to start a beautiful relationship. Don't you agree?'

'Yes, of course,' I replied and tried to think of something to say next. 'Gosh, I see you have a picture of Oscar Wilde there. Was he a client?'

'Not so much a client, more a friend. It was a shame what happened to him in your country. Such a talented man driven into exile. We were lucky that he chose Paris to see out his days. But let's focus on you, my friend. What can we do for you? We can offer you a nice relaxing steam bath and a massage, or maybe you'd prefer a visit to our dungeon for a little punishment if you've been a naughty boy.'

'I haven't been a naughty boy yet, but I'd like to become one. For now, I'd just like to spend some time with one of your chaps, please. I need a bit of relief from the war, if you see what I mean,' I told him.

'Relief is what we specialise in, Captain. Did your friend recommend one of our boys or do you want to try pot luck, as you English say?'

'Actually, my friend recommended Valentin, if he's here. I believe he has particular oral skills?'

'You're lucky, Captain, Valentin is free right now. It's still a bit early in the day for his regulars. He is usually very busy on a Saturday. Jamal here will take you up to his room and I'll ring ahead to tell him to expect you,' said Albert, first indicating his African servant, and then the ornate telephone on the side table.

'My, er, wounds, won't be a problem?'

'No problem, Captain. In fact, for a hero such as yourself, I can give you a discount for your first encounter.'

'Thank you. And exactly how and when does one pay for services rendered?'

'You can pay me on the way out if you like, or we can set up an account for you. We have several staff officers with accounts,' said Albert, eyeing the red tabs on my collar. I hoped that Albert's eyesight wasn't sharp enough to realise the colour wasn't the official British Army scarlet, but the red of my hotel's curtains which were now missing a few inches from their hems. I'd had McIlhenny sew them on to make me into a staff officer and hopefully a more attractive candidate for blackmail.

'Maybe I'd better try it first, before we go too far too quickly,' I said.

'Going too far is exactly what we're all about, my dear Captain, although we don't want you to come too quickly though, do we? We want you to enjoy your time here.'

'Yes, thank you. Now I'd like to meet Valentin, if you please.'

In French, Albert ordered Jamal to take me up to Valentin's room, before switching back to English. 'Enjoy yourself, my friend,' he urged me, with a smile and a wink.

I followed the giant up a set of marble stairs with a wrought-iron balustrade and oriental silk hangings on the walls until we arrived one floor up opposite a red door. I knocked, and a voice inside said '*Entrée*', so I abandoned my minder and went in.

I could see right away that I was in the room where the incriminating photographs of Church-Fenton's blackmail victims had been taken. There were two large sash windows on one side of the room, one of them sporting a large aspidistra in a Chinese cloisonné vase on its sill. The red brocade curtains on the windows matched the red flock wallpaper. I surmised that the aspidistra had been placed as a mark for the hidden photographer. On the wall opposite the windows was a large black and gold fireplace below a gilt-framed mirror. I couldn't see any hole for a camera lens. There were a couple of armchairs either side of the fireplace, and a bed in the far part of the room. A brass bowl sat on a small table, smoking gently, and the room smelt of oriental incense.

'*Bonjour*, I am Valentin. Pleased to meet you,' said a young man standing in the centre of the room.

He had a slightly camp way about him and spoke with an effeminate lisp. He was probably mid-twenties, although this was difficult to tell due to the make-up he was wearing. His hair was well-oiled, he had black eyeshadow around his large, dark eyes, thick mascara on his eyelashes, and his lips were pillar-box red. He was wearing a maroon smoking jacket over black silk pyjama trousers and matching velvet slippers, and was no doubt done up to be exactly what his clients expected. He also spoke in English, seemingly a requirement for the job.

'Hello, I'm Jock,' I said, using the first name that came into my head.

'Hmm, I get a lot of Scottish clients called Jock,' said Valentin, with a smile. 'I like the duelling scar – so romantic. Was it a fight over a man?'

'Sort of,' I replied, somewhat truthfully.

'And what can I do for you, Jock? I am open to anything that pleases you. You are obviously a war hero with your wounds and it's always exciting to be with a strong, brave man.'

'Yes, well, thankfully now I'm on the staff, there's no chance of future injuries!' I now found myself talking more loudly than normal, even more nervous than downstairs.

'That's good news. Now what can I serve you from our menu?'

'I'd like some oral relief if that's all right with you. You have a great reputation amongst my friends for it.'

Valentin smiled and knelt down in front of me. I lent heavily on my walking stick and took a few deep breaths. Valentin began to undo the fly buttons on my trousers.

'Aargh!' I screamed loudly.

Valentin sprang back, asking, 'What did I do wrong?'

'No, sorry, it's not you. It's me. Sometimes I get these terrible pains in my leg. I need to take some medicine. I need to get back to my hotel and get my pills. I'm really sorry. I was so looking forward to this. I'll come back again soon, and make sure I've taken the morphine next time,' I blathered.

Valentin looked relieved and said with a smile, 'It is not a problem, Jock. Don't worry. Just make sure you don't drug yourself up so much we cannot get you aroused, eh?'

I made my way downstairs to see Albert and explained my early departure. He actually seemed pleased that I was in pain and had not suffered a premature ejaculation or some other dysfunction. I promised to come back soon, and said I would arrange an appointment by telephone. Albert confirmed the password and gave me a card with the number for such a call. I offered to pay Albert for the time I'd wasted, but the *propriétaire* refused, asking me to be discreet about my visit and to only share the Marigny's details with "people like us".

Jamal showed me out, and I had a quick look up and down the street to be sure there were no British officers approaching. I found the parked Lanchester around the corner as I'd instructed. McIlhenny and Hodgson must have been sitting on the running board on the opposite side of the car from my approach, for I couldn't see them, only wisps of smoke. However, I could hear them and it sounded like they were discussing the taste of the French Gauloises they were smoking. McIlhenny had apparently bought a packet the night before and was intrigued by the distinct flavour and aroma, which was quite different from the British brands smoked by most Tommies.

'Forget the smokers' debate you two, it's time to go,' I shouted over the top of the car. They both jumped up and ground out their smokes under heel.

'Aye, but first, sur, yer Egyptian medals are showin',' said McIlhenny, pointing at my groin. Sure enough, two of my fly buttons were undone.

'I can assure you that nothing happened in there, and that I stopped before anything did happen,' I told them, blushing as I did up the buttons.

'If you say so, guv,' said Hodgson, po-faced.

'Ye know, Ah once got off with this lassie back in Glesga. She was a real stoater. Well-built if ye know what Ah mean. Ah got her up a close, and do ye know what? *She* was a *he*! She'd a tadger bigger than ma arm, and Ah'm not kiddin'. Ah've never been so scunnered in all ma life. Ah punched his lights out and ran away. Ah'm just sayin', Ah know how ye feel, sur.'

'Thanks for the support, McIlhenny,' I said, trying not to smile. 'Now, we need to move on. We need to go and get some help.'

'Where's that then, guv?'

'Back north. I need to take out some insurance.'

*

The journey was ten long hours of driving, broken only for occasional refuelling, the consumption of tea and chocolate bars, and latrine stops. For the latter part of the journey, I joined the other two in singing the popular songs of the day to be sure that Hodgson stayed awake. We worked our way through an extensive repertoire of "Just a Song at Twilight", "Bicycle Built for Two", "Oh, Mr Porter", "Nellie Dean", "I'm Henry the Eighth", "Good Bye-ee", "Pack up Your Troubles", the inevitable "Tipperary", and a dozen more. McIlhenny taught Hodgson some old Scottish favourites by Burns, plus newer renditions by Harry Lauder, while Hodgson introduced us to cockney ditties like "Any Old Iron". As a result of the singalong, I learned some new, and rather vulgar – but amusing – versions of my music hall favourites. It was in the early hours the next morning when we finally got back to Montreuil.

Sunday,
21st May 1916

CHAPTER 32

'A nice Sunday mornin', so it is, sur,' said McIlhenny when he brought me in a cup of tea. He opened the heavy brocade curtains to let in the bright early-morning sunlight of a beautiful spring day. I was still tired from the previous day's long drive, but let McIlhenny cajole me into my morning ablutions. As always when McIlhenny gave me a shave, he took advantage of my enforced silence during the razor's application to my lathered throat and chin to prattle on.

'Ah've been told there's a battalion of our regiment billeted near here as Étaples is full, sur, if ye want to go to Mass. Sorry, Ah mean Sunday Service, sur. Ah can't get used to yer Proddie names.'

When the shaving was completed and I was dressed, I asked McIlhenny to tell Hodgson to get the Lanchester ready as, based on his news, I had indeed decided to go to church. Villiers made a few inquiries for me and confirmed that a Cameronian battalion was billeted in the nearby village of Beutin, about five miles away along the River Canche. McIlhenny took up my option of missing out on the trip as he had no appetite for a Protestant service.

By eleven o'clock the Lanchester was parked outside a chapel on the aptly named Rue de l'Église. There were no Tommies to be seen, and only a small crowd of elderly French churchgoers, interspersed with a few younger women, were milling around outside the small grey building as its solitary bell pealed mournfully. I assumed all the young men had been called up.

'I don't think this is the right place, guv,' said Hodgson.

'Oh, they won't be here, Hodgson. This is a Catholic chapel, and the regiment is fiercely Presbyterian. They'll be nearby somewhere.'

Sure enough, we found a crowd of Tommies in Cameronian uniforms gathering for a drumhead service on the village football pitch close by. Four armed pickets stood guard outside the main throng with bayonets fixed to their rifles.

'Are they expecting trouble, guv?' asked Hodgson. 'We're a bit far behind the lines here.'

'No, it's a regimental tradition,' I explained. 'Back when the regiment was formed in the 1600s it had to hold secret church meetings, or conventicles as they were known, as it was being persecuted by the then government in Scotland. The sentries are to ensure the service isn't interrupted. It's ceremonial now.'

An officer suddenly shouted, "All clear!" and at this signal a padre, no doubt a Church of Scotland minister, stood up on a makeshift pulpit and the service began.

After the hymns and psalms were sung, and the padre had delivered a sermon strong on fire and brimstone, the attendees dispersed as the battalion band played "Within a Mile o' Edinburgh Toun", the regimental march. I went up to the officers present, but found I knew none of them. A couple of old boys from my school remembered me from my days as their house prefect, but I had to confess I didn't recall them. Although this was all very disappointing, perhaps it wasn't surprising, I thought, as I knew there were now many battalions of Cameronians.

When we arrived back at the chateau, I gave Hodgson the rest of the day to prepare for our next journey, which, I informed him, would start early in the morning. I then made a phone call to take out what I thought of as an insurance policy. Finally, I telephoned Albert at the Marigny, and, after giving the *hirondelle* password, arranged an afternoon appointment with Valentin on the coming Tuesday. I then caught up on the newspapers in the library, enjoyed a very English roast beef dinner, and went up to my room for an early night.

*

I sat in bed that night with a copy of The Memoirs of Sherlock Holmes *which I'd borrowed from the Prof. Although I found it faintly amusing that an erudite law professor should be an avid reader of Conan Doyle's canon of detective fiction, I decided to put that aside and see if the Great Detective could give me any pointers on how to be a better investigator. However, after a few pages of the first short story,* The Adventure of Silver Blaze, *I realised that the disappearance of a racehorse wasn't holding my attention as my mind wandered hither and thither on my own case in hand. I fetched myself a whisky and pondered over my evolving investigation as I sipped the golden malt liquor. Soon, however, my mind was drifting back to the church service earlier in the day.*

As I peered down into my glass, I realised that the conventicle I'd attended that morning was my first time at church since I'd been on home leave as part of my convalescence. I'd found the hymn singing a comfort only on par with belting out my music hall favourites and that the padre's sermon had no effect on me. I also realised that instead of saying a prayer at bedtime, I was now more likely to be seeking solace in a wee dram. I wondered what had happened to my faith. It had certainly been sorely tested by the loss of Hugh and so many good friends and comrades. Now, my past clarity on homosexuality being a sin was being clouded. I wished I could speak to my Uncle John, for, although he was a clergyman and much older than me, he was also my friend and a bit of a philosopher. Unfortunately, that was an option that would have to wait. I finished my whisky and put out the light.

Monday,
22nd May 1916

CHAPTER 33

We left early on the Monday morning for the long drive back to Paris. I had dreamed that my brother had asked me from a church pulpit why I had not avenged him yet, a headless sergeant beside him, and my dead platoon in the congregation looking on. As a result of this nightmare, I had only slept fitfully, and so I dozed most of the way to Amiens.

The greatest excitement of our journey back to the French capital was racing a troop train between Amiens and Montdidier where the railway line ran parallel to the road for several miles. As the Lanchester passed the carriages of French soldiers, many of the poilus, clearly drunk on the red wine they were brandishing at the windows, made all sorts of rude gestures at our staff car. The French soldiers were safe in their anonymity, separated from what they thought were senior British officers in their grand automobile, and so the hand signals were crude, imaginative, and of great variety. I just laughed and waved, although McIlhenny couldn't resist flicking the odd hand gesture in the direction of our rail-bound allies. The friendly rivalry ended where Hodgson had to slow down to pass through a village and the train steamed regally on at speed.

On reaching Paris once more, we drove to the Gare du Nord to collect my insurance policy. Afterwards, we headed over to the same billets as on our previous trip. I then retired with Sherlock Holmes for the night and, for once, read myself to sleep without a medicinal nightcap. I wondered if the Prof would have approved of me using his favourite detective as a cure for insomnia.

Tuesday,
23rd May 1916

CHAPTER 34

I was back outside the Marigny after lunch the next day. As before, I had replaced my green Intelligence Corps collar tabs with the red of the staff, so as not to arouse suspicion.

After an exchange of *papillon* through the door hatch, I was shown in by the giant doorman, Jamal, and was greeted by Albert. This time the *propriétaire* was wearing what I had to admit was a rather chic turquoise number. The dress couldn't compensate for Albert's badly rouged face and smudged lipstick however, and I detected alcohol on the transvestite's breath. It seemed Albert was quite the dissolute.

'Captain, so good to see you back. And so soon. I hope you are in good health to appreciate our offerings this fine day?'

'I feel very well, thank you, Albert. I've taken my medicine and feel ready to give Valentin a good run out,' I said with an enthusiasm I scarcely felt, accompanied by what I hoped was an appropriate hand gesture of a thrusting fist.

'Just so, Captain. I'm sure you will have a very good time. Enjoy!' said Albert, before switching languages. 'Jamal, take the Captain up to his appointment.' He made it sound more like a visit to the dentist than the sort of oral examinations that went on in the Marigny.

Valentin, dressed and made up as before, welcomed me with open arms and kissed me, over enthusiastically I felt, on both cheeks.

The young man then locked the door before leading me into the centre of the room. I was now in line with the aspidistra, I noted.

'Now, my dear Jock, where were we?' asked Valentin, with a cheeky grin. 'Ah yes, I recall. You've taken your medicine, but not enough to dull the pleasure, I hope? Pain and pleasure are the two sides of the same coin in my experience.'

I assured him that I was very alert and ready for an afternoon of pleasure. Valentin knelt down again in front of me while I held my walking stick by my side. As the young Frenchman reached for my buttoned flies, I undid a catch on the stick.

'This is the only prick you're going to feel today,' I told him as the blade I'd extracted from my stick drew blood from the neck of my erstwhile fellator. 'Don't jerk your head away or this blade will cut your throat. It's a very sharp Japanese tanto blade, made of the best steel in the world.'

Valentin froze, but the wall opposite the window bulged, and a large, bearded man holding a pistol burst into the room out of a concealed door beside the fireplace. As the gunman rushed towards me, there was a crescendo of crashes that sounded like one large explosion to my ear. The first crash was the window with the aspidistra in it shattering, the second was the bearded man's head disintegrating, and the third was the mirror over the fireplace breaking into thousands of shards.

I grabbed Valentin by his hair, which wasn't easy given how much oil was on it, and dragged him to an armchair where I secured him with the tiebacks of the curtains. This proved quite difficult with only one good hand, but was soon achieved as Valentin offered me no resistance.

Putting down the blade from my walking stick, I picked up the dead man's pistol, a French Army Lebel revolver, and pointed it at Valentin, telling him, 'If you try to escape, I'll shoot you, just as your friend here tried to shoot me. Do you understand?'

Valentin nodded. The young Frenchman seemed in shock. I meanwhile was elated that my ruse to find out where Valentin's accomplice was concealed had worked, and was even more pleased that my insurance policy had prevented me being attacked. My elation cooled somewhat as I remembered there was a man dead.

I quickly inspected the fallen interloper. The man's head had a small entry wound in the brow, but a large exit wound on the back of the skull where a mush of brains and blood was seeping out. A typical sniper kill, as described by Sneddon. I stepped over my unfortunate assailant and went into the secret room revealed by the bearded man's sudden appearance. The man had clearly been the photographer. In his small den was a large camera on an easel, a stool, a volume from Proust's À la recherche du temps perdu, and a case of photographic plates. The camera was pointed at the hole in the mirror created by the shot.

Upon inspecting the mirror frame from the inside of the hidden room, I noted a small label in the corner indicating that it was a "transparent mirror" and the product of Bloch's of Cincinnati, Ohio. Sure enough, by looking through the broken parts remaining in the frame, I could see out into the room next door with its aspidistra and a shaking Valentin. It was a mirror on one side, and a window on the other, and an invention I had never come across. However, it did explain why I couldn't detect a port for the camera in the wall. Given the light from the large sash windows, the photographer had been quite skilled to get the photographic exposures exactly right, although I worried that this was because of a lot of practice.

The door of Valentin's room was being shaken by now and Albert's voice was yelling through it. I unlocked it and Albert rushed in followed by the doorman, Jamal.

'What has happened? Oh my God, he's been shot!' exclaimed Albert in French upon seeing the dead photographer. Jamal went to grab me, pistol or no pistol, but suddenly the African collapsed on the floor. Behind the giant stood a grinning McIlhenny with a cosh in hand.

'He'll be all right in the mornin'. Ah only gave him a wee tap. Big bugger, isn't he?' said McIlhenny, who had let himself in via the establishment's back door, as ordered, in my anticipation of events.

I used my pistol to encourage the shaken Albert to take the armchair opposite Valentin's. I then posted McIlhenny outside the door in case the brothel's other clients arrived to find out what the commotion was. I reckoned that a Tommy with our corps' armband, obviously standing guard outside of a room, would prevent anyone being too inquisitive. If anybody did stick their noses out of the door of their male paramours, I expected that they would soon be planning an exit route. I pointed the pistol at Albert as he seemed still to have his wits about him. Valentin was meanwhile staring fixedly at the fallen photographer, turning from being as white as a sheet to a light shade of green.

'Right, Albert, I need some quick answers. How did you know Brigadier General Church-Fenton and how were you blackmailing your British clients?'

'What are you talking about? It is not in my interest to blackmail anybody! I don't know any general by that name,' said Albert, indignantly.

'But you and the Brigadier used the photographs that man down there on the floor took to extort money from your customers.'

'No, you are wrong. We hand over the plates with the victim's rank and name, if we have them, to a man who comes to collect them. We were given a diagram with British officers' badges so we could tell their ranks. We try to get the officers' names and regiments from their pocketbooks when they are asleep. Someone calls me once a week to ask if we have some new photographs of interest and, if we do, then they send a man to pick them up. They always call me and I don't have a number for them.'

I didn't understand. 'But why would you do that? Who are these people?'

'I don't know exactly who they are, but they are clearly part of the government.'

'The government?' I asked, astonished.

'I think so. They warned me that if I did not cooperate, they'd close us down. They were blackmailing me. I am the blackmail victim here!'

'Where do the plates go? Do you know?'

'I don't know, Captain.'

I'd had enough experience from my advocate days in court to know when a witness was lying, and I felt Albert was doing so now. I cocked the revolver for effect and held it against Valentin's head before saying, 'If you don't tell me by the time I count to ten everything you know, I'll shoot Valentin here. And if you still don't tell me by the time I count to ten again, then I'll shoot you. Am I being clear?' Albert looked terrified and Valentin fainted.

'But he is my best boy. Please, stop, I will tell you. I am a curious person, so one day after the man collected the photographic plates, I followed him.'

I was speculating how a drag queen as flamboyantly dressed as Albert could possibly have inconspicuously followed anybody. He was obviously reading my mind and said, 'I dressed down, of course. I looked more like a lady's maid, wore glasses, and smoked a cigarette so that my face was veiled. I was quite the secret policeman, or policewoman, if you like.'

I wondered why the transvestite didn't just dress like the man he was, but needed to stay in character as a female. I filed this behaviour away as another piece of my education into human nature, an education that was getting broader by the day.

'Anyway,' continued Albert, 'the man took the plates to an address on Rue de Portfoin, about three kilometres away in the Third Arrondissement. He was let in by what looked like some sort of guard. There's no sign on the door to say what happens inside. There's a service alley round the back, and I even looked there for clues, but there was nothing except that I could see another guard through the window. I've no idea what's done with the plates after that, I swear.'

From the frightened look on his face I now believed him. Once before in this investigation I'd thought things were getting "curiouser and curiouser", and the same thought entered my head again. 'All right, I believe you,' I said to a relieved Albert.

275

There was a pen and paper beside the telephone used to alert Valentin of his clients. I handed them to Albert, telling him, 'Write down the address you followed the man to.' As Albert wrote out the address, I pulled the photograph of Church-Fenton from my pocket and asked him, 'Do you know this man?'

'*Bien sûr*, that's *Nounours*.'

'*Nounours*? What does that mean?'

'I think in English you call it a "teddy bear"?'

'Ah, I should have guessed. A bear. Of course! Well, this is Brigadier Church-Fenton.'

'I only know him as *Nounours*.'

'Did this man come here often?'

'Yes, at first he was a frequent visitor, but he has not been here lately. Valentin was his favourite boy. Is he something to do with all this?'

'Did you ever give him the negative plates directly?' I asked, ignoring Albert's question.

'No, I am not stupid. If I gave photographs of all my clients to everybody else then my business wouldn't last very long. I am the soul of discretion, but I had to cooperate with these government people otherwise I'd have no business at all. They were very threatening. Strangely, I did see *Nounours* go into the same building as the negatives that time I followed the man who collected the plates. *Nounours* was dressed in civilian clothes though. He looked – how do you say in English? – "shifty".'

I felt that Albert had just given me a missing link.

'Right, I'll be off now after just checking the last plates in your secret room.' I went into the den and made sure I exposed all of the plates, both in the camera and in the spare box before throwing them on the floor to smash to smithereens. I wasn't sure if the photographer had taken any images of me before any sex act was committed, but I wasn't taking any chances. Finally, I used the point of my tanto blade to dig out the bullet from the wall. The bullet was no dumdum, but a distorted full metal jacket round, which explained why it had passed through the photographer's head before smashing the mirror and embedding itself in the lathe and plaster. I pocketed the bullet then reassembled my walking stick.

'What am I going to do with him?' asked Albert pointing at the dead man.

'I'm sure you must have had the odd client over the years who passed away during his exertions in your house. You'll find a way. Oh, and one last thing. You saw what happened to your photographer. If you tell any of this to anybody, including the Gendarmes, the plate collector, or the government men who threatened you, I will find out somehow. You won't see who kills you – just like your friend here,' I said, making my threat while waving the revolver in Albert's face. I then emptied the gun and threw it into the corner of the room.

'What are you going to tell the British Army about what goes on here?' asked Albert, an anguished look on his made-up face.

'Nothing yet. And I suggest you don't mention it to your clients on the British Staff either. For now, tell the government people who collect the plates that your camera's broken and you're waiting for a new one. I'll decide what to do about you and the Marigny later.'

With that I left a shaking Albert comforting Valentin, who by now had recovered consciousness, but had vomited down his smoking jacket. After stepping over the groaning form of Jamal, I collected McIlhenny outside the door, and we went in search of Hodgson.

CHAPTER 35

We found the Lanchester as planned, one street away, Hodgson in his driving seat, and Sergeant MacLeod in the back, a Lee-Enfield rifle with a telescopic scope on it resting between his knees.

'Ye'd better wipe that lipstick off yer face before we go, sur,' warned McIlhenny, offering the hankie that already had both our bloodstains on it.

'I don't suppose any more red will make this any dirtier,' I said, as I rubbed my cheeks where Valentin had kissed me. 'Now, Hodgson, let's get out of here. I'm sure somebody must have reported a gunshot to the Gendarmes and they'll be arriving here soon.'

'Right ho. Where to then, guv?'

'Let's drop Sergeant MacLeod here at the Gare du Nord, so he can get a train back to St Pol.'

When we arrived at the station, the area outside was teeming with troops. Some were off to the front, and others were returning in the opposite direction on leave. One set was serious and grim, and the other laughing and jolly. It wasn't difficult to tell which was which.

I got out of the car with Sergeant MacLeod and joined the throng. As we walked into the station, I thanked the old soldier profusely for his critical intervention. I was pretty sure the photographer would have killed me if I hadn't had the sniper as my insurance.

'It was nothing, sir. The shot was easy. Just across the street. That's why I only needed the Lee-Enfield. And, anyway, I didn't like to see an officer who'd helped me, like yourself, being threatened. I didn't like killing the man, but it was difficult not to, under the circumstances. My main worry was getting into a room opposite you, but McIlhenny found an empty flat and let me in,' said the old man with a smile.

As we walked through the Victorian-aged station to Sergeant MacLeod's platform, I noted that it was just like its British counterparts, a vast cathedral of wrought-iron and glass, filled with steam and smelling of coal dust and sweating soldiers. The station concourse was a heaving mass of troops and surrounded by bistros and bars, tabacs and charity stalls. The trains bringing men back on leave had no lavatories, and, as the carriages emptied, the troops relieved themselves on to the tracks, and there was a strong whiff of urine in the air near the platforms. The returning soldiers were assailed as soon as they set foot on the station concourse by young ladies that, from their provocative dress, were certainly not wives and sisters, but local prostitutes. These ladies seemed to quickly appraise the Sergeant and myself as too old and too disabled respectively to be of interest as customers, and quickly made way for us.

At his platform, I shook Sergeant MacLeod's hand in farewell. As the older man turned to go, he said to me, 'There's one other thing that's been troubling me, sir. I don't know if it's important, but it's a bit strange.'

'What's that, Sergeant?'

'Well, I share a tent with a fellow called Danny Kelly. Irish chap. He's not the tidiest soldier, despite having been in the Guards. He's always leaving his kit lying about. The other day there was a pile of letters on his camp bed and out of one of them was peeking a wee photograph.'

'What's so unusual about that?'

'It was a photograph of you, sir.'

'Of me!' I exclaimed, dumbfounded.

'Aye, of you, sir. Do you know him?'

'No. No I don't,' I replied, my memory drawing a blank on any connection.

'Isn't that a wee bit odd, sir?'

'Yes. I agree. Did you ask him about it?'

'Och, no, sir. I didn't want to seem like I was prying into his business. When you share a tent, it's always best to try to rub along.'

'Thanks for letting me know, MacLeod. I wonder how that happened? I'll try to figure it out.'

We shook hands once more and the old soldier turned and quickly merged into the station's bustling crowd. The sniper seemed to have an uncanny knack of disappearing, even when not wearing a ghillie suit.

As I walked back to the car, I wondered why Danny Kelly had my photograph and also why MacLeod thought the Irishman was a Guardsman, when I'd been told by Hesketh-Pritchard that the other sniper was in the Connaught Rangers.

CHAPTER 36

'Where to now, guv?'

I pulled out my Paris map and located Rue de Portfoin. The Third Arrondissement was just south of the Tenth where we were currently parked.

'Let's swing past our next point of interest. It's not far from here.'

As we cruised along the targeted street, a small man in a large homburg hat exited from the building that Albert had given me as the destination of the photographic plates. He looked to be saying goodbye to a guard in a French soldier's uniform on the door as he did so. The man flagged down one of Paris's famous red taxis.

'Nice cab,' said Hodgson. 'They're very reliable are these French taxis. Lots of the ones we have in London are French-built Renaults and Unics. My uncle's got a Unic. I think that one there's a Renault, though.'

I told McIlhenny and Hodgson that earlier in the war the Parisian taxi drivers had rushed large numbers of troops out of the city to defend Paris in the Battle of the Marne. This had made the cabbies even more popular with Parisians, although the French government was less pleased about being presented with a large bill for the drivers' "patriotic services".

'Well, guv, a fare's a fare.' said Hodgson, in solidarity with his French transport brothers.

'Yes, and this fare here looks like an important sort of chap given his large hat and expensive overcoat. I dare say he knows what goes on in that place. Follow his taxi and let's see where he goes next,' I instructed Hodgson. 'We'll come back here later tonight.'

*

The taxi eventually stopped at the Place Vendôme in central Paris and the man-in-the-hat got out, looked at his watch, and then settled himself at a table outside La Coupe D'Or, just off the square. I had Hodgson immediately stop and drop McIlhenny and myself off too, and told him to circle the square until further notice. I set McIlhenny to watch from a distance, while I went and sat at a table within earshot of the man-in-the-hat. By now the man had taken off his homburg and had ordered two pastis, which soon arrived with a glass jug of water. For some reason, now that the man was hatless, I thought I'd seen him somewhere before, but couldn't place him. He had a droopy moustache and a mole on his right cheek, but no other distinguishing marks. The man was obviously waiting for someone and had decided to take out a cigarette from a slim case and light up.

An elderly waiter appeared by my side and raised a quizzical eyebrow. '*Monsieur?*'

I ordered a pastis and water in French as I'd never tried the drink before. In my old student days in Paris I could only afford cheap wine and even cheaper beer.

'Ricard or Pernod?' asked the waiter.

'Erm, Ricard,' I said, not knowing if there was any difference between the two brands.

A glass of dark yellow transparent spirit soon arrived at my table along with a water jug. Not knowing how much water to add, I looked around and reckoned most drinkers of the popular liqueur were adding about five parts water to their glasses, and so I copied the practice and watched as my drink turned a milky soft yellow. I sipped it tentatively and tried not to grimace as the taste hit my palate. It immediately reminded me of childhood aniseed balls or liquorice allsorts, both favourite sweets of my grandfather, but not to my taste. I decided to stick to whisky in the future.

While I was gurning in reaction to my drink, a tall, bald man with a long face decorated by a narrow grey moustache had settled beside my subject of interest. I tried to listen in on the men, but they were keeping their voices low. My eavesdropping was made all the more difficult by the loud braying voices of a table of British subalterns who had obviously taken too much liquor on board. However, I could make out some of the two men's words, and I was astonished to hear them talking in German. They seemed to be discussing some French Army redeployments and I heard *Départment de la Somme* mixed in with their German at one stage.

My subject of interest eventually finished his drink, put on his hat, got up from the table, shook the other man's hand, and left the café. I signalled to McIlhenny, who was leaning on a nearby lamp post smoking a cigarette, that he should follow the man-in-the-hat. The tall companion had by now also left the café and disappeared into the crowd. Eventually McIlhenny returned and we were picked up after flagging down Hodgson on the adjacent square.

'Yer man-in-the-hat went down a street with a name that sort of combined "castle" and "lion",' said McIlhenny, as we drove along.

'Castiglione, Rue de Castiglione?' I asked, after looking at my map.

'Aye, that's it. Anyways, he went into a posh sort of tenement block. Ah picked the lock, and managed to get in soon after him, but he'd got into a lift. Ah ran up the stairs and was just in time to see him goin' in through a door. He had his arms around some young lassie, a lot younger than him, that's for sure. Ah doubt if it was his wife.'

'We need to find out more about this chap, but that can wait until we find out what he does in that building he left earlier this evening.'

'Where to now, guv?'

'Back to our billets. We'll get some rest and something to eat. We've got some more work to do tonight, including McIlhenny putting the green tabs back on my collar.'

CHAPTER 37

Just before midnight, we coasted to a halt at the end of the service alley for Rue de Portfoin. McIlhenny and I got out, and Hodgson drove back round to the front of the street and waited. We'd synchronised our watches, although I was rather dubious about the accuracy of my driver's given it was Hodgson's old London General Omnibus Company issue. In my experience, few buses ever arrived on time. I was, however, proven wrong when a number of fire-cracker intensity explosions came from the front of the property. The makeshift fireworks had been prepared earlier by McIlhenny from revolver cartridges, and had been thrown out by Hodgson as he drove by.

McIlhenny used his lock picks to gain entry at the rear of the building and the two of us crept quietly inside. The two guards could be seen out at the front of the building through an open door, distracted by the small explosions. McIlhenny closed the front door silently and then used his tools to lock the guards out.

I switched on my little Orilux trench torch to search around the building, shielding it so that the guards outside would not see any movement inside their charge. McIlhenny stood sentry, armed with his cosh in the entrance hall, just in case. Based on the reasoning that glass photographic plates were individually quite heavy, and that a lot of plates would therefore be a lot heavier, I expected the targeted

285

material to be on the ground floor, or possibly in a basement, to save carrying the plates up and downstairs as there did not appear to be a lift shaft in the building.

The ground floor had only a few offices, populated by desks and the odd typewriter. However, down in the basement I found what I was looking for after I'd called McIlhenny to pick another door lock. It was a dedicated room with American-style steel filing cabinets lining the walls. The drawers of the cabinets were also locked, and so I had to get McIlhenny to assist in opening one. Its contents were revealed to be a series of photographic plates in individually named files.

'Christ, there must be hundreds of them here, sur! We'll not have time to smash all these,' exclaimed McIlhenny.

I had just come to the same conclusion, but was still none the wiser as to the purpose of the office we were in. 'You're right, McIlhenny. We'll have to come back. Relock this, then get back on sentry duty. I'm going upstairs to the first floor.'

After creeping up the stairs, I came to a set of larger offices and meeting rooms. Through the clear glass door of one large room which was set with chairs around a long table, I could just make out in the gloom a huge map of the Western Front. On it were pins of many colours that I surmised were representing infantry divisions, cavalry, colonial troops, etc. There were a lot of pins concentrated around where I knew Verdun to be, and another cluster where the French line met the BEF at the Somme River in Picardy.

Adjacent to this meeting room was a door with a frosted glass pane with the title *Directeur* picked out in gold on the glass. Beside it was another door labelled *Armée Coloniale*. I was most intrigued, however, by a third door marked *Armée Britannique* on its glass. The building seemed to be some sort of French government establishment, but one which appeared to have a German spy in its midst. The man-in-the-hat must be a fount of useful information for the Germans just from this office alone, without the additional intelligence he'd glean from blackmailing British officers. The sheer audacity of the scheme amazed me. I was just about to ask McIlhenny to come up and pick the office door locks when my batman appeared like magic anyway.

'Ah'm awful sorry, sur, but those boys downstairs are gettin' really fed up. Ah think they'll break in any minute now,' warned McIlhenny and he'd only just finished speaking when there was a crash below as the exiled guards forced their re-entry.

'*Scheisse*. Let's get out of here,' I ordered.

McIlhenny led the way, cosh in hand. I pulled my Japanese dagger from my walking stick. The guards seemed more intent on trying to fix the front door than anything else and so didn't notice us sneaking past behind them, and thus we avoided any confrontation. We made it back to the alley undetected and got into the Lanchester idling quietly at its end.

'Where to now, guv?'

'Back to our digs, then we're off to Étaples early in the morning. You won't get much sleep tonight.'

'Eat Apples it will be, guv.'

Wednesday, 24th May 1916

CHAPTER 38

We left before six o'clock on the Wednesday and had breakfast in Amiens, en route to the coast. While there, I took advantage of the stop to call Villiers from a BEF post and ask him to find yet another of my past contacts who I knew was now in France, and was probably based in Étaples if he wasn't up at the front.

I also called Albert at the Marigny. I now knew what Church-Fenton was using to blackmail his victims, but I still didn't understand why, beyond that it was something to do with French gangsters according to Major Fairbrother. Private Leeming had also mentioned seeing the Brigadier with some unsavoury types in Paris.

'Albert, this is your favourite captain. I need to speak to someone who knows about French gangsters and organised crime. Somebody mentioned a gang called the "Apaches", for instance. I cannot believe you've been allowed to run your house of ill repute for so many years without you knowing someone in the police or Gendarmerie. Do you have contacts I can talk to?'

'And why should I help you, Captain?' asked Albert.

'Because if you don't, then I really will tell the British Army about you, and they'll issue an edict warning off officers from visiting you and facing cashiering and prosecution if they do. You'll be ruined.'

'Ah, blackmail, Captain! All right. I know someone. Let me call him. Get back to me in two hours or so. It may take me some time to track him down.'

We drove on through rain showers to Hesdin, where I made my follow-up calls to Villiers and Albert from the BEF base there. After a quick lunch we continued on our way to Étaples as fast as the roads and traffic would allow. Within the base our destination was the Royal Engineer's camp. I went in to find the information I needed, and my luck was in, and I soon returned to the car with a letter and a set of directions.

*

Using the new directions, we headed off for one of the recreation grounds on the north-east side of the base. For the British Army, recreation largely meant playing football. We arrived to find a team in red and blue vertically striped shirts with blue shorts, playing a team in solid blue shirts with white shorts. There were few supporters straggled along the touchlines as the wind blowing off the Channel that day was quite fierce. Thankfully, the rain had stopped. A handwritten sheet whose ink had run in the drizzle was flapping in the wind and attached to a pitch-side noticeboard. It revealed that we were watching the Royal Engineers' tunnelling companies in stripes, versus a battalion of Liverpool Pals of the King's Regiment in blue.

The Pals were volunteers recruited from one district, often from only a few employers or trades. The idea was that men would be more comfortable volunteering and fighting with their friends or "pals". The Liverpool team was winning by three goals to one as half-time approached, partly due to the tunnellers being a man down.

'Not a fair game of fitba' is it, sur, ten versus eleven? One or two of these Scousers are quite good, but their backs are awfully slow, are they not?' was McIlhenny's opinion when the whistle went to finish the first half.

I waited at the halfway line as the players trooped off for a reviving cup of tea before restarting. As the soldier who had been playing centre forward in stripes approached, I shouted out to him.

'Hey, George, can I have a word with you?'

The tall, imposing player came over. 'Mister Brown! Well, this is a surprise. I'm glad to see you, sir, but sorry to see you've had a hard time of it,' he said.

'I need to talk with you after the game, George.'

'Aye, no problem, sir.'

'It looks like a tough game.'

'Aye, the Pals are quite good. We're a man short of course, and that doesn't help. One of our players called in sick just before kick-off. The MO says he's too ill to play, and none of our other blokes is either good enough, or fancies it on a day like today.'

I introduced McIlhenny and Hodgson to George Cook, another acquaintance from my past. I had defended George after he had been wrongly accused of causing affray by fighting and defeating a crowd of young drunks one night. It turned out that the youths had been put up to it by unknown sponsors as George was seen to be a bit of a troublemaker due to his leadership position in the local miners' union. My defence of George had been another chapter in my often-fraught relationship with the provincial colliery owners.

'Ah'll play for ye if ye want,' offered McIlhenny.

George looked at McIlhenny, doubt on his face. His small stature and bandy legs didn't make my batman an obvious athlete of the highest calibre.

'Ah play on the left. Left-footer, left-winger, that's me, religiously and politically, as well as at fitba',' claimed McIlhenny with a grin.

'He's actually quite good, George, I promise you. He played for our old Cameronians' team and we were division champions. He even had a trial at Glasgow Celtic,' I added as a reference for McIlhenny.

'Aye, but ma trial at Celtic coincided with another trial Ah had in Glesga Sheriff Court the same day, if ye get ma drift, so Ah never made it to play for the Bhoys,' revealed McIlhenny, shaking his head at the memory of the lost opportunity to play in his heroes' strip of green and white hoops.

'All right, you're in. I'll get you some kit and a pair of boots. You can get changed in the tent over there,' said George.

The Liverpool Pals and the referee all agreed that the Engineers could bring in a new man since he wasn't a substitute for a previous player on the pitch, and this was, after all, a friendly match. As we watched the game unfold, in between shouting exhortations at McIlhenny, Hodgson and I chatted away as supporters do, our ranks set aside for the moment.

'Did you play football, Mister Brown, or were you more of a rugger man?' asked Hodgson.

'A bit of both, although I wasn't very good at either, to be honest. I was fast, but not very skilful. What about you, Hodgson?'

'I'm more of a cricket player myself. I bowl for Gosseley's in Newham, an amateur club up the East End. Did you ever play cricket, guv?'

'Only on the beach. It's not very popular in Scotland, I'm afraid.'

'And do you support a football team, Mister Brown?'

'Yes, I support what was my old school team, Hamilton Academical. They're now in the Scottish Football League. What about you?'

'I'm a West Ham United supporter myself.'

'I'm not sure I've heard of them?' I had to admit.

'We're in the Southern League, so we haven't made it to the English Football League proper yet. But we will one day, I'm sure of it. We've got a nice little ground at Upton Park in the East End of London. The Boleyn Ground, it's called. I'm looking forward to going back to watching them again after this is all over,' said Hodgson wistfully.

As we were exchanging memories about our home clubs, McIlhenny was working wonders for his adopted team. On one memorable run down the left wing he beat his full back easily before crossing with pinpoint accuracy for George to head into the opposition's net. On his next run, McIlhenny cut inside, and after a one-two with his inside left teammate, smashed a driving shot into the Liverpudlian goal.

The Liverpool Pals were reeling, and their right back decided to solve their main problem with a scything tackle on McIlhenny. A twenty-man brawl then ensued, with the goalkeepers looking on from either end of the pitch. It was several minutes before the referee could restore order. As it was a friendly, the referee decided not to send anyone off. The next time McIlhenny came up against the full back, he embarrassed him with ease, and left the defender dumped on his backside before crossing once more, this time for George to volley past the Pals' hapless goalkeeper. It was the last act of the game, as the referee blew his whistle for full-time. The Engineers carried McIlhenny off the pitch in triumph at their 4-3 victory.

After the players had changed and then feted McIlhenny with cigarettes, chocolate, and RE badges and buttons, I drew Sergeant George Cook to one side into a more serious conversation. I handed over the letter I'd been given at his camp headquarters, temporarily transferring George from the 182nd Tunnelling Company to my command in the Intelligence Corps. I then told him the minimum I felt he needed to know, to act effectively on the mission. I also outlined what I wanted George to do, so he would know what to bring with him. After the briefing, I left the centre forward to celebrate with his team, but warned the tunneller to be ready the next afternoon to be picked up with all the necessary equipment. I prised McIlhenny away from his happy teammates.

'Where to now, guv?'

'Back to the chateau. It's been a long day. Tomorrow we'll rest, then we're off back to Paris yet again.'

Thursday,
25th May 1916

CHAPTER 39

I awoke early on the Thursday in a sober frame of mind after recalling another nightmare, this one involving my dead Cameronians playing football in no-man's land against German *Jaegers* who all had their faces shot away. It was a far cry from the happy sketches I'd seen of the fraternal football games during the unofficial Christmas truce of 1914.

The Prof called me into his study after breakfast. It was too early for Laphroaig, so we made do with a pot of tea, with my CO playing mother.

'Now, Jamie, do you recall Henry Linton at the college?' asked the Prof.

'Do you mean Doctor Linton, the lecturer on "The History of Law"?'

'Yes, that's the one. I met him at the officers' club the other night for dinner as he was up at GHQ for a briefing. He's now a staff officer with the 51st Division. He'd heard about the attempt on the King's life. He went on to say that regicide is a rare crime. He mentioned the case of England's Edward II who was killed by his nobles through the insertion of a red-hot poker up his backside.'

I winced involuntarily at the thought and could almost smell the singeing hair. The Prof continued.

'Apparently the nobles thought this was an appropriate way to kill the King as he was accused of sodomy with his lover, Piers Gaveston. I then, as innocently as I could, asked Linton if there were any other royals who had been accused of homosexuality. He then told me about our James VI, England's James I. Apparently, he had three male lovers during his reign, including the Duke of Lennox, the Earl of Somerset, and the Duke of Buckingham.'

'Wait a minute,' I interrupted. 'Do you mean King James as in *The King James Bible*?'

'The very same. And there's another example of pious royalty you wouldn't expect – William III.'

'William of Orange?'

'"Good King Billy" as our fellow countrymen in the Orange Order call him. Yes, the hero of the Battle of the Boyne didn't only bring Queen Mary with him when he came over from Holland, but two male Dutch lovers that he made into the Earl of Portland and the Earl of Albemarle.'

'Well, they certainly didn't teach that at school in our history classes!'

'No, quite. And then finally, Linton mentioned the current King's brother, the late Prince Albert. He was linked to "The Cleveland Street Scandal". You won't remember it as it was about the time you were born, but it involved a homosexual brothel in London, a number of aristocrats, and some telegraph boys. So, as you can see from Linton's history lesson, the current Prince of Wales, whether sexually adventurous, bisexual, or even just plain homosexual, is in good company with several of his forebears.'

'Given what you've told me and the "Divine Right of Kings" and all that, especially when we had absolute monarchs, I'm surprised these royals didn't change the laws to make their own preferences legal.'

'Yes, exactly. Now, changing subjects, I've got some additional information for you, Jamie, which I think may complicate your investigation further,' said the Prof. 'You'll recall that I'd never heard any rumours regarding Church-Fenton being a German spy. Then we were told by Lord Ross that the rumour was in fact all an invention to get Sergeant MacLeod to snipe the Brigadier as a traitor. However, by then I'd already put in motion some inquiries of my own about Church-Fenton, based on what you had told me MacLeod had said when you interviewed him. The answers to my questions came in yesterday from my contacts at the War Office. Here, take a look at these.'

The Prof handed me two large photographs. The first showed a number of British officers accompanied by some German counterparts, the latter distinguished by their pickelhaube helmets adorned with spikes and eagles. The second showed a jolly trio comprising a British Army major linked arm in arm with two Germans.

'These are two of the official photographs of our observers at the German Army's manoeuvres in 1906. In the foreground of the first photograph are Winston Churchill, General Hamilton and Lord Lonsdale. God knows what Churchill's doing there as he was at the Colonial Office back then. At one stage the Security Service were concerned about Lonsdale being a German agent as he'd hosted the Kaiser a couple of times to hunt on his estate and was even given a German knighthood. However, he's now formed a Pals battalion and is heavily involved in recruiting men and horses for the war effort and is in the clear. Note in the background that there are some other British officers. If you look closely, you'll see that one of those is Church-Fenton, then a mere major.'

'Oh yes, so it is,' I agreed, after peering at the photograph.

'As you can see from the second print, it's the same major, that is Church-Fenton, with two German friends. The one on the right has been identified as *Oberleutnant* Kurt von Holstein. He was an officer in the *Gardes du Corps*, the Kaiser's personal bodyguard despite the French name, and he was accused of homosexuality back in 1907. He committed suicide.'

'That makes you wonder exactly how friendly Church-Fenton was with his German hosts given his record, doesn't it?' I said. 'Who's the other fellow?'

'The other one with the crossed duelling scars on his face is Maximillian von Drexler. We believe that von Drexler is now quite high up in *Abteilung IIIb,* that's German Military Intelligence. He's based at a place called Wesel and works for my equivalent, a Lieutenant Colonel Walter Nicolai. We thought the *Abteilung,* and their predecessors, *Sektion IIIb,* focused mostly on France and Russia, with German Naval Intelligence looking after Britain. That might have been a ruse if you follow von Drexler's interactions with British contacts.'

'What do you mean, Prof?'

'Apparently von Drexler visited Church-Fenton in England when the latter was on the strength of the Camberley Staff College. That was where Church-Fenton met General Wilson, who was the then college commandant. Wilson later took Church-Fenton with him to the negotiations with the French on the BEF's deployment planning back before the war. Church-Fenton would have spent a lot of time in Paris at the time.'

'It sounds like the Brigadier had German connections after all,' I said looking at the photograph of the three apparent comrades-in-arms. In the picture, von Drexler had a wide smile with crows-feet creases around shining eyes. He sported a thin moustache with waxed tips and had two linear scars on his left cheek in a St Andrew's cross pattern. The scars had the effect of pulling his lips up and his smile was slightly lopsided. It added a sinister dimension to his otherwise happy appearance.

'There's more,' said the Prof. 'Several years before these photographs were taken, a young Church-Fenton was a subaltern in the British contingent that relieved Peking during the Boxer Rebellion in China in 1900. During that campaign he was acting as our liaison with the German leadership of the eight allied nations' occupation force. We were friends with Germany then. It turns out that von Drexler was also on that mission.'

'So, the Brigadier's links to Germany go much further back than his apparent Francophile leanings?'

'It would appear so. Then, as if to emphasise that truth is stranger than fiction, I checked Church-Fenton's record as an infantry brigadier. You'll remember that MacLeod was told that the Brigadier wasted his men's lives? Well, even allowing for him having been in staff posts for some time with little active service, the Brigadier's record was indeed poor when he did have a field command. The casualty rates from his units are very high, even for this war, and the ground gained by his infantry brigades was minimal. With all the other circumstantial evidence, you do have to wonder if some of his battle orders were designed to be more positive for the Huns than for us. It's all in here.'

The Prof handed me a report of all the actions that Church-Fenton had commanded in the field along with their casualty statistics. It was indeed sorry reading, but one particular action stood out to me, the date and location resonating in my brain. I refocused.

'I've also found out that our Brigadier may have another German connection,' I told the Prof after my scan of the report. 'I've found out where the photographic plates are stored that Church-Fenton used for his blackmailing activities. I've also found a German-speaking fellow who appears to have a senior role in the storage building. Furthermore, this suspect has a German accomplice, and I witnessed them meeting to discuss military matters and no doubt pass on secrets. They've fooled the people who took the photographs in an all-male brothel that it's a French government operation. It therefore seems that Church-Fenton had another German connection, but in Paris, since, as corroborating evidence, I have a witness who saw the Brigadier visit the German spy at the latter's office.'

'Yes, well it does make one wonder, and the proposition does seem to be getting tighter,' said the Prof.

'If the Brigadier was an enemy spy after all, he and the Germans must have communicated somehow. Perhaps I'd better go and take a look at his old room and effects again to see if there's anything I've missed. I was going into Montreuil anyway.'

CHAPTER 40

After lunch, I had Hodgson drive McIlhenny and me over to the RAMC headquarters where Villiers had set up another appointment with Brigadier Poulson, the ADMS and brothel expert.

'What can I do for you now, young man?' wheezed Poulson, before taking a puff on his Black Cat. If anything, the ADMS looked even less healthy that during my last visit.

'I'd like to ask you how prevalent you think homosexuality is in the Army, sir,' I said in reply.

'That again? Hmm, well, I expect it's about the same as it is in society in general,' replied the ADMS.

'Yes, sir, but that's something I'm not sure about. How prevalent is that?'

'Well, it starts at the top,' he countered.

'The top?' I croaked, alarmed that the ADMS somehow knew the Prince's secret.

'Kitchener!'

'Lord Kitchener?' I exclaimed.

'Do you know of any other Kitcheners?'

'But he's "Kitchener of Khartoum" for God's sake. Hero of the Sudan and the Boer War. I mean, he's the man on the recruiting poster. "Your country needs you!" and all that. He's our Minister for War, sir!'

'What difference does that make? It's been rumoured in the Army for years that he's a closet homosexual. He's never married. They say he developed a taste for buggery when he was in Egypt and his acolytes were known as "Kitch's Band of Boys". His constant companion for the last nine years is a young Captain Fitzgerald, twenty-five years his junior.'

'Surely he's just the Field Marshal's aide-de-camp?'

'Camp may be the operative word. Apparently, they like flower-arranging and collect porcelain. That's a bit effeminate, wouldn't you say?'

'But most of the gardeners who exhibit at flower shows at church fetes I've been to are men. I'm sure they can't all be effeminate. My uncle collects fine china from his time in the Orient and I'm sure he isn't queer in any way. He's got three daughters. Not every unmarried man is a homosexual, surely? I must say, sir, as a lawyer, this evidence is all very circumstantial. If what you say is true, why has he not been court-martialled?'

'For the very reasons you mentioned, Captain. He's "Kitchener of Khartoum". The government can't let the personal peccadilloes of a great leader like him get in the way of the National Interest.'

'I'm not sure there's a case to be made in law anyway from what you say, sir. I knew several effeminate students at university and they were great ladies' men. Girls seemed to find them more sensitive and understanding than some of the sporty chauvinists. They were always in demand, and at least two of them are married now.'

'Yes, well, you may be right. Nevertheless, we keep an eye on effeminate types like the concert-party drag artistes. I mean people like Bella Epoch. Did you see her – I mean him – at *The Follies* here in Montreuil? Quite ravishing! I could almost fancy him myself.' The image of a portly, naked ADMS frolicking with Bella Epoch suddenly filled my mind and I thought that this would be my next nightmare. 'Still, we won't pursue any action against him and his fellow female impersonators. They're very popular with the troops, and so it would be bad for morale. We also watch out for sensitive types, poets and the like.'

'Poets?' I said, flabbergasted. 'These seem to be a lot of ill-informed prejudices, sir, if you don't mind me saying. However, to return to my original question, sir, how prevalent is homosexuality in the Army?'

'Well, we've had one or two cases in the higher ranks. For instance, a fellow brigadier committed suicide just last Wednesday. The note he left behind suggested he might have been that way inclined.'

'Yes, I heard about that,' I said, my mind filled with guilt that I may have driven the poor man to his death.

'In general terms, in the cases we've had, officers prefer officers, and privates prefer privates or at least other men's privates, if you get my drift,' chortled the ADMS. 'As you know, the punishment for homosexuality is imprisonment and then cashiering for officers. After Oscar Wilde's well-publicised trial and the damage to his reputation, we suspect many have gone to ground. There must be many celibate homosexuals in our ranks.

'Others, however, have been deliberately overt. There have been a number of cases of soldiers dressing in women's clothing when home on leave and getting themselves arrested to avoid coming back over to France and a tour in the trenches. Then we've had a few cases of subterfuge where men have made sure they were caught in indecent acts with other men in barracks or billets so they could avoid duty at the front. They'd rather spend time safely in the glasshouse than on the battlefield and their reputation be damned.

'All this is why, when you were last here, Captain, asking about brothels and those catering for homosexuals, I wasn't that concerned. I'm more worried if such men deliberately get discovered buggering on military premises than what they get up to in private in a bordello. We need every fit man we can get for the fight and it's better these chaps practise their sodomy out of sight in brothels than in the barracks where they'll be caught and imprisoned. Prisoners can't fight.'

'Does that mean there have been a lot of courts martial for this offence, sir?'

'Not really. Despite what I've said, as far as I recall, we've had less than half a dozen cases of officers being charged and about a hundred other ranks. Many are quietly discharged using Paragraph 392 of King's Regulations as being unfit for duty. Although it's normally used for the mentally and physically unfit, Para 392 is also used by many units to weed out homosexuals on the quiet.

'However, as I keep saying, at the end of the day we need men at the front and so, if they're not disruptive to the good of morale of a unit, a blind eye is often turned rather than deprive the ranks of fighting soldiers.'

I thought that this is exactly what Sergeant Hunter had practised with Baird and Livingstone in my own platoon and that I'd unwittingly gone along with it.

'Thank you for your time, Brigadier. As I told you last time, I'm investigating whether officers entertaining themselves at brothels are potential blackmail victims. The scope has been widened to concerns that homosexual officers may divulge secrets and so on to their blackmailer rather than face imprisonment, dismissal, and a stain on their reputation.'

'I suppose it's a possibility. While we often turn a blind eye as I've said, if something incriminating becomes public with solid evidence it would be very difficult not to prosecute and dismiss such officers.'

I left the ADMS as he lit yet another cigarette to add to the pollution in his smoke-filled office.

CHAPTER 41

I next had Hodgson drive us over to Church-Fenton's former billet once more. As the Lanchester's top was down, I was glad of the fresh air after the ADMS's office. McIlhenny and I went in to look for Leeming. He was still there, awaiting reassignment, although the Brigadier's room had been taken by a new officer. The room's occupant was out, so I ordered Leeming to allow McIlhenny to search the place once more, but it was to no avail and we found nothing new. After our failed search, I sought out the Brigadier's former batman.

'Where are all the Brigadier's effects?' I asked Leeming. 'Have they gone back to England yet?'

'No, sir, they're down in the basement. I'm still waiting for someone in the Pay Corps to give me the address of where to send them and confirm if it's his aunt or whoever. I wish they'd hurry up. I'm still getting the Brigadier's mail, and this arrived for him this morning. I think it's from the auntie, and at least there's a sender's address on it that I've copied. I hope she's been told about his death before I deluge her with his things, if it is her who's to get them.'

Leeming handed over a wrapped, thin parcel approximately twelve inches square addressed to the Brigadier and with a sender's name and address on the back. It appeared to be from a Winifrid Church-Fenton in Eastbourne in Sussex. I decided to unwrap it. The parcel's brown paper hid a second inner layer, which revealed that the package had in fact been redirected from England to France and was originally sent from Holland to Miss Church-Fenton. Inside the Dutch wrapping was a box and I opened it and found a set of four Deutsche Grammophon records covering Beethoven's *Fifth Symphony*.

'Huh,' grunted Leeming. 'I don't know why she keeps sending the Brigadier these recordings. He hardly ever used that gramophone of his. I know that several other officers suggested he bring it to the mess and share his records with his fellows, but he was dead against that. Got quite shirty, he did, when anyone suggested it, even if he didn't play them much himself. Even when he did play them, he kept the volume down so low I'm surprised he could hear it.'

'Thank you, Leeming, we'll put this with the other material,' I said.

We left Leeming and went down into the basement to look through the Brigadier's packing cases and trunks to see if we'd missed anything in our last search.

'Wind up the Brigadier's gramophone, please, McIlhenny. We might as well enjoy some music while we work.'

After McIlhenny had done the necessary, I went to put one of the Beethoven discs on to the turntable and, as I extracted the record in its paper sleeve from the box, I noticed that the packet still had the price label on it. I was surprised that it wasn't in Dutch guilders, but was in marks, suggesting a German origin. *That's odd* I thought. I then gingerly placed the machine's needle on to the record and the distinctive notes of the symphony's opening bars blared out from the horn amplifier on top of the gramophone.

'It's not exactly a good tune to sing along to, is it, sur?' was McIlhenny's opinion of the orchestral masterpiece.

'True,' I agreed. 'Pity it's not *The Choral*, then we could have joined in at the end.'

McIlhenny shook his head; my joke being lost on him. We continued to rummage through the Brigadier's belongings. I found a flat rounded dark-green opaque bottle labelled *Vieil Armagnac*. I vaguely remembered Leeming mentioning the Brigadier sent brandy to his aunt back in England, and, as its wax seal around the cork was unbroken, I presumed this may have been the next present for the deceased's aged relative. Since the Brigadier wasn't going to drink it now, and the aunt wouldn't be expecting anything from a dead nephew, somewhat guiltily I decided to take it back to share with the Prof and Villiers.

'What's a grown man doin' with one of these?' McIlhenny asked me, pulling a teddy bear out of one of the trunks.

I took the soft toy from him. I was already a youth when teddy bears became popular after the turn of the century, but I'd since bought one for Marjory, my niece. As I looked at the light brown toy covered in mohair fur with big metal eyes and a cheeky sewn grin, I was reminded of her delight upon receiving the gift. Then, I remembered the bear connection to Church-Fenton. Perhaps it was the Brigadier's lucky mascot and why he'd picked his pseudonym of *Nounours* for the Marigny? It had a metal button in its ear with the word *Steiff* on it. From my childhood days in Duisburg I knew that Steiff were famous German toy manufacturers. When I turned the bear over, I noticed that some of the stitching on a back seam was different from the rest, as if the toy had been repaired. As I squeezed the bear, I felt something hard inside.

'I think there's something in here,' I said to McIlhenny. 'Can you open it up and look inside? I think we need to do our own autopsy. Cut along the stitches, though, and don't damage it.'

I passed the teddy bear back to McIlhenny who took out his cut-throat razor and sliced along the seam I'd indicated. A letter wrapped round a bronze medal was soon produced from amongst the stuffing.

The medal was on a multi-coloured ribbon and the obverse side depicted a crowned eagle vanquishing a dragon, while the reverse had the Kaiser's Imperial cypher above the word "China" and the dates 1900-1901. I presumed it was a German campaign medal for the Boxer Rebellion. The letter was written in German, dated 1907, and said:

Dear Braunbär,

Kurt would have wanted you to have this to remind you of your time with him in China. They were good times. However, I will never forget discovering last year while we were on manoeuvres that the two of you were lovers. It is a pity you corrupted him. While it is sad that he took his own life, perhaps it is for the best. However, you must carry on for the glory of the Fatherland, because if you do not, your secret life will be revealed.
Greif.

As I was trying to understand the note's implications, the first movement of Beethoven's *Fifth* ended. I got up to turn the record over as the needle clicked in the subsequent silence, when suddenly the gramophone erupted into speech through a gruff voice in German.

'Hello *Braunbär*, Greif here. We have not heard from you in some time. As before, make sure you do everything you can to stop the British going on the offensive until we finish off the French at Verdun. If that is not possible, then relay the date of the British attack as soon as you find out. Remember, if you do not deliver, we know what sort of creature you really are, and we know who to tell. Blackmail is a dirty game, but so is war.'

CHAPTER 42

I sat down, stunned. The last sentence about *erpressung*, German for blackmail, certainly struck a chord, and one out of tune with Beethoven's soaring music.

'What was all that about, sur?' asked McIlhenny. 'It sounded like a Jerry givin' orders.'

'That's exactly what it was, McIlhenny. Now quickly, find all the other recordings in the Brigadier's collection. We need to play them one by one to find out if there are any more hidden messages.'

For the next two hours we worked our way through the pile of records. About every third recording had a short voice message inserted into the disc after the musical piece appeared to end. If you weren't listening out for them, you would almost certainly have missed the message, thinking the recording had finished. I could understand now why the Brigadier hadn't wanted to share these with the mess. The messages were all from the Greif and addressed to Braunbär or Brown Bear, continuing Church-Fenton's themed nickname from his school years. I wondered if the messages would reveal if the Germans were using the Marigny's photographs to blackmail British officers into giving up secret information or if they knew about the Prince. At the end of the two hours, I had my answer.

I got McIlhenny to pack up all the records into a box and carry it and the gramophone up to the Lanchester, while I stuffed the bear and its contents, plus the bottle of Armagnac, into my briefcase. As we left, Leeming looked on disapprovingly once more.

'I thought you said, sir, that you weren't planning to remove any more of the Brigadier's effects?' he said in an accusing tone.

'Yes, well, I've changed my mind. Goodbye, Private Leeming.'

As I went out of the door, I heard McIlhenny growl at the other batman, 'Ye better shut yer face pal, or Ah'll rearrange it for ye.'

*

Once back at the chateau, I sent Hodgson and McIlhenny to pick up George Cook from Étaples. I then had a quick look in the chateau's library, which still contained the French owner's books from before the war. Later, ensconced once more in the Prof's study with the gramophone and records, I let my CO hear a message to Braunbär from the Greif.

'Bloody hell!' said the Prof. He rarely swore, so this was a strong reaction indeed. He was quite agitated by the message although I knew he didn't speak German.

'It seems your suspicions were correct, Prof,' I told him after we had listened to a message. 'It appears that the gramophone records were made in Germany, posted in neutral Holland to an English address, and then rewrapped and forwarded on to the Brigadier here. Our Security Service mail interception people probably thought they were just Dutch records going to some old lady. Then the Army Postal Section would just see a British parcel addressed to a senior officer and not know that its contents had originally been purchased in Germany, recorded over, and then sent via the neutral Dutch postal service.'

'Do we have any idea who this code-named Greif is?'

'I've checked in the library here at the chateau. I found an old book on the coats of arms of the aristocracy of Europe. I suppose it's the kind of book that this chateau's owner used to keep tabs on other aristocrats – it's a sort of Continental *Debrett's Peerage*. The von Drexler family is in there and their heraldic crest contains a griffin. That's *greif* in German. It seems that Church-Fenton's contact from the Boxer Rebellion and the 1906 war games was still in the picture right up until the Brigadier died.'

'Do we know if he passed on to the Germans that he had embarrassing evidence of our Prince's indiscretion?'

I told the Prof the gist of the various messages I'd translated from the recordings.

'And there's this,' I said, producing the teddy bear and the contents from its innards, which I told the Prof were also sent to the Brigadier from the Greif. 'I presume that the Kurt referred to in the note is the Kurt von Holstein you mentioned earlier and who was in the photographs. It seems they were all friends at one stage when together in China. That seems to have changed when von Drexler found out the others were queer. He blamed Church-Fenton for seducing von Holstein. Von Drexler's tone now is very much of someone in control of Church-Fenton through blackmail about his homosexuality.'

'Well, it appears our Brigadier Church-Fenton had many secrets. A practising homosexual, a German spy, and a blackmailer – all in one! That's quite a charge sheet. It's rather ironic that Lord Ross was correct after all. The more I hear about him, the more I think our Establishment friends did the right thing with respect to Church-Fenton, even if it was for the wrong reasons.'

'Exactly! And now we know how the Germans sent orders to the Brigadier. However, I still haven't been unable to ascertain how he communicated back to his spymaster.'

'Nevertheless, I think, Jamie, that you'd better carry on with your plan regarding the warehouse with the negatives in it, and then you should interview this other German agent who works there. He may be able to tell us more about this whole episode,' said the Prof. 'Now, in my opinion the sun is over the yardarm. Time for a dram.'

'Why don't we try the Brigadier's Armagnac for a change?' I suggested, handing the Prof the dark bottle. 'This was meant as a present for his aunt in England, but she'll never know.'

While the Prof attended to the drinks, I went and changed the record on the gramophone to one I knew was uninterrupted by the Greif. The Prof broke the wax seal on the brandy bottle, pulled the cork, and tried to pour out the expected amber liquid, but nothing happened.

'I think there's something in here!' exclaimed the Prof, staring into the mouth of the bottle. He stuck a finger inside the neck and pulled out a string which was soon followed by a tiny parcel wrapped in oilcloth. 'Well, well, what have we here?'

The Prof unwrapped the waterproof covering to reveal a small metal cylinder with a screw-top. He opened it, and extracted a piece of paper. 'Hmm, it's in code, I'm afraid,' said the Prof as he handed the paper over to me for a look.

'Numbers in groups of five. Doesn't mean anything to me,' I told him.

'Probably a book code,' suggested the Prof. 'We can send it to our cryptanalysts to see if they can work it out. Did the Brigadier have any books in his belongings?'

'Yes, there were a few. I'll send McIlhenny over to retrieve them. So, this is the Brigadier's last but unsent message. He must have sent his messages in brandy bottles to his aunt. The bottles would be easy to reseal with their waxed tops. I recall the package with the records in it came from a lady by the name of Winifrid Church-Fenton, but I don't recall the address other than it was in Eastbourne. I believe the Brigadier's batman, Leeming, might know it. McIlhenny can find that out, too. I wonder if it was a real aunt? I dare say she sent the messages on to German Intelligence, probably via Holland, and they sent her recordings in return. We need to find out who she is and get Special Branch to round her up.'

'Waste not, want not,' said the Prof, who returned to pouring two generous brandies.

'I'm not sure I know the difference between cognac and Armagnac,' I said as I sipped the vintage brandy appreciatively. 'But I think I like both.'

'Me neither,' said the Prof. 'I daresay a Frenchman would know in the same way I can tell an Islay malt from a Speyside whisky. I must say this is damned good though. You know, Jamie, you've got to hand it to Church-Fenton, he hid all this evidence you've chanced on today in plain sight. The records, the toy bear, and the brandy were presumably all on open view in his billet. He also hid his homosexuality from his superiors for decades. He really was a master of concealment.'

'Yes, pity he wasn't as good at soldiering.'

We lapsed into silence for a while and listened as one of Bach's Brandenburg Concertos filled the room with its Baroque musical grandeur.

'It's a great pity so many of these wonderful recordings are ruined by the Greif's messages to Church-Fenton,' I sighed. 'Such a shame that a country that can produce such wonderful musicians as Beethoven and Bach can also produce some real stinkers like those brutes who ravaged Belgium. I still have a hard time thinking that any of my old school friends in Duisburg could have behaved so badly.'

'That reminds me,' said the Prof. 'Don't be fooled by a little civility. I also did some inquiring around Lord Wokingham. He's from a pretty standard privileged background of Eton, Sandhurst, and the Guards, before a career governing the colonial masses beckoned. Then, after spending some time as a Whitehall Mandarin, he was taken on by the King. He's one of what they apparently call the King's "Three Musketeers" of Keppel, the Master of the Household, Stamfordham, the Private Secretary, and Wokingham, the Special Adviser – although he's also known as the "Grand Vizier". From what I understand, amongst other things, he sorts out any problems the royals may have in terms of scandals and publicity. Lord Wokingham, my sources tell me, is not a man to be trifled with, so make sure you get the answers he wants, Jamie, and stay on his good side.'

*

Later that evening, Hodgson duly arrived back with his passengers and the three of them reported to me.

'Where have you been?' I demanded. 'I know the roads around Étaples are packed but you've been ages.'

'Och, well, there was this ASC quartermaster bloke who refused to fill up the car,' explained McIlhenny. 'He threatened to impound it as he wouldn't believe we were out in such a smart vehicle without an officer. He wanted to get the polis involved and ye know, sur, how Ah hate fuckin' Red Caps, beggin' yer pardon. It was all the boys here could do to stop me givin' him a Glesga Kiss.'

'So, what did you do? Can I expect a call from the Military Police at Étaples?'

'It's all fixed, sur. The Sarge here sorted him out.'

I looked over at George and wondered exactly how he'd sorted it and whether it had been legal.

'It's all right, sir. I just showed him what we had in the boot, warned him that it was a bit unstable, and that if he didn't give us what we wanted quickly, then the longer we stayed there, the more at risk he and his precious fuel dump would be of being blown to kingdom come. He let us fill up the car and even gave me a few extra cans of petrol, too. He was glad to see us go.'

'What exactly did you show him?'

George opened the boot lid to reveal several cans marked "Ammonal".

'What's ammonal? Is that your explosive?'

'Aye, sir, it's what we use to blow up mines below the German lines before the infantry go over the top.'

'And is it unstable?' I asked, suddenly worried about the journey planned to Paris the next day.

'Och, it's fine, sir. Bob's the best driver I've met and we'll be fine. Mind you, I think I'd better sleep in the car tonight to be sure no stupid sentry or scrounger decides to have a look in the boot.'

'I'm afraid I've got one more task for you two this evening,' I told McIlhenny and Hodgson. I ordered them to go over once more to Church-Fenton's billet and collect all his books from the basement, and find out from Leeming the Brigadier's aunt's address in England.

As I sipped my nightcap that night, my mind kept returning to the German-speaking man-in-the-hat and I wondered exactly what he and the Brigadier had got up to.

Friday,
26th May 1916

CHAPTER 43

I shook myself awake the next day. When I thought about what we were about to embark on in Paris, I had to admit to feeling a thrill of excitement. I had McIlhenny ensure the others were ready to leave after breakfast and soon our expanded four-man team took the long drive back to Paris where we arrived late on the Friday evening.

Villiers had arranged for us all to stay in a small hotel in the Tenth Arrondissement, just north of our target. I had decided that McIlhenny and I had been too conspicuous during our last burglary and had therefore ordered the men to change into rough dark-blue denim typical workmen's clothes. I had to admit, though, that it would be difficult to explain, if we were stopped by the Gendarmes, why a party of Tommies were dressed in mufti as French manual workers, while driving around in a large British staff car filled with explosives.

*

We set off in the Lanchester for Rue de Portfoin after ten o'clock. Luckily, we arrived at the end of the service alley undetected. George, McIlhenny and I proceeded to blacken our faces with boot polish, which, with our blue denims, made us very difficult to see in the darkened alley or through the windows when inside the building we were about to enter. We all put on gloves and balaclavas to complete our ensembles.

'What do you think?' I asked Hodgson.

'Like a troop of blackened minstrels, guv. You can give the guards a chorus of "Dixie" to distract them if you meet them,' joked Hodgson, making us all laugh and relieving the tension in the group.

We got out of the car and I looked them over. George with a blackened face looked exactly like he would after a normal work shift, emerging from the cage of a pit in Motherwell covered in coal dust. At the coalmine, George was the leading underground shot-blaster; a skill-set that explained his NCO status in a Royal Engineers' tunnelling company. It was for those exact skills that I had recruited him.

McIlhenny in camouflage looked like the professional cat burglar he was, all set for his usual night-time antics.

I caught a glimpse of myself in the Lanchester's small wing mirror and decided I looked the least like my normal pre-war persona. Not many advocates blacked up to appear in court as far as I was aware, and not many soldiers went on a raid carrying a walking stick and a briefcase either. At least my eyepatch was now indistinguishable from the rest of my face. We left Hodgson on watch and set off down the dark alley.

As per last time, McIlhenny picked the lock at the back of the building where the photographic plates were stored. The batman silently crept in with cosh in hand to try to locate the two guards. George followed behind. I waited outside by the door. After some scuffling noises, George brought one of the guards out. He was an old soldier in his late forties who was probably grateful for what he thought was a safe assignment in the centre of Paris, but who was now unconscious after being coshed by McIlhenny. While George went back in to help McIlhenny with the second guard, I tied up the first with the thin rope we'd brought along specifically for that purpose. I then gagged the man with a length of pillowcase torn from our hotel bed linen. After a resounding thump emanating from inside the property, the second guard, a younger bespectacled man, was brought out in a similar comatose state to the first and processed by me in the same way.

The three of us entered the building and went down directly to the basement. I risked putting the lights on in the file room. McIlhenny quickly picked the lock on each filing cabinet, taking only seconds to do the last one.

'Practice makes perfect as they say,' said McIlhenny, before I sent him back upstairs to watch the front of the building to balance Hodgson on sentry duty at the rear.

George returned to the vehicle and collected the cans of explosive from the boot. The Sergeant set to work with enough ammonal to ensure that every photographic glass negative plate in the room would be destroyed, despite being packed together and in metal filing cabinets. Meanwhile, I searched for my main prize. Within each cabinet there seemed to be up to four plates per file, each file labelled with the subject's name, rank, and unit if known, plus the brothel frequented. Some had all four fields filled in, others only had question marks for the relevant military information. The files in the cabinets were individually bulky, I was relieved to see, and so the number of officers contained in the files was far less than I'd thought when I first saw the banks of cabinets. Higher-ranking officers seemed to patronise *maisons close* such as Le Chabanais and La Fleur Blanche. I imagined these must be classier and more expensive establishments.

One wall had a set of cabinets separate from the rest and marked for the *maisons tolérées,* including, it turned out, patrons of the Marigny. I was perversely pleased to see that the Anzacs had a whole drawer to themselves. Another drawer was marked "General Staff" and this was quite full, while others were half empty.

I caught George looking at one of the plates from the Marigny, a look of consternation on his face, so I told him, 'Put it away, George, and forget you ever saw what you just looked at.'

'You don't get that sort of behaviour in the pit showers,' said George before obeying my order.

Within the other regiments I found a drawer marked Fusiliers. I opened the drawer to find fusiliers of the Royal, Northumberland, Lancashire, Welsh and Scots varieties inside. The 10th Royal Fusiliers was the cover unit for many in the Intelligence Corps. I knew, however, that there was also a true 10th Battalion, nicknamed the "Stockbrokers" and filled with brave volunteers from the London Stock Exchange. It was a sort of posh Pals battalion. A name under "V" caught my eye and I pulled the file and put it in my briefcase.

I thought I'd found the files I'd been searching for when at last I came upon a drawer marked "Brigade of Guards" since the Prince was a Grenadier. However, his file wasn't in it, although one name stood out for me in my quick perusal of the rest of the drawer's contents and I pulled a plate out and placed that in my briefcase, too.

I felt my frustration mounting, but then noticed a small safe in a corner of the room. This was surely the most obvious place to keep the most contentious negatives. I went and got McIlhenny to come down and have a look at it.

'It's an old lock and key safe. Looks last century. Made by somebody called Fichet. Ah've never heard of them, but Ah'll give it a go.'

'Right, as fast as you can, McIlhenny, we can't stay here all night. If you can't open it, we'll have to try and take it with us.'

Fifteen minutes later the safe door swung back, and I quickly reviewed the few plates it contained. We'd finally hit the bullseye, and I loaded the safe's contents into my briefcase.

'Excellent work, McIlhenny!' I told my safecracker, before sending him back upstairs to his post. 'We still need to destroy this lot, though, George. Half the Empire's officer corps seems to have visited some sort of brothel in Paris. There's a German spy in this place, and he can't be allowed to blackmail the British Army through these, so go to it.'

George soon announced himself satisfied by the disposition of his explosives. He placed gun cotton primers in the ammonal cans with detonators in each, and ran leads from them out of the room and up the stairs. He returned with several khaki-coloured containers marked "War Department, Highly Flammable, 2 Gallons" and proceeded to slosh the petrol over the open drawers of the filing cabinets. The fumes were terrible, and George and I quickly left the basement, me with my briefcase and George with his empty cans. On the way out, George ran into each room and opened the valve on the gas heaters he'd noticed earlier. Soon the smell of coal gas was mixing with that of petrol and I was terrified the whole lot would blow before we'd exited. Again, I'd had no time to inspect the upstairs offices.

Outside in the cool, clean air, I watched McIlhenny and George drag the two guards well away from the planned explosion. We had previously confirmed on a drive-by earlier in the evening that the buildings either side of the target were empty that night, or at least were not showing any lights. It was the best I could do to minimise collateral damage.

George put the final touches to his task and wired up the cables from the detonators in the basement into a firing box at the end of the alley beside the waiting Lanchester. The firing box was labelled *Siemens Gluzundapparat* and had been captured by George in one of his ferocious fights with the enemy deep below the conventional trench warfare lines. It would certainly help confuse French investigators.

'All done,' said George finally, his white teeth grinning within his blackened face.

We all piled into the staff car with the firing box and Hodgson started the vehicle.

'Do you want to do the honours, Mister Brown?' asked George.

I felt a sudden rush of childish pleasure at the thought of setting off a large bang. I turned the T-shaped handle of the firing box with my right hand and threw the apparatus out of the car. Almost simultaneously to the Lanchester accelerating away came a huge flash and very loud bang, followed by the sound of crashing rubble as the targeted property disappeared in a cloud of smoke and brick dust before being engulfed in flames.

'Where to now, guv?'

'Let's go and get this boot polish off our faces and then I've a bottle of good malt whisky in my valise at the hotel that I think we deserve to share tonight.'

Saturday,
27th May 1916

CHAPTER 44

Early on the Saturday morning, back in uniform, tired after a few drams too many, and with pink faces from scrubbing off boot polish, we drove back to the scene of the previous night's sabotage. We couldn't drive down the Rue de Portfoin to view our handiwork up close as it was closed by a Gendarmes' rope cordon. Our target had seemingly disappeared, and its former site now looked like a missing tooth in a row of dentures.

I used field glasses to get a closer view from the end of the street. The two guards from the night before were off to one side being interrogated by a senior officer. While both would undoubtedly be glad to be alive, having seen the site, they'd have the embarrassment of explaining why they'd failed in their duties. From his angry gesticulations, this seemed to be the point the officer was making to them.

A squad of *pompiers* were hosing down the building's remains from a pre-war fire engine, while what looked like French Army engineers were poking around the edges of the rubble under the command of a young officer. The firing apparatus was lying at the officer's feet.

A red taxi appeared at the far end of the street. Out of it stepped the small man in the large homburg hat that we had previously followed. He was allowed inside the cordon after showing one of the gendarmes some sort of pass.

The man-in-the-hat was saluted by the officer haranguing the two guards. The guards then seemed to take it in turns to make statements to him. Next, an elderly pompier, who was presumably the local fire chief, gave his viewpoint to the new arrival. Finally, the engineering officer gave an opinion, which included showing the man-in-the-hat the German-made evidence.

To my surprise, a soldier, drenched from the firemen's efforts, appeared out of the wrecked building from a ladder which must have gone down a hole into what was formerly the basement. The individual shook his head and spread his hands. The pompiers were ordered to stop pumping and the man disappeared back into the hole taking the end of a rope with him. A few minutes later the engineers were hauling out of the ground a small safe with its door almost hanging off. The man-in-the-hat knelt down and peered into the safe as if he was expecting its contents to still be inside, despite all the evidence to the contrary. He stood back up, hands on hips and then slowly looked around him.

'Well, well,' I said to the others, 'Our man-in-the-hat from Rue de Castiglione seems to be confirmed as the boss around here. A great position for a German spy! Now, he really is a man we need to talk to.'

Just as I finished speaking, our suspect appeared to spot the Lanchester at the end of the street. He frowned and then stared straight at us.

'Right, let's get out of here,' I ordered and Hodgson duly obliged.

'Where to now, guv?' he asked as we drove off at speed.

'We need to go to the Left Bank. You can drop me off at a café near Boulevard Saint-Germain, and then find yourselves a cup of tea or coffee, while I speak to someone.'

CHAPTER 45

After being deposited at Le Bonaparte Café, I identified the man I was looking for sitting at a table outside the establishment. My contact was an elderly gentleman in a brown suit with matching bowler hat and the ruddy complexion of a heavy drinker above a white toothbrush moustache. I knew from Albert's description that this was former Police Inspector Henri Bloch. He was a "former" inspector as he'd been expelled from the police for taking bribes. Albert claimed the inspector knew everything that I would need to know about the capital's gangs and criminal organisations. After our preliminary mutual identification and me handing over an envelope full of francs, we started a conversation in French.

'You come highly recommended by Albert, Monsieur Bloch,' I said, to get things going.

'I'd be careful of anything that Breton upstart recommends, *monsieur*, even me,' said Bloch, with a smile. 'What do you know about your contact at the Marigny?'

'Very little, I have to confess.'

'Well, his full name is Albert le Cuziat. He came to Paris as a footman to a Polish prince and ended up wheedling his way into high society as a pimp for well-to-do pederasts and sodomites. He set up the Marigny with some money from the likes of Proust and other so-called liberal socialites. In exchange, it's said he lets his sponsors spy on his paying clients as they enjoy their young men in the steam baths, the bedrooms, or even in the dungeon they have for sadomasochists. It is rumoured that the Marigny is riddled with spy holes for voyeurs. Albert pays off the *Groupe des Homos* – they're the special police squad who occasionally raid such establishments. I wouldn't trust Albert as far as I could throw him.'

'Thanks for the warning. I'll certainly be careful in my dealings with Albert going forward, Monsieur Bloch, although I hope never to see him again. Now, what can you tell me about gangs called "Apaches"?'

'Ah, yes, Albert mentioned you wanted to know about the Apaches. Well, the Apaches first appeared at the turn of the century. They get their name from our press imagining that their savagery was similar to the Red Indians of the American Wild West. There are several gangs or tribes of Apaches, and the police have never really achieved full control over them. Each gang wears a distinctive outfit, almost like a uniform. Now they're full of deserters who should be in the trenches defending Paris instead of stealing and extorting money from its citizens. They have a reputation for fighting dirty and have all sorts of nasty tricks. Some so-called artistes have romanticised them, and even made a dance performance out of their fighting style. They are basically parasites on this city, my friend.'

'Are there any that are particularly into gambling or bookmaking at racecourses?' I asked, playing a hunch like a horse racing punter – ironic under the circumstances.

'Yes, of course. The Belleville Apaches are famous for that and run all sorts of illegal bookmakers at Longchamp and other racecourses.'

'And how would they treat someone who hadn't paid their gambling debts?'

'As a warning to others they would threaten his life and even kill him if he didn't pay up. Simple as that.'

'How would I get to meet the chief of the Belleville Apaches?'

'I'm not sure that would be wise, my friend. These are savage people and their leader is known locally as "The Terror". Belleville has a certain reputation for toughness in this city and their barricades were the last to be removed before the Commune was dissolved back in '71. If you go snooping into their business, they could kill you, soldier or not.'

'It's a risk I need to take. Where will I find them?'

Bloch gave me the address of a café in Belleville in the Twentieth Arrondissement in north-east Paris that acted as a front for the local gang.

'*Bonne chance*, my friend. You'll need it.'

I was picked up at the time I'd prearranged and settled in the back of the Lanchester beside George Cook.

'Where to now, guv?'

'We're off to a Wild West show to meet some Apaches,' I told them.

'Great,' said McIlhenny with enthusiasm. 'Ah once saw Buffalo Bill's Wild West Show in Glesga. Must have been about ten or twelve years ago. It was magic, so it was.'

'Well, this time you're going to be in the show, and you'd better be prepared for a fight. It's us British cowboys against some French Indians,' I warned them as we headed through the city to Belleville.

CHAPTER 46

I had Hodgson park the staff car a short distance from the aptly named Geronimo Café that was the headquarters of the Belleville gang, and told Hodgson to keep the engine running in case we needed to make a quick getaway. I briefed the other two and then sent McIlhenny round to the back of the property. I pushed open the door of the café with the considerable bulk of George behind me as an obvious bodyguard.

Silence fell on the establishment as we entered. I presumed they didn't get many British soldiers in their café. I went up to the bar and asked the man behind it in French if I could speak to the boss, "The Terror of Belleville" as I believed the chief was known. The barman seemed astonished at my brazen approach, but indicated we should wait while he went off into a back room via a door beside the bar. In the mirror behind the counter I watched the café's customers, while George had turned to survey the room's occupants directly. One or two were whispering to each other. They were rough-looking fellows, dressed exactly as Church-Fenton's batman had described them, and were by inference Apache foot soldiers.

The barman returned and bid the two of us enter the back room, before retreating and closing the door behind him. It was a gloomy, windowless room lit only by two feeble arc lamps and with another door in the wall behind a dark wooden desk. A large man with long greased-down black hair, his chin ravaged by smallpox craters, and with a badly-stitched scar on his left cheek, sat at the desk. After we'd entered the room to stand before him, we were grabbed from behind by strong arms and two bodyguards frisked us. One of the men removed my Webley revolver from its holster.

'We don't get many British Tommies around here,' said the seated man in French. 'How can we help our dear allies?'

'Are you the gentleman they call "The Terror", the leader of the local Apache gang?' I asked.

'I go by many names, my friend. All of them well deserved,' said the man with a terrible lopsided smile, which, if anything, made his face even more menacing.

'I need to ask you about this man,' I said, pulling out the desktop photograph of Church-Fenton and showing it to the gangster.

He glanced at the photograph, and then said, 'I don't have to tell you anything about anybody. Now, I suggest you leave before you wish you'd never left the trenches.'

'I'd like some answers first,' I insisted.

'Throw them out, but make sure they learn never to come back here,' he ordered his henchmen.

'Now, McIlhenny!' I yelled at the top of my voice and my batman burst into the room, having silently unlocked the back door.

The two bodyguards went for George and me. The one attacking me didn't seem to expect a cripple to produce a dagger from a walking stick and so was surprised to receive a series of short stabs that left him collapsed on the ground. The other tough, meanwhile, learned that he was not so tough after all. Even though he was an experienced street fighter, he had never engaged anyone like George who'd fought in vicious hand-to-hand combat in mine galleries deep under the front line. The two Apaches were soon felled. Unfortunately, the scuffle had not been completely silent, and I was worried that the noise would have alerted the men in the café.

I looked up to see the tables had been turned and that the gang leader was now looking slightly terrified due to the four-inch blade of a cut-throat razor that McIlhenny was holding against the criminal's neck. McIlhenny had nicked the Frenchman for effect and a dribble of blood was running down into the gangster's collar.

George disarmed the two groaning thugs and borrowed McIlhenny's cosh to give them each a sharp blow behind the ear to ensure they would not take any further part in the proceedings. As he was doing so, I locked the door to the bar.

'Now, Monsieur Terror, I ask you again to tell me how you know this man in the photograph, as I know for a fact that you do. If you don't answer my questions, my friend here will give you a scar across your throat to match the one on your face, only you'll not live to see it in the mirror. And by the way, I'm not worried about the police, as I suspect you'll not be sorely missed if you're found dead on your premises.'

'All right, I'll tell you all I know, which isn't much. He is a British general. I know him from a contact we have at the Jockey Club de Paris. Before the war he used to frequent the club and visited various racecourses around Paris. Longchamp, Auteuil, Chantilly, even as far as Le Touquet. He bet frequently, but he was a poor judge of horses. He lost a lot of money and, like all bad gamblers, he tried to win his way out of trouble. Instead he just dug himself into a deeper hole. My organisation was one of his bookmakers and he ended up owing us a lot of money. Our interest rates are very high for fools like him. We warned him that if he did not pay up, he would first be cut on the cheek, then have a hand amputated, and then his throat would be slashed. We could not be seen to be soft as we have a reputation to protect! Then one day he disappeared from France without settling his debts.'

'Yes, he was posted back to England, before the war,' I confirmed.

'Then, suddenly, out of the blue, a few months ago, he reappeared on the scene. He still owed us a fortune from before the war, and we do not forget uncollected debts. One of my men waiting to rob some rich people coming out of a hotel recognised your general, so my men followed our debtor. They found him up an alley with a young boy doing things that no man should be doing to other men. We pulled the boy away and gave the general a beating, and then my men brought your officer back here. He was told to pay his old debts or else we'd reveal his terrible habits to the British authorities. We let him know we'd kept the boy as a witness to his deeds and that we'd made the youth one of our gang. Your man was terrified by our blackmail and promised to get the money.

'However, to be sure he knew we were serious, we sent him a message by having his army servant run over and killed, and then letting the general know it was no accident. Sure enough, a few days later he paid off some of his debt, which by now, with accrued interest from the years before, and for the cost of our silence on his love of young boys, was several thousand francs. He assured us that he had a way of getting the rest of the money and started to pay us every time he came to Paris. He didn't turn up this week to pay us off, so we are out looking for him now at all his usual haunts.'

The man had used the word *chantage,* French for blackmail, in his confession and I added him to the long list of blackmailers in this investigation, a list that seemed to be getting longer by the day. I also added the poor predecessor of Leeming to the list of men killed due to the Brigadier's actions.

'Well, you'll not be getting any more money from this man, that's for sure. He's dead and buried now, so your goose that laid that golden egg is no more. In fact, it's cooked.'

By now there were shouts from the bar and fists banging on the door from the other room. 'Time to exit stage left,' I told my two men.

I ordered George to recover my Webley and give the gang chief a "wee tap" to ensure none of his tribe would follow us once they'd broken the bar door down. The three of us left via the back door of the café to find the Lanchester.

'Where to now, guv?'

'Let's head back across the Seine and find a quiet café off the beaten track. Now we need to plan a kidnapping.'

'It's all go, guv, and no mistake,' observed Hodgson as we headed out of Belleville.

'Aye, and, the cowboys beat the Indians, just like in the films,' said McIlhenny, a smile on his face, no doubt dreaming of Hollywood stardom.

'Just be glad we didn't get scalped,' I said in reply. 'I tend to agree with Private Leeming. The French could do with one or two of these toughs at Verdun.'

CHAPTER 47

Two hours later, I had Hodgson park the Lanchester on the Rue de Rivoli, just around the corner from the Rue de Castiglione, hoping the man-in-the-hat was a creature of habit. I told Hodgson to wait with the car and gave George and McIlhenny their instructions.

I took up a position at an outside table of the same café as before, just off Place Vendôme, appearing to read a copy of *Le Figaro*. Despite my limp, I was sure that I could keep up with the shorter pace of the smaller man-in-the-hat if the German spy appeared, but to be ready for a quick getaway, I paid for my coffee in advance. I'd decided to forego the pastis this time, as my tastebuds hadn't recovered from their last exposure to the aniseed-flavoured drink. The coffee was so expensive that I ignored the service charge, much to the annoyance of my waiter.

As if on cue, a red taxi duly deposited the man-in-the-hat at the corner of Place Vendôme and Rue de Castiglione, just along from my café. I got up quickly and followed the homburg as it proceeded down the road under the arcade of the street's buildings, past the expensive boutiques and cheaper tabacs, and into the entranceway of one of the apartments set above the street-level shops. I followed the man in through the door before it shut and found myself in a hallway with a wrought-iron staircase running round a lift shaft in its centre.

I called out, '*Monsieur!*'

The man-in-the-hat turned and seemed surprised that there was a British officer close behind him. As a result, he didn't see the pre-positioned McIlhenny step out of the shadows in the poorly-lit hallway and raise his cosh to deliver a blow to the side of the man's head. The victim fell like a sack of potatoes. George, emerging from the other side of the hallway, hoisted the slack body into the lift cage.

'Ah always wanted to be a lift operator. Ah used to love goin' into Goldbergs' in Candelriggs in Glesga and ridin' up and down in the lifts. What floor do ye want, sur? Haberdashery? Ironmongers? Gentlemen's outfitters?' joked McIlhenny as he shut the lift's concertina gate and took over the brass controls.

'Stop messing about and take us up to the floor you saw him visit before.'

'Aye, very good, sur.'

It was a short ride for the would-be lift operator. George pulled the man-in-the-hat out of the lift and propped him up against the wall beside the apartment door McIlhenny had indicated. Our victim was completely out of it.

'I think you might have been a wee bit heavy with the cosh there, Mac,' said George.

'Ah wasn't sure how much to give him, what with that big hat on his head.'

I rang the doorbell with my left hand, while in my right I held my revolver. The door was opened by an attractive blonde lady in her early thirties dressed in a Chinese-patterned silk dressing gown and holding a bottle of Guerlain's *Jicky* perfume in one hand, and a hairbrush in the other. She opened her mouth to scream when I put my pistol against her neck, but I managed to cut her off with my left hand over her mouth. I had to admit that close up she felt very soft and smelled delicious, and her lipstick was moist under my hand. I gestured her inside, quickly followed her, and was in turn followed by George carrying her lover and, finally, McIlhenny, carrying the man's homburg. The door was closed, and I asked the lady in French to show us into her parlour. We soon established that she spoke good English and that her name was Claudette.

'We don't plan to harm you, *mademoiselle*,' I told her. 'We just needed somewhere private to talk to your friend here.'

The friend in question was showing no signs of coming round, but was thankfully breathing quite regularly on the settee where George had placed him. The comatose victim was quite a small man with crinkly black hair, flecked with grey, and a droopy black moustache. There was a large mole on his right cheek. His dark suit and grey silk waistcoat were well tailored. Up close, I was now certain that I had seen the man somewhere before.

'Do you have any smelling salts, *mademoiselle*?'

'Yes, in my bathroom.'

'McIlhenny, go and fetch them with her. Then, tie this lady up in as gentlemanly a way as possible in her bedroom, making sure she can't scream and doesn't have a telephone in the room with her.'

I proceeded to empty our kidnap victim's pockets. I found a small MF-branded pocket pistol, an identity card holder, a pocketbook, some keys, a cigarette case, and a box of matches.

McIlhenny arrived back a few minutes later with a bottle of lurid-coloured crystals in a bottle labelled *Sal Volatile*.

'Did you tie her up?'

'Aye, it was easy, sur. Her bed's got all sorts of cleats and loops for tyin' people up with. Ah think she likes that bondage stuff. Or maybe the bloke here likes it? A Boy Scout could have a great time, practising his knots and havin' "how's your father" at the same time.'

'Thank you, McIlhenny, that's enough of that. You and the Sergeant can wait in the hall. The hall, mind, not the bedroom.'

I placed the smelling salts under the man-in-the-hat's nose and, after a few unconscious snorts, he soon came round, groaning and rubbing the side of his head where a golf ball-sized purple lump had appeared. I sat well back from the man and held his MF pistol in my hand, pointing it at the recovering victim.

'Can you hear me?' I asked the man in German.

The man nodded tentatively, a frown on his face.

'Please do not try to escape or do anything silly as I have a gun on you and in the hallway are two of my men. I have also retrieved your pistol from your pocket, so you are both unarmed and outnumbered.'

The man groaned in reply, but opened his eyes a fraction.

'Now, I see from your ID card that you claim that your name is Pierre Joubert and that you are a colonel in the French Army. Well, I'm afraid Colonel Joubert that your game is up.'

'Why are you speaking German?' demanded Joubert in a groggy voice.

'Because, sadly for you, I know that you are a German spy.'

'What are you talking about?'

'We're speaking fluent German now, you were speaking German to a contact of yours in a café on Place Vendôme two days ago, a known German spy was seen entering your building, and your accent gives you away as a native German speaker. I used to live in Germany myself and you don't sound like a Frenchman speaking German to me.'

'You fool, of course I'm French. I'm from Alsace. The man you heard me talking to is also Alsatian. Between ourselves we speak a form of German. It's a German dialect, but I am French. I was born in Mulhouse. Check my ID card, you idiot, and you'll see for yourself! My family left Alsace when the Germans took it over back in 1871 after the last war against the Boche. The area has changed sovereignty many times, but I am French and proud of it. And you, *monsieur*, are in a British uniform, and you are in big trouble!'

Joubert had switched from German to English for the last sentence, as it seemed to have finally sunk in that he was being questioned by a British officer. I switched to my native tongue too.

'I may be in big trouble with you, Joubert, but I'm the one holding the gun.'

'Go to hell,' growled Joubert. 'You'll pay for this, whoever you are. A junior British officer assaulting and kidnapping a senior French officer! How dare you? They'll throw the book at you!'

'I don't think so, as I am here on behalf of the men who own the book,' I explained.

'I work for our High Command, the GQC, and I've been vetted for my post. My job is top secret. Of course I'm not German. I wouldn't be in such a job if I were a *Boche*. My father was decorated in the War of 1870.'

'For which side?'

'For France, of course. Do not insult my late father, *monsieur*,' said Joubert indignantly, sitting upright and looking as if he was going to attack me, gun or no gun.

'So, who was the other German?'

'It is a dialect, I'm telling you. We are both French patriots. He is not a German either.'

'If your job is so secret, why were you discussing troop dispositions with the man in the café?'

'He works at the Prime Minister's office. We were discussing the cooperation with you, our British allies, in the next big offensive. I have contacts like him at the highest level in our government and that's why you, Captain, are in deep *merde*.'

'Not as deep as you, Colonel. Your masters will not be happy about your collusion with a fellow German spy.'

'What German spy?'

'Are you claiming you don't know this man?' I asked, showing him the picture of Church-Fenton.

'Are you saying he's a German spy?' said Joubert in a trembling voice. His face had gone white and he looked at me with wide eyes. 'I need a drink.'

I gave the Frenchman a bottle of Rémy Martin from a side table and Joubert took a hefty swig of the cognac direct from the bottle.

'We have proof that this officer, Church-Fenton, was a German agent. Before he conveniently became a Francophile immediately pre-war, he spent many years on and off cooperating with the German military. We have actual copies of instructions being given to him by German Intelligence.'

'*Merde!*' said Joubert. 'That is *l'Ours*.'

'*L'Ours*? Ah, of course – as in "bear". His German code name was *Braunbär*. Strikingly similar, wouldn't you say?'

'*Mon Dieu*, what does he know?' Joubert whispered to himself.

'What he knows is of no consequence as he's dead. What he passed on to the Germans on the other hand may be very important.'

'Dead? How did he die?'

'Ironically, he was shot by the Germans as they tried to assassinate our King,' I lied.

'Ah, I heard about that and knew that a British officer had been shot, but I didn't know it was *l'Ours*,' said Joubert in a surprised voice while shaking his head.

I thought that Joubert was either a very good actor or he was indeed a patriotic Frenchman. Based on my years interrogating criminals and witnesses in cells and courtrooms, I finally decided on the balance of probabilities for the latter, but needed proof.

'All right, Colonel Joubert, if you are who you say you are, prove to me you're not a spy too by answering my questions. Tell me about your activities at Rue de Portfoin, and what you know about the man in the photograph. You must know that he is really a British Army brigadier general called Church-Fenton.'

'I will not admit to anything. I have told you already, I will tell you nothing.'

'So, you keep saying, Colonel, but please cooperate, or, as I've warned you before, we'll tell your masters that you're a German spy.'

'Please go ahead. They will not believe you,' said Joubert in a complacent tone and then he took another swig of brandy.

'All right, then maybe we'll have to tell your wife or your employers about your mistress, Claudette, and your penchant for a bit of sadomasochism?'

'Don't be ridiculous. Most men my age and in my position have a mistress. My wife knows about it and it's almost expected of me by the class of people I work and associate with. This is France! You can't blackmail me for having an affair, you fool. Now let me go.'

'So, how will your wife and your peers react to you being a homosexual?'

'What are you talking about? I'm not a homosexual.'

'Well, I have some good contacts at a *maison tolerée* who will claim otherwise. Let's just call it the Marigny and call them Albert and Valentin for now. They will help me prove that you are not what you seem. Valentin can make any man dance to his tune when he blows their trumpet, if you understand what I mean, and Albert has an excellent photographer. I'm sure a few staged photographs of you with your cock in Valentin's mouth will help your wife and your associates understand what kind of man you really are.'

Joubert looked as if McIlhenny had coshed him again as the weight of my words sank in and he realised he'd been hoisted by his own petard. 'That's blackmail!' he exclaimed, but I just shrugged. 'Now I need a cigarette,' he said, and I tossed him the case and the matches, and he took out and lit a Gitanes.

'Now, Joubert, please tell me what you were up to in Rue de Portfoin? From my observations, you seem to be the boss. Are you the Director?'

Defeated, and with his image as a classic French lover under threat, Joubert blew out some smoke and sighed. He then began to explain. 'I work for the *Premier Bureau* of the French GQG, our High Command. For some time now we French have been trying to convince your British politicians to form a single unified command on the Western Front – under a French generalissimo of course – to better coordinate our Allied attacks against the Germans. We have had a lot of talks at your GHQ in Montreuil.'

'Wait a minute,' I said, suddenly realising where I'd seen Joubert before. I now remembered a short French colonel with a mole on his cheek coming out of GHQ as I went in to meet Lord Wokingham. 'Were you there a few days ago, but in uniform? I think our paths may have crossed unwittingly back then.'

'Yes, I was. When in Paris I feel more like a civil servant and so adopt civilian dress. I think it inappropriate to go to work in an office

345

every day in uniform. It is almost an insult to those fighting at the front to sit at a desk in a uniform so far behind the lines.'

'I remember overhearing you say something about a Plan B. So, what is it you actually do?'

'Let me explain my role. In France the GQG is split into several desks or offices. You will probably have heard of the more famous *Deuxième Bureau*, our main intelligence service. My *Premier Bureau* looks after personnel and organisation. In anticipation of a future unified command, the *Premier Bureau* was tasked with finding out as much as possible about the British Army and its officer corps to make integration easier once your stupid politicians finally understood our logic. We wanted to know everything about your senior officers – and I mean everything. We were very thorough, so, as a matter of routine, we kept files of which British officers visited which brothels.'

'You were spying on your ally's generals?'

It was Joubert's turn to shrug and he said, 'We do the same to our own senior officers. The brothels are largely regulated and inspected, so we've always had an excuse to visit and gather information. We've always thought such information may come in useful at some stage in the future. It's a big job as there are nearly forty major brothels in Paris, although luckily only a few are dedicated to officers, and only the most senior officers can afford the better establishments. In this case, selected prostitutes fed us information overheard from British senior officers about what they were really thinking about our negotiation for a unified command. It is amazing what men, in their pillow talk, will tell women that they think of as of no consequence. We also had some secret photographs taken of them in flagrante delicto too.'

As Joubert talked, I was beginning to understand why there were so many filing cabinets in his old basement.

'As we progressed, it came to our attention from the police vice-squad that several British officers were using a new brothel called the Marigny, and that it was for those who preferred boys to girls. We started to keep a watch on who was using it and just added the information to our files as pointers to the reliability, vulnerability, etc., of the officers concerned. We were worried that if in the future they were to be part of a single Anglo-French army command, and their proclivities became known to German agents, that they could be blackmailed. The way things have evolved, this proved to be quite ironic,' said Joubert with a half-smile, before continuing.

'Then, late last year, we got very concerned when your GHQ started to prevaricate after your losses at Loos, Aubers, and the other 1915 battles. During the various meetings of generals and politicians from our two countries, your leaders kept changing their minds and would not commit to a time or place for all those volunteers of Lord Kitchener to finally take to the battlefield and aid France as we had been promised. We needed a forceful ally who was going to help us drive the damn Germans out of France.

'A plan therefore evolved in case you British went back on your promises of a "Big Push" this year. We decided we'd need more influence inside your GHQ and beyond to ensure you complied with our wishes. If we couldn't get to your damned politicians, we hoped to get to enough of your generals to influence outcomes, and we didn't care how we did it. We called it "Plan B". And so, we put a camera into the Marigny and started photographing your senior officers to give us proof of their indiscretions. We also needed some officers in the British Staff who would support us in this strategy. We paid particular attention to those who had accompanied General Wilson to the coordination talks between the two armies before the war began, as many of them seemed quite Francophile.'

'And so, you chose Church-Fenton?'

'We got Church-Fenton on camera one time and shared his photographs with him. We basically blackmailed him into working with us. We certainly had no indications that he was a German spy. We thought that he was sympathetic to France. We even let him have his own negatives as a sign of good faith and recruited him into our scheme. He was given the code name *l'Ours* at his request. We briefed him on a visit to Rue de Portfoin. He was instructed to drop hints to targeted British senior officers that there was evidence they'd be cashiered and publicly humiliated if they didn't use their influence via military, political or newspaper contacts to promote the idea of a unified command and a "Big Push" this year.'

'And you gave him some of the photographs?'

'Yes, he needed evidence if he was going to blackmail these officers. Then it all became critical once Verdun started in February this year. We have intelligence from our sources in the German High Command that their intention is "to bleed France white". Well, my friend, I have to tell you that they were succeeding, and we were getting very pale! We became desperate for your help. So, I am ashamed to say, that when your Prince of Wales appeared in our camera lens, we thought we had the perfect opportunity to force your politicians and GHQ to act to relieve the pressure at Verdun or suffer a different type of national humiliation to ours. *L'Ours* was to warn the Royal Family that we had embarrassing material on the Prince. He was to say that we were willing to release the photographs to the international press if the British did not agree to launch an offensive.

'However, suddenly it didn't matter anymore as Pétain stabilised things at Verdun, and your politicians and generals finally committed in April to the "Big Push" this summer. Even now your divisions are moving into place. Better late than never is all I can say! As a result, Plan B wasn't needed any more and was shelved. *L'Ours* was instructed to stand down. And now we couldn't execute the plan anyway as all the photographic plates were destroyed last night in an explosion by saboteurs.'

'What a sordid tale of blackmail and deceit from our supposed allies! I'm surprised your government would stoop so low,' I told him. These words didn't begin to express my shock. A blackmailing operation by the Germans I could understand, but one by our ally was difficult to comprehend. To think the French had the temerity to talk about "Perfidious Albion"!

'Our government knows nothing of this,' said Joubert. 'No one at the top knows about our special operation. Not Poincaré, not

Briand, not Joffre. We deliberately did not inform our ministers so that it was deniable by them. Even the general responsible for the *Premier Bureau* at GQG, General Pelle, didn't want to know the details after we described our plan, although he didn't stop us either. I'm sorry to say that possibly my department went a little too far on this. But we did it for France. For us, desperate times required desperate measures.'

'Well, your Plan B was certainly pretty desperate!' I agreed.

'You British will never understand. You are an island race and have suffered no invasions since our Normans nearly a thousand years ago. We have the painful memory of 1870, and now these dreadful times since August 1914. We have French soil under German boots, and our men, women and children in Lille and the Département du Nord under German command. Our coalfields are confiscated, our pride is hurt, and thousands are being slaughtered daily at Verdun. Wait until you have suffered humiliations such as these before you judge us or say what you would not do for your country under the same circumstances!'

'Hopefully, that will never be put to the test. You should know that I was not joking when I said I worked for the men who own the book. Some of them may have been on your photographic negatives for all I know. I don't know how they'll react to this. I'm sure representations will be made at governmental level.'

'I expect so. As I said, our government will deny any knowledge of this plan. My bureau will be dubbed "rogue elements within the State", I expect, and we will be pensioned off, or worse, I will be wearing my uniform again and be sent to the front.' Joubert took another pull at the brandy bottle.

'Yes, I expect it will be something like that. Your government will have to be seen to take action, although, given the embarrassment on both sides, I suspect that it will be very discreet.'

'I understand. I see you are a captain, and a wounded one at that, so you are a brave man and have fought for France, and so I salute you,' said Joubert, starting to slur his words. 'Tell me though; since you've been following me and knew about our office, were you responsible for the explosion last night? You destroyed everything, you know? *Les pompiers* say the basement is like a sheet of glass. It means it was so hot down there that many of the negative plates must have melted and fused together. You did a very good job. And I presume it was you in that British staff car I saw at the end of the street earlier today? I wondered why it had stopped. Seemed rather a coincidence, despite the false clues of German involvement. I am impressed, Captain.'

'I cannot confirm or deny your accusation, Colonel,' I replied, but couldn't stop myself smiling.

'So, Captain, the key thing is what has *l'Ours* told the Germans about Plan B and its cancellation because the "Big Push" is on. I don't think I showed him anything that would be useful to the Germans regarding details of the offensive, but he had access to the photographs for blackmail purposes!'

'What about the map on the wall of your meeting room?'

'Ah, so you saw that, too? You have been busy before you destroyed my office. All it shows is troop concentrations around Verdun and the Somme. If the Germans haven't worked out yet that the Somme is where our next Allied offensive will be from the volume of troops, ammunition and supplies moving into the area, then I'm sure the bombardment of their trenches for many days before the assault will give the game away. But what about the blackmail? Do you know if he was passing information on to the Germans that he'd got from blackmailing British officers?'

'I'm afraid we don't know the answer to that one, Colonel,' I lied, deciding not to tell Joubert about Church-Fenton's need for money to pay the Apaches.

'I am very sorry, Captain. I cannot turn the clock back, so what will be, will be. I still do not know your name, Captain? Who has succeeded in revealing our plot?'

'Captain James Brown, British Army Intelligence Corps.'

'I salute you, Captain,' said Joubert, raising his bottle before drinking a toast. 'What now?'

'Nothing more from my side. I'll leave you to think about what you've done and its possible consequences and inter-government repercussions. Your mistress is tied up next door. You can release her once we've left.'

'Why would I release her? I don't have to be home for another hour, and I need to do something to take my mind off what you have just told me,' said Joubert, with a wolfish grin.

I was amazed by the man's powers of physical and mental recovery. This whole investigation had opened my eyes on what people got up to behind closed doors. I collected my men from the hallway and we soon found Hodgson and the car.

'Where to now, guv?'

'I think Amiens will be far enough for this evening, Hodgson. There's an old friend of mine there that I need to see. Once I've got us billets, you three can enjoy a well-deserved night on the town before we go back to reality. Also, I need to telephone Colonel Ferguson and tell him that we've successfully accomplished our mission.'

'Amends it is, guv.'

CHAPTER 48

When we got to Amiens, I was in luck and there was space for me at the Carlton. After registering at the hotel, I sought out my old friend Harry Stewart, and, thankfully, he was available that night for dinner. Before our meal, I visited a perfumery and bought a bottle of *Jicky* scent, and then went to a stationer's to buy wrapping materials.

Later, over a pleasant meal, Harry and I caught up on mutual friends such as Iain Sneddon, and many others, and, as always now, toasted "absent friends" to those we had known and who had already perished in the war. Harry told me the "Big Push" was definitely on given the rail traffic passing through Amiens on its way to Fourth Army. I thought once more that the impending offensive must be the world's worst kept secret as everyone I talked to seemed to know about it. We ended our dinner with a toast for success for the BEF in the forthcoming battle.

Before we got up from the table, I asked Harry for a favour. 'The last time I was here, Harry, you said you were going on leave soon?' I said, as I reached into my briefcase.

'Yes, a quick one, starting on Monday. By the time I get to Edinburgh it will be time to come back here again. I'll probably just say "hello" to my parents on a platform at Waverley Station, and then get back into the carriage,' joked Harry.

'Can I ask that when you get to Edinburgh that you post these for me? They're both fragile. One's a Limoges porcelain plate for my aunt and uncle that I picked up in Paris and the other's a bottle of perfume for my girlfriend, Jeanie. Great though the Army's Postal Section is, I don't want them smashed.'

'Yes, of course, Jamie, I'd be glad to. Consider it done.'

I handed him a sealed padded package addressed to my Uncle John at his church manse in Hamilton, and a second for Jeanie at her student digs in Glasgow.

'Now, come on, I'll walk with you to the Carlton, and maybe we can have a nightcap along the way. There are plenty of good cafés in Amiens,' said Harry.

'As long as it's decent Scotch and not pastis or barbed-wire whisky, I'm your man,' I told him as we set off in the direction of my hotel.

Sunday,
28th May 1916

CHAPTER 49

Late on the Sunday afternoon, after completing a pleasant journey in fine weather back to the chateau via Étaples to drop off George, I went in to see Villiers.

'The Old Man's not here,' Villiers informed me. 'However, he asked me to give you this.'

Villiers handed over an envelope, which I opened. Inside was a letter ordering me to report back on my investigation the following afternoon in the Prof's study to the gentlemen who had commissioned my inquiries. In exchange for the letter, I handed Villiers a package, heavy for its size.

'Christmas come early, old boy?' he asked with a smile.

'Let's just say it's a gift to say thank you for your help in rescuing me that night in the stable.'

Villiers opened the package and slid out four glass photographic plates. He held one up to the light and then gasped, his smile fading as he turned a bright shade of red.

'I suggest you smash these up with a poker in the fireplace in your room before Colonel Ferguson comes back. I also suggest you be more discreet in your liaisons in the future.'

'I wasn't aware of this at all. My God, I could have been blackmailed or cashiered. How can I thank you?' asked Villiers in a trembling voice.

'You don't have to thank me, Villiers. Just make sure you don't get caught again. And don't worry, your secret's safe. By your detective work and finding me the other night, you helped save my life. Let's call it quits. Come on, let's go to the mess for an early dinner. I've got some work to do this evening and I need you to do some more research for me.'

'Anything, old boy, anything.'

'All right, then please see if you can find any connections between these three people,' I said handing Villiers a list of names. 'You might have to dig back into their records using that network of yours.'

'It's a Sunday, old boy. The Records Department at the War Office in London will be closed. I won't be able to do anything today.'

'That's all right, but I'll need an answer before my appointment with our betters tomorrow.'

'I'll get on to it straightaway in the morning.'

*

After my meal, I went up to my room to prepare a report on my findings. I'd had Villiers send up a typewriter and a portable machine now sat on my small desk. Villiers had made sure that I had a ream of paper and a few blue carbon sheets too. I decided that my report was so sensitive that I'd better make only one copy, and so I eschewed the latter as I loaded the typewriter.

I decided to constrain my report by self-censorship, as I felt Lord Wokingham and General Maldon did not need to know the names of witnesses and others I'd talked to in my investigation. I pecked away at the typewriter's keyboard with my good right hand. It took me two hours to produce a scanty four-page report following some retyping, a bit of redacting, and a few handwritten corrections. I went down to Villiers' now empty office and collected some more stationery items to take up to my room. I put my report in a brown cardboard cover, tied the pages together with a Treasury tag, and then used a rubber stamp and an inkpad to mark it "Top

Secret". Finally, I initialled each page, before I signed and dated it for completeness.

Since I had the typewriter in front of me, I decide to write some letters home, as I'd last written nearly two weeks previously. My mind immediately filled with what I couldn't write about, rather than what I could. I wasn't sure how my parents would react to my involvement in a trail of blackmail which stretched from the Royal Family down to a humble highland crofter. For sure they would have been shocked at the string of deaths by assassination, murder, suicide, and misadventure surrounding my investigations, some of them directly due to the activities of their loving son. Now wasn't the time either to discuss my faltering faith or my changed attitude towards homosexuality with my Uncle John. I certainly couldn't tell Jeanie about my exploration of Parisian brothels.

In the end, I wrote three short anodyne letters. To my mother and father, I wrote about the latest ex-university chums I'd met on my travels, some of them familiar to my parents from their visits to Edinburgh. I avoided telling them of friends who had become casualties, as I knew this would be upsetting and they'd have seen the grim lists in the *Glasgow Herald* and *Hamilton Advertiser* anyway. To my Uncle John, I wrote about the various Gothic cathedrals I had seen in the cities that I'd visited across northern France, contrasting them to his simple charge back in my hometown. I warned him to expect a fragile package in the post and that under no circumstances was it to be opened, and that he should follow the attached instructions in the event of my death. Finally, I told Jeanie to look out for a parcel and that she should only wear its contents when next walking out with me. I told her about Paris and its famous sights and how I hoped to take her there when the war was over, before confirming my love for her at the letter's end.

*

Later, as I sat on my bed, I thought again about what I'd just written to Jeanie, and my wish to take her to the French capital when the current conflict was over. I also wondered if any of what I had done in the last few weeks would make any difference whatsoever to bringing that conflict to an end.

Such a thought would have kept me awake all night if I'd let it, so I resorted to my usual nightcap and poured a large whisky. As I sat sipping the malt, my eye rested on the Brigadier's teddy bear, propped up on my desk. I thought about its previous owner once more, and how my pursuit of his crimes had changed my views over the last few days.

CHAPTER 50

Thinking about Church-Fenton prompted me to me revisit the whole issue of homosexuality, and I wrestled once more with my own feelings towards it as a crime. Its criminalisation was at the very heart of the feasibility of the French Plan B. Until recently I would have thought it would have had little chance of success, but now that I'd seen first-hand the lengths that men would go to protect their reputations and avoid the criminal and military implications of their behaviour, I was not so sure. If blackmailed, I felt certain that a number of officers might well have gone along with the French plan rather than face public exposure and its humiliating consequences. I thought about those I'd learned were either proven homosexuals or had been accused of being one.

The lawyer in me certainly found the evidence against Lord Kitchener somewhat flimsy, and its circumstantial nature had not convinced me that the Field Marshal was indeed that way inclined. Given his great deeds for the country, did it matter anyway? I was somewhat rankled, however, by the fact that Kitchener may have been protected because he was part of the Establishment. Then again, wasn't that behaviour exactly what I was helping facilitate to protect the Prince?

I had felt very positively towards Major Fairbrother after my interview with him. The Major seemed a decent and brave man, a VC winner who, by all accounts, took the welfare of his troops seriously, and was apparently well respected in his regiment. Any accusations against him would be devastating for the Major and a real loss to the BEF and his men.

Then there was Villiers, who had saved my life and who had tried to come to my aid when I was kidnapped. I also knew that Villiers sincerely wanted to fight. As the Prof had said at the beginning of my acquaintanceship with Villiers, the man was a bloody good adjutant and very valuable to the Intelligence Corps. Both Fairbrother and Villiers were therefore, in their own ways, good soldiers, as well as good men. However, I wondered if I just felt differently towards these two because I'd got to know them better, and indeed now counted Villiers as a friend. How did I feel about others who shared their sexuality that I didn't know?

On the subject of good soldiering, my thoughts returned to McIlhenny's comment on Livingstone and Baird in our platoon. I now recalled Sergeant Hunter warning me that he was keeping an eye on that pair as they were getting too chummy and were always sharing a blanket in their billets. I had dismissed Hunter's speculation at the time as Baird was a coal miner and Livingstone a foundryman. Both were big burly lads and surely such men wouldn't be queer? Maybe they were, after all? I'd found out from McIlhenny that both had been "Mentioned in Despatches" and had been killed side by side in the street fighting of the village of Loos itself, well after I had been felled. I now thought that it really didn't matter one jot what their feelings were for each other, as they'd obviously died not only as good, loyal soldiers, but, since they were both volunteers, as patriotic citizens into the bargain.

As I thought about the gallant Major and my brawny platoon members, I felt somewhat confused, as none of them had the effeminate ways of Valentin and Albert. In my ignorance I had previously thought all such queer men would be "artistic types" like Oscar Wilde, Proust, and the others in Albert's photographic Hall of Fame, or the literary tourists mentioned in the Brigadier's postcard from Squidgy on Capri. While not expecting them to dress like Albert as a drag queen, I thought I would see other physical signals and lisping voices. The Army's uniform regulations and predilection for khaki on active duty certainly gave no *licence for flamboyant dressing or effete touches. I had to admit to myself that my past mental stereotypes of such men were completely inaccurate and frankly ridiculous.*

From the historic figures Linton had mentioned to the Prof, like King James and William of Orange, and the fact that the Ancient Greeks seemed to indulge in this sort of thing, homosexuality was obviously not a new phenomenon. If it wasn't constrained by historical age, it didn't seem constrained by physical age either, as witnessed by the fact that Pevensey College schoolboys through to elderly men, like my Edinburgh accoster, all seemed to indulge. I wondered what that meant with respect to people being born that way, rather than growing into it, but it was all beyond my knowledge of both physiology and psychology.

I now also realised that men with these feelings must be found across the whole spectrum of society. I had been sent out to protect the reputation of the Heir to the Throne after all, but now saw that these tendencies stretched all the way down the class structure to the working class. From the files I had seen in Paris, which included Anzacs and Canadians, and with my run-in with the South African Cronje, this clearly wasn't just a British issue, but Empire-wide. I recalled that Lord Wokingham had called homosexuality the "German Disease" and that Church-Fenton had a German lover. And then there was a special brothel for practitioners, here in France. It therefore seemed there were no boundaries of class or nationality to men who felt this way.

While I expected that most of my fellow officers and their troops were almost certainly heterosexual, I had now met or been in contact with several who clearly weren't, and the evidence from the basement in Paris certainly supported that the number was significant. I recalled that was why the ADMS, Brigadier Poulson, was so ambivalent about special brothels. Poulson's focus was on ensuring that there were enough men to continue the fighting, and he implied that if all the homosexuals were combed out of the Army, it would have had a significant effect on numbers. That seemed to be why the ADMS wasn't addressing it vigorously, but concentrating on VD, a temporary disease, instead.

With these thoughts in mind, I worked out that the Army must statistically have a large number of soldiers that had sexual feelings for their fellows. Most must be suppressing these feelings for fear of a court martial for so-called "indecency" and were therefore largely celibate. Surely that number would also be reflected in society as a whole? If this was true, then was it fair on such a large proportion of the general population that their sexual preferences were denied under law? This didn't make sense to me for consenting adults.

My legal training made me rationally evaluate a law which drove men like Cranbrook in Amiens to hang himself rather than suffer being exposed as a homosexual. Did that officer force himself to marry to provide better cover in society for his own true desires? If that was the case, then how dreadful for his poor wife. Was such an act common or just a rare occurrence? What was the value of a law which forced men like the Colonel and the Captain in the stables to be willing to murder a fellow officer rather than be labelled homosexuals? Surely murder was the more heinous crime?

Earlier, I had read in a newspaper in the mess that rabble-rousers back in England, through magazines such as Pemberton-Billing's The Imperialis were raising the spectre of all sorts of homosexual conspiracies via a pro-German secret society called "The Unseen Hand", to add to their usual ridiculous accusations against the Jews. Why scapegoat all these men?

So far, the trail of blackmail over homosexuality that I had uncovered had regrettably led to the deaths of at least six men, if Church-Fenton was included. The accusation from the hanged Brigadier Cranbrook's suicide note that I was actively hunting down such people was an unsettling thought. In truth, it had unnerved me more than I'd first admitted to myself. I certainly didn't see myself as the avenging angel on behalf of generals like Maldon, aristocrats like Oscar Wilde's nemesis, the Marquess of Queensberry, or lunatic fringe politicians like Pemberton-Billing.

I realised that, in a way, Church-Fenton was a victim too, blackmailed by the Germans because of his sexuality. He had been forced to betray his country because that nation's laws made him a criminal. Those same laws had then made him a target for exploitation by both *the French and the Apaches. However, my sympathy for him evaporated due to his extortion of his own kind to pay off his gambling debts because of his betting addiction. This exploitation of others, combined with his treachery, forced or not, meant I had, as a lawyer, little professional empathy for his victimhood. That professional assessment was before I even considered the personal angle on how I felt about him.*

All these different thoughts chased each other in my brain. Ultimately the logic of my lawyer's mind dictated that since this sort of behaviour was statistically significant and not as unusual as I'd previously thought, it should therefore be accepted by society as a whole, and that the current laws should be revised. I knew, however, that the path to legal acceptance of homosexuality would be long, with centuries' old prejudices, religious and temporal, to be overcome.

I finally realised that I'd had a sort of epiphany, and I felt strangely liberated. It had taken a while to sink in, but I had learned from the investigation that there were people with all sorts of feelings and needs dissimilar to my own. This didn't make them bad people, just different people.

Monday,
29th May 1916

CHAPTER 51

At the allotted time on the Monday afternoon, I was standing nervously outside the Prof's office having a stilted conversation with Villiers. I'd spent the morning rehearsing my case and then absorbing the information on the three names on my list that Villiers had brought to me just before midday. As before, for meeting the expected dignitaries, I had been dressed for the occasion by McIlhenny in best tunic, tartan trews and Glengarry, with my black belts, buttons and boots highly polished. I had my walking stick in one hand and my briefcase in the other.

'Good luck, sur,' McIlhenny had said as I had left his charge to go downstairs.

'Good luck, guv,' Hodgson had echoed as I'd passed him in the foyer.

Eventually the Prof called me into his office. This time there were only the red-faced General Maldon and Lord Wokingham sitting alongside the Prof, all with their backs to the fireplace. I was waved to a seat strategically placed in front of my superiors. I saluted, removed my Glengarry, sat down, and took a deep breath.

'Captain Brown, welcome. What's happened to your face? You seem to have additional wounds since we last saw you?' said Lord Wokingham.

'It's nothing, sir, a minor run-in with some rough types during my investigations.'

'In the line of duty then? Thank you, Captain. Now, Brown, let's hear your report, please. We are keen to know if you've been successful or not.'

'Yes, sir. I began by revisiting Church-Fenton's room and, despite the previous search by Lord Ross, found a hidden cache of materials. These materials revealed that the Brigadier himself was in fact a homosexual.'

This statement produced a 'My goodness!' from Wokingham and a 'Bloody hell!' from General Maldon. In the meantime, I continued.

'Additional evidence eventually led to someone who helped establish Church-Fenton's past history of money problems and about his liking for men over women.'

'Who was this other person? Is he a serving soldier? If so, I'll be obliged for a name if he's also one of these damned sodomites. We can't have these queer types of fellow in the British Army,' the General demanded.

'I'm sorry, sir, I can't say who it was,' I replied.

'Can't say or won't say? Damn you, Brown, buggery is an offence against King's Regulations. If your informant is a soldier, he'll have to be court-martialled. And you should be too, for your dumb insolence!'

'Then I can presume that the Prince, as a serving soldier, will be similarly treated?' I asked.

The General's head looked like it was going to explode.

'*Touché*. The Captain makes a good point, General. Please calm down and let the man finish his story,' said Wokingham. 'Continue, Captain Brown.'

'On the advice of my informant, my investigation led me to a brothel in Paris that caters for those who prefer men to women. I visited the brothel where I found that there was a hidden camera which took pictures such as those you've seen of the Prince.'

'I'm glad you found this establishment in Paris after all,' said Wokingham. 'I now know the Prince has visited such places in other cities in France. I would have hated to widen the scope of your investigation any further.'

'Under interrogation, the brothel's owner revealed that the photographic plates were collected and taken to an address not far away. I'm afraid I had to break into this building one night. In its basement were several filing cabinets of plates and other material. The Prince was not the only one photographed, and if the entire cellar's contents had been revealed, it would have been highly embarrassing for several high-ranking officers in the BEF. I believe only a half-dozen officers have been charged with homosexual behaviours so far in the war, but the number of files would suggest this is an under-representation of such practices.'

'Are you suggesting the officer corps is full of damned pederasts?' demanded General Maldon.

'Strictly speaking, General, pederasty is committed between an adult male and a boy,' interrupted the Prof. 'The word's derived from the Greek, *paid* for boy and *eros* for love. Brown's talking about consenting adults here.'

General Maldon clearly didn't appreciate the Prof's etymology lecture, and so I plunged on quickly to divert his attention. 'Unfortunately, I was disturbed in my search, and had to leave, but I returned later with a demolition team, and we destroyed the building and the evidence. We tried to make it look like German sabotage. However, before detonating the charge, I located and retrieved the incriminating plates showing the Prince.'

'Splendid,' interjected Wokingham. 'Well done, Captain. Please continue, I can tell you've more to relate to us.'

'Yes, sir. Well, before and after our raid, when the property was under surveillance, I noticed a man who seemed to be involved in whatever the goings-on were at the property. I kidnapped and interrogated him. He was a senior French War Office official.'

'You kidnapped a French official!' exclaimed Wokingham.

'Yes, sir. I was remembering your request for urgency in completing the investigation. By threatening the man with his own method of blackmail, I managed to get an explanation from him. It seems that the French were planning to blackmail our High Command, or even the government or Royal Family, by using the photographs they'd obtained. They were worried that we kept changing our minds on supporting an offensive to relieve the pressure on Verdun. They were desperate. If we hadn't agreed to the "Big Push", they'd have threatened to make the photographs available to the international press.'

My audience were now sitting open-mouthed as they tried to take in what I'd just told them.

'The man I questioned claimed that the upper echelons of the French government were not aware of this plan to blackmail us, but I have no way of knowing if he was telling the truth.'

'Thank God for that!' said Wokingham.

'Yes, sir. Those who were involved had chosen Brigadier Church-Fenton as a strong Francophile to be their go-between to start the blackmail process. He was known to them from his time in Paris with General Wilson, thrashing out the military response required by the *entente cordiale,* although they also had similar compromising photographs of him.'

'So, confirmation that he was a sodomite, too. Well, I'll be damned,' said the General.

'Unfortunately for the French, the Brigadier went off on a private extortion racket using their photographs to get the money he needed to pay off old gambling debts due to Parisian gangsters. It seems he was a serial gambler. I interrogated the gang leader who revealed that not only did the Brigadier owe them money for his gambling, but that they'd evidence of his homosexuality, too, and were using that against him as an additional power over him and to garner larger payments. So, you see, the Brigadier had significant money problems, hence his blackmailing exploits.'

'So that was the motive. Well, well,' said Wokingham, shaking his head.

'Yes, sir. One of Church-Fenton's blackmail victims was, of course, the Prince and that's what eventually led you to arrange his assassination. Killing him therefore brought this whole chain of events to a close.'

At the end of my report there was silence in the room as Lord Wokingham and the General considered what might have been, given the evidence I had described. By the General's requirements it would have meant a lot of courts martial, and several holes in the British Army's command structure.

Then the General finally did explode, shouting, 'These goddamned Frenchies! Imagine the audacity of it. Trying to blackmail an entire nation to get us to send our young men to die on their behalf. Don't they think we're doing enough? We've already lost most of the Old Contemptibles and are about to feed in huge numbers of our volunteers, and soon enough, we'll be burying our conscripts on their damn soil. How dare they?'

'Calm down, General,' interceded Wokingham. 'Now we have this knowledge we must seek to use it to our advantage with our dear French allies at an appropriate time. It will be our turn to blackmail them.'

'Yes, and we damn well should! Whatever were the French thinking? Did they honestly think that the King would rather protect the honour of his son than preserve the lives of British soldiers? I'm sure that the King, like Wellington, would have said, "Publish and be damned!",' claimed the General.

'Thankfully, that is a moot point, Maldon,' said Wokingham, not looking at all convinced that this would have been the King's reaction. 'In the meantime, we should thank Captain Brown for his success. Now, Captain, please hand over the plates which show the Prince's indiscretion.'

I opened my briefcase and passed over three negative plates to the Peer. The civilian held them up to the chandelier for a better view, and to see for himself that they were indeed the correct ones. He shook his head as he looked at each of them. Satisfied, he then took them to the fireplace and proceeded to smash the plates to smithereens with the poker and put them in the fire in an attempt to melt them. I also handed over the single copy of my report on the investigation. I was rather annoyed that after all my late-night soul-searching, pecked typing, and judicious editing, that the Peer placed it straight on the fire, too, without even glancing at the contents, and then made sure it went up in flames.

'We don't need any records of what happened here to embarrass the Prince or others if someone discovers it in a dusty file in a few years' time, do we? The Prince will eventually be our King, after all,' said Wokingham, as he stoked the fire.

I sighed and nodded in understanding, before Wokingham continued. 'Thank you again, Captain. As we agreed last time, Lord Ross's highland feud with Private McNicol has been settled. McNicol has been released and transferred to another regiment. He is now as safe as any soldier can be at the front in wartime. Sergeant MacLeod has been informed that his orders were legal and Lord Ross has guaranteed his family's tenancy of their crofts.'

'Thank you, sir, for following through.'

'Meanwhile, the press back home have been having a field day with what we've promoted as an assassination attempt on the King. Not only has it made the introduction of conscription for married men more palatable to the general populace, as we predicted, but it's even resulted in a fresh crop of volunteers coming forward before their own conscription was required. The Kaiser has denied it, of course, but nobody believes him.'

'That's very good, sir.'

'President Wilson of the United States has expressed outrage, and anything that makes America angry with the Germans is bread and butter to our cause. The propaganda battle is an important war front, and the Ministry of Information and the War Office are very pleased with the result of our subterfuge. So, you see, Captain, this whole messy affair has been of great value to our country.'

'Well, actually, sir, I'm not sure Lord Ross's order to Sergeant MacLeod was in fact illegal in the first place.'

'What the devil do you mean?' demanded the General.

CHAPTER 52

'I'm afraid to have to tell you that I have proof that Church-Fenton was in fact a German spy after all.'

'You mean that even though we thought we'd made it up, it was in fact true?' asked Wokingham in astonishment.

'Christ Almighty!' blasphemed the General, his face as red as Valentin's lipstick.

'Exactly, sir. We've studied the Brigadier's service record and it turns out that it crosses several times with a German officer called von Drexler. They were together in China, Britain and Germany, several years before Church-Fenton's work with General Wilson on the BEF deployment. Von Drexler is now a senior officer in German Intelligence. Lord Ross's implication that the Brigadier wasted his commands' lives needlessly is, upon detailed analysis, almost certainly the truth. We also have copies of actual communications from von Drexler to the Brigadier with orders for information and sabotage. Ironically, it appears the Germans were blackmailing the Brigadier into working for them because they too knew of his homosexuality.'

The Peer had gone white, his usual urbane and unflappable expression replaced by one of deep concern. Even General Maldon was now only a pale rose pink in complexion, as the blood had finally drained from his face.

'Do you mean to say that the Germans know about the Prince and these other officers, after all, via Church-Fenton?' whispered Wokingham.

I decided to put them out of their misery, but only after a long pause. 'Actually, no, sir, that is not the case. From the communications to the Brigadier from von Drexler, it really does look as if he was using the photographic material solely to blackmail individuals for money to pay off his gambling debts. I don't think that he ever shared this information with the Germans.'

'Thank God for that! What a relief,' said Wokingham, with a huge sigh.

'Why the hell didn't you just say so in the first place, Brown? There was no need to be so damned theatrical,' thundered the General, his usual ruddy hue returning at an alarming rate.

'Thank you for clearing that up, Captain Brown. I am much relieved.'

'By the way, sir, to put pressure on the French official I interrogated, I let him know that he'd been using a German spy working as a double agent. I did not tell him that the Germans know nothing of the French blackmail plans or Church-Fenton's redirection of those for personal gain. As far as the French are concerned, their plan may have been compromised, and they do not know what the Brigadier may or may not have shared with his German spymasters.'

'Excellent, Captain Brown. That will give us additional leverage over our French friends. Well done.'

'However, in conclusion, gentlemen, I'd also like to inform you that we intercepted the message the Brigadier was intending to send to his German controllers. Luckily, since the Brigadier was shot, it never reached them.'

'Do we know what it said?' asked the General.

'I'm afraid I don't know,' I replied.

'No, but I do,' said the Prof. 'It was a book code based on Goethe's autobiography and our cryptanalysts at MI.1b have deciphered it. I got the answer at lunchtime from London. It said, quote, "Somme sector, 1st July", unquote.'

'My God!' exclaimed the General. 'That would have put the cat among the pigeons.'

'The Brigadier was sending messages, such as this, to his Aunt Winifrid in England. She was then passing them to German Intelligence in Wesel, via neutral Holland,' I explained.

'I've got more information on that, too, which I haven't had time to share with Captain Brown yet,' the Prof said. 'Church-Fenton was the only child of an only child on his father's side, according to the birth records at Somerset House, and so there is no Aunt Winifrid Church-Fenton. Interestingly, Winifrid is a common Teutonic lady's name, and, ironically, I believe it means "peaceful friend". Perhaps the Germans have a sense of humour after all! Anyway, we must assume his contact was a German agent.'

'Right, well, I presume, General, that you will clear up the mess created by the Brigadier's antics and have this agent arrested,' said Wokingham to Maldon.

'I'll get straight on to it as soon as I get back to the War Office, believe me,' replied the General.

'There's no need, sir,' said the Prof. 'I alerted Inspector Wetherby of Special Branch in London once we found out the supposed aunt's address and Scotland Yard sent a team down to Eastbourne. It's an empty house. It looks like it was used as a dead letter box. Special Branch are watching the place in case anyone turns up, and if they do, they'll nab them.'

'Thank you, Colonel. That's very thorough,' said Wokingham. 'I'm sure Lord Ross will also be pleased to hear this, too. Now, Captain Brown, as a symbol of His Majesty's recognition for your efforts, he has asked me to give you this in the event of a successful mission, and so I am most happy to do so.'

Wokingham passed over a slim box to me. I opened it and inside was an enamelled white cross with a gold crown on a red boss at its centre. The medal had a blue-red-blue vertically-striped ribbon attached.

'The Distinguished Service Order?' I said, recognising the ribbon colours, a bit surprised to be given it, and not sure I warranted it.

'You don't seem impressed?' said the General, who himself sported a DSO ribbon bar on his uniform.

'No, I appreciate it very much, sir. It's just that the DSO has been awarded to a lot of staff officers who've never been under fire, and I know my front-line colleagues have not been impressed by that. I wasn't under fire this time either. They call the DSO the "Dukes' Sons Only" in the trenches.'

The General's face reddened yet again, but Lord Wokingham intervened before he could speak. 'I'm sure that whoever sees it with your MC ribbon and your wounds, Captain, will not doubt your valued service to your King and Country. The award will be gazetted shortly. Now, is there anything else you'd like to tell us, Captain Brown, before we leave?'

'Well, I do have a confession to make, sir.'

'What now? Spit it out, man,' demanded the General.

'There were four plates of the Prince enjoying himself, but I've handed over only three for you to smash.'

'But you were ordered to pass over everything you'd found associated with this matter. You'll now be court-martialled for disobeying an order, by God!' said General Maldon.

'I don't think you'll do that, General, as all this story would come out. No, you see I was afraid that if the Establishment is happy to assassinate one of its own, and a brigadier general at that, then I'm sure an accident could be arranged for a mere plebeian captain. I've therefore taken the fourth plate as my insurance.'

'Where is the negative?' asked Wokingham in a dry whisper.

'It's on its way back to Britain and will be kept by an acquaintance of mine. It is being carried privately and so cannot be intercepted by the Postal Section. The plate is in a sealed envelope which its keeper is sworn not to open. It will be released to the press upon intimation of my death, unless my demise is clearly the result of enemy action. That's to the American press by the way, as I realise you'd slap a

D-Notice on Fleet Street. My acquaintance has instructions to send the plate to Buckingham Palace upon cessation of hostilities and never to return it to me, so you can rest assured that I will not be using it to blackmail anyone at a later date.'

'I see,' said Wokingham, who I could have sworn had turned quite pale again. 'What you're saying is, of course, quite preposterous. We would never contemplate such an act against you, Captain.'

'Really? I see you're wearing a Guards tie, Your Lordship,' I said, pointing to the blue and red strip of silk in his wing collar.

'What?' said Wokingham, discomfited by my turn in direction. 'Yes, I was in the Guards. I fought with them in the Boer War. What's that got to do with anything?'

'I believe you started in the Grenadiers, sir, and then you were one of the cadre of officers transferred from that regiment to form the Irish Guards in 1900 at Queen Victoria's behest to recognise Irish service in the Boer War?'

'Yes, that's correct.'

'I gather that some ninety Irishmen from the Grenadiers went over with you and your fellow officers to create the core of the new Guards' unit and that one of them was a Sergeant Daniel Kelly. Army records show that Kelly was one of the men you designated as a sharpshooter in South Africa after you were much impressed by the Boers' sniping tactics. Tactics which you wished to emulate. Kelly retired from the Army in 1907 and returned to Ireland.'

'I'm not sure I understand where you're going with this, Captain, or its relevance to what we've been discussing.'

'Kelly was dug out from retirement as an experienced NCO and asked to join the 6th Connaught Rangers, a New Army battalion formed in September 1914. They arrived in France about a year later, and then recently he was transferred to the Sniping School as an instructor due to his shooting skills. Kelly was in London recently on leave. I wonder if you met him when he was over there?'

'London is a large city, Captain, and, as I'm sure you'll understand, people in my position don't socialise with the likes of this man Kelly,' said Wokingham, looking very uncomfortable. I mentally thanked Villiers once more for his research skills.

'I just thought there may be a bond between the two of you as you were "Mentioned in Despatches" for saving him from capture by the Boers at the Modder River while under fire. He would owe you for that, wouldn't he? Anyway, apparently, he returned from London with a photograph. A photograph of me. How would he have got that and why would a trained sniper need my photograph?' I said, leaving the last sentence hanging.

'I'm sure I don't know what you mean, and I resent your implication,' said Wokingham testily. 'Now, we thank you once more for your service, Captain Brown, but we must be going.'

'Major Brown,' I said.

'What?' spluttered General Maldon.

'I think "Major Brown" sounds much better than "Captain Brown",' I told them.

'Who the hell do you think you are?' shouted the General, his red face finally turning the same shade of crimson as his collar tabs.

'I think I'm the man who knows where the last photographic plate of the Heir to the Throne engaged in an illegal act is.'

'That's blackmail, godammit!'

'Yes, it seems there's a lot of it about these days, sir.'

'I will ensure your "request" for promotion is processed,' said Wokingham calmly, seemingly having recovered his composure. Since my accusation that the Peer had planned my execution, the Grand Vizier seemed to be assessing me in a new light.

'Then it will be "acting" only,' insisted the General, meaning that the promotion would be only temporary and with no pay rise.

'Oh, I think we'd better make it substantive, General, don't you?' said Wokingham, meaning permanent. 'Is that all, *Major* Brown?'

'Yes, sir.'

'Then the General and I will leave you now. Notwithstanding your last-minute disclosure, and your unfounded accusations, you did a very good job, Brown, and we are indebted to you. You are of course on your part bound by the Official Secrets Act that you'll keep all this confidential, but I trust you anyway. Please do not betray that trust as I'd really hate for something bad to happen to you. Goodnight,' said Wokingham getting up to shake my hand and then going over to do the same to the Prof.

General Maldon came over to me and spoke in a low voice. 'You're on thin ice, Brown. You'd better watch your step in the future. Protecting sodomites, making accusations against a Peer of the Realm, blackmailing superior officers for promotion, withholding evidence. You might have your wounds and your gongs, but I can assure you, you are not untouchable.'

'I understand, sir. For what it's worth, I could find no connection between you and the Irish sniper, Kelly.'

'I should bloody well think not! In the meantime, consider yourself lucky that I don't have you transferred from this soft assignment to running a warehouse in Salonika or some other godforsaken hell-hole.'

'Yes, sir. You're quite right, sir. But, before you go, General, there's one thing I forgot to give you.'

I pulled out from my briefcase the photographic plate I'd removed from the Brigade of Guards drawer in the Rue de Portfoin basement. I dropped my voice to match the General's. 'I believe this is your younger brother, General. The resemblance to you is uncanny. A Guards' lieutenant colonel, isn't he?'

The General looked at me in disbelief, then grabbed the plate and stalked out. Lord Wokingham had witnessed all this from his position beside the Prof and had said nothing, although when the Peer passed me, he gave me a wink.

EPILOGUE

With his visitors gone, the Prof rearranged the chairs and invited me to sit opposite him beside the fire after giving me a glass of his favourite Laphroaig. He then lit his smelly pipe and settled back in his armchair with his whisky.

'Well, well, Jamie, that was an interesting tale you told. I don't think I've heard of blackmail on such a scale before.'

'Yes, it's been an international web of British blackmail, German *erpressung*, and French *chantage*, all at the same time, with no party aware of what the others were up to, other than the spider in the middle, Church-Fenton. I was struck by a quote from von Drexler in one of his messages to the Brigadier where he said "blackmail is a dirty game, but so is war", and that seems like a good excuse for everyone in this case.'

'I'll say. We've had nations blackmailing nations for military advantage, both friend and foe alike, and individuals blackmailing others for money to pay off people blackmailing them!'

'Blackmail is just another form of bullying, and you know how I hate that.'

'Well, you'll have to be careful on the slippery slope then, won't you,' warned the Prof, 'as you've blackmailed witnesses and suspects for information, and then, finally, pulled that stunt just now by blackmailing Wokingham and Maldon for advancement.'

'Yes, I'm sorry about the last. I hadn't planned it, but the General was really annoying me. And yes, I was a bit uncomfortable using blackmail as a tool in my interrogations, particularly on the Brigadier's former lover. However, I tried to make it up to him by giving him the incriminating evidence. You'll note I didn't mention him by name in my report. Not that it matters now the document's incinerated.'

'It's good that you took out some insurance,' said the Prof. 'Do you really think they planned to kill you to keep you quiet when this was over?'

'I can't think of any other reason that Kelly had my photograph other than to help him identify his target. If they were willing to eliminate me, Prof, you may also have been on their list.'

'Yes, that's a sobering thought,' said the Prof, taking an extra-large slug of whisky.

'I have no firm evidence of this plot other than the word of a man I trusted with my life. It all fits with your warning about the Establishment after the last time we met with these gentlemen, plus your insight into Lord Wokingham's character. You heard His Lordship's threat at the end, too? While I expect them to call off Kelly for now, he, or someone like him, will be lurking in the background if I ever spill the beans on the Prince, or attempt my own blackmail of him.'

'You know, Jamie, it's very appropriate that two Scots should be discussing blackmail. Did you know it's a Scottish word originally?'

'No, I didn't,' I admitted, waiting for the inevitable etymology discourse.

'Well, it is. It was used by the Border Reivers along the Scottish-English Marches in Tudor times. Basically, the reivers wouldn't come to your lands and steal your cattle or harass you in other ways if you paid them tribute or blackmail. It's believed to be from two Gaelic words: *Blathaich* meaning to protect, and *Mal* meaning payment. A protection racket really. So, in effect, you were just carrying on an old Scottish tradition. Come, let's drink to your promotion, Major Brown,' said the Prof with a grin.

'Well, I can do with the extra twenty-five shillings a week,' I said, returning the Prof's smile. 'I intend to buy an engagement ring next time I'm back home on leave.'

'Now you can get a bigger diamond,' laughed the Prof. 'I hope you'll be very happy together when the time comes.' He raised his glass once more in a toast.

Then the Prof's smile faded and he turned serious. 'Now, Jamie, I have a confession to make. Just before the war, when Andrew was up visiting us in Edinburgh from Cambridge, he brought one of his chums with him. They seemed the best of friends. Then one day, by accident, I went into Andrew's bedroom and found him in bed with this other fellow. I was shocked at first. I promised him I wouldn't tell his mother. I'm only telling you now as he's dead, and it hasn't made any difference about how I feel about him, how I grieve for him, and how I'll always love him as my son.'

'I know, Prof. I do understand. Everyone's different, and maybe we should celebrate that and not maintain laws that don't recognise it. It's taken me some time to come to this realisation. I've struggled a bit along the way, but I'm certainly not sitting in judgement on the men involved in this case who were blackmailed for what they felt was natural to them. Fairbrother and others are just like us, and brave men, too. However, I will sit in judgement on Church-Fenton and how he tried to exploit their weaknesses. Now, if you'll excuse me, Prof, it's been a long day. I think I'll go up to my room and have a hot bath before dinner.'

'Before you go, Jamie, there's one last thing that bothers me. At the beginning of all this, when you knew that our Establishment had killed Church-Fenton after finding him guilty without a trial but via some sort of modern "Star Chamber", and before you even knew he was a German spy, you accepted his execution quite readily. The firebrand student Jamie of old, believer in the Rule of Law and Due Process, would have made something of that and created merry hell, even despite what you've just said. A man was assassinated after all, without a fair trial or formal court martial. What happened? Why so passive?'

I looked into my whisky glass and then after taking a sip of the golden liquid, I turned to the Prof and could feel the anger burning in my eyes.

'Why didn't I care about Church-Fenton's murder? Because Brigadier General Arthur Horatio Edward Church-Fenton was the man who ordered my brother Hugh's company of Cameronians on a suicide mission in appalling weather, with no artillery support, and no wire cutting, to take a German redoubt against the will of the battalion colonel. The battle was already lost. It was a futile gesture. Hugh and his men never made it past the first fifty yards after going over the top. The German machine guns scythed them down like corn. His colonel later committed suicide. Church-Fenton was, however, awarded a medal for his part in the battle, and quietly moved back to a cushy staff position liaising with our French allies, enjoying an easy life with trips to Paris to pleasure himself. My brother was one of those statistics we analysed that showed what a deliberate butcher Church-Fenton was. The report you gave me confirmed it. So, no, I don't really mind that he was assassinated. From my point of view, the bastard deserved it.'

AUTHOR'S NOTES

Homosexuality was an offence under British Civil and Military Law at the time of the First World War. Eight officers and 153 soldiers were court-martialled for "indecency" on active service during the war. Punishment for officers was cashiering and two years in military prison. The rumours around **Lord Kitchener's** sexuality are well documented, but remain unproven.

The ruling British Royal Family in 1916 were members of the German ducal house of **Saxe-Coburg and Gotha.** Many Britons and sections of the press thought this Germanic family association to be unpatriotic, particularly as the King and the Kaiser were cousins through their shared grandmother, Queen Victoria. Anti-German sentiment came to a head in March 1917 when **Gotha**-type aircraft bombed London. This strong public outcry, when coupled with the Czar of Russia being forced by his populace to abdicate, convinced King George V to change the Royal Family name to better reflect British public opinion. The "House of Windsor" was created to remove any lingering German links to the Royal Family name. The King visited his troops near the front at least seven times during the war, but no regicide assassination attempts are recorded.

Before the war, a number of Kaiser Wilhelm II's entourage and *Gardes du Corps* officers were accused of homosexual practices and cross-dressing. Several officers committed suicide and the accusations led to a string of well-publicised libel trials and courts martial. Based on the name of the most senior accused, the scandal became known as the **Eulenburg Affair**. In the British press, homosexuality became known as "**The German Disease**" as a result of the controversy.

There have been persistent rumours since early last century that the then **Prince of Wales,** who later became Edward VIII, and then the Duke of Windsor, was bisexual. There are also many rumours that he frequented the brothels of Paris and Calais during his time as a soldier in France. The Prince was a frequent and popular visitor to the front, but was forbidden from taking part in the actual fighting.

The British Expeditionary Force, or **BEF**, was the British Army on the Western Front. It evolved continuously during its five years in existence and was ultimately led by General (eventually Field Marshal) Sir Douglas Haig, whose staff and general headquarters, **GHQ**, were located in **Montreuil**. The BEF itself was divided into armies, which in turn had several corps made up of divisions. These divisions were composed of infantry brigades comprising several battalions, backed by support troops such as artillery, cavalry, engineers, medics, etc., plus a logistical tail. Battalions were made up of companies, which in turn were composed of platoons. A platoon was led by a lieutenant or second lieutenant. These junior officer ranks were known as **subalterns**. The British soldier was almost universally known as a **Tommy** due to example forms in the Army being signed "Tommy Atkins".

In August 1914, two days after war was declared, **Lord Kitchener**, the newly appointed Secretary of State for War, appealed for **volunteers** to allow the small professional British Army to expand rapidly. The volunteers were formed into "Service" battalions of existing county and rifle regiments. These battalions collectively made drafts of the so-called "New Armies". Several units were formed of men from the same district or profession and known as "**Pals**" battalions. Most of the Kitchener volunteers were sent to the Western Front to become part of the BEF.

The British introduced **conscription** for single men in January 1916. This was a politically contentious issue, but the public received the Act of Parliament in May that year, to extend conscription to married men, even more poorly. British politicians were desperate to have conscription accepted so that the projected losses of troops could be replaced in what was by then becoming a war of attrition.

A **Brigadier General** was a British Army rank, nominally in charge of an infantry brigade, but which was used for all arms of the service as a general officer rank. It sits between the ranks of colonel and major general. Confusingly, its holders were sometimes given their full title, while at other times they were referred to simply as brigadier or general. The equivalent rank is now that of brigadier, and it is a non-general rank.

The **Cameronians (Scottish Rifles)** were an infantry regiment which had eleven active battalions serving at various times with the BEF. Four of these were Service battalions of Kitchener's volunteers, including the 10th Battalion. Members of the regiment won three VCs in the war. Its principal recruiting grounds were Lanarkshire and the Clyde Valley, and their regimental HQ was in Hamilton, near Glasgow. Formed to defend the Presbyterian faith in the seventeenth century, it had many traditions and uniform peculiarities associated with this original role. The Cameronians disbanded in 1968 rather than merge with another regiment.

The **Seaforth Highlanders** were a Scottish infantry regiment that had nine battalions with the BEF. The regiment was also known as the "**Ross**-shire Buffs" and their recruiting grounds were the north-west Highlands and the Hebrides. Members of the regiment won seven VCs in the war. The Seaforths are now part of the Royal Regiment of Scotland.

The **Intelligence Corps** was formed in August 1914. It had responsibility for providing intelligence to GHQ gleaned from spies and observers, signal intercepts, and aerial photographs. Its roles included counter-intelligence immediately behind the lines. Recruits not already affiliated to a regiment were nominally enrolled in the

10th Fusiliers. The corps' officers wore green hatbands and had green tabs on their collars, while other ranks had brassards or armbands marked "IC". There was no Section X.

To offset German marksmen's early wartime successes, the BEF formed **Sniping Schools**. Many of these were manned by ghillies or gamekeepers from the Scottish estates of the landed gentry. The **Lovat Scouts** were a regiment of sharpshooters from just such backgrounds. Snipers to this day in all armies wear ghillie suits to blend into their surroundings. Captain, later Major, **Hesketh-Pritchard**, was the principal architect and driver behind the schools. The longest officially recorded sniper shot in the First World War was of 1400 yards by an American Sergeant Major Sleigh using a standard issue Springfield rifle.

Dumdum bullets were first developed by the arsenal of that name near Calcutta (now Kolkata) in what was then British India. They were designed to expand on impact, which slowed the bullet down, and transferred the kinetic energy to the target, causing a larger and more deadly wound channel. The loss of energy meant that often they did not leave exit wounds. Used by the British in colonial wars and for big game hunting, they were eventually banned by the 1899 **Hague Convention** via an amendment raised by Germany. The Hague Conventions addressed weapons of war, as opposed to the **Geneva Conventions**, which addressed how humans involved in wars should be treated.

Kitchener's volunteers were bloodied at the **Battle of Loos,** which started on 25th September 1915 and ran until 13th October. It was fought amongst the coalmines and mining villages of northern France, close to the Belgian border. The battle is also historically noteworthy for the first use by the British of **poison gas**. Earlier that year, the Germans had been the first to use poison gas on the Western Front.

The **Battle of Verdun**, starting in February 1916 and lasting ten months, was the largest and longest fought in the First World War between German and French forces. It was planned by the Germans to be a battle of annihilation and was one of the costliest battles in history with nearly a million casualties in total. The French were close to defeat several times and were desperate for the British to attack elsewhere along the Western Front to distract the Germans. This eventually led to the "**Big Push**" of the **Somme** offensive in July 1916. Verdun is to the collective French memory, what the Somme is to the British.

Britain and Germany were allies in the suppression of the **Boxer Rebellion** in China in 1900-1901. Britain held three rounds of talks with Germany between 1898 and 1901 about joining them in their Triple Alliance with Austro-Hungary and Italy. These friendly discussions and the shared Royal Family relationships often led to observers attending each other's military manoeuvres, such as those of 1906. The two powers eventually became rivals as exemplified by the naval arms race immediately before the war. By then, Britain had joined France in the *Entente Cordiale*.

The **Alsace** region of France sits adjacent to Germany and Switzerland and has been disputed territory for centuries. After Germany won the Franco-Prussian War of 1870-1871 it annexed Alsace. Over 100,000 French-loyalist refugees fled to France. Alsatian is the traditional language of the region and is linguistically closely related to Swiss German. Alsace became French again after the war.

The **Marigny** was a brothel in Paris which catered for homosexuals and was nicknamed "The Temple of Shamelessness". It was, however, opened in 1917, but I have taken artistic licence and brought its opening date forward to fit the plot. It was popular with British and French officers. The Marigny was run by **Albert** le Cuziat and one of his sponsors was the author, Marcel Proust. Proust was a notorious voyeur of sexual acts being committed in the brothel. The Marigny on Rue de l'Arcade is now a four-star hotel. It should not be confused with Baron Rothschild's former home in a different part of Paris, which is now a government guest house.

While the *Deuxième Bureau*, the French equivalent of MI5, is quite well known, the *Premier Bureau* is less famous. The French general staff was divided into bureaux or departments which handled different aspects of their army, i.e. 1st for organisation and personnel, 2nd for intelligence and security, 3rd for operations, 4th for logistics, etc. The bureaux were manned by a mix of soldiers and civil servants.

The **Apaches** were organised criminal gangs of particularly vicious thugs in Paris in the early twentieth century. They often dressed flamboyantly in uniforms which distinguished their particular gang. The Belleville Apaches were led by a man dubbed "The Terror" by the Parisian press, and they were particularly involved in illegal bookmaking scams.

Lanchester was a luxury car manufacturer based in Birmingham which produced only a few of their Lanchester 40 model before the war started. It was a more expensive vehicle than a Rolls-Royce Silver Ghost. Large staff cars were called "chariots" in BEF slang. The company eventually ceased independent trading in 1931.

Alcohol and nicotine were the drugs of choice in the British Army in the First World War. Officers were allowed access to spirits, more often than not **whisky**, even in the front line, and there were several cases of drunken officers poorly executing their duties. Officers often received whisky from home, or brought it with them when returning from leave. They often also had access to cognacs and fine wines through their messes. Other ranks made do with beer and cheap wines when out of the line, and were issued **SRD Rum** at specific times in the trenches and especially before going into the attack. The RFC pilots were notoriously hard drinkers, while the Scottish, Irish and Australian regiments upheld their national stereotypes in terms of numbers of soldiers charged with alcohol-related offences.

Smoking cigarettes, also known as **fags,** gaspers, coffin nails, and many other synonyms, was deemed to have a calming effect on soldiers, and so was encouraged by the military authorities. Tins of cigarettes from home were a popular present to the BEF's troops. They were not only given directly by soldiers' relatives, but were also distributed by well-meaning charities.

Post-Traumatic Stress Disorder, PTSD, and its associated

symptoms, was not recognised fully as such in the First World War. The stress of battle manifested itself in what was officially known up until 1917 as **"battle fatigue"**, and from then on as **"shellshock"**. The Army medical staff's reaction to this mental illness at the time was mixed; GHQ would have preferred that it didn't exist, and many field commanders saw it as an excuse for cowardice. Understanding of the illness only progressed as the war wore on through pioneering work by doctors at special hospitals, such as Dr William Rivers at Craiglockhart.

The **Glaswegian** dialect spoken by McIlhenny mixes local vocabulary with Scottish English and Standard English. I have watered it down in the story to enable a wider readership to understand his wit and wisdom. For the unfamiliar, the first person singular, "I", becomes "Ah" in the Glasgow vernacular. Other common differences result in the "g" being dropped from words ending in "-ing". For those seeking greater authenticity, another change concerns compound words where "'not" becomes "nae" as in where "would not" becomes "widnae", "cannot" becomes "cannae", etc., and these words can be spoken as such in the reader's mind. Although Hodgson is a London cockney, I have avoided him talking in rhyming slang to minimise further confusion. In a military setting, additional soldiers' slang words, many gathered from across the Empire, were of course added to the mix resulting in an enriched patois. One of these words is **"Blighty"**, the corruption of an Urdu word from India, meaning home, England or the British Isles.

ACKNOWLEDGEMENTS

My thanks to the following for their advice and encouragement:

Janet Walker, Nichola & Kristian Kolsaker, Rachel & Matt Wilkinson, Lindsay Freeland, Ruth & Iain Richardson, Nick Thripp, Andrew Massey, Susan Wade, and Rachel Marsh.

IF YOU LIKED
BLACKMAIL
YOU'LL LIKE THESE OTHER FORTHCOMING BOOKS IN THE JAMIE BROWN SERIES...

SMALL PRINT
November 1916

Major Jamie Brown investigates why an Australian attack on the Western Front went so badly wrong. Are the Aussies right to blame incompetent British generals? Or is something more sinister afoot? And what is the unexpected Irish connection?

CHINESE MEDICINE
September 1917

Major Jamie Brown investigates strange connections between the Chinese Labour Corps and the Welsh Regiment's battle successes on the Western Front. The trail leads Jamie from France to an East End of London under aerial attack, and then back to the Continent, and into the murky role of neutral nations in wartime and their exploitation by both warring sides.

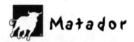 Matador